IN A PICKLE
THE ANNIE PICKEL SERIES, BOOK I

By Karen Robbins

Martin Sisters Publishing

Season life with humor!
Karen Robbins
10-19-12

Published by

Ivy House Books, a division of Martin Sisters Publishing, LLC

www. martinsisterspublishing. com

Copyright © 2012 Karen Robbins

ISBN: 978-1-937273-55-2
Fiction
Printed in the United States of America
Martin Sisters Publishing, LLC

For my mother, who always said she seasoned her recipes with marijuana when she really meant marjoram.

An imprint of Martin Sisters Publishing, LLC

Chapter One

I'm not ordinarily a violent person, though I beat up the newspaper deliveryman once. I whacked him with the newspaper from the end of the driveway to my kitchen door. It didn't hurt the paper none since he'd rolled it up and tucked it into one of his skinny orange plastic bags.

"You can take the time to bag it, but you can't take the time to put it into the special box the newspaper people made me install?" I yelled as I swatted him. It gets my dandruff up when I have to bend down and pick up a newspaper that ought to be in its proper place.

He wasn't hurt any because he really wasn't there. I have a good imagination. I conjured up a picture of a cowardly deliveryman, arms flailing to protect himself, yelling, "Have mercy! Have mercy!" Yes, I could see him in my mind running for his car or truck or whatever he drives, a trail of orange bags blowing in the wind behind him. He's lucky he wasn't really there when I went to retrieve the paper that morning. I just might have given him a few whacks, or at least a piece of my mind.

The gray misty November morning didn't help my mood any. A cold chill hung in the air as the weather wavered between giving us more of an Ohio Indian summer and hitting us with an early arctic blast.

"No excuse," I mumbled as I fumed over the paper I had to pick up from the ground. There wasn't even any snow yet to keep him from getting his car near the box. "Just no excuse."

Sometimes I wonder if people think they can take advantage of me because of my white hair. Yes, it's white, not gray. It used to be chestnut until I stopped dying it on my 55th birthday and went au naturale. That was ten years ago and I haven't been sorry. Not only have I saved lots of money on dye jobs, but I've gotten plenty of compliments on it.

"Annie Pickels," people say, "your hair is as white as a fresh snow fall in December." Still, lots of people see a white or gray head, and they think it's a sign of senility. Let me tell you, I'm far from being senile. You can't be senile and run a business.

I pickle pickles and sell them to local restaurants and diners near the farm where I live. I have my own recipe, and my pickles have quite a reputation in the area. The money the pickles make isn't important. My Russell, rest his soul, provided well for me before his untimely death.

I also make a little money renting out plots of land on what's left of my acreage to the city folk who want to come and play in the dirt and pretend to be farmers. Some of them are successful at it and some aren't.

That November morning, the morning I imagined I beat up the deliveryman, the heavy leafy smell of autumn mixed with the pungent odor of rotting vegetables. Some folks hadn't harvested everything before the first frost and what lay in the fields was returning to the soil. It was a good smell though. It reminded me of Russell.

I don't mean to say Russell smelled earthy. No. I mean it reminded me that Russell would have been out turning over those fields and making them ready for the next spring planting. He knew how to farm. He'd gone to Ohio State University to learn all about it. These city folk—they just played at being farmers.

My nose dripped like a leaky faucet by the time I got back inside the house. I gave it a swipe with a tissue from my pocket, and then exchanged my muddy outdoor boots for my warm cozy slippers. I left my boots to dry on the landing that sits between the three steps up to the kitchen and the ones that go down into the basement. The basement is where I keep all my canning supplies and inventory. It's cool down there and the cucumbers keep well until I can get them all pickled.

Last year, my brother built me some shelves in the basement for storing jars. Trouble is, my business has outgrown those shelves, so I have to pile up the empties alongside those that are full and it can get a little precarious. I recycle the empties. I sterilize them and refill them, putting on new lids to seal in the freshness after I fill them with cucumbers and brine and seasoning.

Once I got my slippers on, I thought about trudging down those steps to gather some empties and the rest of the cucumbers, and get started on finishing up the year's crop. It seemed like there was no end to pickling. Either I planted too many cucumbers or the Lord blessed too much.

I didn't feel up to pickling just then or my usual two mile walk. I had a cold coming on, and my bones ached. My robe comforted me with its softness and warmth. I wasn't about to give that up for regular clothes yet. I hung my jacket on the hook and took the picked-up-off-the-ground newspaper into the kitchen.

Now, I usually don't imbibe, but my daddy did teach me how to make a good medicinal hot toddy. My symptoms called for something that would warm the joints and chase the sniffles, so I fished under the sink for the bottle of whiskey that someone had given me ages ago. Does whiskey ever go bad? I sniffed. Whew! The smell went clear up my nostrils and hit something inside my head. I guessed it was still good.

I drained the little that was left of the caramel colored liquid into a saucepan and added lemon, honey, cinnamon, cloves, nutmeg, and water, then left it to simmer on the stove. The spicy aroma floated through the kitchen. I filled my mug and blew on it to cool it a bit. Just a few minutes with the morning news show, I thought, and I'll get to work. I sat in the big easy chair, propped my feet on the ottoman in front of the TV, and took a few sips. The sweetened whiskey burned a bit as it went down, but its warmth began to spread with a tingle from the top of my head right down to my toes. My eyelids grew heavy.

Suddenly my body jerked me awake. What time was it, ? I could feel the hairs on the back of my neck begin to rise. I shivered. Something wasn't right. My ears tuned in to listen for the familiar sounds of the house. Then,

CRASH! I heard glass shatter against the basement floor, as if someone had run into my stash of empty pickle jars.

CRASH! More jars hit the floor. I sprang from the chair. A cold breeze blew through the open door just above the steps that led to the basement. Panic shot through me like a lightning bolt cuts the sky. I hadn't shut the kitchen door! My heart beat like the big bass drum in a marching band. Someone was in the basement!

Cordless phone in hand, I raced back into the living room. Crouching behind a chair, I punched in 9-1-1. The hot toddy must have done its work on my joints because I don't remember feeling any pain as I bent down on my knees and hit those numbers.

"What's your emergency?" the dispatcher asked.

"This is Annie Pickels," I whispered. "There's someone in my house."

"Where are you?" she asked.

"I'm in my living room."

"Ms. Pickels, you need to get out of the house," she urged. "Get yourself out of danger." I nodded at the voice on the phone.

"Go to a neighbor if you can. I'll get the sheriff there right away."

I thanked her, but I wondered how I was going to get my jacket and get out the kitchen door with no one seeing me from the basement. I grabbed the old sweater I'd left on the couch and flew out the front door instead.

My friend's house across the road from me looked safe, but the moment I started for it, my Bohemian temper, from my mother's side, got the best of me. I was not going anywhere until I knew who was in that basement. I couldn't go back in, but I could stand my ground in front of the house with a view of both doors. I dug my heels into the frosty ground, my fists clenched. No one was getting out of there without me seeing him.

At that moment, two men in a white Econovan passed by, slowed to a stop, and backed up. I could see them out of the corner of my eye, but I didn't turn to look. No way would I chance missing the culprit in the basement should he decide to come out. I wanted to be able to pick him out of a lineup.

"Anything wrong, lady?" one of the men called out to me.

"There's someone in my basement!" I sounded a little more frantic than I meant to, but I was chilled. My teeth clicked like the wind-up ones you find in a joke store.

I heard metal scrape against metal as the door of the van slid open, then closed with a bang behind me. But I wasn't about to turn around. My eyes were glued to the doors of my farmhouse. When the two men reached my side, I realized one held a crowbar. He was the larger of the two, broad shouldered and muscular. He gave me the confidence that he could handle whatever he found in my basement. His shorter and smaller framed sidekick looked like he could run fast if he had to.

"Why don't we check it out for you?" the shorter guy offered.

"Th-thanks," I stuttered.

"You can get warm in the van," the taller man suggested. He raised his cap a bit revealing a balding head, and gave me a curious once over look. It was then I realized I was standing in a soggy pink chenille bathrobe with pink fuzzy slippers that were now matted from the rain and mud in the yard. The green sweater I had grabbed was still clutched in my hands. I tossed it over my shoulders.

"Th-thanks," I told him raising my chin in defiance of his patronizing look, "but I'll watch the doors. I want to see who comes out. B-be careful in there."

I pointed to the side door that led to the basement, and the two men disappeared inside. It seemed as if they were gone for an eternity. Rivulets of water ran down my face as my hair shed the excess dampness accumulated from the mist and drizzle. I wiped my forehead with the inside of my sweater while I kept one eye trained on the door.

The faint wail of a siren could be heard in the distance just as my two heroes emerged from the house. The big guy held something carefully cupped in his large hands. Both struggled to contain a smile, but failed. Their shoulders shook from the effort.

I wondered what was so insufferably funny.

"It's just a bird, lady," the smaller man said. I peeked inside the enormous hands that were closed around a frightened little brown bird. When I nodded and stepped back, he threw his hands into the air to release his prisoner. The wren took flight just as the screech of tires and a final whoop of a siren announced the sheriff's arrival.

The door to the police cruiser popped open. The sheriff struggled to pull his large frame from behind the steering wheel. He pitched forward and hopped on one leg until the other leg followed him out.

"Hands in the air!" The sheriff shouted even before he could draw his gun. He planted his feet shoulder width apart, knees slightly bent. His left hand supported the right hand that held the pointed gun. The shocked heroes complied.

"And drop the weapon!"

The crowbar fell with a thud.

The sheriff growled into the microphone clipped to his shoulder. "I need backup!"

Bewildered, I looked to the men, then to the sheriff, and back again. I tried to absorb the fact that a little bird was responsible for all this confusion, a host of activity involving the sheriff and a gun and two fellows who were getting paler by the minute.

Relief that there was no one in my house blended with my embarrassment over all the commotion made my hands begin to shake. Then I did something I rarely do, I started to cry. I hate to cry.

"Lady," the shorter hero pleaded, hands held above his head. "For Pete's sake, lady, tell him it was a bird."

I couldn't talk. My mouth felt frozen and my chest tightened as I sobbed. I nodded my head but the sheriff didn't see me. His eyes were locked on his two prime suspects.

"Please lady, tell him we found a bird," came the plea again. The taller man's face blanched as he stared down the business end of the sheriff's gun and waited for me to answer.

I took a deep breath and finally muttered, "Bird, they found a bird. H-helped me."

The sheriff got the message at last and holstered his gun. The suspects turned into heroes once again and eagerly agreed to tell their story to the newly arrived deputy.

"Let's get you out of the cold, ma'am," the sheriff said. He took my arm and led me into the house. I didn't even get a chance to thank those wonderful men. Of course, maybe it was just as well. I'm not too sure they were happy with me after their discomfort.

I excused myself for a minute to change into dry clothes. When I came back into the kitchen, I saw the sheriff place the empty whiskey bottle back on the counter. He turned to me. "Now, Ms. Pickels, you're going to have to tell me exactly what happened here."

"Yessir," I said my mouth going dry, "but I need a drink first." I winced. That didn't come out right. Land sakes! I was sure he'd think I was a foolish old woman who was pickled from drinking a bottle of whiskey. Heat crept up my face as I reached for a glass and filled it with water. I gulped it down, trying to drown my embarrassment.

My composure restored, I cleared my throat and turned to the sheriff. "Well, it all started with pickles."

"Okay, Annie, Pickles, " He began writing in his book. "Do you spell Pickles, P-I-C-K-L-E-S?"

"Yes, but my name is spelled P-I-C-K-E-L-S."

The sheriff scratched his head. "Your name is Pickels, P-I-C-K-E-L-S? Not Pickles, P-I-C-K-L-E-S?"

I nodded.

"Let's back up." The sheriff took a deep breath. "You said it started with pickles. Well, was that P-I-C-K-E-L-S or P-I-C-K-L-E-S?"

"It's Annie Pickels' Pickles."

His pen poised above his notebook, he merely stared back blankly.

"I, Annie Pickels, E-L-S, make pickles, L-E-S. Annie Pickels' Pickles."

"Aha." The sheriff's head bobbed.

I nodded at the empty whiskey bottle. "I know this looks suspicious, but I assure you I'm not pickled."

The sheriff scratched his head again as if he had a bad case of dandruff. If he did that too often, he was going to get a bald spot right in the middle of all that red hair. For the first time I noticed the name above his badge, Sheriff Redd Stewart. Well, that was appropriate.

A few minutes later, Sheriff Stewart finally had enough details for his report. He returned to his car juggling two jars of my best pickles. I couldn't let him leave empty handed after all I had put him through.

The sheriff was no sooner out the door, when the phone rang. Of course, I thought, I'm surprised Elma waited this long. Elma Thompson's my best friend and neighbor. She lives right across the road where she can keep an eye on everything that goes on at my place.

"Annie, are you all right?" Elma sounded genuinely concerned. "The deputy wouldn't let me come in."

"Yes, I'm fine." I sighed. "A little embarrassed, but fine."

"You sound, " Elma let the sentence hang in the air for me to finish. Elma can always tell when I'm down whether it's from a cold or just missing Russell. The just-missing-Russell doesn't happen as often anymore as it used to.

"I'm coming down with a cold and standing outside in the rain like a fool didn't help any," I said.

"What happened?"

I spent a few minutes telling her about the bird, my heroes, and the sheriff who made out his report. I left out the part about the hot toddy. I didn't need a lecture from Elma on the evils of alcohol.

"Wow, you've had quite a morning. I have some chicken soup in the fridge. I'll be right over and we'll warm you up with that." Elma was just too eager, and all I wanted at the moment was a little peace and quiet to collect my thoughts and let my face recover from its blush of embarrassment.

"Thanks, Elma, but I'll pass on the soup. I just need to rest a spell. I think I'll take a little nap." I hoped that would keep her at bay for a bit. She is a petite dynamo, a little shorter than I am, probably about 5'4", and she hasn't let her hair go to gray yet. It's more a golden brown color. "Iced Mocha" I think she called it. She has a big heart and a curious mind to match it.

"Well, don't you worry about what to make for dinner. I'll be over later with some soup. You get a good nap in. You'll feel much better." Elma was determined for me to have that soup.

It was nice to have someone care about you like that, gives you a warm feeling even without the soup. Elma and her husband, Warren, built a house across the road a few months after Russell died. I always told her she was God-sent. She was never afraid to ask me questions about Russell, not like other people who avoided the subject altogether. She knew more about me and Russell than any other human being on this earth.

The soup would be good. I knew where she got it. We attend the same church but Warren doesn't go to church in the middle of the week. So it's just Elma and me who go for the Wednesday night dinners and Bible study. The chicken soup was leftover from Wednesday night. Elma is in charge of the cooking and she doesn't like to waste anything.

I took a nice hot shower, washed my hair and dried it before I got busy with the cleanup in the basement. With all those jars crashing, that poor bird was probably half frightened to death in its panic to get out.

Once the basement was in order again, I forgot about my oncoming maladies and got involved with my pickling. The rest of the afternoon passed quickly. By the time I noticed Elma heading across the road, I was ready to face her, her questions - and her chicken soup.

Chapter Two

A ray of sunshine managed to sneak through the blinds and play across my face to force me awake the next morning. Sunshine? I had overslept! I jumped out of bed, tossed on my walking clothes, and grabbed a cup of coffee that was still warm. My kitchen coffeemaker had started automatically at 6 a.m., my usual rise and shine time. I groaned. I hated to jumpstart the morning. I much preferred warming up to it.

The crisp bright morning took the edge off of the bad start and I began my two-mile constitutional. Back straight, chin up, arms swinging, eyes looking toward the horizon. I mentally ticked off the checklist of proper exercise form in my head. "Count your blessings, name them one by one," played in my head as I set my pace. While I walked, I began my spiritual exercise as well. I pride myself in being ambidextrous, able to walk and meditate at the same time. Meditation always leads to prayer and God and I have some great conversations. I don't like long prayers. Mine are usually very short. Like I told Elma once, "No sense wasting God's time with a bunch of chit-chat. Get to the point. He's a busy person."

Lord, I prayed, thanks for Elma. *She's a great friend even if she is a bit too nosy at times.*

Old Route 47 wasn't too busy this time of the morning so I didn't have to play dodge 'em cars all the way to the development. The heavy traffic was above me up in the air. Gaggles of geese honked a warning to "look out below." I was careful to watch them with my mouth closed as their wings swooshed through the quiet morning.

Why were they called Canadian geese? If they were Canadian shouldn't they stay in Canada? Everyone complained about the mess they created on lawns. I had to smile at them though every time they perched on top of my roof. They looked like guard geese. Thankfully, it wasn't one of them in my basement.

I focused on the road again and saw a big truck coming at me. It grew larger by the second. I jumped onto the loose gravel on the side of the road. The rush of wind created by the monster whipped my hair across my face. Route 47 never used to be busy but now that suburbia sprawled across the farmland between Bellefontaine and Sidney, traffic was increasing. With a shaky hand, I patted my hair back into place. I needed to be more careful. I wasn't ready to join Russell and Jesus yet.

Once I got to the newer development of homes about a quarter mile up the road, there was a nice smooth sidewalk that kept me out of harm's way. Most of the development used to be part of our farm. It seemed so long ago and yet only like yesterday that Russell had struggled to grow crops where the homes now stood.

Lord, thank you for the return on Russell's investment. He just didn't know we'd be growin' houses instead of corn and tomatoes.

Neat little homes with shuttered windows and manicured lawns lined the street. Children rushed outdoors to await the yellow school bus whose daily route snaked around the twists and turns through the maze of homes. The bus driver seemed friendly enough. He always waved at me every time he saw me. Actually, it was more of a salute than a wave as if I were an officer of rank. I liked that. Respect. Even if it was for my snow-white head.

As I approached one driveway, I watched a mom fuss with the stiff collar of her boy's blue jacket while her toddler danced beside her. Suddenly the little girl took off and ran in my direction. She gained speed as her tiny feet pattered down the cement driveway.

I stopped and prepared to catch the human missile flying directly toward me before she could hit the street. She caught me instead, right around the knees. The impact took me by surprise.

"Ga-ma, Ga-ma," she babbled as her mother huffed and puffed behind her.

"I'm sorry," the breathless woman said as she pried the little arms from my legs. "My mother has a jacket that same color. She must have thought you were Grandma."

"That's okay." I went down on one knee to look into the cherub face. She turned away quickly to hide behind her mom. "I'm just glad she didn't get past me into the street."

"Me, too." The mother turned to look up the road for the bus and any other traffic that might have been a danger.

"So what's your name?" I said to my new little friend. "My name's Annie."

The little girl's curiosity caused her to peek at me again with big brown eyes open wide and a thumb stuck in her mouth, I assumed for security. Instead of an answer, she quickly buried her head in her mother's jacket again.

"Tell Annie, your name." Her mother's prompt did no good.

I stood up. "That's all right. She doesn't need to talk to strangers."

"Her name is Sarah, and you're not exactly a stranger. You're the lady in the farmhouse around the corner, aren't you?"

"Yes," I replied.

"Hi, I'm Sarah's mom, Jennifer. It's nice to meet you." Jennifer shook hands with me just as the bus rumbled around the corner. She called to her son to pick up his schoolbag and get ready.

"Well, I'm off," I said. "Nice meeting you, and you, too, Sarah." I bent over and wiggled my fingers in a wave.

Sarah pulled her thumb out of her mouth and gave a little wave and a smile. How sweet, I thought. If Russell and I could have had a family, I might be a grandmother instead of just looking like one. How nice it would have been to have a little one wrap her arms around you and call you "Ga-ma" for real.

Before I could get into that just-missing-Russell mood, I quickened my pace and turned my thoughts instead to the cruise brochures stacked on my kitchen table, brochures that advertised warm, green places in the sun. John Grisham, my favorite author, had sparked an idea when I read his book, "Skipping Christmas." Not his usual legal thriller, this story was about a couple whose grown daughter wasn't coming home for Christmas, so they decided to go on a cruise and forego all the folderol of the holidays.

When I thought of all the work it would save me, the obligatory family get-togethers I could avoid, and the pampering I'd receive on the ship, a Christmas cruise sounded wonderful. Why not? I deserved a little vacation, I told myself. Questions filtered through my mind. How was I going to choose a ship? Where could I picture myself for Christmas?

The Tahiti cruise looked enticing but it required air travel on Christmas day. I wanted to skip having Christmas at home, but I didn't want to skip remembering Jesus properly on his birthday.

The sleek lines of the Queen Mary 2 had impressed me. The brochure featured a "Yuletide Caribbean Cruise" that was fourteen nights. I had never been to Dominica or Tortola, two of their ports of call. Best of all, the dates of the cruise worked perfectly into my schedule.

All my mental vacation planning had slowed me down, so I started swinging my arms a little faster to pick up my pace again. For incentive, I promised myself a cinnamon roll and cup of coffee when I got home. My mouth watered at the thought.

As I finished my circuitous route and approached the farmhouse, I saw a familiar car parked in the drive. It was an older model Chevy, big and heavy, with a homemade paint job that included some red and yellow flames exploding from the wheel wells as if the wheels were so fast they could burn up the highway. I'm not a mechanical wizard, but I doubted Tommy could get that heap up to speed fast enough to burn anything.

Tommy was a young man in his early 20s who had rented a garden plot from me for a couple of summers now. He took good care of it, got a nice crop of corn and marjoram each season. Tommy was of medium height but a little on the skinny side and had long dark hair. It took me a little while to get used to his body decorations though. He had a few tattoos and some metal things stuck in various places that were never meant to be poked and studded. I have a hard time looking people in the eye and talking with them when they have a silver ring in their eyebrow or a stud in their tongue. How do they blow their nose with metal stuck in their nostril? I was tempted, but too polite to ask.

The trunk of the old Chevy was open and Tommy was lifting out a tiller.

"Mornin', Tommy," I said.

"Hey, Mrs. A," Tommy grunted as he set the gardening machine on the ground. He always calls me "Mrs. A." I told him he could call me "Annie" but he insisted on "Mrs. A." Kind of reminded me of Happy Days and the Fonz calling the mother Mrs. C.

Tommy's a sweet boy—a little strange but very nicely mannered.

"Have a good walk?" Tommy asked.

"A good walk and a good talk," I told him glancing heavenward so he'd know it was God I'd been talking to and not myself. As Tommy stood before me, all those thoughts about being a mother and a grandmother flooded back. I felt a twinge of regret. If life had gone differently, Tommy might have been a grandson.

"Would you like to join me for some hot chocolate?" I blurted out. "Or coffee?"

"Some coffee sounds good, Mrs. A." His smile revealed a beautiful set of teeth that only needed some whitening to make them perfect. "I could use some joe. I skipped breakfast this morning so I could get started a little faster."

"Good grief, child, don't you know breakfast is the best meal of the day?" Now, I really felt that grandmotherly thing. His sparkling brown eyes told me he had just baited me into giving him something to eat with his "joe." That was okay. The Bible said old widows should practice hospitality. I figured I might as well do a little practicing.

"C'mon in, I'll fix you some eggs to go with that coffee. You're going to need some energy to handle that thing." I pointed to the contraption he had hauled out of the trunk that now sat on the driveway and waited for its opportunity to chew up the ground.

"Thanks, Mrs. A!" Tommy followed me into the house like a puppy dog that knew his food was going into the dish any minute. He stopped to take his muddy boots off before he walked into the kitchen. I appreciated the gesture. Tommy was such a good boy.

A few minutes later the smell of bacon and toast filled the kitchen. I sipped a second cup of coffee and watched Tommy munch on crisp salty bacon. He dipped his buttered toast into the molten egg yolk and raised it to his lips. The yolk dribbled down his chin and he scooped it back into his mouth with a deft finger.

"Mmm, good. Really good, Mrs. A," he said his mouth still chewing on bits of egg and toast.

I had to smile at him. His head moved like a bobble-head doll approving every bite. It was fun to feed someone who obviously liked eating.

Hunger satisfied, Tommy leaned back in his chair, poked his fingers in his belt loops and sighed. "Well, got to move on. Lots to do today. I have to get things ready for my Mary Jane."

I raised an eyebrow. Mary Jane? This was the first time Tommy had ever mentioned a girlfriend.

"Yessiree. If I take good care of my Mary Jane, she takes good care of me." He sat up straight and smiled like a kid with a secret he itched to tell.

"My Mary Jane takes good care of me, too," I said as I thought of my niece and her muddle-headed need to be my caretaker. Facetiously I added, "I don't know what I'd do without her some days."

Tommy leaned forward and grinned at me strangely. "Really?" he said slowly. "How does Mary Jane help you out?"

"Well, there are days when my arthritis kicks up and Mary Jane helps me get the lids screwed on my pickle jars tightly and the labels in the right place."

"Mary Jane helps me get through life," Tommy went on. He shrugged "Otherwise, I couldn't make it through the day." He looked at me, a sly silly grin on his face, like he'd just discovered peanut butter and jelly sandwiches. Young love, I thought. How sweet.

Something bothered me about Tommy's crop of marjoram though. He'd asked me when he rented the plot if I minded him growing it. He didn't want it to be a problem. I didn't know how growing marjoram could be a problem unless it took over the other plots I rented out. That wasn't likely since Tommy's plot was way in the back corner. But I'd snipped a little and put it in my pickles and I was beginning to feel guilty about it. I really needed to come clean and get it off my chest; confess my sin and ask for forgiveness.

"Tommy, I need to tell you something." I took a deep breath. Confession may be good for the soul but it certainly made the body quake. "I have to confess that I've snipped a little from your plants for my own use. I didn't think you would mind. You have so much. It seems to grow so well alongside the sweet corn."

Tommy's grin broadened. "It's okay, Mrs. A. I'm only using it for myself. It's not like I'm trying to make a profit from selling it." He drummed his fingers on my stack of cruise brochures. "I can bring you a little dried stuff if you need anymore. I got plenty this year."

"No, but thanks, Tommy," I said grateful to be forgiven. "I prefer the fresh green leaves and I'm all done with my pickling for the year."

"Goin' on a vacation?" He pointed to the pile of cruise literature and then picked one up to examine it closer.

"I'm thinking about it." I retrieved the pot of coffee and poured him a second cup.

"I've never been on one of them big boats. I'd be afraid of gettin' seasick." He pointed to the picture of the Queen Mary 2 in the brochure.

"Actually, it's not bad. They have some kind of gadget that comes out the side of the ship that keeps it from tilting too much." I couldn't for the life of me think of what the thing was called.

"I've been considering a cruise on the Queen Mary 2."

Tommy opened the brochure. "I hate to say it Mrs. A, but this ship looks like the Titanic."

"Funny you should say that. Both ships are from the same cruise line, Cunard or at least White Star became Cunard sometime after the Titanic," I explained. "I think they have that lifeboat thing figured out now, though, and there aren't any icebergs in the Caribbean."

"Would you like me to keep an eye on the house while you're gone?" Tommy offered eagerly.

"Thanks, but that won't be necessary. My friend Elma will check on things and the sheriff is always kind enough stop in and have a look."

Tommy choked. I think he took too big a gulp of hot coffee. I hoped that stud in his tongue wasn't loose and giving him trouble.

"Th-the sheriff stops by?" Tommy cleared his throat.

"Yes. If I tell him I'll be on vacation, he does." The bird fiasco of the previous morning came to mind and I chuckled. "Actually he was just here yesterday."

"He was?" Tommy's eyes grew wide like a little kid who was in awe of his hero. It was refreshing to see a young man respect officers of the law and look at them as heroes. After all, when the police weren't chasing birds out of basements, they were arresting criminals.

I told Tommy the story about the bird. I could laugh about it with a day's distance now between the incident and the storytelling. I still felt a little embarrassed, but that would fade with time.

"Does the sheriff ever check the fields?" Tommy leaned forward. His facial muscles tensed making the ring in his eyebrow stand out a bit more.

"No. He just checks to see that the house is secure. Nothing out in those fields to interest him." He released a long breath of air and relaxed. I was puzzled. Tommy seemed so concerned about the sheriff getting into the fields. Was he afraid the sheriff would trample his plants?

Tommy's chair scraped against the wooden floor as he stood. "Well, uh, I'd better get that field turned over. I only rented the tiller for half a day."

His eagerness to work in the field reminded me of Russell. He used to love the rich aroma of freshly tilled soil. He always said it was the smell of the earth that told you it would yield a good crop.

Soon, the distant noise of the tiller's motor drifted in through the opened window along with the fresh air I so enjoyed even if it was a bit chilled. The dryer hummed and thumped in the laundry room as I sipped another cup of coffee, decaf this time, and perused the cruise brochures again. My mind was made up. Icebergs or no icebergs, I would book the Yuletide Cruise on the Queen Mary 2.

The dryer buzzed and I went to retrieve the clothes before they had a chance to wrinkle from setting too long. As I passed the window, I noticed Tommy load the tiller back into the trunk of his car. He stepped back for a moment and leaned against the telephone pole next to the drive. He seemed to struggle to catch his breath. The tilling hadn't taken very long. It wasn't quite noon yet.

He put a hand to his forehead, and then used his shirtsleeve to wipe sweat from his brow. The air was chill and the sun was muted behind the clouds. Had he worked that hard to break a sweat? He bent and grabbed his leg with both hands and began to massage it slowly. He straightened again, his hands on his arched back. He grimaced as though in pain.

I stuck my head out the door and called to him. "Everything all right, Tommy?" He waved to me.

"Yeah, Mrs. A. I just ran out of gas." He clipped a bungee cord onto the trunk lid to secure it on top of the machine, and walked stiffly over to the landing where I stood.

"Did you get all your plowing done?"

"Not quite but it will do until spring." A cold breeze lifted some of the stray strands of black hair that had escaped Tommy's ponytail. I pulled my sweater closed against the chill. Winter was in the air.

"Would you like another cup of coffee and a cinnamon roll before you go?"

His face looked pale and drawn.

"No thanks, Mrs. A. I'd better get that machine back to the rental place before they charge me for the whole day."

"I won't see you until this spring then?"

"I guess," He set one foot on the bottom step and massaged his leg a bit again. "I'll miss your coffee and rolls though."

"No reason you can't stop by for some." He winced as he straightened. He really seemed to be in pain. "Tommy, are you sure you're all right."

"I'm great, Mrs. A., just a little twinge. Thanks again for breakfast! I'll be seein' ya." He grinned weakly and winked.

Tommy limped to his car, his boot strings dragged behind him in the dirt. He waved once more and then took off. I hoped he would stop by during the winter. I enjoyed his company and he seemed lonely, even though he had his Mary Jane. Such a character, I mused. I smiled as I thought of all that marjoram he had harvested. But what was he doing with it if he wasn't selling it? He had grown enough to season a whole herd of cattle.

Chapter Three

"Annie, it's just a few relatives, I think you know most of them already."

I frowned. My grip tightened on the phone. I know Elma had good intentions, but maybe I should have planned to skip Thanksgiving as well as Christmas.

"At least I think you know most of them," Elma continued. "Besides, with Mary Jane and your brother out of town. . .well, you don't need to spend Thanksgiving by yourself."

"Really Elma, I'll be fine," I insisted. "I have to get some shopping done and gifts wrapped so I can have an early Christmas with my brother and his family."

"Thanksgiving day is not for shopping," Elma said emphatically. "And I promised Mary Jane I'd make sure you weren't alone for Thanksgiving."

So that was it. My niece, Mary Jane, had gotten to her. My friend was not easily intimidated but if anyone could do it, Mary Jane could. Mary Jane could lay the track and push a trainload of guilt at you and you'd never see it coming. Out of consideration for what I was sure she had been through, I accepted Elma's invitation.

On Thanksgiving afternoon, I arrived early to give Elma a hand with the turkey and trimmings. Being the organizer that Elma was, there wasn't a lot left to do but take dishes from people as they arrived. The smell of turkey and dressing and homemade gravy wafted through the air. As each person arrived, they breathed deeply as if they had arrived at a spa that smelled of wondrous mysterious scents. All sorts of food was carried in, hot casseroles, cold Jello salads, soft rolls, pies, and one curious dish with pink marshmallows and fruit.

"Elma," I said holding a casserole in one hand and cranberry sauce in the other. "Where am I supposed to put all of this?" She had arranged a buffet style meal in the kitchen, and set places at her dining room table, kitchen table, and a few long folding tables from church for folks to eat at. The kitchen counter was almost full and her card table threatened to collapse under the weight of all the pies.

Elma shrugged. "Start putting stuff in the middle of the tables and folks can pass it around," she said. I put the casserole on one table and the cranberry sauce on another. I wondered if an army could eat all that we had to offer.

"How many did you say were coming?" I asked as the house began to fill with people.

"Oh, I don't know. Just a few relatives and some friends."

A "few" turned out to be a small army, thirty if I counted right—maybe there were more. Kids never stand in one place long enough to be counted.

Elma seated me next to a cousin who was obviously interested in more than a mere acquaintance. He studied me with beady eyes that all but disappeared into his puffy face when he grinned. He draped his arm on the back of my chair like it belonged there and leaned into my personal space a little too often for my comfort. The large class ring on his finger clunked against the wood back of the chair as he tapped his finger nervously. He was obviously a proud alumnus since I noticed that his tie bar bore the same blue stone and insignia as the ring. The tie bar held his napkin in place over a substantial midriff to protect the blue and gold striped tie that clashed with his green plaid sport coat.

More than once, he leaned in my direction as pickle juice dripped from his mouth, to say, "You make a mighty fine pickle, Annie." Chomp. Chomp. "Mighty fine."

"He's harmless," Elma said later when Thanksgiving dinner was over. "Just a little lonely. He was married years ago but his wife left him for a doctor she met at an ice cream social, poor thing."

Poor thing? Did Elma mean him or the wife who left? No matter, I didn't appreciate Elma's matchmaking and I told her so. She promised to behave, but that kind of a promise was easily forgotten by someone like Elma. I knew how to even the score though. There was a way to get under Elma's skin and I knew just how to do it. I chuckled. She'd probably be expecting me to do something.

A few days later, I smiled as I put the bow on Elma's present, and the tag that read, "Do Not Open Until Christmas!" Now that's payback, I thought. Elma will go crazy if she has to wait that long to open her gift and I would insure she did with a promise from Warren to see that she didn't open it before then. He was a man who could keep a promise and he would especially enjoy keeping this one. He loved to see the little girl in Elma squirm at Christmas when it came to packages and surprises.

Just as I rolled up the last of the Christmas wrap and put it in the storage box, I heard Mary Jane's familiar knock on the door, two short raps followed by a pause and then three quick ones. It was a signal for me that it was safe to answer the door. She was concerned that I would open the door to strangers, hardly the case since I could see who was there through the glass in the kitchen door. Maybe she thought someone would wear a disguise to look like her, you know, like a Mission Impossible thing where they rip off a rubber mask and reveal the villain is there. That was an unlikely scenario, since I had no government secrets to harbor for safekeeping.

I pushed the curtain aside and looked through the window in the door so she would know I checked to see who was there before I turned the door handle. Dark blonde hair framed the face of a woman whose blue eyes flashed with impatience and brow furled with determination. Yup, it was Mary Jane all right. No hope that a mask would peel off and expose an imposter. Her three boys weren't with her. They were obviously in school terrorizing someone else. They weren't bad children, just rambunctious.

"What took you so long? I was beginning to worry about you," Mary Jane said as she brushed past me. "I was ready to let myself in." She put the extra set of keys back in her purse.

"You could have. It's not locked," I wanted to bite my tongue as I said it but the words were out before I could stop them. Words tend to escape my mouth before they are ready to be aired. A carpenter always measures twice and cuts once. I should apply that rule to what I say.

"Not locked? Auntie, what have I told you? It's not a safe world any more. And what, with the traffic picking up on 47, well, anyone could be passing by and decide this looks like a promising place to hit."

I didn't know what would make my old farmhouse look so promising for a "hit." The new homes down in the development looked a sight better if someone wanted to commit a robbery and get something of value. The only break-ins I knew of were caused by birds.

"I'm sorry, Auntie," Mary Jane continued as I followed her to the kitchen table. "It's just that I pictured you lying on the floor, I was afraid you might have fallen and couldn't get up."

Now I really had to hold back the chuckles. Next thing you know, she'd have me wearing one of those emergency calling devices around my neck.

"I didn't mean to worry you, MJ. I was putting away my Christmas stuff and I had my hands full." Even with all of her dramatics, I do love Mary Jane and know that she cares about me. I guess I wouldn't want it any other way.

"Do you have any coffee, Auntie Ann?" Mary Jane slung her blue fur trimmed parka over the back of a chair. "I could use a cup. It's been a busy morning." She made herself at home as she opened the cupboard and inspected the cups. Assured they were all clean, she chose one. She sniffed the coffee in the pot. Satisfied it was fresh, she poured it into the cup and then turned toward the refrigerator. I knew what came next. It had become ritual.

Mary Jane watched talk television programs and read books and articles on the care and feeding of the elderly. She knew how to recognize the signs of a senior whose living skills had slipped. The refrigerator open before her, she "looked" for the milk while she inspected to see that the vegetables were fresh and the meat wasn't green.

"There's some vanilla flavored cream that you like in there, MJ," I said to her.

"Ah, yes, here it is. Thanks." Mary Jane straightened up, nodded as though pleased that she didn't have to lecture me on spoiled food, and poured the flavored cream into her coffee, after she sniffed it of course. She placed it back in my amply stocked refrigerator.

"Well, now that I have the boys off to school, how can I help you today?" She sat down and settled against her parka on the back of the chair. As I watched her raise the cup to her lips I couldn't help but imagine she was being embraced by a polar bear with all the white fur on her jacket.

"Abby's Grill on Rockside would like a case of pickles. Could you run them over for me?"

"Sure. Are there any groceries I can pick up for you? Errands I can do?"

"No, but thanks."

I smiled. Mary Jane had just seen the refrigerator. Surely she knew the grocery shopping was done. I still drove my own car. I wasn't that feeble yet. As a matter of fact, if Mary Jane thought about it, she would realize that I was far from the feeble stage of life. At 56 I took up golf. I loved the challenge of that but not as much as the snow skiing I learned to do at age 60. Being active kept the energy level up and the arthritis at bay. Wouldn't she just sizzle if she knew I was contemplating scuba diving?

Over the top of her coffee cup, Mary Jane scrutinized the table top. She set the cup down and dove into my pile of cruise brochures. She waved one in the air and asked, "What's this?"

My cruise tickets had just arrived and they lay on the table in an impressive leather case that Cunard provided. She picked that up next and began to peruse the contents. The excursion booklet sat opened next to it. She flipped through that as well. Mary Jane allowed nothing to escape her attention.

"Are you planning another trip, Auntie Ann?"

Mary Jane still called me "Auntie Ann." It was left over from childhood when she couldn't say "Aunt Annie."

"I thought I might," I had hoped to break the news gently to her eventually but her keen sense of perception honed by the television programs she watched had sniffed me out.

"Are you going with a group?" She pursed her lips as though she'd just popped a sour lemon drop into her mouth. "You know how I hate you traveling alone."

I'd traveled alone many times since a few years after Russell passed on. I liked the sense of adventure, of self-discovery. You don't get that with a tour group.

"No." I took a deep breath and prepared myself for the lecture. Mary Jane was unusually quiet, seemingly immersed in the cruise information before her, so I took advantage and plunged ahead. "I thought I'd like to skip Christmas this year and do a cruise. You know, like in that book by Grisham I loaned you."

"You mean 'Skipping Christmas?'"

"Yes. That one, only I plan to actually take the cruise."

"But don't you want to be home for Christmas? Won't you feel lonely not being around the family?" The look on Mary Jane's face was one of incredibility, or was that incredulity? I always get those confused. "Won't you miss the snow you love to play in?" Sarcasm tinged her voice.

"Actually, I'll be back in time for the best snow." I passed her the brochure with the picture of the Queen Mary 2 on it. "I'm very interested in seeing this ship. I saw a film on the Travel Channel about its construction."

A shadow crossed her face. "It looks like the Titanic." Mary Jane always worried about ominous signs.

"I assure you there are no icebergs in the Caribbean. It will be quite warm and quite safe."

"Oh." Mary Jane sounded disappointed. What would she worry about now? "How long will you be gone?"

"About two weeks, fourteen nights to be exact."

Mary Jane opened the brochure as she looked for another reason why I shouldn't go. She couldn't understand my penchant for travel. I was younger than Mary Jane when Russell joined Jesus. The traveling helped me through some of the loneliness. It gave me goals. Helped me pass the time as I planned my next adventure. I wished she could have met Russell. Maybe she would have understood better what a great hole had been left in my life to try to fill.

As I watched Mary Jane inspect the excursion booklet, I thought back to that first summer when I'd gotten to know Russell. I was only 15. He arrived at our farm near Mansfield just after spring planting.

"So, you're a senior at Ohio State University?" I had asked as my fingers destroyed a piece of grass I held. I was nervous talking to a college student and one who was exceptionally handsome with his blue eyes and sandy brown hair that had a way of falling over his eye as if it had a mind of its own. He had strong arms and a ruddy complexion, traits earned from hard work in the fields.

"Yup. I'm majoring in Agricultural Economics and Rural Sociology." He laughed. "It's a fancy way to say I'm learning to be a farmer. Your father agreed to let me intern here for a few months."

My family took an instant liking to Russell. I watched each morning as he crowded into the front seat of the old pickup with my father and brother, and headed out to work the fields. Then, in the evening, my mother would lavish him with her special meals and warm rolls from the oven. Russell was handsome, smart, witty, and when I looked into his eyes, I saw the warmth of his soul.

I was in love.

"Just because you're older than me, Russell Pickels, doesn't mean you can pick on me," I said when he pulled my ponytail. I relished the attention.

"Hey, short stuff, where I come from you'd be a grizzly snack!" He laughed.

Russell was from Alaska. My heart broke when he left just after Thanksgiving to spend Christmas with his family but letters began to come, almost daily. Then he returned to Columbus to finish school and said he would visit when he could.

Then, on a fresh spring morning while I sat in church waiting for the service to begin, I sensed a presence next to me. I looked up into familiar smoky blue eyes that crinkled with mischief.

"Hey, short stuff." His greeting had set my heart racing. Russell had a nickname for everyone. I wondered as I studied Mary Jane, would he have called her Miss Kitty? Purring one minute and claws extended, ready to pounce, the next.

"Hey, stranger." I made room for him to sit beside me.

Russell sat down and held my hand throughout the morning. I never wanted him to let go. Our hands fit perfectly together. I knew our futures would too.

After Sunday dinner and a short chat with my father, Russell took me for a stroll in the apple orchard. The trees were in full bloom. We sat down under one and leaned against its gnarled bark.

"Annie, I want you to be my wife." A few petals floated down from the tree onto his head. "I realize you're much younger than I am, but I've never met anyone quite like you. I've prayed and prayed and the answer's always the same, you're meant to be mine."

For a moment, I couldn't breathe. And then he kissed me, a slow and gentle kiss on my forehead.

"What do you say?"

My eyes—my head—everything swam. I swallowed hard.

"Russell, I, I. . . "

"I love you, Annie Fisher. Do you love me?"

"Yes," I whispered. I was spellbound.

He kissed me again. This time it was a real kiss, soft and tender and sweetly scented by apple blossoms.

The apple blossom thoughts turned to pumpkin candle scent as Mary Jane brought me back with a poke of her finger at an ad for a big fancy tanzanite ring in the brochure. "These cruises seem to be all about getting you to spend money frivolously."

I sighed. "MJ, if I spent all my money on those baubles and bangles, I wouldn't have anything left to book another cruise with."

She harrumphed.

The jewelry ad reminded me of the simplicity of Russell's engagement ring. High school graduation day came and with it, a beautiful solitaire diamond set in a shiny gold band. I loved to watch it sparkle in a sunbeam. Along each side of the diamond were tiny hearts engraved in the band. It was as though the diamond was there to unite the two hearts forever.

I glanced down at the engagement ring I still wore on my finger. My heart was forever united with Russell's. What would life be like now if he were still here, I wondered? Would I be more like Mary Jane, children and a husband to hold me at night? Did Mary Jane appreciate what she had? I swallowed a lump that formed in my throat.

"Well, I suppose there's no talking you out of it," Mary Jane said as she looked up at me. She had finished her thorough investigation of the excursion booklet. She gave me that lemon-drop look again. "You will keep us up to date, like before?"

"Yes," I sighed impatiently. "I have a prepaid calling card and I will be sure to check in so that you don't think I've fallen off the face of the earth." I was afraid if I didn't promise to call, Mary Jane might pack a bag and come with me or arrange for one of those travel companions she always threatened to look up and hire. I quite preferred to have my own adventures and choose my own companionship, thank you.

With a wave from my kitchen door, I sent Mary Jane on her way, her hands cradling the box of pickles she was to deliver. Abbey's Grill was on her way home, an easy errand I could have run myself. Of course, if I hadn't asked her to deliver pickles, she would have snooped around the house and found something to clean or move or reorganize. The girl was always on a mission. Someday perhaps, I would be in need of her attention. For now, I just wanted her to feel she was needed and appreciated. Maybe she wouldn't be so uptight about trying to look after me then.

Thoughts of apple blossoms swirled in my head long after Mary Jane left. Was it too late to plant a couple of apple trees? Maybe I could get Tommy to help me. He seemed to have a green thumb, like Russell, my wonderful, handsome Russell.

Chapter Four

Mary Jane did not help me pack for my cruise. That job fell to Elma.

I didn't need the help, I just thought it would be fun to have her around, giving her opinion on what I should or shouldn't wear. Elma considers herself something of an authority on my haughty culture. Of course my haughty culture usually consists of a long sleeved flannel shirt, short sleeved cotton in the summer and a pair of jeans. That's just when I'm at home though, working with my pickles. I have a whole other closet full of clothes for travel, non-wrinkle slacks, some knit tops, a skirt for informal night dining and, of course, some sparkly beaded tops and a fancy long skirt for formal nights.

My bedroom was a mess, clothes scattered everywhere, with a shoe thrown in here and there. Hats, tote bags and scarves were distributed according to a mix and match system Elma concocted. She was like a chicken fluttering around and scattering feathers in an excited frenzy, repeating over and over, "The Queen Mary! The Queen Mary!" You would have thought I was going to meet a real queen at court.

"It's the Queen Mary 2," I said emphasizing the 2. The first Queen Mary had been retired, moored at a pier in Los Angeles, and turned into a floating hotel.

"Imagine, Annie," Elma clasped her hands together and sighed. "All those fine English gentlemen, warm sea breezes, moonlit nights, " She sighed, a scarf pressed against her cheek, her hazel eyes all misty as she floated in a daydream.

I watched as Elma paused to imagine herself on the ship. Then just as quickly she went back to pulling more clothes out of my closet to judge their appropriateness for my next once-in-a-lifetime cruise. I began to wonder if asking her to help me pack was such a good idea.

I didn't have a big enough suitcase or clothing budget for all the paraphernalia Elma insisted I take. Two swimsuits with cover-ups to match, sun hat, matching tote, and sandals, just in case I went to the beach; a heavy sweater, two jackets, one tailored and one casual, just in case it got cold; and sleeveless blouses, shorts, another sun hat, matching tote, and sandals, just in case it got too hot. We hadn't even discussed eveningwear yet.

"I like this one," she said pulling a sleeveless pink cotton dress from the depths of my closet. She held it up to me. "Cotton candy pink brings a blush to your cheeks, makes you look sweeter." She batted her eyelashes at me.

"Honestly, Elma, you'd think I was going off man-hunting the way you're carrying on." I took the pink dress and hung it back in the closet. I thought it might be a little tight. I wasn't going to try it on in front of Elma and bust a seam to send her into peals of laughter. "I need to take things that won't wrinkle easily. I don't want to be spending all my time in the laundry room ironing."

"They have a laundry room?" Elma looked shocked. "I thought you would have a butler or something."

"No." I laughed. Even if I could afford it, I wouldn't feel comfortable having a butler fuss with my things. "They probably have butlers in the suites, but I'm not in first class. I can't imagine paying all that extra money just for a butler and a special dining room."

Much to my relief, Elma abandoned my wardrobe and retreated to the big reading chair in the corner of my bedroom. She picked up the leather folder from Cunard and began paging through the information that arrived with my tickets. Her petite form settled into my overstuffed chair, her feet tucked neatly under her.

She was almost as old as me. Why wasn't I that flexible?

Elma was a good friend. She'd been my friend for almost 30 years. When the Thompsons moved into the Old Miller farmhouse across the road, Elma and I had hit it off right away. Well, except for Elma's nose problem. It took me a while to realize she meant no harm. She was just naturally curious and questions popped out of her mouth like popcorn in a hot pan without a lid.

"Pity the man who sees you in this," Elma said. She set aside the cruise brochure and reached for my new black evening dress. It was made out of one of those fabrics that travel well. You could roll it up in a ball, pack it in a suitcase, and just shake it out again with no wrinkles. She held it to her body and swirled around the room.

"Pity the friend who gets it dirty and has to have it dry cleaned," I shot back at her with a grin. Actually, the dress was washable which had made the purchase a no-brainer and a permanent part of my cruise wardrobe.

"I really need your opinion about these." I slipped on a pair of apricot Capri pants I had bought the same day as the dress. All the store windows had mannequins dressed in Capri pants. We used to call them pedal-pushers, so I figured it must be one of those retro things.

"They don't make me look like a teeny bopper, do they?" I asked.

"They're great!" Elma's hazel eyes glowed behind the new glasses she'd recently bought. They were almost frameless and flattered her face. I had helped her with her fashion choices last week at the eyeglass store. I liked the thin band of gold across the top that held the lenses in place instead of the heavy black plastic she used to wear. Elma still fussed with the new trifocals though. She raised her head a bit, and then lowered it until she found the right spot to look through.

"You sure?" I asked. "I don't want to be lookin' like an old fool."

"I'm sure. Although I don't know why you won't wear shorts and take advantage of all the sunny weather. You got legs. Show 'em!" Elma gave me a wicked wink.

"Yeah, I got legs sure enough, , and varicose veins to decorate them. They look like I went to a tattoo artist who needed glasses. I'm not about to flaunt those, sunny weather or not."

"Come on, Annie. You still cut a nice figure and you're active. Good golly, you're more athletic than I am, and you're older than me."

"Fine. Rub it in. I'm older than you." I stuck my tongue out at her. "That only means I've got more sense." There wasn't a whole lot of difference in age, only a few months between us, but we liked to tease each other about it. I took the tack that she should listen to her elder, me.

"I just don't want you to rule out the possibility of meeting someone, some nice man, and having a little fun, maybe develop a friendship."

She tread on dangerous ground and she knew it. We'd been through this before.

"Elma, this isn't the Love Boat. It's the Queen Mary 2. And I'm not looking for any male companionship."

"Why not?" She pushed on. "I'm just saying you shouldn't rule it out. There's a lot to be said for companionship with the opposite sex, especially at our age."

"Oh, so now you're 65?" I made an effort to shift the conversation to something else.

"Not until this Saturday and don't you forget it."

I wouldn't forget it. Elma and I have a standing date for our birthdays. It consists of lunch followed by a trip to the greeting card shop. We scour the racks for clever cards and exchange them in the store. The funnier the card the better we like it. We read the cards and then put them back on the shelf. It never costs us a penny in postage.

"Your birthday's why I want to get my stuff together today," I explained. "I can't traipse around with you all weekend, and be packed and ready to go by Monday morning."

"What time did you want us to pick you up? I think Warren wrote it down but I want to be sure."

I relaxed. My ploy worked. I got Elma off the subject of men and romance.

"I need to be at the airport by 6 a.m. I figure we need to leave at 4:45."

"4:45!" She rolled her eyes.

"I can call a cab if that's too early for you and Warren."

"It's way too early." Elma rolled her eyes again. "But we'll suffer through it. I figure I can get Warren to buy me breakfast that morning. There's sure to be a breakfast place along the way back."

Suddenly she jumped up and grabbed a sleeveless top off the dresser. "This would look great with those pants. See, now you have an outfit and you didn't even know it."

I didn't tell her I had purchased the two pieces together just like they'd been displayed in the store.

Elma looked at her watch. "I guess it's time to go home and feed Warren." She put her hands on the back of her hips and swayed back and forth, stretching taut muscles as if she'd put in a full day of physical labor. She told me one time that she and "Arthur Ritis" were becoming close friends. I said I didn't think that was a good idea, her being married and all.

"Is Abbey's Grill okay with you for your birthday lunch tomorrow?"

"Sounds good," Elma replied. "I hear they serve great pickles with their corned beef sandwiches." She giggled.

Saturday came and went in a hurry. Why is it time moves faster the older you get? Elma and I had lunch at Abbey's and they surprised her with a cupcake sporting a lit candle. The waiters and the cook sang "Happy Birthday" and Elma basked in all the attention. We found some funny cards at the drugstore to exchange for her special day and put them neatly back on the rack. I bought a special Christmas card to send to Mary Jane. I'm sure the clerk wondered what took us so long to pick out one card.

Sunday, after church and dinner out with the Thompsons at Elma's favorite buffet place, I began packing in earnest. Most of the stuff fit into my new large suitcase with rollers on the bottom. Some clever young man I supposed had come up with that nifty invention that made the rollers move in any direction. I could push the suitcase or pull it, whatever was most convenient. I packed a small satchel with shoes and a few items to get me through a day or two in case the airline sent my suitcase in the wrong direction. I stuck in a book I wanted to read as well. It was a murder mystery, something to distract me from the tedium of air travel and challenge my power of deductive reasoning.

I was putting my tickets and passport into my travel tote when I heard a knock at the door. It wasn't Elma; she'd walk right in. It couldn't be Mary Jane either. There was no telegraphed identifying knock. I stepped around the suitcases and went to the kitchen door. Tommy's big grin greeted me.

I swung the door open and motioned for him to come in. "Tommy. What a pleasant surprise!"

"I wasn't sure if you'd left yet," he said as he removed his boots.

"I just finished packing. I leave tomorrow morning." We went into the kitchen. I didn't have any coffee to offer him and the cinnamon rolls were all in the freezer. "Can I get you some tea? I didn't make any coffee this afternoon."

"No, thanks, Mrs. A. I'm not staying long. I knew you wouldn't be here for Christmas and I wanted to give you something." He blushed like a little boy who's about to hand his first girlfriend a bouquet of daisies. Then he held out a small package loosely wrapped in Christmas paper. It had one of those stick-on bows on top that didn't want to stick properly. It popped off when I took the gift from him then bounced on the floor.

"I'm sorry. I'm not very good at wrapping things," Tommy scooped up the wayward bow and held it out to me.

"I'm not either," I said trying to ease his embarrassment. I stuck the bow back in place and admired the decoration. "I try to use those gift bags whenever I can."

I nodded at the small gift in my hand. "May I open it? Or do I have to be good and wait until Christmas?"

He smiled that winning smile I loved so much. "Sure, open it."

I carefully peeled back the paper and watched as a snow globe emerged from the layers of Christmas wrap. It was plastic, full of liquid and snowflakes, and had a small skier crouched between a few pine trees.

"It's beautiful!" I held it upside down and shook it to make the snow fly.

"I just wanted to get you something, kind of a thank you, you're always so good to me, you know, the coffee and cinnamon rolls." He shuffled his feet and looked down to hide his reddened face.

"How did you know I liked to ski?"

"I remembered you saying something once." He beamed up at me, obviously proud that he remembered and happy that I was pleased by his gift.

I hugged him.

He stiffened, as though he wasn't used to being hugged, but then returned the gesture by patting me awkwardly on the shoulder.

"Are you sure I can't make you some tea?"

"Naw, really, I can't stay." Tommy started for his boots. "I just wanted to make sure you got a Christmas present before you left."

"Thank you, Tommy. This is really very special, so unexpected. It's a beautiful surprise." I couldn't think of anything that would truly express what I was feeling. I was overwhelmed by his thoughtfulness.

I walked him to his car and watched him drive away. The painted flames of his car glinted in the late afternoon sunshine. If I had a grandchild I would have liked it to be someone as thoughtful as that young man.

I placed the snow globe next to the basket of napkins on the kitchen table to remind me of my special friend. I reached up to my eye and felt a drop of moisture in the corner.

Was I crying?

I hate to cry.

I took a deep ragged breath and blinked away the annoying moisture in my eyes. Turning again to my packing list, I scratched off passport and tickets, and murder mystery. I was tempted to sit down and open my mystery book but I didn't want to start something I couldn't put down. Four o'clock would arrive early in the morning and I needed a good night's rest.

A light snack, a couple of sit-coms, and I was off to bed. Sleep came easily. It just didn't seem to last long.

Chapter Five

The alarm clock shrieked its warning at me. However, the clock didn't know I was up and half dressed. I just needed to don a pair of sneakers and a sweater and jacket to peel off as I migrated south. I scurried from the bathroom to turn the alarm off.

It was too early to expect Warren and Elma, so I brewed some tea in a disposable cup left over from last month's ladies' Bible fellowship at my house. I didn't want to leave any dirty dishes lying around for Mary Jane to find when she checked on the house, which I knew she would do even though I told her it was unnecessary.

I fished out a can of Slimfast from the back of the refrigerator where it hid from Mary Jane's disapproving eyes. She was sure to have a reason I shouldn't be drinking the stuff. I thought it was nutritious enough to substitute for a meal once in a while. I wasn't sure when I'd have breakfast this morning, if at all. The gourmet breakfast on a plane usually consisted of a dry muffin and bitter coffee. "Won't be long and they'll be charging us for that muffin and coffee," I grumbled to myself. Most of the airlines already charged for meals.

I settled into my chair at the table. As I sipped tea and chocolate Slimfast, my thoughts turned to Russell. A small wave of melancholy washed over me. What fun we could have if he were cruising with me. There were still times, even after 30 years, that I felt the emptiness of my loss. Thankfully, a knock on the door brought me back to my senses again before I was awash in the might-have-beens.

"Ready?" Warren asked when I opened the door. Warren was the opposite of Elma, quiet, unassuming. His physical size would make you believe he could hold his own on a football field but his thinning gray hair and paunch told you he was an armchair quarterback.

"I'm ready." I passed my larger bag to him and grabbed the smaller one.

"This all you got?" Warren looked surprised but obviously pleased. "Elma would have packed the kitchen sink as well."

"She tried, but I took it out."

Warren exploded with laughter. He chuckled all the way out to the car as I followed behind him.

Snow drifted down gently and rested on my hair and nose. The quiet December morning smelled fresh and crisp. We put the suitcases in the trunk, and I climbed into a nice warm car behind Elma. She turned and peered over the seat at me.

"Good morning," Elma sang with excitement as I closed the door and reached for the seat belt. Warren slid into the driver's seat next to her.

"Morning. Thanks again you two; I really appreciate this."

"Not a problem," Warren's arm swung out and his hand reached for the back of the seat as he looked over his shoulder to back the car out the driveway. Elma automatically ducked her head as the arm swept past her.

I smiled. The move was a choreographed dance that a couple learns from many years of being together.

Elma babbled about their Christmas plans all the way to the airport, detailing the dinner they expected to have with the family, including their daughter and son-in-law from California. "This has to be the year they tell us we're going to be grandparents. It's the only Christmas gift I want."

"Well then, you can give mine back."

"No way." Elma was absolutely a child at heart. "Do I really have to wait until Christmas to open it?"

"Yes, and I'm counting on you, Warren, to see that she does."

Warren saluted me in the rearview mirror.

When we arrived at the airport, Warren pulled into the lane marked "departures" and Elma's conversation turned to house watching, my house in particular. "I'll grab the mail each day and take it in," she reminded me. "That way I'll know the furnace is still running. No need to have the pipes freeze while you're away."

"Thanks, Elma. I appreciate all you do for me, both of you. I expect someone from the sheriff's office will be by too. I called them to let them know my vacation plans and asked for a house watch. So if you're there and someone yells 'Freeze!' you better comply."

"If I get shot trying to help you out," Elma said semi-seriously, "it'll be all your fault."

"It's okay. I gave them a good description of you and Mary Jane."

"Have a good time, kiddo." It sounded like Elma was about to cry. Warren pulled up to the airline's departure door and popped the trunk to get my bags.

"Thanks again for the ride," I said, my hand on the door handle. "There are a couple of jars of pickles on my kitchen counter for your Christmas dinner. Don't forget them."

"My mouth's watering just thinking about them," she cooed.

Elma and I got out and stood beside the suitcases Warren unloaded from the trunk and set on the curb.

"Remember," Elma lectured, her index finger jabbing at me. "I want to hear all the romantic details."

Warren laughed. "She has it in her head you're going to meet a man and fall madly in love on this cruise."

That remark earned him a punch in the arm from Elma. "Just don't rule it out," she warned as if she were a prophetess.

I hugged them both. We waved to each other as they drove away from the curb.

Thanks Lord, for such good friends. Watch over them while I'm away.

I yanked up the handle of the large suitcase and balanced my little one on top, then wheeled them into the ticket area. Elma's words kept ringing in my head. A man. Romantic details. That woman fantasized enough for the both of us. She should be a romance writer.

I moved to the counter to check in and answer all the packing questions, "Did you pack your own bag? Has this bag been out of your sight? Did anyone ask you to carry anything for them?" The young man drilling me with questions was handsomely dressed in a blue blazer and mock turtleneck with ID tags hanging from his jacket pocket. His picture looked as bored as he did. Tommy might not be so well dressed but he certainly made conversation more interesting. He would do well in a job like this. What kind of job did Tommy have? He had never talked about a job. I made a mental note to ask.

The young man took my suitcases and attached the destination tags to the handles. He slung the suitcases onto the moving belt where they promptly disappeared behind strips of plastic hopefully to reappear again in Fort Lauderdale.

With a forced smile, the natty young man handed me my boarding pass. "Gate 50, Concourse C, to your left. Have a good trip."

"I hope to." I hooked my travel tote over my arm, and headed for security.

When I saw the lines were short, I sighed with relief. I could take my time. It was always a hassle to know what to remove so the metal detector would remain silent. I took off my shoes. It didn't matter if they had metal or not, I learned the hard way that you had to put them through the x-ray machine, otherwise they'd have you step aside, and assume the stance while they ran that fat wand up and down your body. Wouldn't be long before they'd be sending us through those new-fangled machines that saw absolutely everything. Well, I'd deal with that when I had to. For now, I just tried to get all the metal off me.

Along with my shoes went my jacket. I didn't shed my cardigan. Beneath it, I wore a sleeveless blouse, and it was too cold to stand there with my arms exposed.

A man came up behind me, obviously in a hurry. In the time it took me to fill one bin, he had filled two with a laptop, a coat, briefcase, shoes, and loose change. Mr. I've-Done-This-A-Thousand-Times tapped his stocking foot. It was cell phone withdrawal, I was sure. He couldn't carry it through the metal detector.

As he pushed his bins forward, I caught a whiff of a very unpleasant but familiar odor. This guy must have been out walking his dog before he left home and wasn't careful where he'd stepped. I glanced in the bin. Too bad. They looked like really expensive shoes. I hoped he had enough time for a shoeshine. Oh, the poor shoeshine man.

When I pushed my travel tote and shoes onto the moving belt for the x-ray machine, the guard waved me on. I held my breath and stepped through the arch of metal detection. Alarms sounded. Drats! What did I do?

"Please step over here, ma'am," the female guard with the big wand said.

What had set the stupid detector off? I knew I didn't have a wire in my bra. The clerk at the store had assured me I was supported by plastic, not metal.

Unfortunately, I knew the drill. I stood with my feet shoulder width apart, arms outstretched, and looked straight ahead. The electronic bloodhound sniffed around my arms and chest. When it got to my waist, the wand buzzed with excitement.

Dumb. Dumb. Dumb.

I had forgotten to take my belt off. The buckle was big enough to trip all the alarms. I removed the belt and used one hand to hold up my pants.

"Ma'am, you have to hold your arms out," the guard said.

"I can't. My pants will fall down." I always wore pants that were a little larger around the waist for travel. They were more comfortable and allowed for those extra five pounds I always carried home around my middle after a vacation.

The woman folded her arms over her rather large bosom and narrowed her eyebrows. "Arms out."

Did I really look that dangerous? Besides, she'd already checked my armpits once. "I don't want to embarrass either one of us with my pants falling down," I insisted.

"Your pants aren't going to fall down."

"Isn't there somewhere else we could do this?" People were beginning to stare at the obvious confrontation.

"We could go to a private room but that would waste a lot of your time and mine. I don't think you want to risk being late for your plane." The guard crossed her arms, her wand sticking out and pointing in an awkward position. She impatiently shifted her weight from one foot to the other.

I took a deep breath. "Okay but do this quickly. And if my pants start to fall, I'm going to grab them. So don't pull your gun and start shooting."

The guard rolled her eyes.

I spread my legs further apart to keep the pants from sliding all the way down in case I wasn't fast enough. Then I extended my stomach muscles as far as I could to enlarge my circumference. I raised my arms and prayed.

The guard started the wand in its usual path from shoulders to underarms. I could feel the smooth lining inside the pants begin to crawl down my leg. The wand moved down one side of me and up to my waist then down again. Sure enough my pants started to slide just as she was bringing the wand up the last leg. The tip of the wand caught on the flap of my pants pocket saving me from certain exposure.

"Gotcha," the guard said as she held her wand in place until I could grasp the waistband and pull it back where it belonged. She looked so proud of herself.

Once we established that I wasn't a threat to anyone's security, I dressed and hurried to my gate. "Stupid terrorists," I mumbled under my breath with every step. They were the cause of all this. I wondered if whacking terrorists with a rolled up newspaper would do any good. Probably not.

I rounded the corner of Concourse C and found Gate 50. There was just enough time left to make a potty stop before boarding. I avoided in-flight restrooms whenever I could. The ladies room was right across from my gate. I was in and out quickly. Much relieved, I boarded my plane for Fort Lauderdale.

I found my seat and slid across to the window. My carry on barely fit under the seat in front of me. I thought about putting it in the overhead bin but figured the flight wasn't long enough to worry about leg space so much. I began to relax. An interrogation at check in and a strip tease through security, hopefully, nothing else would go wrong with my flight. I settled back into my seat and opened my book, *Murder in the Marketplace*. The back cover indicated it was a suspense thriller that had more twists than a bag of pretzels, and a surprise ending. I turned to the first page and began to read:

"It was a dark, stormy night."

Not a good start. I checked to make sure the author wasn't Bulwer-Lytton, or Snoopy.

A rather large lady huffed and puffed down the aisle and stopped at my row of seats. She looked left then right and said, "Oh, here I am." She plopped a square canvas bag with a mesh top onto the aisle seat beside me, then struggled to stuff a large bag in the overhead bin until a gentleman finally got up and helped her push it in far enough for the door to close.

"Oh, thank you," she said sweetly. "I couldn't have done that on my own. You are so kind. Your wife must be so proud of you. You are married aren't you? I wouldn't think someone as nice as you are would still be available."

I watched the man turn beet red as he returned to his seat.

She turned to me. "He really is a nice man, don't you think?" She didn't give me time to answer. "It's hard to find those kind of men anymore. It's this entire equality thing between men and women. It's spoiled it for us ladies."

I had nodded at her first remark but I wasn't sure how I wanted to react to the rest. It seemed she was going to rant on whether I agreed or not.

Carefully she took the square bag and stowed it under the seat in front of her. "Okay, honey. We're on our way. It won't be long now."

I looked to see if she had one of those hands-free devices people talk to. Nope. She was talking to herself. Surely she wasn't calling me honey. Was she addressing someone in the bag? Did she have someone's ashes in there? Now I was worried. What kind of a person was I sitting next to?

She rearranged her clothing a bit, smoothed her skirt and pulled her knit top down over the back of the skirt's waistband. Her hands examined the short-cropped platinum hair that crowned her head in a spiky cut. Satisfied all was in order, she carefully lowered herself into the seat. Producing a mirrored compact from the purse in her lap, she flipped it open and fussed with the layers of makeup on her face. Makeup is high maintenance. That's why I don't wear it much.

"I almost missed the plane. I had to run from the security area all the way to the gate," my seatmate began again. "I knew I couldn't count on my brother to get up on time. I should have taken a cab. I hate rushing like that. It's not good for Mopsie either." The woman hardly took a breath when she talked.

Mopsie? I raised an eyebrow. Was Mopsie the entity she was talking to in the bag?

Just as I was about to ask, she leaned forward and unzipped the mesh top of the bag beneath the seat. Instantly the head of a Skye terrier adorned with a bright red bow popped out. Good grief! She'd smuggled a dog on board!

"Oooh, how's my little baby? Are you thirsty? I'll bet you are, and hungry too. Poor baby." She turned to me. "I didn't feed her or give her any water since last evening. I didn't want her making a mess in her little bag."

She continued with more information than I wanted to hear about the bodily functions of a small dog but eventually the woman, and her dog, settled down. The plane lifted off the runway and to my amazement, the dog never whimpered. I returned to my murder mystery only to be distracted moments later by two eyes outlined in black and heavy with mascara peering oddly at the front of my paperback.

"Great read," the dog lady commented as she sat back in her seat again. "I read that on my last trip to Miami. Let's see if I remember correctly." Her face scrunched together in the middle while she concentrated. "They find a body in the farmer's market in a cooler and suspect the butcher but then the baker looks guilty when they find out that he'd been seeing the victim's wife, of course they suspect the wife too. Then when the CSI guys find beeswax under the victim's fingernails, they realize he was killed because he was in debt to the guy who was selling candles, but actually, the candles were just a cover for the bookmaking operation he was running."

All in one breath! She'd told the whole story all in one breath! Trying to stop her would have been like trying to stop a Mack truck rolling downhill with no brakes.

"Oh, dear!" She raised a hand to her mouth. "I suppose I shouldn't have told you how it ended."

Duh, I thought.

"Oh well, now you can just enjoy reading it. You won't have to worry about how it comes out in the end."

Finished. Taken care of. Her job was done. She had helped me avoid the consternation of trying to figure out a who-dun-it. Like I said before, I'm not a violent person, but I clutched my book tightly and willed my hands to stay put. In my head though, I could hear, "Whack! Whack! Whack!"

Mopsie behaved in her little bag until the smell of food began to permeate the cabin. When you begin to unwrap a hundred or so muffins from their plastic covering in a confined area, the smell fills the air. Mopsie's little stomach must have been churning from lack of food. She began to whimper.

Dog Lady rescued Mopsie from the bag and held the furry animal to her abundant chest. The stewardess stopped in the aisle and gently reminded her that the dog would have to go back in the carrier before we landed.

"Yes, ma'am," Dog Lady replied. "She just needs a little air. I'll put her back in a minute."

Since when were animals allowed out of their carriers on a plane? Weren't they concerned about people's allergies? Or canine chaos if there were more than one onboard? Doesn't anyone follow rules anymore?

Mopsie and her owner shared the cinnamon bran muffin bite by bite. I like dogs, but not well enough to be eating from the same muffin. Their muffin disappeared quickly, and Mopsie put her nose to the air sniffing for more to eat. She spied the half eaten muffin on my tray table.

Little legs pumped and pushed until Mopsie had wiggled her way to my muffin. In an instant it vanished. My mouth hung open in amazement. This petite little thing had swallowed that muffin like a python swallowed a pig. I looked to see if her throat was bulging.

"Mopsie! Bad girl! Tell the lady you're sorry."

Did the dog talk too?

"That's all right. I wasn't very hungry," I said to Mopsie. "You needed it more than I did." I felt sorry for the dog. She hadn't asked to be shut up in a bag, stuffed under a seat, and starved for a day just so her owner could travel without the guilt of leaving her behind. Dog Lady on the other hand was getting my dandruff up.

The stewardess came by and politely asked again that Mopsie be returned to her bag until the flight was over. It seemed okay with Mopsie. The muffins were gone. I worried about where those muffins had gone and what kind of havoc they might play with Mopsie's delicate little digestive system. We still had an hour of flight time left.

Chapter Six

Mopsie managed to keep her muffin down—at least until we got to the terminal and deplaned. I heard a gasp, and saw Mopsie's head juggle up and down in her bag as her owner dashed for the ladies room to clean up whatever it was she'd discovered in Mopsie's carrier.

I walked toward baggage claim until I found the appropriate hand-held sign that read "Cunard." Joining the other passengers who had gathered under the white sign with blue letters, I felt my tension ease a bit. Let the pampering begin.

We were led to waiting buses to be transported to the cruise terminal. They were touring buses contracted by the cruise company to transport us comfortably to the ship in Port Everglades about fifteen minutes away. I shed my sweater as I waited to board. The weather was a perfect sunny 74 degrees with little humidity. The kind of Florida day that makes you want to be a snowbird, someone who spends her winters in the Sunshine State instead of battling the cold and snow and slush of a northern winter.

We were well cared for but not as pampered, I'm sure, as the first class passenger I saw waiting on the dock with her luggage when we arrived. I spied her through the tinted window of the bus. I guessed from the wrinkles in her face, she was about 80 unless she hadn't weathered the years well. Some people can look eighty and be sixty, especially if they are ardent sunbathers.

Despite her aged looks, this lady posed like a senior super model atop her trunk. Who travels with a trunk anymore? She was thin but stately, dressed in dark navy pants, with a matching sweater of white and navy stripes embellished mid-chest with a gold anchor. Atop her head perched a saucy little cap of the same colors nestled at a slight angle into a neatly coiffed head of silver hair. Her makeup was impeccable, defining her features but not making her look painted.

Even from a distance, I could tell she had those fake nails. A woman with acrylic nails gestures in a way that draws attention to her nail work. Posture perfect, she demurely crossed her legs and dangled delicate black patent leather slippers as she sat waiting for, well, whatever or whomever she was waiting for.

Lord, forgive me for being materialistic, but I don't have anything that comes close to that in my wardrobe. And, I'll never look that perfectly groomed until the undertaker does it for me.

Were my careful choices packed away in my suitcase appropriate enough for this cruise? I knew it would be more formal than other ships. This was an ocean liner with a heritage of elegant liners before it. Would I just look like some kind of yokel trying to mix with the upper crust?

Of course, I thought, as panic subsided, I'm in steerage and she's obviously in first class, probably not even the Princess level. She's all the way up to the Queen's level, I bet. A suite, a butler, and a privileged dining room. Normally I wouldn't worry so much about how I'm dressed, but I didn't want to appear dowdy in the midst of such high-class cruisers. I probably wouldn't even run into people like that where my stateroom was. Yes, she was definitely a Queen's level cruiser. I was willing to bet she'd give her butler a run for *her* money.

After going through security for the second time in one day, albeit successfully this time, I joined the stream of passengers ascending the escalator to the reception area where we would check in for our cruise. I automatically headed for the long counter that held the terminals to complete the process.

There were no lines. This looked to be a snap. I headed for one of the open spaces.

A lady in a cruise-blue jacket and skirt with a bright red scarf at the neck stuck out her hand and stopped me cold. "I'm sorry ma'am. I need to see your ticket before you can get in line."

No problem. My documents were in the handy-dandy side pocket of my travel tote. I pulled out the booklet that held the tickets, vouchers, and a dozen pages of small print that exempted the cruise line from any responsibility for absolutely any catastrophe, big or small. That fine print guaranteed Mary Jane would never take a cruise if she read it.

The woman scrutinized my ticket and exclaimed, "Oh, I'm so sorry. We're only processing the 12:15 passengers now. You aren't scheduled to check in until one."

"But there are no 12:15 passengers." I pointed to the empty spaces in front of the computers. I knew I sounded argumentative, but it seemed obvious.

The woman looked as though it were a revelation. For the second time in one day, my mind reached for the rolled newspaper in its little orange bag. The image of one good whack to get some sense into this woman's head helped me keep my patience.

The woman adjusted her little red scarf and looked at me with the professional smile of a person who dealt daily with the perceived impertinence of others. She patted me on the hand. Calmly and slowly, enunciating each word, she stated, "The cruise company has to stick to its schedule so that embarkation will go smoothly for you and all the other passengers. If you'll just find a seat, I'll be happy to see that you are in a line and ready to check in at one o'clock."

Patronized again! Did people think gray heads, or white for that matter, meant they had to talk slower and louder for us to understand them?

I mentally whacked her all the way back to one of the molded plastic chairs that was empty in the fifth row. By the time I was done, her hair was askew, her scarf was untied and hanging precariously over one shoulder, and she had lost one shoe. This kind of anger management was akin to a speaker who had to imagine an audience dressed in their underwear so she didn't feel so nervous. But everyone knows you can't harbor bad thoughts long in your head, so I asked the Lord to forgive me and help me to think more kindly about the lady in cruise-blue who had a job to do.

The molded plastic chair conformed to someone else's behind, not mine. Rather than be uncomfortable, I chose instead to exercise my legs by wandering around the large reception room. Three times around the Promenade Deck of the Queen Mary 2 was said to be a mile. I estimated six to eight times around this room would do as well.

There was nothing much to look at. A snack bar sold packaged sandwiches, candy, and canned drinks for those who couldn't wait for the lunch buffet aboard ship. The only place of interest was a display set up way in the back corner. Men dressed as waiters in smart white jackets and black trousers stood around it. I ventured over.

A table was arranged with dinnerware and menus from the various specialty restaurants aboard the ship. I picked up one menu that read "Todd English." The pre-cruise material had stated that this was the specialty restaurant where, for an extra $30 for dinner, you could enjoy the famous cuisine of award winning chef, Todd English.

"Would you like to make a reservation, madam?" asked a man dressed in black with a linen cloth draped over his forearm. I could tell he was the maître 'd just by the difference in his stature and dress. While the other men were wearing short white jackets with black pants, his outfit looked more like a tux. He seemed a bit anxious to get me to sign up. I wondered if he had a quota to meet before we embarked on our voyage.

"Oh, no thanks," I said as pleasantly as I could. I didn't want to say I had no one to dine with. I felt you should have a dinner partner for a place like that. My face flushed with heat. Why was I blushing? Was I embarrassed to be alone? At my age, I should be done with that. Maybe menopause was returning. Perish the thought!

"Ah, but you can come and have a quiet dinner and enjoy conversation with our waiters, and me." Had he read my thoughts? His smile adjusted, as he tried to put me at ease.

I set the menu back down and said, "Thanks, I'll think about it," and moved on.

I was just about to lower my bottom into one of those uncomfortable seats again when a voice over the loud speaker barked, "Those with a check-in time of 1 p.m. may now proceed to the counter."

I looked at my watch. It was only 12:50. My goodness I hoped this wouldn't upset the cruise company's whole system. Why, it could lead to all sorts of changes to the schedule. A wry smile crossed my face. Hoisting my bag onto my shoulder again, I dug out my cruise documents and marched forward.

The lovely cruise hostess unclasped the red velvet rope to let me through. I smiled at her to show there were no hard feelings, and she smiled back as if nothing had happened. I planted my feet in the first empty space I found in front of one of the computers.

The man behind the counter paged through my documents and clickety-clacked the computer keys. His eyes concentrated on his screen, not giving me a second glance. Head still bent, he raised his hand and pointed to a ball perched on top of the screen.

"Look right up here," he instructed.

I stared at what looked like an eyeball staring back. Just as I squinted to get a better look, I heard a click. I pulled my head back. That was strange, I thought.

"All right." He said, shuffling my leftover documents and handing them to me. I stooped to stick them in my tote. When I straightened, he was holding out a plastic card to me.

"This will be the key to your stateroom and your boarding pass as well," he continued, pointing to the card in his hand. "You won't need extra identification. It will also be the way you pay for purchases aboard ship. Enjoy your cruise."

I was puzzled. On all of my previous cruises, we had to carry a photo ID, a passport or driver's license for security in a port. This was something new, a picture on my sea pass. As I walked away, I looked down at the card. A white haired lady with a prominent nose, eyebrows raised, mouth skewed, and one eye half closed stared up at me. That little eyeball had been a camera. It had captured my image and put it on the card. This would be my required picture ID. This is how I was going to get on the ship? Who would let such a crazy person board? Should I protest or was one run-in with cruise staff enough for the day?

I wavered. I couldn't live with that picture for fourteen nights, or days for that matter. I turned back to the counter, but the man had abandoned his computer.

Now what? A little voice in my head said, "See, that's what happens to people with bad attitudes and rolled up newspapers."

I forged ahead. Why not try boarding? If the photo didn't work, I'd come back. I passed the photographers rounding up people for welcome aboard pictures. They looked like cattle being sorted out for branding. I didn't stop. One bad picture for the day was enough.

Security looked at my card, inserted it in a little machine that binged its approval, and waved me through without so much as a smile to indicate the absurdity of my captured image. Did they think I actually looked like that?

Maybe I did. Scary thought. I needed to find a mirror.

There were two essential things I always looked for when I first reached my stateroom upon embarkation for any cruise. The first was the little daily newsletter the ship produced. It told you the serving times and locations for all meals. You could eat all day but without that little paper, you'd have a difficult time finding the food. The Daily Programme lay on the beige bedspread next to all the "Welcome aboard!" sales ads from the various shops on Deck 3.

The second thing was the map of the ship. The QM2 had a pocket-sized fold out map laying on the vanity in the room next to the housekeeping card that said, "Hello, my name is Marcus." The map was a handy size but it was of little help to the directionally challenged. It showed the side view of the ship rather than a layered version of each deck. I tucked it in my pocket in case I got desperate.

I checked in the bathroom. It was standard cruise ship size— large enough for one person but too small to be shared by two, or used by one who indulged too much in the midnight buffets and had a large circumference.

The room was brightly lit from the glassed door that looked out onto the balcony. Unfortunately the balcony was cut from the hull of the ship and didn't allow for a view when you sat in a lounge chair since the railing was chest high. If you wanted to see the view, you'd have to stand.

I returned to examine the rest of the room. There was a wooden mirrored vanity, a small settee and glass coffee table, the advertised "spacious closet" with plenty of hangers, and a safe, which I would try to program later. I glanced at my reflection in the mirror. I relaxed a little. The image wasn't as bad as the picture on my ID.

A knock on my stateroom door startled me; perhaps the butler bringing tea? No Annie, this is steerage, remember?

"Yes?" I called out. If he were the butler, he'd let himself in.

The door opened. "Ms. Peekles?" It was the cabin steward. A butler would have been dressed in tails.

"Yes."

"Hallo, I am Marcus, your cabin steward. The room is all right?" Marcus was dark skinned with wavy black hair and couldn't have been much older than Tommy. I didn't recognize his accent, maybe Indian, maybe Filipino. I was never very good at that.

He continued his practiced welcome speech. "If there is anything you need, please let me know."

So, all right, he wasn't a butler, but he was charming and I was sure he could handle anything I needed just fine.

"Everything looks great, Marcus. All I need is my luggage."

"Oh, I will check. Some luggage is here."

Sure, some luggage was here, but I knew better than to hold my breath waiting for it. Luggage on a cruise ship had a way of not showing up until the last minute before dinner. "Thank you, Marcus. I'll just freshen up and go find some lunch."

"Yes, ma'am." He bobbed up and down as he backed out the door.

I caught myself bobbing in return. Marcus was a nice young man, much more approachable than those people had been on the dock during embarkation.

I glanced at the card in my hand again. Well, I didn't seem to scare Marcus. I peered in the mirror. I needed to be sure I really didn't resemble that picture, at least not all the time. The woman looking back at me appeared somewhat normal, although there was a bit of fire in her eyes.

My rumbling stomach drew me away from my inspection of the old woman in the mirror. I set out to find the buffet.

The Daily Programme announced that the lunch buffet was in the Kings Court restaurants located on Deck 7. How hard could that be to find? Just get in the elevator, go to Deck 7 and follow the smell of food, I figured.

My plan worked. I got off the elevator on Deck 7 and moved in the direction of the arrow on the sign that said, "Kings Court." Well, that was easy.

When I entered, I immediately saw the trays and silverware at the start of the queue. This being an English ship, I assumed it to be a queue, not a line. I reached for a tray containing silverware neatly wrapped in a white cloth napkin. To my surprise, I found myself in a tug of war with the server in charge of the trays.

"Pleeze," she said and nodded to some place behind me.

I wasn't letting go, please, or no please. She nodded again trying to direct my attention to something. I wasn't going to fall for any tricks. I kept a grasp on the tray, and turned slightly to the side. A couple entered, stopped, and placed their hands under a little dispenser that hung on the wall. It spit a glob of disinfectant into each of their hands and they rubbed them together. They moved forward, and the server eagerly handed them a tray with silverware.

Well, why didn't she just ask if I'd washed my hands?

I turned around, rolled my eyes, and let the dispenser deposit its spit on one of my palms. I rubbed my hands together, inhaling the smell of rubbing alcohol mixed with some sort of herbal scent. When I turned back again, the server beamed with approval and held a tray out to me.

I thanked "Mom" and took the tray.

The Kings Court consisted of four different buffet lines. One featured Italian dishes, one, Asian style cuisine, another, grilled items, hamburgers and hot dogs could be found in the last queue. After being coaxed to wash my hands, I felt like a kid so I opted for a hot dog and fries. I'd worry about my cholesterol later.

It took me a bit longer to figure out where the drink station was, but once I had everything I needed, I found an empty seat near a window. I gazed out at the sunny weather and watched people parade by on the promenade deck.

While it was warmer than back home in Ohio, it was still a little cool for Florida weather. Many people wore sweatshirts or light jackets. I loved to people-watch so this was as good as eating lunch while viewing The Price Is Right. Bob Barker and now Drew Carey always brought out the fun side of people, so did a cruise ship.

The passengers I noted were mostly middle-aged. There were not a lot of kids but once in a while a stroller would go by or I'd see a small bundle of energy skipping alongside a parent or grandparent.

I bit into my hot dog. A blob of mustard squeezed out of the bun and slithered down my chin. I leaned over my plate and glanced down to where my napkin lay. Before the napkin could zero in on its target, I saw the senior super model from the dock saunter past the window. Wouldn't you know it? She slowed and stared right at me in apparent disgust as I wiped mustard off my chin.

Why me? Guess they wouldn't let me eat in first class even if I could afford it. That was all right with me. First class probably didn't have hot dogs and this one tasted really good.

The deck chairs outside the window beckoned to me, padded wooden loungers that begged to be sat upon. Some filled with bodies that reposed in absolute peace, eyes closed, a few of them with mouths open. I'd have to retrieve my book from the room. At least if I fell asleep, it would appear I was reading. Thanks to the Dog Lady, I could even tell someone what the story was about.

A server in a crisp white shirt and vest scooped up my tray of dirty dishes. I took my leave of the buffet, resisting the temptation to grab a cookie on the way out. While I waited for the elevator, I mentally reviewed *Murder in the Marketplace*. The book involved a butcher, a baker, and a candlestick maker. Wasn't there a poem about them? The doors opened and a handsome gentleman dressed in a yellow sweater emerged. He swept to one side as if I were the queen herself and held a hand against the elevator door until I was safely inside. I blushed a bit and thanked him. I could almost feel Elma beside me, poking me in the ribs, saying, "He could be the one, the man of your dreams."

Chapter Seven

With *Murder in the Marketplace* tucked under my arm, I hunted for an empty chair on the Promenade Deck. It was only four o'clock. I was sure my luggage wouldn't arrive for at least another hour. There was plenty of time to sit back and relax, or sleep.

The wooden lounge chairs on Deck 7 were padded with soft blue striped cushions that comforted a weary body. I settled into a sun-warmed chair and adjusted all my bodily appendages until I felt comfortable. The gentle breeze and soothing sunshine chased away the last of my jangled nerves. My eyelids fluttered.

A moment later, a shadow cooled my face. Sensing the presence of someone beside me, I opened one eye.

"Is this chair taken?" a deep charming voice asked.

I looked up into a tanned face that appeared to be about my age, maybe a few years younger. He wore casual khakis and a yellow sweater pulled over a crisp white shirt that accented his complexion. It was the gentleman from the elevator! His blue eyes crinkled slightly as he smiled, anticipating my answer.

"Why, no," I said almost stammering. My nerves sprang to life again. What had affected me? The blue eyes? The handsome face?

The distinguished silver highlighting his gray hair? It wasn't often I looked at a man and assessed his physical attributes, but then it wasn't often a man like this paid me any attention.

"It's a little cooler than I expected," he commented. "I was hoping to enjoy the warm sun today. We haven't seen much of it in Indiana."

"It's a little chilly when the sun hides, but it's comfortable otherwise."

I gazed out over the harbor not trusting myself to look into those eyes again. I should have said something about being from Ohio. Experienced cruisers exchange that kind of information when meeting new people. It's part of the fun of cruising, but by the time I got the courage to say more, he had opened his book and leaned back into his chair.

The conversation obviously over, I leaned back again and pretended to read.

Lord, if I fall asleep here, please don't let me snore.

I dozed. When I awoke, the chair next to me was empty. Had I snored him away? I checked my mouth and chin. At least I hadn't drooled in my sleep. It was silly but I missed not seeing him there in the chair next to me. I felt, abandoned, by a complete stranger! Was I losing my mind?

The sun began to fade. I headed back to my stateroom with the hope that my suitcase had arrived. Casual dining or not, a shower and fresh clothes would feel good before going to dinner.

The main dining room, Brittania, could be reached from both Deck 2 and Deck 3. I entered on Deck 3. Beautiful wood paneling graced the walls of the two-tiered room with a large winding staircase as the focal point. I stood at the top of the staircase and paused. The maitre'd had read my dining card and directed me to use the stairs to go down to my table on the lower level. The brochure had described the staircase as the way to make an entrance into the grand dining area. I stepped carefully. I didn't want to make an unforgettable entrance by tumbling down the stairs into the table full of exotic flowers at the foot of the steps.

As I neared the bottom, my sandal caught on the step and I could see disaster in my future. As I lurched forward, a waiter extended his hand and rescued me. He smoothly secured my hand in the crook of his arm and escorted me to the table number on my reservation card as if it had all been planned.

"Thank you so much," I said gratefully.

He bowed slightly from the waist. "My pleasure, madam." He turned and walked off to his other duties.

I stood before an oblong table with places set for eight. The door to the kitchen was just beyond a half wall that separated the waiter's station from the dining area. I hesitated. There was no one else here. Where should I sit?

On the end? Then everyone would have to pass around me.

In the middle? That might break up a couple if they wanted to sit beside each other.

Once again the waiter saved me by pulling out a chair and motioning for me to sit down. I accepted the offer. He adjusted my chair as I settled into it, putting me at a comfortable distance from my plate and the twenty or so pieces of silverware surrounding it. He quickly placed my napkin across my lap and opened a menu before me. I turned to thank the kind waiter but he had scurried off to help another damsel in distress.

A moment later, a couple in their late sixties was shown to the table. They were quite a pair. She was elegantly dressed in a silky orchid blouse and casual pants. Her blonde hair accentuated the fairness of her complexion and framed a classic face with large brown eyes. Her escort was neatly dressed in resort casual, tan trousers and a white shirt unbuttoned properly at the neck to reveal just a hint of silvered chest hair that matched the thick wavy hair on top of his head.

They nodded in my direction and greeted me with a "Bon Jour!" as they took their seats.

I nodded back. "Good evening," I said in my very best American.

Next a couple in their early fifties, I judged, approached the table. They were dressed in knit tops and Dockers. Both shirts had logos on them depicting a diving resort in the Bahamas. He was medium build with a slight paunch, his hair mostly dark with distinguished gray on the sides. She had a cheery round face and medium length brown hair pulled back by sunglasses that perched on top of her head. Their animated conversation with each other ceased as they were seated.

The man reached across and shook everyone's hand before he sat down.

"Hi. I'm John and this is my wife, Carol." They looked expectantly at the rest of us.

"I'm Annie Pickels," I said. "Glad to meet you."

John looked to the French couple who finally got the idea. "Charles," he said touching his chest. Then he pointed at the woman I assumed was his wife from the gorgeous set of wedding rings she sported on her left hand.

"Madelaine." She nodded and smiled.

"Where are you from?" John wanted to know.

I thought it was pretty obvious from the accent.

"From? From?" Charles wrinkled his brow.

"Yes," said John. "Where do you live?"

I noticed that John was speaking slower and louder now. Was it the gray hair or the fact that they spoke a foreign language?

"Leeve? Ah, leeve! We leeve in Nice. Nice, France."

I couldn't help but think of Maurice Chevalier in the old movie Gigi. I loved the way he spoke English with a French accent.

"And you, Annie?" John turned to me seemingly reluctant to push the limits of Charles' English.

"I come from Tinkers Creek, a little town near Mansfield, Ohio," I replied.

"Oh, a Buckeye!" Carol exclaimed. "We both graduated from Ohio State! We live in Maryland now, just outside Washington, D.C."

The waiter interrupted the conversation by beginning his liturgy of the menu choices and his opinion of the chef's creations. He flipped open his small black notebook and looked at Madelaine.

"Madame?" They began conversing in French. I was impressed with our waiter's language versatility.

"Is someone joining you?" Carol asked. She indicated the empty seat next to me.

"No, I'm traveling by myself."

Carol's expression changed to one of pity. I could imagine what she was thinking, an old woman traveling alone at Christmas time, probably doesn't have a family, or a life. I suddenly felt the urge to defend myself.

"I've already had Christmas with the family." I explained. "When I saw the Queen Mary 2 on the Travel Channel, I couldn't pass up the opportunity to enjoy some warm weather and see what all the fuss was about. This is my Christmas present to me."

Carol seemed relieved to know I had a family. "Oh, I know what you mean. It's been a cold winter so far. We had our Christmas with the kids and grandkids last week. We left them to enjoy their own families while we seek out the sun."

"Are you," I didn't finish the sentence. All eyes were suddenly looking past me. I could feel someone at my side. I looked up into the same blue eyes I had met on Deck 7. And then, I blushed.

What is going on with you, Annie? Get a grip. Everyone's watching.

My handsome lounge chair acquaintance settled into the seat beside me and was promptly "napkined" by the waiter and handed a menu.

"Good evening, everyone. Sorry to be late. I'm Arnie," he said, his eyes sparkling like blue tanzanite over the top of his menu. The scent of his after-shave stirred my senses. He had obviously received his luggage for he looked crisp and fresh in a cotton shirt and slacks that hadn't lost their crease.

John went around the table introducing everyone, finishing with me, "And this is Annie."

"Annie." Arnie repeated my name as he looked at me appraisingly for a moment. Then he nodded to the group. "It's nice to meet everyone."

The waiter quickly intervened to take his order. While he tried not to show it, the waiter obviously wanted to keep things moving along. Early six o'clock diners needed to move out on time to ready the tables for the late diners who would enter at eight-thirty. Arnie spent a few minutes, head bowed together with the waiter, discussing his dinner choices.

I put my hand to my face. My cheeks felt hot. What was it about him that did this to me? I remember telling Mary Jane once that although I was sixty-five on the outside, I felt like seventeen on the inside. I hadn't meant to suggest that I acted like a teenager, although I'm sure she took it that way, but I was certainly feeling like one now. I clutched the napkin in my lap a little tighter and tried to engage Carol and John in conversation.

"I noticed the logo on your shirts. Are you divers?" That question opened the floodgates and started the two of them into a series of adventuresome stories of shark encounters, dolphins, and critters of the deep. Charles and Madelaine just smiled throughout each story, occasionally commenting to each other in French. Arnie and I commented with an "Oh, really," now and then.

"Have you ever been diving?" Arnie asked me when Carol and John dove into their entrees in earnest.

"No," I said. I turned to him to tell him I'd been snorkeling but the thought left me when I saw his blue eyes soften as they met mine. I lingered for a moment in the shadow of his gaze. The eyes are said to be the windows of the soul. I liked what I saw.

The spell was broken by the waiter who placed a perfect crème brulee before me. Carol and John picked up the conversation again. Leaning toward Arnie, Carol asked, "So, Arnie, we never found out. Where are you from?"

"I live near Indianapolis," he replied breaking the crusty top of his dessert with a spoon. "How about the rest of you?"

John had a great memory. He rattled off everyone's hometown. "Are you retired, Arnie?" he asked reaching the cream for Carol's coffee.

"Yes and no," came the reply. "I'm a lawyer. I retired from my practice a few years ago, but I take on a case now and then when it strikes my fancy." He patted his mouth with his napkin. "I enjoy traveling. I get to see a lot of places by signing on as a gentleman host aboard cruise ships."

"A gentleman host? Really?" Carol chimed in. "That sounds like a lot of fun."

"Sounds like a lot of sore feet," John quipped. "Don't you have to dance with all the single ladies?"

"Actually, it is a lot of fun, and a lot of sore feet." Arnie chuckled. He had a pleasant laugh. "We have to be at all the dance opportunities aboard ship." Arnie checked his watch. "As a matter of fact, I need to be down in the Queen's Room in a few minutes. I'll have to excuse myself." He rose and pushed in his chair.

As I looked up to say goodbye, Arnie bent down. For a moment, I thought he would kiss me.

I felt panic and another hot flash.

Instead, he whispered in my ear. "Would you join me later for a dance around the beautiful ballroom floor?"

My cheeks reddened. "I don't think so. I'm not much of a dancer," I stammered.

"I promise not to step on your toes." He straightened and stepped back a step as though I had offended him.

"I don't think so. Thank you though." I tried to look in his eyes but I feared my fluttering eyelashes would give away my discomfort.

Arnie cocked his head to one side and gave a slight shrug of his shoulder. I watched him walk away, wondering if I were going to make a fool of myself at dinner for the next thirteen nights.

"Oooh, Annie. If I were single, I'd have taken him up on his offer. I'll bet he's a great dancer," Carol gushed. For a moment I thought she sounded just like Elma.

"I don't think I'm quite up to his standards. He was just being kind." I hesitated to tell her I wasn't ready for male companionship. I still had my memories of Russell to hold onto.

"I'm sure he wouldn't have offered if he didn't mean it, " She left the sentence hang just like Elma would. I smiled and dug into my crème brulee. Elma would be on me like white on rice if she were here. At least Carol backed off.

When desserts and coffees were finished, we all said good night and left to attend to our own agendas. I fished out my little map hoping that I could find the theater without any trouble. I was ready to be entertained and distracted from the stupid school girl feelings that were causing me all sorts of consternation.

The map showed the theater in the front of the ship. I stuffed it back in the little clutch I carried. Certainly if I followed the parade of people out of the restaurant, I would find the way.

As people descended the small staircase just outside the entrance to the Britannia, they broke into three lines of traffic. One went to the right, one to the left, and one down a center hall. I made a hasty choice to follow the middle line.

Just past a set of elevators, I found myself between the casino on my left, already pinging with rewarding noises, and a lounge on the right preparing to provide dance music with a small group of musicians. I continued on through a huge center hallway that exhibited four large pieces of artwork. They were bronzed reliefs depicting various continents. I made a note to look more closely at them later.

I reached the Grand Lobby where a stairway ascended to the upper decks. A second entrance to the casino gave passers-by another opportunity to try their luck. I kept moving straight ahead.

Just past another set of elevators, I ran into a wall, literally, while fishing in my clutch for the map. I rubbed the top of my head a bit and turned to see who had noticed. Everyone politely diverted his or her attention and I mentally tossed a coin to see which way I should go.

A young lady in a white nautical uniform caught my attention. She smiled sweetly and waved an arm toward a door. "Are you here to see the show?"

"Why, yes. Thank you." I followed the pointing fingertips and found myself in the Royal Court Theater. Meandering down the aisle, I heard someone cry out.

"Annie! Come sit by us."

Carol waved an arm high above her head.

Why not? I threaded my way between knees and the backs of seats to get to the middle where they sat.

"This place is half empty." John gestured to the upper balcony and the seats on the sides of the theater. "It's the first night. People are probably trying to get their sea legs, if you know what I mean."

I knew. One does not mention seasickness to another when you are aboard a ship or boat. Half the problem of being seasick is thinking about it. The other half, well I won't go there.

Lights dimmed and the cruise director started his first night cruise shtick. I think all cruise directors get their material from the same book. When he finally got around to introducing the comedian, I was more than ready to sit back in the comfort of a darkened theater and enjoy a good laugh.

My comfort only lasted until John started roaring with laughter. His laugh was an attention-grabber. The comedian was also a ventriloquist and he and his "partner" immediately singled us out.

"Ma'am," he said to Carol. "You'll have to control your husband. We're trying to do a show here." John wiped tears and Carol just shook her head.

Suddenly a spotlight shined down on us. The dummy on the comedian's knee was a craftsmen's interpretation of an old man, big jowls, gray hair, squinty eyes. The crafty character did a double take as he gawked at us.

"Yowza! Who's the babe on the other side of that guy?" The light narrowed in on me.

Please, Lord, just let the floor open up and deposit me on the bottom of the ocean. I hated being singled out in a crowd like this. What a mistake to sit this close to the stage. I knew from experience that comedians usually picked on people in the audience. I preferred to be an observer rather than a participant.

"Be nice, Stanley. That's the man's mother," the comedian warned his wooden sidekick.

I tried to hide my eyes from the glaring light. I wished I could just hide me completely.

"Hey babe, you got a date after the show?" Stanley was raising his bushy dark gray eyebrows up and down in my direction.

I shook my head.

"Back stage, door 2. Just knock on top of the luggage case. I can be ready in two seconds. Yowza!"

John bellowed even louder.

"Leave the kids in the room, though. They'll just cramp my style."

"Stanley, what kind of talk is that? That's no way to woo a lady." Stanley looked at his human buddy in surprise.

"It's not?"

"No." From there a conversation ensued about the art of dating and the spotlight faded.

I felt a trickle of perspiration run down my spine.

John shook with giggles. Carol continued to shake her head. I hid my eyes behind one hand. *Why me, Lord? Why me?*

The embarrassment began to fade after a while. The nice thing about being aboard the QM2 was that there were many Europeans whose English was a little slower than the performer's. While John laughed himself silly throughout the welcome aboard show, he was among the minority. A lot of the comedian's patter was lost on an audience that wasn't all English speaking and didn't understand American humor. That was lucky for me, but unlucky for the comedian, and Stanley.

The lights came up at the end of the show and I stood to leave. John was still wiping the tears from his eyes. "Aw man, that was good." He chuckled one more time and got up. "Don't wait up for us, Mom. We kids are going to party tonight."

"John!" Carol reddened. "I'm sorry, Annie. Sometimes his mouth works before his brain does."

"You two have a good evening," I said. In the spirit of good fun and partly to hide my discomfort over the whole thing, I shook a finger at them and added, "Now behave yourselves kids."

Carol smiled back at me as I turned to exit the theater. I moved in the direction I thought would take me to my room but found myself at a dead end facing two huge double doors. I stopped and stared for a moment, causing the people behind me to change course to avoid knocking me over. They circled around me and disappeared through the doors. One gentleman held the door for me, thinking I was going in as well. I didn't want to disappoint him, so I entered.

Soft barrel-shaped chairs were grouped around tables on two levels of a carpeted area that led down to an enormous polished wooden dance floor in the center. Above the dancers' heads, were two large chandeliers sparkling with color as small spotlights in the ceiling played on the shimmering shards of crystal. The atmosphere was romantic. Despite the enormous size of the ballroom it felt intimate.

This had to be the Queen's Room I'd seen pictured in the brochures. It was supposed to have the biggest dance floor of any ship on the ocean. A small orchestra at the front played a waltz.

I wound my way around the back until I found a spot against the wall where there were few people. I planned to fish out my handy-dandy little map and try to find my way out of there and to my stateroom. As I rifled through my clutch, I felt a tingling sensation on the back of my neck as though all the little hairs were trying to stand up. I reached back and rubbed it.

"Hello. Did you change your mind?"

I almost jumped out of my skin. There, standing before me, was Arnie. My cheeks reacted with a hot pink flush again.

"No, I was just wandering around and happened upon this room. I decided to have a look."

He leaned toward me and extended his hand. "We shouldn't waste this beautiful music."

The band was playing a favorite of mine from the late fifties but for the life of me, I wouldn't have been able to name it if I'd been asked.

"Oh, I couldn't possibly," I started to protest as his hand went to mine and his magnetism lifted me from my seat.

"Oh, but you could." He led me to the dance floor.

My body, having a will of its own at this point, followed him. I was perplexed. This wasn't me. It had to be someone else. I don't do things like dance with strange men or let them lead me around. I wasn't a lonely old woman looking for companionship. What was happening to me? I felt shaky, nervous. Would I be able to follow him without stepping all over his shiny shoes? I wasn't sure my feet would even move once we were on the dance floor.

Arnie gently placed his arm around my waist. My hand rested comfortably on his shoulder, and I fell into step with him as though we had been doing this together for a long time.

He is good. I don't feel the least bit clumsy in his arms even though I haven't danced like this since,

I stopped abruptly.

"I really must go," I insisted. And, feeling just like Cinderella, late to catch her pumpkin carriage, I hurried off the dance floor and out of the room. I had no idea where I was going. I just kept on moving until I felt that I could breathe again. My heart raced at a dangerous pace. I found myself in front of a bank of elevators and pushed the call button. I waited. Something was on my cheek and I brushed at it.

A tear.

Oh, great. Could I embarrass myself any more tonight?

More tears fell as the elevator doors opened. Luckily I had stumbled into the elevator at Stairwell C and it was empty. I recognized the picture on the wall when I exited onto Deck 4. I turned the corner and checked the numbers on the doors until I found the right one. My hand shook slightly as I passed the key through the slot in the doorknob and sought the solace of my private space.

Sitting on the bed, I started to sob. *Lord, I miss Russell. I know it's been a long while you've had him up there with you, but I still miss him.*

I took a deep breath and turned on the television to create a distraction as I got myself ready for bed. A surprising question nagged at me. Would I dream tonight? Whom would I dream about?

Sometimes it was a comfort to dream Russell was near—to feel him put his arms around me again and to hear his voice. Arnie had a nice voice. It was a little smoother than Russell but Russell's voice was the one I wanted to hear. Russell had always been fun on a dance floor. We'd laugh about getting out of step with the music and he'd twirl me around and we'd try again. Arnie was a polished dancer. He'd probably taken lessons. It felt like dancing on a cloud with him but it was Russell I wanted to dance with. Russell I wanted here with me. Russell.

I slipped into bed. It was Russell I wanted to dream about tonight.

But would I?

Chapter Eight

A steady cool morning breeze gathered mist from the sea and gently sprayed my face. I felt refreshed as if I'd been to the spa and paid for a facial. At least I imagined that's what a facial might have done. I'd never had one. There were other things I'd rather splurge on, like a manicure. I didn't mind someone fussing over my fingernails. I didn't like them rubbing my face or massaging my body.

I finished the coffee in my cup before it became seasoned with the saltiness in the air. The water was a bit choppy but those thing-a-ma-jigs that kept the ship stable were doing a good job.

My dreams of Arnie and Russell had given me a restless night. One moment I was dancing with Arnie and the next moment it was Russell. The two men seemed to blend into one by the time morning came. I was eager to get on with my day and forget the night before.

A guided tour of the ship was first on my morning agenda. I moved from my observation spot near the deck railing and placed my cup on a table near the pool with other dirty dishes from someone's breakfast that were about to be rescued by one of the wait staff. The doors to the inside opened automatically as I approached. I hoped the tour would help me navigate the confusing corridors that sometimes came to a dead end or brought you to the rear door of the Britannia dining room when you couldn't pass through because people were eating. Stumbling upon the Queen's Room the night before had been pure chance. I could never have found it using the map.

Was it really chance? Or did God want me to find Arnie? What a thought! I pushed it from my mind.

The beginning of our tour took us to the Queen's Room and the disco at the rear of the huge ballroom. To the left of the entrance were four or five steps down leading to another corridor lined with impressive artwork. We passed by landscapes, cartoon celluloid's, brilliantly colored interior scenes whose furnishings sat at odd angles, and the occasional black and white artsy photograph. Much of it was up for auction in the afternoon.

As the guide stopped to explain the auction of artwork, I glanced down the corridor and spied a man about Arnie's height. My pulse quickened. I hurriedly turned my attention to the guide. Russell always claimed I was part cat, the part that's curious. I couldn't help myself. I looked down the hall again. He was gone.

Why did I care if it was Arnie? Russell is, was my husband, is the love of my life. Arnie is just a good dancer. I tried to concentrate a little harder on what the guide was saying.

We walked through the Chart Room, which was a lounge designed around a navigational theme using nautical maps and instruments. It blended into a small niche that housed the champagne bar.

"This is a quiet little place for you to relax and enjoy the fine champagne and caviar the Queen Mary offers," said the perky young lady in uniform who led our tour. It would have looked a lot cozier without the thirty or forty people on the tour trying to squeeze into it.

"Next stop is the library," she announced as she pushed through the group of onlookers.

The library was hidden on Deck 8 in the front of the ship opposite the beauty salon. Lighted bookcases of rich cherry-stained woods held an impressive collection of fiction and non-fiction books in almost any area of interest imaginable. Most were in English but a respectable number were in French and German. I walked over and perused some of the titles. What kind of books does Arnie read? I shook my head. Where were these thoughts coming from? I needed to concentrate on something other than Mr. Arnie whatever-his-last-name. I'd forgotten.

At the end of the tour, our perky guide gathered us together in the Winter Garden lounge. We huddled before a mural of tropical fish. The fountain in front of them resembled a spring shower with water droplets running down thin threads of plastic. It was the first time I had ever seen fish swim through rain.

"Thank you for joining me this morning," our guide said. "I hope that our tour has been informative. Do you have any other questions?"

"Yes," I injected quickly, feeling more directionally challenged than I had before the tour started. "What's the best advice you have for those of us who keep getting lost?'

Everyone laughed. I thought it was at me, but then I noticed heads nodding in agreement. I wasn't the only one ending up in places I hadn't planned to be.

"The best advice I can give is to refer to the Daily Programme, or the map, to find the closest stairwell, A, B, C, or D, to your destination. Then take the elevator or stairs to the deck you need."

That was easy for her to say. You still had to figure out whether to turn right or left. One wrong move and you could find yourself walking a mile in the wrong direction. At least I would get plenty of exercise.

All that navigating must have made everyone hungry or else it was the smell of food wafting into the Winter Garden from the Kings Court. The group headed in the direction of the buffet. I opted to indulge in something a little more English for lunch and backtracked to the Golden Lion Pub. On the tour, I had noticed a sign advertising fish and chips, or as we Americans call them, French Fries. I went in, found a seat, and ordered. The fish was delicious, breaded and deep-fried. It was a huge piece accompanied by crispy fries. I sprinkled on a little malt vinegar as suggested by the server and was delighted with the taste combination. When I was finished, my hunger was more than satisfied and I felt quite British.

The planetarium was next on my day's itinerary. Earlier, I had miraculously found the place where I needed to get a ticket. The planetarium was popular and the free tickets were gone quickly I was told. Luckily I got the last one but unluckily, I fell asleep watching the film that explored all the constellations in the night sky. How could you not relax? The chairs were soft and cushy, and reclined for viewing the stars as they slowly rotated overhead in the darkened room. Harrison Ford talked in hushed tones through the journey. I didn't wake up until the lights came on.

Next, I moved on to the beauty salon for a manicure. I don't fuss much with my nails usually, but it was fun to indulge on a cruise. They tried to talk me into a pedicure as well, but I plain out told them, "I'm not exposing my feet tonight, just my hands."

According to the Daily Programme the evening dress was formal. When I returned to my stateroom, I pulled my long black dress and silvery jacket from the closet and laid it out on my bed. I studied the sleeveless evening dress stretched across the bed Marcus had so neatly made up while I was gone. The silvery jacket lay next to it. I liked the two-piece outfit. The little bit of sparkle added to the festive feeling of the season. I wavered between wearing the shimmering ensemble or saving it for New Year's Eve. I had purchased three other tops for the dress to give me a different look for each of the four formal nights during the cruise.

I went back to the closet and pulled out my other pieces and arranged them around the dress on the bed. As I contemplated my choices, my mind wandered to the little senior super model I had seen on the dock. What was Ms. Perfect asking her butler to pull out of the closet for her tonight? Would she even make her own choices, or leave the decisions up to him?

I pushed the picture of butler and senior super model from my mind and I studied my wardrobe choices. The silvery jacket went back into the closet. Instead, I selected the black lace jacket, another bargain update to my collection of cruise clothes. I loved a good sale.

After donning my evening attire, I stood before the mirrored vanity. It was the closest thing to a full-length mirror in the room. The black lace jacket and dress accented my white hair. I was pleased. I could picture myself gracefully gliding across the dance floor with ...

Whoa, Annie, don't go there. Just when I was confident I had my thought processes under control, they would slip over the edge again. I straightened my shoulders and wiggled a finger at the wicked woman in front of me. That's the third time today, Annie, or was it the fourth?

I pushed thoughts of Arnie away again and assembled my pitiful supply of cosmetics on the narrow shelf in the tiny bathroom. I don't usually wear makeup, maybe a little lipstick on Sunday. For formal cruise nights however, I decided to go all out and even use some tinted moisturizer. I liked it better than all the foundation and powder some women plastered on their faces making them look like an old woman with a desert-dried mudpack. All that stuff seemed to find its way into every new age crease in a face as old as mine.

I daubed a little eye shadow on my lids but it seemed to disappear into the deep creases of my eye sockets. I chalked it up as a waste of money. A little mascara, however, helped to make my eyelashes more visible. I liked that effect.

Smiling in the mirror, blusher brush poised, I tried to decide whether I needed a little color on my cheeks or if it would just add insult to injury should I find myself flustered again at dinner. Just the thought of Arnie brought pink to my face. I stuck my tongue out at the image in the mirror. Behave Annie Pickels!

Feeling sufficiently self-chastised, I smiled and spread a light blush on the cheeks that popped up. Lipstick finished the job. Da Vinci couldn't have done it better. My smile was just as mysterious as Mona's.

I turned to exit and then remembered my cologne. I misted lightly with the same scent I had been using for years. It was my scent, a mix of vanilla and spice, the one Russell called my "smell." For a second I felt a little stab of pain in my midsection. Lord, help me not to miss him so much tonight.

I scooped up my small black evening bag, another bargain at ten dollars, and the key card with the crazy lady pictured on it who in no way resembled the glamorous woman that walked out the door. With an air of confidence, I wound my way through the maze of the QM2 successfully to the Britannia dining room.

When I arrived, the French couple, Charles and Madelaine, and the divers, Carol and John, were already seated in the same places as the previous night. How quickly people became creatures of habit.

Our waiter pulled my chair out for me and expertly dropped the napkin into my lap. His shiny brass name badge told me his name was Esmond. I tried to think of ways I could remember it. Waiters like to have their names remembered. It always bothered me when people on a cruise ship would ignore the waiters and other crew members and treated them as if they didn't exist. Didn't they wonder how their food got to their table and in front of them?

Tonight Esmond was dressed smartly in a short white jacket that pointed to a waist encircled with a black cummerbund. I couldn't imagine having to get all gussied up every day in formal wear to do my job.

There was an empty chair beside me. Arnie's chair.

I caught myself looking for him once or twice. His absence annoyed me. If I were going to feel embarrassed over the previous night of dancing, I wanted to get it over with then and there, not wait for another time when I wasn't prepared to face the music. We were past our appetizers and into our salads before anyone expressed concern about Arnie. Carol started it.

"I wonder where Arnie is?"

"Maybe he's off dancing through dinner," John tossed in then turned to our French dinner companions. "Saaay, you and Madelaine make a beautiful couple on the dance floor."

"Eh?" Charles looked at John and raised an eyebrow."

"In the Queens Room, you and Madelaine," John made motions with his index and middle finger as though they were two legs walking. "You dance well."

"Ah! Yes, yes. Many years." Charles translated for Madelaine.

"Oui," she answered and nodded her perfectly coiffed head. "Merci."

I concentrated on my Caesar salad hoping beyond hope that none of them had seen me with Arnie or noticed the hasty Cinderella exit from the dance floor.

"Arnie was a busy guy last night," John continued.

I almost choked.

"He had one lady or another on the dance floor every time I saw him."

I fidgeted with my napkin and stared at my water glass, slowly turning it by the stem.

"In fact, I thought I saw him leading you out onto the dance floor, Annie." John sipped his white zinfandel.

I opened my mouth but nothing came out. I patted my chest a bit as though something had caught in my throat. Just as I drained my glass of water, Esmond arrived with the main course. I breathed a sigh of relief. The Lord's angels come in many different forms. Sometimes they wear white jackets and black cummerbunds.

"Oh, does this look wonderful!" John was distracted by the delectable array of food in front of him.

In front of me was a plate exquisitely arranged with chateaubriand, four spears of asparagus tied together with a thin strip of some other green vegetable, and three small red potatoes peeled around the middle to reveal the soft white inside, all sprinkled with parsley. I released the knot around the asparagus to give it room to breathe. I wished there was some way I could breathe. If John continued his line of questioning about Arnie and dancing, I was going to hyperventilate.

Everyone but Madelaine had ordered the chateaubriand. Madelaine had a rack of lamb standing in the middle of her plate atop a daub of mashed potatoes accompanied by a similar bundle of asparagus and three petite round yellow squash.

The first bite of the beef sent everyone into ecstasy when the tender piece of meat almost melted in the mouth releasing the juicy flavor of a prime cut cooked to perfection. Dancing was forgotten and great meals of the past remembered.

The knot in my stomach dissolved. I silently gave thanks.

The dessert menu arrived as soon as the last tidbits of food disappeared from the dinner plates. One glance and I knew immediately what I would have. Pavlova. A few years back, I had visited Australia and indulged in their famous pavlova, a baked meringue topped with berries and sauce and a dollop of whipped cream.

The description on the Britannia's menu mentioned strawberry ice cream but I figured I could set that aside. Ice cream sometimes gives me a stomachache and strawberry ice cream wasn't worth chancing that. With great anticipation, I ordered the pavlova.

Esmond scraped crumbs from the tablecloth with his nifty little scraper that captured the crumbs which he then emptied onto a plate in his hand. Next he set out more silverware. I could never understand all that folderol. I hadn't used half of what I'd started with and he'd taken that away. Cups were arranged neatly and Esmond poured the coffee. Desserts arrived from the kitchen and he placed one in front of each diner. I stared down at mine in disbelief. I was sure I had someone else's order. A baked meringue cup filled with a scoop of strawberry ice cream looked back at me. It was barren, not a berry or drop of sauce or even a dollop of whipped cream. My shoulders drooped. The disappointment must have shown on my face.

"What's wrong?" Carol asked.

I looked up and sighed. "I was really looking forward to this, but it isn't anything like pavlova is supposed to be."

"Tell him you want something else," Carol prompted, her spoon poised to dip into her lump of strawberry ice cream.

"Oh, I hate to be a bother."

"You're not a bother. You paid for this, and you deserve to have something you like." Carol caught Esmond's attention. "Esmond, Annie needs to have something else. The pavlova is not what she expected."

Immediately Esmond was by my side apologizing. "I'm sorry, Ms. Pickels. Is something wrong with the pavlova?"

"There's nothing wrong," I started to say. My heart pounded in my throat.

"But you don't look happy. I can get you something else?"

I could beat up a newspaper deliveryman and a cruise lady with a wadded up newspaper. Why couldn't I complain about the pavlova? I certainly wasn't myself. Something was throwing me off kilter. Carol was right. I had paid a good buck for this cruise and I should be able to enjoy my dessert. I forged ahead.

"It's just not what I expected. The pavlova you get in Australia isn't anything like this. It has berries and sauce and whipped cream on the meringue, not strawberry ice cream."

"Oh, the chef, he make it different, no?"

"Yes. He made it different. Not like in Australia. Maybe he's never been there." I peered down at the melting ice cream.

"May I get you something else? You want berries? I can get you strawberries."

Esmond hovered like a mother hen and I could feel everyone's eyes on me, expectant, urging me on. I raised my head again to refuse his offer but one look at his eager face changed my mind.

"Some strawberries would be very nice, Esmond. Thank you."

A moment later, he presented me with a huge bowl of the largest reddest strawberries I had ever seen. There was way too much for me to eat, so I passed the sweet gems around to the others. I was feeling kind of foolish. If I had just said something about the pavlova when I first saw it, there wouldn't have been so much fuss.

Just as we finished our desserts, the maitre'd arrived at our table. "Is everything excellent? Esmond is taking good care of you?"

We all nodded and praised Esmond, who beamed at the good review.

"Ms. Peekels, I understand you did not like our pavlova?"

My eyes darted around the table, trying to discern who had betrayed me to the maitre'd. They just stared back at me as they waited for my response.

"It just wasn't what I expected." I flushed. So much for the blusher. I knew I didn't need it.

"What did you expect? Please. I should tell the chef. He needs to know."

I was sure the last thing in the world a busy chef, preparing five course meals for almost 2,000 passengers wanted to know was my opinion of his pavlova. There was no reason to make his job any more difficult.

"It's fine," I said. "Esmond brought me some beautiful strawberries that we have all enjoyed." I tried my best sweet smile and hoped that would end it, but he persisted.

"No. No. I need to know. We want your dinner to be excellent. What did you expect of the pavlova?"

I figured I might as well explain. He wasn't going to leave until I did. "Well, the pavlova I've had in Australia had a baked meringue like this one tonight, but it had berries, blueberries, strawberries, raspberries on top, with a berry sauce over it and whipped cream on top of that. I was disappointed to see the ice cream. But everything is fine, really. Thank you. "

The maitre'd wasn't convinced that everything was fine. "We will have your pavlova for you, not tomorrow but in a couple of days. You will see. I will tell the chef."

"No, no. That's not necessary. I'm fine with the strawberries tonight." I could feel everyone's stares again. John and Carol were silent, waiting, watching. People at the tables around us turned to see what the commotion was about. Disappearing into the chair would have been a great trick if I could have pulled it off right then. When had I become a magnet for so much unwanted attention?

"Oh, but it is necessary. I do not want my guests to be disappointed. Esmond!"

He gestured for the waiter to come to his side. I had seen restaurant staff on a cruise ship fawn over people before. Often it was because they thought they would get a bigger tip at the end of the cruise. I didn't mind the extra pampering but I didn't appreciate being made the center of attention in our area of the restaurant. Esmond bustled to the table.

"In a day or two we will have pavlova for Ms. Peekels. You will make sure she has it?"

"Ah, yes, yes!" Esmond grinned ear to ear, so happy to be of service and have the attention of his boss.

When the two walked away, John leaned over the table and said quietly, "So, that's how he earns his tip." He pointed over his shoulder with his thumb in the direction of the maitre'd. "I always wondered why we were supposed to tip him too."

I laughed weakly.

"When you have to have your lobster removed from its shell, he's the man to do it." Carol said. "That's where he really makes his tip money." She finished the last of her coffee and set the cup down with a clink of china against china.

Madelaine refreshed her lipstick, clicked her gold compact closed, and smiled at all of us as she and Charles rose to leave. John followed Charles' lead and held Carol's chair for her as she got up. Wishes for a good evening were exchanged and everyone departed.

I looked at Arnie's still empty chair. I wondered if he skipped dinner because of the way I treated him the night before. I hoped not. It wasn't my intention to hurt his feelings or, for that matter, to discourage his friendship. I just felt awkward in another man's arms, even if it was just to dance. All of my musing during the day led me to the conclusion that I wasn't hurting Russell or his memory by having a gentleman friend. Perhaps that was just what I needed to help ease the pain that should have subsided years ago.

Elma's words echoed in my head. Maybe you'll meet the man of your dreams. But the man of my dreams was Russell. Always had been. Always would be.

However having a gentleman friend, well, why not? I smiled. My chin lifted and my step lightened as I steered through the crowd that made its way to the theater for the evening performance. My confidence was returning. I turned over a new leaf.

The evening show featured a pair of comedic jugglers. I cringed as they looked for a stooge from the audience. The spotlight searched in about the same place I had sat with John and Carol the night the ventriloquist entertained. True to habit, Carol and John sat in the same place tonight. The spotlight passed over them and returned; stopping to narrow on John's graying head.

"There's a brave-looking man!" One of the jugglers motioned for John to come up on stage. "No need to be afraid. The ship's doctor is in the audience, always at the ready."

John acted reluctant, but I could tell he enjoyed all the attention. They did their best to frighten him with how sharp their huge knives were. Then they blindfolded him while they tossed the knives through the air in front of him, behind him, and over his head.

Their next proposal was to do it again, only this time they would wear the blindfolds. John talked his way out of that while the audience roared with laughter at the comedians and their patter. John's adventure, I was sure, would make great fodder for conversation at the dinner table tomorrow night.

The cruise director closed the show with his usual patter about upcoming events for the evening and the following day. As soon as he was done, I slipped into the traffic that was slowly moved out of the theater. I needed to find a ladies' room.

To my surprise there was a ladies' room right outside the theater. I hoped the good luck would continue and there would be no line once I was inside. When the door opened, my eyes could not believe what I saw.

Chapter Nine

There was no line in the ladies room. It was my lucky night. I took care of nature's call and went to the sink to wash my hands. I checked my mascara. After laughing so hard at the comedic jugglers that performed in the Royal Court Theater, I wanted to be sure it was still on my lashes and not smeared across my face from swiping at laugh tears.

A petite lady stood at the mirror next to me patting her hair into place and smacking her lips to spread her lipstick. I paused with my own lipstick midway to my lips when I recognized her.

The Senior Super Model was a little shorter than I had imagined. Upon closer observation, I could see that her stature ruled out any possibility of her being a runway model. She was dressed to the nines in a glittery but conservative deep purple dress that complimented her complexion and silver hair. Did that make her a winter or a fall? Elma would know. Elma knew all those girlie things.

As I studied her out of the corner of my eye, stunning was the word that came to mind. Expensive came next. Her hands were laden with diamond cocktail rings that flashed like blinking Christmas tree lights, but no more so than the diamond tennis bracelets that dangled from her wrists. She snapped her bejeweled evening bag shut and turned to leave.

As the door closed behind her, I rolled my eyes at my mirrored image. I'd be afraid to walk around with all those 'carrots,' I thought. Some bunny just might want to feast on them.

Outside the ladies' room, I stopped and looked both ways. Should I go to the piano lounge or try to find the Queen's Room again? If I chose the Queen's Room, I was obviously looking for trouble. Arnie was sure to be there engaged in his professional duties. I knew there would be an awkward moment, maybe two.

If I chose the piano lounge, I was avoiding confrontation, in other words, chickening out. Sooner or later I was bound to run into Arnie and would have to explain my hasty exit the previous night. I couldn't use the old carriage-will-turn-into-a-pumpkin excuse. Cinderella had that one all sewn up. I'd have to tell the truth and hope for the best.

My inner conflict continued until the thought of the old time dance tunes got my feet moving in the direction of the Queen's Room. I didn't need to dance. I would just listen to the wonderful old tunes. My pulse quickened.

The ballroom dance enthusiasts strutted their stuff on the dance floor under the sparkling lights of the crystal chandeliers. I noticed Charles and Madelaine right off. They stood out, he in his handsome white tux and she in her cobalt blue gown, sequined on the top with a full chiffon skirt that swirled as Charles led her across the dance floor. John was right. Those two were great dancers.

I found a seat where I could observe the dance floor from a safe distance and ordered a decaf cappuccino. My intent was to enjoy the old tunes and watch the talented dancers compete with the not so talented for space on the polished hardwood floor. If Arnie and I should meet, so be it. I would face the music. Right now, I would just sip my cappuccino and enjoy my evening people watching.

Most people were dressed in black and white. Those who wore colorful dresses like Madelaine, stood out. The purple dress on my Senior Super Model instantly got my attention. Even from a distance her collection of diamonds glittered as much as the chandeliers above her. Her dance partner swirled her deftly and brought her back into his arms. My breath caught in my throat.

She was dancing with Arnie! The conflict began in my head again as I watched them glide across the dance floor. It's his job. Yes, but does he have to make it look so good with her?

My cappuccino arrived and I played with the foam while I watched Arnie cha-cha the Purple Dragon around the space they had claimed on the dance floor.

Purple dragon!

Where had that come from? I had regressed from Senior Super Model to Purple Dragon in the swirl of a spoon through coffee.

Lord, forgive me. I don't know what's gotten into me. It's not right to call someone a name like that when I don't even know her.

After my little prayer, I raised my eyes and who should be standing right in front of me but Arnie. He extended his hand.

"May I have this dance?"

"Are you sure you want to try this again?" I tried to stall. I wasn't sure I was ready. What would this lead to? Another sleepless night? More thoughts of what it would do to Russell's memory? Did I dare?

"I'll try not to do anything to scare you off this time." He took my hand and smiled.

"And I'll try to behave." I smiled back at him. Yes, I would dare. Something in me said this was okay. Russell had been with Jesus for thirty years now. Would he really object? And it was just a dance. One dance.

We waltzed to a couple of favorites of mine. I tried to concentrate on the conversation rather than the feeling of his arm around me. I'm ambidextrous, as I pointed out before. I knew I could dance and talk too.

"You said you were a semi-retired lawyer. What does that mean exactly?" I hoped the question wasn't too personal but I didn't know where else to begin. Men usually liked to discuss business, even when they didn't have any.

"I take on a case occasionally just to keep the mind sharp. I used to be a prosecutor but now I'm on the other side of the room. A defense lawyer. It's quite different, a challenge."

He swirled me a bit and slowed again.

"And you? Are you retired or just semi-retired?" he asked.

"I guess I'd have to say 'semi.' I have a little business I run on my farm."

"What kind of business?"

"Pickles. I can pickles and sell them to local restaurants."

"Ah, a pickle entrepreneur." Arnie had a pleased look on his face.

"I've never thought of myself as an entrepreneur, but I like the way that sounds."

The music moved from a waltz to a fox trot and Arnie adjusted his steps smoothly. It was easy to follow someone who knew how to take the lead with his dance partner.

"Was dinner good tonight?" Arnie asked.

"Dinner was very good, except for dessert. The pavlova wasn't exactly what I expected but Esmond brought me a delicious bowl of strawberries to make up for it."

"I'm sorry I missed it. I had to escort someone to dinner at the Todd English."

I wondered if the someone was the Purple Dragon.

"The food there is pretty good," He added. "You ought to try it."

"Oh, I don't know," I hated to say I didn't want to go because I had no one to go with. That would look like I was hinting for him to join me.

"What are you doing Christmas Eve?" Arnie asked. He did a little turn that gave me vertigo for a moment. "Will you join me for dinner at Todd English? Please, say yes. I'd like to say I'm booked for that night if anyone else should ask."

He didn't give me much time to think about it. Before I could answer he said, "I'll meet you at the entrance to the restaurant, say six o'clock? It's on Deck 8."

I nodded before I thought it through.

The music ended and the band geared up for another cha-cha. Arnie led me back to my cappuccino.

"Thank you, Annie. I'll make those reservations. I'm looking forward to a quiet dinner with an interesting lady." He patted my hand and went back to his hosting duties.

Somehow I managed to find the chair and place my behind in it properly. What had just happened? I had a date! I hadn't had a date since, well, there was no need to think back that far. Did I really want to do this? Arnie was a nice guy but still, a date?

This required quite a bit more thought and I figured I'd better throw in a lot of prayer as well. The Lord was going to have to help me out with this one.

My cappuccino was lukewarm. I finished it in one big gulp and left before I had to watch Arnie dance with any more ladies, especially the one in the purple dress.

I wandered a bit through the public areas of the ship, stopping here and there to snatch a bit of the live music. In the Winter Garden, a harpist played Christmas songs in front of the rainy fish fountain. I settled into a cushioned chair and rested my elbows on its arms.

A young boy, a passenger, sang with the lovely strains of the harp music. His childish voice, sweet and innocent, was pleasantly in tune with the melody that came from the strings of the harp. Everyone applauded when they were finished and encouraged more.

A yawn caught me unaware, and I hurried to cover it with the back of my hand. I needed to be up early in the morning for my excursion to see plantation homes on St. Kitts. It was time I took myself to bed. I rose to wind my way back to my stateroom.

Thoughts wound through my mind and took as many twists and turns as the corridors of the QM2. After St. Kitts we were scheduled to stop in St. Thomas and then it would be Christmas Eve. Christmas Eve. My dinner date with Arnie. I sighed like a silly schoolgirl as I reached my stateroom. Absently I passed my cruise card through the slot on the door. The little light turned red, not green.

I swiped it again.

Red.

I gave it a minute to reset before I tried another pass through with my card.

Still red.

What now?

I looked up and down the empty corridor. Marcus was done for the evening and was probably in his own room resting for tomorrow's daily routine. I guessed I would need to go down to the Purser's Desk on the main deck to get someone to help.

Suddenly the door opened.

Huh?

A hand appeared wrapped around the edge of the door. The hand was followed by the appearance of the top of a man's head and two beady eyes.

"Hallo mum. Havin' trouble with your key?"

"Who are…? What are you doing in my room?"

The eyes opened wider.

"Why, you're not my missus. Your room?"

His head poked a little farther past the door and I could now see a rather bulbous nose. I had the distinct feeling the gentleman was not dressed. He kept himself discreetly hidden behind the door.

"Sorry, mum. This is my room. I thought you were the missus having trouble with her key again."

He peeked around the door at the numbers as if to assure himself he was in the right room. I looked at the room number myself. It was 437—not 436. I was on the wrong side of the ship.

"My mistake. I'm sorry," I stuttered, hoping the British gentleman didn't still think the colonists were nothing more than insurgents who had no regard for tea or room numbers. I turned and started back toward the stairwell to cross over to the other side of the ship where the even numbered rooms were.

Coming down the hall was a stout lady who sternly looked me up and down. I smiled at her but she didn't return the gesture. A moment later I heard raised voices behind me.

"Can't turn me back for a moment," a female voice yelled.

"Truly, love. She had the wrong room."

A door slammed. I ducked into the stairwell and scurried across to my side of the ship. I felt guilty. The poor man. I hoped he wasn't in much trouble.

This time, I double-checked the numbers on the door. 4-3-6. I swiped the card through the slot. The light turned green. "The other woman" was back in her own room.

Elma was going to love this story.

We arrived in Charlotte Amalie in the morning. I've never been fond of St. Thomas. It is always a mess of traffic and noise. Unless you take the time to get away to other parts of the island, you feel like you are in the midst of a bustling city instead of a little town with one and two story buildings. But it is the shopping that draws so many to Charlotte Amalie.

I'm not a shopper. That's why I opted to stay in the dock area. There were plenty of opportunities to spend money there and I wouldn't be frustrated with hoards of people and honking horns. I noticed a bank of phones between a souvenir store and a cigar shop that featured hand rolled stogies for five dollars. I decided to phone home. I doubted I would have another chance to call Mary Jane before the holiday. We would be at sea until after Christmas Day. Phoning from the ship would cost about $10 a minute. And even if

I did give in and get one of those phones that are supposed to be smart, it would still cost too much from the ship at sea. I fished out my calling card and walked over to the phone that was in the shade.

Mary Jane answered after the first two rings.

"Mary Jane, this is Auntie Ann." I could hear the boys in the background. By now they were on their winter break from school, probably in front of the TV with joysticks in their hands and their little minds busy with video games.

"Oh, Auntie Ann! How are you?" You would have thought I was a long lost relative who lived thousands of miles away and saw her only once every couple of years. I'd only been gone a few days and I had no doubt she was expecting me to check in.

"I'm fine. I'm in St. Thomas enjoying the beautiful sun and warm breezes. How are things there?"

"Everything is good. The kids are home for two weeks now and, wouldn't you know, it's turned frigid so they can't stay outside too long to play, Harold, don't hit your brother with that controller!" I waited for her attention again.

"I'd love to send them out to play in the snow, but with the freezing temperatures, the snow's not much fun. If you can't make a good snowball to bash your brother with, you might as well stay indoors."

A little part of me enjoyed her frustration.

"How much snow did we get?" I asked.

"Probably four, maybe six inches. Some places got more than others."

"Well, hopefully it will melt before the next batch so it won't get too deep in the driveway."

"I don't think you have to worry there. That Tommy character that rents land from you shoveled your driveway. When I checked on the house, I found a note he left."

"What a sweetheart."

"He gives me the creeps, Auntie. I wish you'd discourage him from coming around."

"Nonsense. He's got a good heart."

"Oh by the way, the sheriff stopped by while I was there." She paused a moment to yell at Harold again. I suspected Harold was taking advantage of Mary Jane being on the phone. "The sheriff said to thank you for the pickles and he wants to talk to you about your recipe when you get back."

"I'm glad he enjoyed them. Don't know that I want to share my recipe, but I'm flattered that he would ask." I felt a bit of pride slip in even if it was the sheriff who probably didn't know the first thing about pickling. Maybe it was his wife who was curious. "MJ, I have to go but I want to wish you and your family a very happy Christmas. I won't be able to call on Christmas day. We will be at sea and the ship's phone costs $10 a minute."

"That's probably wise not to use the sea phone," the prudent Mary Jane remarked. "You have a nice Christmas, Auntie. Harold! Put that down!" Mary Jane was distracted again. "Take care of yourself, Auntie. You know I worry about you traveling alone."

"I've met some very nice couples at dinner and we are all getting along just fine. Don't worry about me. I love you, Mary Jane. Talk to you later."

"Love you too. Thank you for calling. Bye."

All things considered, I had gotten off lightly with Mary Jane, the drill sergeant. Harold, bless his little heart, had diverted the attention away from me.

I purchased a few postcards and decided to write them out before getting back on the ship. Sitting on a bench in the shade, I wrote a few lines to MJ, my brother, and a couple of women from our ladies' group at church. Then I started on Elma's card. The question was, should I tell Elma about Arnie or not?

I decided, not. A postcard was only going to whet her appetite and not give her the blow-by-blow description she would demand. Better to keep it to "Weather is beautiful. Wish you were here."

There would be plenty of time for hashing over the details of my meeting Arnie when I got home. And, there would be more to tell. I still couldn't believe I had a date. What was I going to wear tomorrow night? The black lace jacket was out. I'd worn that the first night. Maybe I'd try the sparkly jacket. To sparkle or not to sparkle, that was the question.

I could already feel my pulse quicken at the thought of a date. I hoped I wouldn't work myself into a nervous fit before Christmas Eve. There were butterflies in my stomach again just like when Russell would come to visit me before we were married.

Russell.

I hadn't thought about him for a while. Did that mean Arnie was coming between us? Seemed silly. After all, Russell was with Jesus and our vows had been "until death do us part." It was the "parting" I didn't like. I didn't want to part with him.

A gentle breeze brought the sweet fragrance of honeysuckle with it. I looked around for the bush but didn't see one. The scent seemed to come from a pink flowered vine covering a fence. The blossoms delicately danced with each puff of wind. Tropical foliage was so unusual and so abundant. Even the plants you were familiar with were difficult to recognize because they grew so profusely here and larger than life. Did the people who lived here appreciate what they had? Sometimes you don't know how good a thing is until it's gone.

Chapter 10

I was glad I had saved the sparkly jacket to wear. It was Christmas Eve. It was a formal night. And I had a date. Schoolgirl giggles fought with grownup fears for attention.

I almost backed out. Arnie had not returned to our table in the Britannia for dinner since that first night aboard ship and I had avoided the Queens Room. I didn't want him to feel obligated to dance with me or think that I sought him out. Truth be told, I really didn't want to see him waltzing the Purple Dragon around again.

It was 5:45 when I left my stateroom to search out the Todd English restaurant. I was fairly certain I could find it again. I had been by there once on the guided tour and again this morning to chart the route from my stateroom. The QM2 was designed like a maze. You could spend hours just trying to find the library. It was hidden away in the front of the ship around a bunch of bends and turns and places that looked like dead ends. I was afraid to check out any books. I feared I wouldn't find my way back to return them. Somewhere in the weird recesses of my mind I pictured someone who watched us to see how we would find our way around much like a scientist who experiments to see how long it takes a mouse to find the cheese in a maze.

The Todd English was a little easier to locate than the library and I felt somewhat confidant that I could reach it without a compass, a map, and a GPS device. As I waited for the elevator, I checked in the mirrored doors to see that everything was in place, no slip showing, no runs in the hose, no hair standing straight up. In the midst of my preening, the doors opened and erased the image. I entered, turned, and pressed the button for Deck 8. Mentally, I checked my path, turn right from the elevator, then right again, go down the hall and it should be straight ahead.

Deck 8 was full of suites, the kind the Purple Dragon probably stayed in. There were fancy carriage lights along the corridor to light the way and a little doorbell to press to announce your presence. As I neared one door, it opened. An elegantly dressed young lady stepped into the hall. Her blonde hair was braided thickly and hung down over one bare shoulder. A thin strap on the other shoulder held a clingy black dress that graced curves I don't think I ever had. I smiled and nodded at her just as her escort joined her side.

At least I thought it was her escort. He looked more like her father but their body language indicated otherwise. I shook my head. I don't care how long I live I will never understand those May-December things, especially when May and December seem to be separated by decades rather than months.

The further I walked the more I began to distrust my sense of direction. I hadn't made any turns, yet I suspected that something was amiss. "It didn't seem like such a long corridor before," I mumbled quietly. "Great, now I'm talking to myself." Get a grip, my inner voice said. My stomach began to tighten like wet rawhide drying out in the sun and shriveling to a fraction of its size.

The corridor seemed endless. I continued on. I figured the worst that could happen was I would make a complete circuit of Deck 8. Sooner or later I had to end up in the right place.

Maybe I could knock on a door and ask directions, I thought. Of course, with my past history, that would most likely get me in trouble, or get some nice gentleman in Dutch with his wife who would see us talking at the stateroom door and think it suspicious. I could almost hear Elma's peals of laughter as I anticipated the storytelling.

I made almost a complete circuit of Deck 8. At the front of the ship, the hallway jutted this way and that and brought me back to a straight corridor that led past the stairwell I had started from, Stairwell C. But of course, I suddenly realized, the restaurant was near Stairwell D and the elevators there face the other direction. I had started from the wrong stairwell, again.

It was 6:05 by the time I walked through the doors to the restaurant's foyer. Since three times around the ship was a mile, I had walked about a third of a mile to get there. I guessed the exercise would cover any dessert calories.

Arnie sat on a huge round padded bench, purple and red, accented with gold braid. Sheer fabric hung overhead and draped across the ceiling and down the side of the walls. I had to suppress a giggle. It looked like something out of Arabian Nights.

Arnie did not, however, look like a sheik. He was very handsome in his tuxedo, his silvered hair neatly brushed to one side with a bit of a wave cresting the top of his head. His tan was deep but showing a rosy glow that indicated he'd gotten bronzed naturally not in a spray-on tan booth. He must have found a little time to himself in the sun.

He rose as I approached. "You look lovely tonight, Annie." He took my hand. "And it must have been a good day. You're wearing a beautiful smile."

I breathed in his freshly shaved scent then looked away quickly before my eyes betrayed my enjoyment of his after-shave and the dashing figure he cut. I purposely glanced up at the sheer fabric and down again at the cushioned seating areas and waved a hand over it all.

"If you must know what's making me smile, I can't help but be reminded of a sheik's harem every time I see this room."

Arnie glanced around as if it were the first time he'd noticed his surroundings. "You're right. It is a bit decadent. You suppose Todd English is really Lawrence of Arabia?"

I laughed. Arnie had a way of putting me at ease and the knot in my stomach relaxed. We were seated at a table for two near the window with a view of one of the pool areas on the ship. It wasn't the best view for a restaurant of this class. There were a few mounds of flesh still lounging in some chairs poolside. I did a double take as I realized one rather grizzled character had metal studs prominently displayed on a very tender part of his chest. I turned away with a shudder. I hoped Tommy hadn't gone that far with his body piercings.

Arnie ordered a glass of white zinfandel wine for each of us and we toasted to a good cruise.

"Did you hear that Santa is due to arrive tomorrow?" He asked, his eyebrows raised.

"No. Is he?" There were a lot of children on board. I had assumed they would do something for them. Arnie made Santa's visit sound like something not to be missed.

"Yes. Listen for the announcement over the PA tomorrow. They're going to build the suspense throughout the morning. He's due to arrive around 11 a.m."

"Our weather man back home talks about radar blips on Christmas Eve. I always wondered what self-respecting child would be up at 11p.m. to listen to the news instead of in bed, trying to go to sleep before the old guy got there."

The arrival of the bread tray interrupted our holiday chatter. It was accompanied by an assortment of spreads made from olives, different although a little too salty for my taste. The waiter hovered nearby.

We concentrated on the menu of impressive choices presented to us. Each item sounded more delicious than the last. I had a hard time deciding, but I finally settled on an asparagus and morel tart for an appetizer, and the sea bass for an entrée. Arnie ordered lobster chowder followed by beef short ribs, a man's dinner.

"I must ask," the waiter ventured as we closed our menus. "Are you considering the house specialty for dessert? It takes extra time to prepare, so we must order it early."

"Of course!" said Arnie immediately. "Annie?"

"What is the dessert?" I hadn't seen desserts listed on the menu. What if it turned out to be strawberry ice cream pavlova again?

"Annie, if you have any penchant for chocolate at all, you have to try it," Arnie began excitedly. "It's called Fallen Chocolate Cake and it's been described as a 'death by chocolate' dessert."

"Well, if I'm gonna die, let it be from chocolate." I nodded at the waiter. He grinned as though he had just sold me the London Bridge and rushed off to place our order.

"So, tell me about your pickle business. How did all that start?" Arnie leaned in a bit toward me. I was pleased. He seemed genuinely interested and not just asking as a way to pass time before our appetizers arrived.

"Some years after my husband died, I decided to start putting up some of my own produce for the winter."

"You still farm the land?" Arnie appeared surprised.

"Yes, well, not all of it. I just made a small garden that I could handle on my own. But a few years ago, I had quite an abundant crop of small cucumbers and I got over zealous with the pickling. I knew I couldn't eat them all, and my extended family didn't want any more, so I offered a few jars to a restaurant where I eat frequently when I don't feel like cooking for myself. They really liked them and asked for more, even offered to pay me for them. I got the idea it might be kind of fun to have a little business to keep me busy so I started planting more the next year and expanded my customer list to half a dozen restaurants and diners in our area. Each year I add on a few more customers."

"It must be exciting. Your eyes light up with the telling of it." Arnie smiled and picked up his fork. "You have the brownest eyes I have ever seen."

I blushed. At this rate, I could stop wearing blusher.

The waiter arrived with our food. In between bites of wonderful sea bass and tender beef ribs, Arnie and I discussed the fine art of canning and pickling. Arnie acted as though I owned some kind of important company on the New York stock exchange.

"You do this all on your own?" He seemed amazed.

"Most of it. My niece, Mary Jane, helps deliver some of the pickles and she's learned to make labels on the computer so I have my own labels now." I didn't tell him that she sometimes helps screw on the lids if the arthritis is kicking up. "I don't make a living from it. Russell planned well enough that I get by nicely, but I do like to travel and the extra money keeps me going places."

"You are quite a lady, Annie Pickels."

I did that blushing thing again. I'm never sure how to respond to such a compliment. Mentally I threw my blusher in the trashcan.

Arnie sighed and began to fidget with a packet of sweetener. "My Ruth was quite a woman too. I lost her three years ago. Cancer. She went fast. I guess that was a blessing."

I noticed his eyes glistening as he looked up at me.

"Thanks for having dinner with me, Annie. Holidays are the worst."

"I know. It's hard not to think about Russell, too."

The arrival of the Fallen Chocolate Cake diverted our attention. I examined the masterpiece before me. A small chocolate cake resembling a soufflé without the dish rose from the center of a pool of red raspberry sauce. A scoop of vanilla ice cream sat next to it, melting from the warmth of the cake. Two large blueberries and a mint leaf garnished the arrangement. I used the side of my fork to cut a small wedge out of the cake. As I pulled it away, rich molten chocolate flowed from the inside of the cake. I watched in amazement, already tasting the chocolate with my eyes.

"How do they do that?" I exclaimed.

"I don't know," Arnie replied. "I just know that a food critic would have difficulty finding words worthy enough to describe it."

We both put a piece in our mouth and moaned in unison. A good laugh followed. It was comfortable being with Arnie. And fun. Lots of fun.

"Would you join me again for dinner, just the two of us, for New Year's Eve?" Arnie asked as we finished the last of the coffee.

"Oh, I don't know if I could eat like this again." I placed a hand on my midriff. It felt twice its normal size. "In fact, I'm not sure I'll need to eat again for a couple of days at least."

"We'll plan something light. How about the Lotus in King's Court? Do you like Asian food?"

"I like to get Chinese once in a while."

"This is much better. It's an assortment of different Asian foods, kind of a sampling of different countries. Shall I make reservations?"

"Sure. I'd love to."

"They don't open until 7. I'll make our reservations for 7 sharp so that we don't have to rush. I'll have dance duty that night, but the Black and White Gala doesn't start until 9."

"I'll look forward to it."

Arnie rose and came around to pull my chair out. He was such a gentleman. I felt his arm lightly around my waist as we walked out of the restaurant. It felt nice, warm, caring, comfortable.

"Where can I walk you to?" Arnie asked as we reached the sheik's harem. "Would you like to join me in the ballroom? I'm on duty again."

"I think I'll take in the show." I needed a little space to breathe, to think actually. Dinner was nice but the ballroom involved dancing and that meant being in his arms again. I was having feelings I hadn't had in a long time. I needed to sort them out.

"Can you set me in the right direction for the theater? I'd be grateful if I could find it before the entertainment starts."

We rode the Stairwell D elevator and walked forward to the theater where Arnie took my hand in both of his. Those smoky blue eyes of his looked into mine. "Thank you for a lovely evening." His eyes spoke the genuine sincerity of his words.

"Thank you," I half whispered, caught in the moment. He was gone before I had a chance to add anything else. It was probably just as well. If I had said anything more, it would have likely been something stupid that would have ruined the moment.

I turned and floated into the theater. I tried to recall for a minute what the show was supposed to be and couldn't. This time, the senior moment didn't bother me. I had more important things to ponder, like the touch of Arnie's hand on my back, the smell of his after-shave, and the wonder of molten chocolate. Most of all, I let his words ring in my mind, "You are one special lady, Annie Pickels."

Would he still think so after a second date?

Chapter 11

The week flew by quickly. I had set foot in five more ports. Curacao, Bonaire, Dominica, Barbados, and Tortola. Dominica and Tortola had been particularly scenic ports. I viewed them from a comfortable shaded lounge chair on the deck of the ship while I read and enjoyed the sea air. Let the beach lovers and water enthusiasts overdose in the sun. I didn't need to encourage more age spots and the quiet ship was just what I needed to reflect on all that had happened on this cruise so far.

I took the opportunity in Barbados, while ashore, to call and check in with Elma. There was a bank of phones just outside the entrance to the visitors' center. Next to me in line for the phone stood members of the crew who were eager to check in with their loved ones. I marveled at the diversity of languages being spoken all at once. Even though cell phones appeared plentiful in the hands of passengers and crew, there were still those like me who preferred a good land line to "can you hear me now?"

When I got through to Elma, she sounded a bit down. "It's snowing again," she said woefully. "I envy you. You'll have a great tan and look so healthy when you get back. And me, I'll be wearing pale winter white."

"It is nice to feel warm," I commented trying not to rub it in too much.

"So, any good looking men on that big ship?" Elma tossed out a little bait for me to bite on.

I hesitated. Should I give her a hint or not? "Well, maybe just one."

"Really? Come on, friend, give."

"His name is Arnie. We sit at the same table for dinner."

"Arnie. I like the name. Sounds like fun with a mix of sophistication." Her excitement crackled over the phone line. "I need more details."

"He escorted me to dinner at the specialty restaurant for Christmas Eve. We have another, um, dinner planned for New Year's Eve." I almost said "date," but changed my mind. A date sounded too romantic. Too promising. I didn't want Elma to make more of the situation than she should.

"He's one of the gentleman hosts on the ship," I continued, "It's his job to dance with us old single ladies." I thought that should put the whole thing into perspective.

"But he took you to dinner and you're going out again. That's more than a little spin around the dance floor, dear." I could sense that famous wry grin of hers spreading across her face. Oh, there would be no containing her enthusiasm and curiosity once I got home.

"He's a nice man and it's good to have someone to try out the special restaurants with, but it's nothing more, Elma." I tried using the tone of voice that implied, "don't push it" but it was useless with Elma.

"Well, it sounds like he's taken a special interest in you." Her comment hung in the air waiting for me to elaborate. Elma was good at pregnant pauses. If she waited long enough, she knew the other person would deliver.

"I'm sure it's just professional. He's just doing his job, keeping an old woman entertained. I really need to go, Elma. I have to save some minutes on my card to call MJ again."

"I'll be waiting for a full report when you get home," she warned me. "Have a great time. Happy New Year!"

"Thanks. Tell Warren I said 'hello' and Happy New Year to both of you. See you soon."

I was sure Elma would buzz like a bee storing up honey the rest of the week until I got home only she'd be making up questions for me. Was I wise to mention Arnie? A part of me had fun keeping a little secret but another part of me wanted the confirmation from a friend that it was okay to have had dinner with a charming man who at times took my breath away.

A thread of fear pricked me. What if she tells Mary Jane? That would create a whole peck of trouble. Mary Jane would be sure to think Arnie was after my money, as if I had that much of it to interest anyone. She wouldn't think I was attractive and interesting enough to catch a man's attention. To Mary Jane I was just an elderly lady who needed looking after. There was some truth to that, not the elderly part but the attractive and interesting part. Was Arnie truly attracted? Or was I just a diversion?

And then there was that nagging little voice in my head again. Annie, are you really trying to attract a man's attention? Just Arnie's. He's the only one I've met since Russell who's as kind and understanding, and caring.

I was so deep in thought about my intentions toward Arnie that I forgot to have my cruise card ready to show for boarding as I entered the gangway. I stepped aside to fish in my bag. As luck would have it, the card was at the very bottom of my tote bag. I dug deep, searched around, and finally pulled it out. The security officer took it and looked at it. He inserted it in the box and listened for the little "bing" that said I could board. As he handed it back to me, he smiled. "You look much nicer in person."

"Thanks," I mumbled. It was the first time anyone had commented on the crazy lady picture. I felt relieved. The opportunity had always been there for someone to make a comment. Now that it was made, it wasn't so bad. Not everyone thought I was really like that person in the picture. It was a moment captured in time by a camera, hopefully never to be captured again. Perhaps this cruise, this time with Arnie, was a just a moment captured in time, never to happen again. I swallowed hard and concentrated on my challenged sense of direction to find the way to my stateroom.

As I was getting ready for my evening with Arnie, I applied my makeup and thought back to my conversation with Elma. I let myself wonder again what my intentions were with Arnie. Funny, it was usually a woman who wondered what a man's intentions were. I hadn't contemplated that. I was more concerned with my own feelings. I felt a change in me since boarding the ship in Fort Lauderdale, since meeting Arnie. Of all the adventuresome things I'd done, I had never entertained the idea of becoming involved with a man. My attitude had changed. Was it a good change?

Russell was still with me. He would always be with me. But, somehow I felt that he approved. Russell's memory didn't seem tarnished by my being with Arnie. My love for Russell wasn't diminished, but rather was somehow enhanced by my newfound friend. Boy, I thought, Dr. Phil should get a hold of this for one of his shows.

What would the good doctor say? "Annie, have you recognized that this is becoming a relationship?"

"No, Dr. Phil, it can't be a relationship. You can't be ambidextrous when it comes to men."

Still, Russell was gone. Arnie was here.

I slipped on my black dress and topped it off with a black silk poncho that had a slightly ruffled edge and draped nicely over my shoulders down to my waist covering the little midriff bulge forming from all the good eating and lack of proper exercise. I was satisfied with what I saw in the mirror. It was fun dressing up though I wouldn't want it as a lifestyle change.

I jumped a bit when I heard a knock on my stateroom door. I thought Marcus was checking to see if I'd left yet. Normally I left earlier for the six o'clock dinner seating and he would turn down the bed and leave fresh towels and put chocolates on the pillow while I was gone, the luxury of cruising. I opened the door and my breath caught in my throat.

Arnie stood there, handsomely dressed in a black tux with white shirt and black bowtie. In his hand was a single white carnation. "Young lady, I'm here to pick up my dinner companion. Is she here?"

I raised a hand to my mouth to suppress a giggle.

"Oh, Arnie. That line is older than we are!"

He handed me the carnation.

"For my lady." He bowed just slightly. "Am I too early?"

"No, not at all. Just let me grab my purse." I turned and smelled the fragrance of the perfect blossom in my hand. It was heavenly. Purse and flower in one hand, I took Arnie's arm with the other and let him lead me down the hall.

We took the Stairwell C elevator to Deck 7 and were the first to arrive at the Lotus in the Kings Court. The buffet had been transformed with panels of Far Eastern artwork and muted lighting. The paintings on the wall that were barely noticeable during the day were lit from behind giving them an almost glow-in-the-dark aura. Tables were decked out with fine white linen and square plates accented with blue bowls and crystal stemware. Silverware and chopsticks completed the table setting giving you the option of stretching your dexterity or eating comfortably with manageable tools insuring that the food would actually get to your mouth.

As we sat at the table, the candle in the middle cast a warm glow across Arnie's face. He really was a nice man, a handsome man, a gentleman, and someone who could be a good friend. I felt it deep in my bones. I was pretty good at judging character. I had looked past Tommy's body decorations and found a nice young man behind it all. I was sure Arnie was all I thought him to be as well.

"You seem deep in thought tonight," Arnie observed.

"Oh, it's almost over, you know, the cruise, that is." I acted as though I was melancholy over facing disembarkation day.

"Two more days and we dock in Fort Lauderdale. Boy, it has gone fast." He put his hand over mine on the table. "Must be the good company I've kept."

I felt the blush. I hoped the dim light hid the flush in my cheeks. Was it possible the older you got the more you regressed to being a teenager again? I gently pulled my hand away and took a sip of water. "Russell always used to say that having good company made a day more pleasant and the hours fly. I'd call that ambidextrous, myself."

"You loved Russell very much, didn't you?" Arnie shook his head. He looked down at the chopsticks and rolled them back and forth on the table. "I'm sorry. That was out of line. I shouldn't be prying into what isn't my business."

"That's all right. I don't mind talking about Russell if you don't mind listening." I took a sip of the hot green tea in my cup.

"I'd love to hear about the man who won your heart."

I told Arnie some about Russell, about how he came from Alaska and studied at Ohio State and how we met and fell in love. "It was a simple wedding," I continued after our waiter had placed a spring roll and sushi appetizer before us.

I picked up a fork and Arnie reached for my hand. "Annie, I want you to continue your story in a minute but I sort of made a New Year's resolution, and even though it's not New Year's Day, I'd like to start now. Would you mind if I say grace?"

"I would love it if you would." I was pleased. *Lord, what a wonderful surprise. I haven't said a word to him about you and here he wants to say grace. Is this your way of telling me he's yours?*

Arnie said a simple prayer of thanksgiving and then asked me to continue on about Russell.

"Like I said, it was a simple wedding. Neither of us was big on parties and we knew Russell's family couldn't make it down from Alaska for the wedding. We had a small reception at the church with my family and friends. Our honeymoon was down in the Hocking Hills in southern Ohio. Russell's friend had a cabin there on some land the state had purchased and he let us stay for a few days. We explored caves and picnicked on the hillsides overlooking beautiful views of the rolling hills and watching the sunset."

I sighed. The memories were sweet now, not painful.

"When Russell brought me home he made me keep my eyes closed as he turned up the road to where his farm was. The last I knew, he'd just had a rough one-room cabin built to live in. When I opened my eyes, I saw the wonderful house he had built for me. He told me it was his wedding present to me. My mother had been there, hung curtains and stocked the refrigerator. There was one of her home baked apple pies on the kitchen table. It had a welcome home note on it." I paused, recalling the savory smell of that pie. "I still live in that house. Russell was a good craftsman."

"He sounds like quite a man," Arnie said.

We ate quietly for a few minutes.

"What was Ruth like?" I ventured as I finished the last spoonful of a bowl of miso soup.

"Ruth was the love of my life. I don't think I was quite the romantic Russell was but we dated in high school, so you could say I married my high school sweetheart. She worked hard to put me through law school. I don't think I ever made that up to her."

Arnie got a distant look on his face. I could recognize the pain, the regret of things unsaid.

"We put off having kids," he continued, "and then had difficulty having one. We wanted a houseful but we were thankful to have a great daughter. Pamela is the spittin' image of her mom, warm brown hair, full smile, brown eyes that sparkle with golden flecks. Ruth was gracious and kind, and put up with me for almost 40 years before she found out she had breast cancer. It had advanced too far too quickly. That was three years ago." Arnie's voice cracked slightly and he reached for a sip of water.

"She suffered for four months before she finally gave in. I think she felt afraid to leave me alone. She always felt like she had to take care of me." Arnie took a few more swallows of water.

"Russell hung on for quite a while. We did the chemo and radiation but the cancer continued to eat him up," I said. I knew how hard it was for Arnie having been through it myself. I wanted him to know I understood. "God forgive me, but in the end, I prayed the Lord would take him and end the suffering."

Arnie nodded his head, commiserating with me. Our common pain seemed to draw us together. We concentrated for a time on our main course sampling of duck and shrimp and rice.

"You were lucky," I said, breaking the quiet between us. "We never had the chance to start a family. We were only married fourteen years. The first five we spent with getting the farm going and the last years we spent in and out of hospitals."

The final course arrived just then. The dessert looked more like Mexican flan than anything Asian. A blob of egg custard in a shallow dish with a honeyed sauce poured over the top. When the waiter walked away, we looked at each other and laughed.

"Ole!" said Arnie and we dug into our desserts welcoming the chance to change the mood the conversation had set.

We strolled out of the King's Court, Arnie's hand lightly pressed against the small of my back. I loved the feel of his hand there. Somehow it conveyed a sense of security.

Once outside, he turned to me and took both my hands in his. "Annie, you wouldn't think badly of me if I didn't walk you to the theater tonight, would you?" he asked. "I need to run back to my room before I go on duty in the Queen's Room tonight."

"Of course not," I answered trying not to show my disappointment. "I can find my own way."

"This has been another wonderful evening," he said softly. "You are a special lady, Annie Pickels." He smiled sweetly and gently kissed my forehead. Then, as if embarrassed by his boldness or perhaps confused by his actions, he disappeared down the stairway.

I sat alone in the theater as I watched the Royal Court singers and dancers present a collection of Broadway tunes and production numbers from some popular musicals. I tried to stay involved with the performance on stage but my mind insisted on wandering back to my conversation with Arnie. His feelings for Ruth, his wife, were still deep. It was obvious in the way he spoke of her. Had he noticed that about me and Russell? Although lately it seemed my feelings for Russell were faded, lost in a foggy recess of my heart. Was I losing Russell all over again? No. Russell was my love. Arnie was a friend.

With that conviction, I permitted myself to relive the evening and enjoy the memory of a nice dinner and conversation. I could have a male friend without being romantically involved. I could even put up with him dancing with other women. Arnie and I shared the loss of spouses. That was a special bond. We could understand each other better because of it. It was nice to have that kinship. I had talked a lot with Elma and she acted like she understood, but until someone has experienced a loss like that, it's hard to imagine the pain. Arnie understood. Still, Elma would be there for me at home. The friendship with Arnie would probably end in two days when we docked at Fort Lauderdale. Or would it? I touched my forehead remembering the gentle kiss.

My thoughts were broken by applause. The show had ended. Half of the audience rose to their feet for a standing ovation and the other half were either too tired or not as impressed with the performance. Then again, I figured some of them might be on their feet only because they were ready to leave. Imagine being a performer and trying to decide if the audience was impatient to leave or truly loved your performance. Either way, I couldn't move until one end or the other of my row cleared out, so I sat and contemplated what to do with the rest of the evening. I wasn't ready for bed yet and I wanted to see the New Year arrive.

The Queens Room seemed the most attractive offering of entertainment and they made a mean cup of decaf cappuccino guaranteeing I wouldn't be up all night from the caffeine, just the fluids. Besides, it was the easiest place to find, since I seemed to be directionally challenged, I kept ending up there anyway. And I'd never been to one of those fancy New Year's Eve bashes where they drop balloons. I was curious. Growing up I had always watched Guy Lombardo on television on New Year's Eve. This would be my chance to see a real welcome to the New Year.

Party hats and noisemakers abounded in the Queens Room. Balloons were suspended in a huge net above the dance floor waiting for the magical moment when one year ended and a new one began. It was so crowded you couldn't see anything if you sat down, that is, if you could find a place to sit down, so I propped myself up against a wall and found a break in the crowd through which I could observe the activity on the dance floor.

People moved on the dance floor but I'd hardly call it dancing. There wasn't much room in the midst of the crowd to do more than wiggle body parts. One couple tried a little swing but all they got for their efforts were a lot of dirty looks over shoulders when they kept bumping into others. With all the gents in plastic top hats and the ladies in glittering paper crowns, I couldn't help but think I was at a Guy Lombardo party. The only thing missing was the bubble machine. The excitement was contagious. My heart began to thump with anticipation of the big moment. This was so much better than viewing a party from a recliner in front of the television. At least I wouldn't fall asleep here before the clock struck twelve or the ship's bell tolled.

At midnight they would strike the ship's bell. It was an old nautical tradition. The bell signified the passage of time. The oldest crewmember would strike it eight times just before midnight, and the youngest member, eight times after midnight. I didn't understand why it was eight and not twelve but I decided I'd stay long enough to hear the bells and watch the balloons drop and then call it a night.

It was hard to pick out Arnie among all the black tuxedos. Everyone was dressed in black and white since it was a Black and White Gala but there were a few women who didn't get the message. A red dress stuck out in one place, a shimmering green in another, but a flash of deep purple caught my eye and kept my attention.

Sure enough, the Purple Dragon stood out in the crowd. What disturbed me though was not what she wore but who she was standing with, Arnie. He smiled radiantly at the little Senior Super Model. The same smile he had used on me.

Does he have to look like he enjoys it so much?

They were in a dance position but, like I said before, there wasn't much room to dance so they were just kind of wiggling. Arnie seemed very attentive.

The countdown began to midnight. 10-9-8 -

The bells began to strike.

7 - 6- 5 -

I watched as the Purple Dragon wrapped her arms around Arnie's neck.

4 - 3 - 2 - 1- she pulled him tightly to her.

The balloons dropped on the heads of the partiers. The crowd shouted "Happy New Year!" Old Lang Syne began to play.

The Purple Dragon yanked Arnie down to her level and planted one right on his lips! He didn't fight it. When he straightened up, he patted her hand and smiled.

I was appalled. The nerve! The Purple Dragon looked in my direction, a smirk of triumph on her face. What was she doing? Arnie was my friend. The urge to escape somewhere to think more clearly propelled me toward the doors. My heart pounded. My vision threatened to blur. I felt like a jealous woman. Maybe I was.

No. Not tears. Not now. I hate to cry.

I hurried through the revelers toasting the New Year with all its promise of new beginnings. I thought tonight was the beginning of a new friendship, but if Arnie was romantically involved with the Purple Dragon, there was no room for me. The ship's bell began to strike again. The old year had died, the new begun.

I retreated into my stateroom and sat on the bed. Distance didn't fade the picture in my head. The kiss replayed like a groove in an old record that the phonograph needle got stuck in. So much for being friends, Arnie. So much for being anything!

I flung my evening bag across the bed. It rolled to the other side, spewed open, and spilled its contents across the floor like the dashed hopes a foolish old lady.

The revelation came. That's all I was to him. A foolish old lady!

Did I look lonely? In need of company?

Well, I didn't need him. I had my Russell. That was enough. I wasn't looking for any more heartbreak. I wiped my face with a tissue and got down on my hands and knees to collect the scattered items from my purse. I prayed while I was on my knees asking God to keep me from being foolish again with Arnie or with anyone else for that matter. Once everything was back in order, I rose to my feet, pleased with the new resolve to protect my heart.

Chapter 12

Disembarkation day arrived. I sat in the back corner of the Royal Court Theater until it was time for the Red 4 group's turn to disembark. I had managed to avoid Arnie the last couple of days. On a ship the size of the Queen Mary 2 it wasn't hard to do. With any luck, I wouldn't see him today either. Let the Purple Dragon have him. I was done worrying over whether we were friends or something more than that, or nothing at all. I didn't need the confusion he brought into my life.

I held *Murder in the Marketplace* open in my hands. The words on the page didn't make any sense. I couldn't concentrate. I found myself looking for one more glimpse of Arnie and at the same time, hoping I wouldn't see him. I reread the same page a dozen times. At this rate I would never get to the end. But of course it didn't matter. The Dog Lady had given me the ending.

Then the prickly sensation of someone standing near me made me lift my head. I knew before he spoke it was Arnie.

"I've been looking for you for two days," his said in a deep soft voice. Arnie set his small travel bag on the floor and slipped into the seat next to me. "You didn't return my messages. I was afraid you might not be well. Marcus assured me you hadn't fallen off the ship. Are you all right?"

"Fine," I replied curtly. I had my pride. I tightened my lips to keep them from trembling. It was a little late for him to make amends now.

"I looked for you in the Queens Room on New Year's Eve, but I couldn't find you."

"I saw you." I said. "You looked busy. I didn't want to bother you." I stared straight ahead at the stage as though I were watching a drama unfold.

Arnie looked down and shook his head. I glanced at him and saw his ears turn red. So, he could blush too.

"Yeah, the Purple Dragon latched on and wouldn't let go. I shouldn't label people but she was always in that purple dress and leeching on to me," he said.

Inwardly, I smiled a bit. So, we had picked the same label for the Senior Super Model. We thought alike.

"We're not supposed to let someone monopolize us like that on the dance floor," he continued, "but I couldn't get that through her head. Matter of fact, short of tying her to a chair, I couldn't keep her from following me all over the ship. I don't know what I did to encourage her."

I watched him weasel through his explanation. I didn't say a word. I wasn't going to help him out. We were only acquaintances, two people who'd shared dinner a couple of times I reminded myself. His problems with the Purple Dragon shouldn't matter to me. There would be no other relationship, spoken or unspoken, between us.

"I'd like to keep in touch with you if you don't mind," Arnie said. "Do you have an e-mail address?"

"Nope." I was going to leave it at that, but my mother didn't raise me to be rude, so I added, "I have a computer but I've never had a need to set up all that Internet stuff."

"May I write then?" Arnie's eyes pleaded with me.

Why was he doing this to me? He could make friends with a hundred other women. Why me? Why not the Purple Dragon?

I steeled myself and looked him squarely in the eye. "I do have a mailbox. I suppose you could do that."

I knew I was making it difficult. I didn't care. There was no use getting close to someone if they would forget you existed when they returned to their old routine. In all my cruising experience, no one had ever corresponded for more than one Christmas card if that.

Arnie extracted a pen and piece of paper from his pocket. He wrote down the address I gave him. Then he pulled out a fancy business card and gave it to me. "If you get hooked into the Internet and get a mail box, that's my e-mail address, or, if you just want to call and talk, my phone number is there as well."

He seemed to be grabbing at any thread I might offer. I refused to hold one out, well, maybe just one.

I took the card.

An announcement hushed the crowded theater for a moment. "Everyone holding Red 4 and Yellow 6 tags may now proceed to the gangway and disembark at this time. Thank you for sailing with us."

"That's me," I said. I rose and pulled the strap of my travel bag over my shoulder. I extended my hand to shake his. Arnie took it, but instead of a handshake, he pulled me to him and gently kissed my cheek.

"Annie you are a special lady," he whispered. "Please keep in touch."

He took me completely off guard. I didn't know what to say. I didn't trust myself to say anything. I nodded, swallowed hard, and walked away. Don't look back. Don't look back.

A mist of tears formed against my will and I fought to see through them. Emotions surged through me too difficult to sort out immediately. Like Scarlett O'Hara, I decided to think about it tomorrow. I forced myself to concentrate on the task before me, getting off the ship and getting on with the rest of my life.

By the time I reached the terminal and found my luggage, I had regained control. The threatened tears had disappeared and I concentrated on the procedure of reentering the country. The uniformed customs officer approved my forms and I made my way out to where the buses were waiting to take us to the airport. Limousines lined the curb with their engines running, waiting on passengers.

Since they were apparently for first class cruisers, it seemed odd that they would be out among the steerage passengers boarding the buses, and not in a special place away from the fray. Curious, I tried to catch a peek inside one of them as I walked toward my bus. Did they really have televisions and champagne bars in there?

Without warning, someone bumped into my left arm sending my travel bag flying into the air. I turned slightly and out of habit, started to say, "Excuse me."

Next to me was the Purple Dragon dressed in the natty little travel outfit I had seen on the first day of our cruise. She was trying to right an errant suitcase that had a mind of its own. I picked up my bag and studied the helpless little woman as she struggled.

"Oh, here," I said in the most polite tone I could muster. "Let me help you." I always liked the Bible verse that said you should heap hot coals of kindness on your enemy's head. Actually, I thought the wadded up newspaper would be more appropriate, but I was willing to give the hot coals a try. I reached over and set the bag back on its wheels. "There I think you can manage that now."

The natty little dragon gave me a sharp look from top to bottom and then continued on her way to a limousine waiting with door open and chauffeur smiling.

"Bye," I said cheerfully and wiggled my fingers at her as if we had been old friends. Maybe Arnie had told the truth after all.

Maybe the Purple Dragon really had latched on to him and wouldn't let go. Maybe she was so desperate that she tried to start something by kissing him that night. Maybe she had been three-sheets-to-the-wind and wasn't entirely in control of her actions. See what heaping coals of kindness did? It gave you a whole new perspective on your enemies.

Perhaps I would give Arnie a chance to prove himself a friend. I'd watch the mailbox and see what came along. Meanwhile I was going to have to do some praying, not only for the Arnie situation but for the Purple Dragon as well. She looked more like just a lonely old lady now rather than the queen of the dance floor.

The trip home was uneventful. I finished *Murder in the Marketplace*. The lady with the dog had correctly identified the culprit, the candlestick maker. Warren and Elma met me at the airport. Elma wore the red hat with the purple boa that I'd given her for Christmas. I'd included the line from Jenny Joseph's poem that said, "When I am an old woman, I shall wear purple with a red hat that doesn't go, " She loved the gift but didn't love waiting until Christmas to open it.

In the car, I finally told Elma about my dates with Arnie. She hounded me all the way home about him. Warren kept saying, "Elma give it a rest." I'm sure he felt uncomfortable with all the girl talk in the car. I appreciated his attempts to quiet her even though it was futile. Elma was excited about Arnie and whether or not he could be the man of my dreams. I was still too confused about my feelings for him to be able to answer her or myself for that matter. I needed some space and time to think. I didn't plan to make snap decisions when it came to exposing my heart.

"What does he look like? What color are his eyes? How tall is he? Does he have an accent? Where does he live? Was he married? Did he have kids? What did he do for a living? How was his dancing? What did he talk about?" The questions popped out of her mouth faster than a ball player spits sunflower seed shells.

Then came the big one: "Did he kiss you goodnight?"

"Elma!" The kissing question broke Warren's patience. "I'm sorry, Annie, I just can't control her anymore."

"It's all right, Warren. I've known Elma to be entirely ambidextrous as a friend, respectful of my privacy but nosier than anyone I know."

"Honestly, you two," Elma protested. "I'm only trying to look out for Annie's best interests."

"No you're not. You're living vicariously through her," Warren threw in. That earned him a scowl and a poke from his beloved wife.

"How can I judge if he's worthy enough for her if I don't know all the particulars," Elma whined.

"It's not your call," Warren told her.

"Trust me, Elma," I said, "No one will ever be as worthy as Russell." I thought that might stop her. I should have known better.

"He doesn't have to be," Elma retorted. "He just has to be a good person who respects and adores you."

I gave up and tried changing the subject by asking Warren to give me a detailed weather report. He summoned it up in one word—SNOW. It was a dirty four-letter word to Warren. He didn't like the snow or the dreary, gray days that went with it. I, on the other hand, was kind of excited. I planned to get out on the slopes the next week and enjoy real snow, not the manufactured kind the ski resort had to produce when the weather didn't cooperate. My membership was all paid up and my skis were waxed and ready.

When we got to the house, I plopped my small travel bag next to the luggage Warren so graciously carried into the kitchen for me and stood in the door to wave as they backed out of my driveway. Elma still grinned ear to ear. The twinkle in her eye was unmistakable. I was sure to face more questions in the days to come.

On the kitchen counter sat the pile of mail Mary Jane and Elma had collected while I was gone. One stack was nothing but catalogs and magazines, a lot of page-shopping ahead, but it beat window-shopping on cold blustery snow days. The other pile consisted of bills and mailings that offered fabulous deals on everything from new windows to credit cards and of course the catalogs from cruise companies eager for me to book the next one. It was obvious that Mary Jane had sorted it all out for me. I had to give her credit for her honesty. She had not tossed the cruise brochures in an effort to curtail my travel plans. Perhaps she had given up. Unlikely.

I looked at the bills stacked neatly in a pile according to the size of the envelope and hopefully not the size of the amount due. I sighed. Back to the reality of life. As if paying bills wasn't enough, there were the dirty clothes to be washed. I hadn't done laundry in two weeks despite the availability of a washer and dryer aboard the ship. I smiled. Maybe if I'd had a butler. . .

The big suitcase was full of clothes that needed to be unloaded. The sooner I faced it the better. I wheeled it into the laundry room and sorted the contents into baskets according to colors and fabric content. I gathered my curling iron, toiletries, and the few souvenirs I'd bought into my arms, and started for the bedroom. Halfway there, the phone rang. I knew without looking at the caller ID that it would be Mary Jane. Honestly, I think she had managed a special ring as well as a special knock.

"Hello," I said as I juggled everything to set it on the counter without having it roll to the floor.

"Auntie?" Mary Jane asked. "You're home?"

I wanted to say, "No, this is the maid. Can I help you?" but I thought better of it.

"Yes, MJ. I'm home."

"When did you get in? I thought you were going to call me."

"I just got in a little bit ago. I wanted to unpack a few things and start a load of clothes to wash before sitting down to call you."

"Well, I was worried. I just wanted to make sure you were home okay."

Mary Jane excelled at laying on the guilt even when there was nothing to feel guilty about. In all fairness though, there was one trip when I had given her reason to worry. I was stuck in Toronto overnight when the bus driver who shuttled us from the cruise ship couldn't find my luggage at the airport. I missed my connecting flight. I hated to call in the middle of the night and wake her up so I waited until the next day. How was I to know she wouldn't go to bed without hearing from me?

"I'm fine, MJ. Thanks for your concern. And thanks for taking care of the house while I was gone."

"No problem, Auntie. I was happy to help out." She paused a moment and then asked, "Did that Tommy get your drive shoveled again? He said he was coming back before you were due home to clean it off one more time."

'Oh, did you talk to him?"

"No but I read the note he left."

Funny, I thought. I didn't see a note here from Tommy.

Mary Jane continued, "I saw him briefly as he pulled away in that pile of junk he drives. He's a creepy kid. I wish you would discourage him from hanging around."

"Well, then I would have to shovel the drive myself and you would be worried about me getting hurt." I smiled. I had here there. "Besides, I wouldn't want to pull a muscle and not be able to ski." That ought to really set her off, I thought. I was having a bit of fun, albeit a dangerous thing to do with Mary Jane. Maybe I had missed her, just a little.

"Skiing? You're not serious. You're going to do that again this year? What if you break a leg or something? Your bones don't heal that well after a certain age, you know."

"When I reach that age, MJ, I'll let you know. I appreciate your concern. But now, I really do need to get unpacked. Will you stop by next week so I can show you my pictures?"

"Sure, I'd love to see them." She sighed. "Someday I'd like to get Bud on a cruise. That's not likely to happen for a long time though."

I hung up, then stared at the phone for a few minutes wondering if I'd heard right. Was there a change in the wind? Was Mary Jane actually thinking of doing something adventuresome? So, she wanted to take a cruise sometime. Hmmm. Had she looked through my new cruise brochures? Maybe I was rubbing off on her a bit. I chuckled and gathered my armload of stuff again. The theme song from the Twilight Zone played in my head. Mary Jane, a cruise, who knew what lay ahead?

Chapter 13

A few days later, against Mary Jane's better judgment, I spent a glorious day on the slopes near Mansfield. The weather people predicted a warm up. I wanted to enjoy the good snow before it melted any. Our Ohio ski resorts are bunny hills compared to neighboring Pennsylvania and further over in New York, but they allowed me to dream. I made a mental note to check into a trip out west to Colorado. I wondered if Arnie skied? I never asked him. There were a lot of questions I hadn't asked. Elma pointed them all out to me.

Late in the afternoon, as I pulled into my drive, the familiar old Chevy with flaming wheel wells was parked to one side. Tommy was shoveling the last of the new snowfall from the night before. It wasn't necessary to keep the drive clean for me. The Ford Escape I purchased last year had four-wheel drive and I used it quite proficiently. I appreciated his gesture even if it meant I had to stock up on hot chocolate and cinnamon rolls. It was nice to have someone to share the rolls and chocolate with.

"Hi, Tommy!" I called as I shut the car door. "Nice job!"

"Hey, Mrs. A.!" Tommy leaned on his shovel. His nose was cherry red and his cheeks were pinked from the cold. He swiped his nose across his jacket sleeve and sniffled.

"Come on in," I offered. "I need to make some hot chocolate and get warmed up. How about you?"

"Sounds good!" Tommy hastily returned his snow shovel to the trunk of the car. When he entered the house, he removed his boots and padded over in his stocking feet to a seat at the kitchen table while I heated the water and mixed the instant hot chocolate.

"My daddy would have had a fit to see me making instant hot chocolate," I said as I poured the hot water into our cups and stirred the mixture. "But it's easier than worrying about keeping fresh milk on hand."

The microwave dinged its message that the cinnamon roll was warm. I only made one for Tommy. I didn't need any more calories than necessary to add to the extra pounds I gained on the cruise.

"So, Mrs. A., how was the skiing?" Tommy stirred his hot chocolate. I always liked sipping hot chocolate when you wanted to talk with someone. You could learn a lot in the time it took for the marshmallow to melt.

"The skiing was great. Makes me want to head for the Rockies before I get too old to keep my balance."

"I don't see you ever getting too old," Tommy said with a grin. "You amaze me with the things you do. You're never bored."

"Are you, bored?" I asked hesitantly. I didn't exactly want to pry, but it seemed like Tommy showed up at my home a lot lately and I wondered if it wasn't just to have someone to talk with. Maybe that girlfriend of his, Mary Jane, had upped and left him with a broken heart. If she did, she was the loser. Tommy was such a nice young man. A great catch for any worthy young lady.

"Well, right now I'm kinda between jobs so I don't really have a lot to do." Tommy hung his head and studied his swirling marshmallow.

"That's too bad." I sent my marshmallow into a dizzying spin with my spoon. "Have you looked for another job?"

"Yes but not successfully. I'd like to do something in the computer field, maybe even work on my own if I could make some good contacts. You know, do some web designing or something. So far I haven't found a place to get my foot in the door."

"You know much about computers?" I raised an eyebrow as an idea came to mind.

"Enough to get by and then some."

Tommy smiled that perfect, easy smile of his. If this kid weren't such a metal magnet, he'd be a handsome young man. How could I tell him gently that businesses might frown on hiring employees with so many shiny protrusions?

"Could you help me out?" I asked. "I'd be willing to pay you. I need to learn about the Internet and e-mailing."

His face lit up." Well, sure Mrs. A. I don't need no pay though."

"No. I insist. If I had to go and take a course somewhere, I'd have to pay tuition and they wouldn't be showing me what to do on my own computer."

He gawked at me. "You got a computer?"

"I do. Don't act so surprised. Come on. I'll show you."

I led Tommy into the spare room that served as my sewing/computer room and showed him the computer that I purchased with some of my first pickle money. It wasn't anything fancy and I was sure it was probably outdated already. Electronic things got old faster than I did.

"My niece uses it to make the labels for my pickle jars and I use it to write letters to missionaries or friends," I explained. "I guess I should confess, I'm addicted to solitaire."

"Who isn't? Especially Spider solitaire." Tommy sat down in front of the computer and pushed the start button. "Let's see what you've got here."

I pulled up a chair beside him and watched as he and the computer seemed to meld. He was in his element.

"O, kaaay. You have Internet Explorer installed already. That's good. And your computer came with Microsoft Office so you have an e-mail program to work with. All we need to decide is how you want to hook into the Internet." He straightened in the chair and looked at me.

"What are my choices?" I asked not having a clue.

"Well, one way is to hook up with a modem that dials through your phone line. That's probably the easiest and the cheapest but it's also the slowest and, unless you get two lines, your phone line will be tied up every time you are on the computer. Anyone calling you will get a busy signal."

"That wouldn't be good if my niece is trying to get hold of me. She'd have a fit if my line was busy too long." I could just imagine Mary Jane making unnecessary trips to the house to see if I'd fallen or died while trying to dial the phone.

"Do you have cable TV?"

"Yes. I got it a few years ago when it came through for the development up the street. It was much better than relying on the antenna for reception."

"The cable company should have a DSL package available to you. We could hook your computer into that. The hookup is high speed and things will download quickly from the net."

DSL, download, net? My head was beginning to spin. Was I biting off more than I could chew?

"What would you do, Tommy?" I asked.

"I'd go with DSL service rather than dial-up. Now, you can get that through the phone company too, but it would require a second line, and I think their service charges are more than what the cable company is offering in their package. I'd have to check."

"I'd appreciate it. Just tell me what I need to do."

"Nothing for right now. Let me find out the prices, then see what you want to pay and we'll go from there."

Something had changed in Tommy since he sat down to discuss my computer needs. He'd become remarkably professional. I was impressed. He would be quite a businessman if people could get past his appearance.

"Thanks, Tommy. Let me know when you have all the particulars," I said as we walked back to the kitchen. "Need some more hot chocolate?"

"Naw, thanks, Mrs. A. I need to get goin'. Got a job interview at Bob's Burgers. It's minimum wage, hamburgers instead of computers, but I gotta make rent money."

"Good luck," I said as I saw him to the door. "I'll say a little prayer for you."

Tommy gave me a strange look I found hard to interpret. Was he uncomfortable with the suggestion of prayer, or thankful for it? I couldn't tell. Whether he knew it or not, my prayers always included him. He was a nice young man and I wanted the best for him.

The familiar sound of the mail truck as it pulled away from the mailbox the next day sent me out into warm sunshine to retrieve whatever junk mail and bills the mailman had been kind enough to put in the box. He was good. He would actually pull up to the box and put everything inside—not like the newspaper deliveryman. No sir. Things hadn't changed there at all. He still rolled up the paper and stuffed it in an orange plastic bag that was then tossed in the middle of the driveway each morning.

It got lost one day. We'd had a heavy snowfall between the time it was delivered and the time I was able to go out for the paper. He must not have pitched it far enough into the driveway. I'm pretty sure it ended up in one of the snow piles lining route 47 when the snowplow went through. I deducted the amount of the paper from my bill and added a note about my disappointment in not having the paper in the box. Like Rodney Dangerfield, I got no respect and no response.

Today it was warmer. The snow melted quickly and the orange paper roll was easy enough to see. The mailbox was full. Seemed like everything decided to show up at the same time, catalogs, flyers, mid-week shopper ads and the like. I bundled it carefully in my arms and carried it into the house to examine.

The contents of the mailbox spilled across the kitchen table when I set the pile down. Before perusing the treasure trove of postmarked propaganda, I grabbed a cup of fresh coffee that had just finished brewing. It was designer coffee today. I decided to treat myself to a little first class flavor, hazelnut. It wasn't cappuccino like on the Queen Mary 2, but it smelled good and tasted great with a little sweetener stirred in.

I separated catalogs and magazines from bills and envelopes of interest. Those were the ones that came with first class stamps, not the bulk mail stamp that indicated it was just another credit card offer. Between two catalogs, I found a hand-addressed envelope. The postmark read "Indianapolis, Indiana". Could it be?

I sliced open the flap with my thumb and pulled out a couple of folded pages of white stationery. Carefully, I opened the letter.

Dear Annie,

How have you been? I'm sorry it's taken so long to write to you but I came home to find that my ex-partner needed my help with a case that was a little more than he could handle on his own. It was very interesting but needless to say put me behind in unpacking and setting about my usual routine.

I understand you've had a lot of snow in Ohio. We've had a goodly amount, but I don't think it measures up to yours. Hope you are enjoying it. We never did talk about whether you like the snow or not? Do you?

Annie, there is still so much more I want to know about you. I really meant it when I said you are a special lady,

I closed my eyes for a moment. I could hear him say those words again. Funny, I remembered so much from my short time with him. The way he smiled. How his hand felt on my back as we walked out of the restaurant. The smell of his cologne as he swirled me on the dance floor.

He went on in his letter to talk about skiing, skiing! He was a skier too! I couldn't imagine the hills being any higher in Indiana though. From what I could remember of my geography in school, Indiana was as flat as Ohio.

Annie, it would be great if you could get e-mail. I enjoy writing but e-mail just seems to bring you closer to the person you're corresponding with. It's quicker, guess that's why they call the USPS "snail mail."

I hope to hear from you soon.

Best Regards,

Arnie

I liked the way he signed his name. I traced it with my finger. It looked lawyerish, a big A followed by tiny letters you could hardly read. Russell was always proud of his signature. It was bold but it was readable. Not many men had signatures you could actually read.

A knock and a "Helloooo!" interrupted my thoughts.

"Hey, Elma." I called out. "In here."

"Mmmm. What smells so good?" she asked as she walked with her nose in the air sniffing like a bunny rabbit looking for a carrot.

"I just made a fresh pot of hazelnut coffee. Would you like a cup?"

"Oooh. Designer coffee." She walked to the coffeemaker and inhaled the aroma. "What's the occasion?"

"No occasion," I said as I got a cup down and poured the steamy liquid into it. "Well to be truthful, I really wanted a cappuccino but since I don't have a machine,"

"Reliving our Queen Mary days, are we?" Elma teased as she sat down at the table.

"Just wishing I could have some of their specialty coffees again." I sat down with a second cup of my own hazelnut brew. "What are you up to?"

"Nothing. Warren is asleep, again, and I was bored so I thought I'd take a nice walk in the sunshine and see what my neighbor was up to."

"Just going through the mail," I said. I pointed to the pile in front of us on the table.

"Anything good?" I could see Elma eyeing the letter from Arnie. I knew I could trust her not to pick it up, but I was just as sure I could trust her to ask about it.

"I got a letter from Arnie."

"You did? Really? He wrote a letter? Longhand? What did he say? Does he want to see you again? Are you going to write him back?" Elma's excitement meter registered off the charts again.

"It's a nice letter. Nothing terribly exciting." I toyed with the idea of letting her read it and then thought better. I didn't want to have it analyzed inside and out. And it was my letter. Something personal and not to be shared, even with Elma. "He mentioned skiing though. I didn't know he was a skier."

"That's right up your alley, isn't it? Something more in common. Something fun."

Elma paused expectantly. She eyed me over the rim of her coffee cup. I knew she was waiting for me to tell her more. There really wasn't more to tell. Not what Elma hoped I would tell anyway. She wanted to hear about romance. It was that latent romance writer in her that wanted to create a good story. I changed the subject.

"Tommy was over on Monday. He agreed to help me get hooked up to the Internet so I can use e-mail."

"Great! Our kids hooked us in and it is so good to be able to communicate quickly. Sure beats phone calls with long distance charges. And the kids send us pictures, places they've been to, things they're doing to the house, grandchildren."

"Grandchildren?"

"I can dream, can't I?" Elma smiled mischievously. "At least now I'm ready to hear about it the moment it happens."

"I thought I might correspond with Arnie by e-mail. He asked me about it when we got off the ship."

"Hmmm." Elma sipped her coffee loudly and raised one eyebrow. How did she do that?

"What do you mean 'hmmm'?"

"Well, for someone you claim is not the man of your dreams, it looks like he's becoming a bigger part of your life. The lady doth protest too much, I fear."

If he had become more important to me, I wasn't going to admit it to Elma, not yet anyway. I put my cup down and tapped her on the forearm. "Why don't we take that imagination of yours for a walk while the sun is still shining? The snow ought to be melted off enough by now to navigate 47."

Elma slipped back into her coat and I grabbed mine from the hook where I'd left it. We donned gloves and hats. The wind was still a bit chilly in our faces as we stepped outside despite the rare January sunshine but the air was fresh and clean.

"How was Tommy when you saw him Monday?" Elma asked as we walked down the drive.

"He was fine. Why?"

"Well, when he was shoveling the drive while you were gone, Warren noticed him doubled over, like he was in pain or something. He came over and asked Tommy if he was okay. Tommy told him he'd forgotten to take his pain medication until late that morning and he was waiting for it to kick in."

"Pain medication? What's wrong with him?" I remembered the trouble he had when he loaded the tiller in his car last fall. He shrugged it off and told me it was nothing. I still didn't believe that and now Elma confirmed it. There was something not right with that boy.

"I thought maybe you knew," Elma said. "He wouldn't tell Warren anything."

"What was he doing shoveling the drive if he was in pain?"

"That's what Warren asked him. But he said that exercise helped, and he wanted to earn some cinnamon rolls."

"I saw him cringe once when he loaded his tiller into the trunk of his car. But he said he just pulled a muscle or something. Maybe he hurt himself more than he realized then." The latent doctor in me continued to make observations. "I've noticed a few times he's looked really tired out, a little glassy eyed, but I just assumed he'd been out late with friends or worked crazy hours. Of course, now he tells me he's out of a job."

"Well, who would hire someone with all that metal stuck in their body." Elma winced. "Especially that tongue thing. Yuck!"

"It shouldn't matter what a person looks like, they should be valued for what's in their heart." It seemed I preached about this a lot lately. First to Mary Jane. Now to Elma. "Tommy's got a good heart."

I must have been a little too defensive because Elma didn't come back at me with anything. We walked on a bit more before she said, "I think Tommy's a good person too, from all you've told me. And I trust your judgment. I just wish he didn't look so much like a street punk."

Elma was right. Tommy's appearance could lead someone to think he had a bad attitude.

"I know, Elma. But Tommy is who he is. And he's a good kid despite what folks might judge him to be by how he dresses." We made our turn in the development to head home. "He really impressed me with this computer stuff. I think we need to pray him into a job where he can use those skills. Would you add him to your list?"

"Sure." Elma grabbed my arm and squeezed it. She gave me her puppy dog look. "You don't mind if I pray a bit about his appearance too, do you?"

"If you must, you must," I said and patted her gloved hand. Elma would always be Elma. I loved her for it. If God saw fit to answer all of Elma's prayers, it could only mean bigger and better things for Tommy.

Chapter 14

It had been almost a week since Tommy called the cable company about setting me up with a DSL service. We made an appointment for the installation of whatever the equipment was and Tommy arrived the same time the cable guy did. He followed the poor man around like a puppy dog, asking questions and supervising his work as he hooked a metal box to my computer and then to the wires that led to the cable box out at the road. I wasn't so sure the cable guy appreciated the supervision. But once he was gone, Tommy positioned himself in front of my computer and began to check things out.

"Okay, Mrs. A.," Tommy said as he wiggled the mouse around to get the little arrow on the computer screen to do his bidding. "I'm going to set you up with a mailbox in Network.com. The mailbox is free."

The little arrow moved around the screen at Tommy's command, stopping here and there when Tommy clicked the mouse button. I lost focus after the first dozen or so pages popped up on the monitor and then disappeared. The pages were difficult to read from where I sat and Tommy never stayed on one page long enough for me to see it all. He certainly seemed to know what he was doing though.

"Aha!" Tommy exclaimed as though he'd just discovered a scientific breakthrough. "We lucked out. There's no 'apickels' listed at Network so you can use that as your address. What would you like to use as your password?"

"My password?"

"Yup. I need to put in at least five letters for a password so you can retrieve your e-mail from the server."

"Well, how about pickles, p-i-c-k-l-e-s?"

"That might be a little obvious with your last name. Someone could get into your box too easily that way," he explained. "What else could we use?"

I thought hard. It had to be something I would remember easily or I wouldn't get into the box either.

"How about dills? Would that work?"

"Dills." Tommy thought about it for a minute. "Sure. We'll use dills but we'll add some numbers after it to make it stronger. What would you remember best? Maybe a special date?"

I thought for a minute. My wedding anniversary popped into my head first but I shook it away. It made me feel guilty that all of this Internet business was for Arnie, not Russell. I couldn't use my anniversary date. "How about my birthday? September 4."

"That works. Your password will be dills94. Okay?"

I nodded. Easy enough to remember but I'd write it down somewhere anyway.

When the mailbox was all set up, Tommy demonstrated how to go on the net as he called it, and open the mailbox to read and send messages. To my delight, there was already a message in my box. It was from Network, reminding me of my address and password. That was nice of them to remind me so soon when I hadn't even asked. I wrote them down on a piece of paper so they wouldn't have to remind me again.

I gave Tommy Arnie's e-mail address and he entered it into an address book along with his own address.

"Okay, Mrs. A." Tommy got up and motioned for me to sit in the chair in front of the computer. "It's your turn. I put my e-mail address into your book. I want you to click on my name, write me a message, and send it."

I did everything as he instructed, wrote a message in the box, and then clicked on the send button. In a flash, it was gone, just disappeared. But where? I sat staring at the screen. It read, "Message sent."

"Now, Mrs. A, this is my cell phone number." Tommy handed me a slip of paper. "If you have any questions, you just call me. I don't want you worrying over anything. I don't care what it is, you just call me. I can talk you through a problem over the phone, and if I can't," He beamed a smile at me, "it'll cost you a cinnamon roll for a house call."

"How will I know you got this message?" I asked still staring at the spot where I had typed, "Hi, Thanks for the help."

"I'll reply."

Reply. That was the button Tommy said I could click on to send an answer back to someone who wrote to me. Why couldn't I just create a message? Would I ever get the hang of this?

"Oh," I said, still amazed by the thought that the simple words I had written were scurrying along some lengths of cable beside thousands, no, probably millions, of other words and Tommy was convinced they were going to end up in the right place. It was probably the same feeling my grandfather had when he first used a phone.

Tommy spent a little more time trying to show me how to "surf the net" but my information quotient was overloaded. I have to absorb new things a little at a time. My brain is an old used sponge. It takes a little longer to sop things up.

"Tommy, I'm so grateful to you," I said when we finally took a break. I handed him an envelope with a thank you card and some money inside. "I couldn't have done any of this without you."

"Aw, Mrs. A., I told you I wasn't charging anything," Tommy whined as he saw the twenties inside.

"Please take it," I coaxed. "And use me as a job reference."

He laughed and pocketed the card with the twenties.

I sent Tommy on his way with a couple of cinnamon rolls for the road and went back to the computer. The screensaver was bouncing linear triangles and waves of blue and green and pink lines across the blank screen. I moved the mouse. The screen sprang to life as it displayed what Tommy described as a home page. Now, what was it Tommy told me to do?

At the top of the homepage was a box where I could enter a word and search for places on the net that were about that word. Hmmm, what do I want to know about?

In the box next to the search button, I typed in the word, pickles. When I clicked on the search button, a new page showed me all sorts of places on the Internet where I could go and find pickles. One in particular intrigued me. "Deep Fried Dill Pickles" was listed on a recipe page. Deep fried pickles? I couldn't resist. I double clicked. Sure enough, there were the instructions for making the delicacy. I wondered if Warren and Elma might be up for a little experimentation. I printed the recipe.

The next website listed on the search results said something about pickles and dancing. Dancing pickles? I decided to take a look. It took a few moments for the page to come into view, but when it did, I covered my eyes quickly. The pickle who was dancing was not a cucumber. I peeked through a crack between my fingers just enough to find the place to click and get me back to the search page. I resolved to be a little more careful about reading the descriptions on the search page before I carelessly clicked again.

When I was done pickle hunting, I successfully navigated to the mailbox page that gave me Arnie's address and clicked on his name. A message box sprang up on the screen before me. I began to feel a sense of power. I heard about people who connected with the world through the Internet. Now I was one of them. It felt like I literally had the world at my fingertips, as long as I hit the right keys, and clicked in the right places.

Now what did I want to write? The little vertical bar kept flashing at me, daring me to put words in the white space. It blinked impatiently as if it were tapping its foot saying, "C'mon you called me here, now write!"

If I wrote a note to Elma, there wouldn't be any hesitation. I'd tell her about the pickle websites and have a good laugh over the dancing pickle. Then I'd mention the new deep fried pickle recipe and challenge her to taste it. But what did I say to a male friend? "Hello," I decided, would be a good start.

Hello Arnie,

I have finally arrived at the world's doorstep and become a surfer. At least that's what my young friend, Tommy, says. He arranged for me to connect with the Internet through my cable TV. Looks like cable may actually have something good to offer after all.

I sat back and reread what I'd written. So far, so good. I described Tommy as "my young friend." I didn't want Arnie to get the idea I had a lot of male friends who were single and his age. Now what?

I continued:

Thank you for the nice letter. I was surprised and pleased to see that you are a skier too. How are the hills in Indiana? Ours aren't so big here, but it's still fun to be out in the fresh air and enjoying some good exercise. We've had more than enough snow to keep the hills fresh. It's enough to break the old records.

The pickle business has been good. I look forward to planting in the spring.

Your friend,

Annie

Actually the pickle business had slowed some but I didn't want to sound like sour grapes. There would be plenty of stock to see me through until pickling time in the early summer, but it didn't concern Arnie and I didn't want to burden him with something that wasn't his to worry about.

The message finished, I reread it just to make sure I didn't make any careless spelling mistakes. Then I read it again just to make sure it didn't sound stupid. When I was satisfied it looked all right, and sounded somewhat intelligent, I positioned the little arrow on the send button—I think Tommy called it a cursor. He assured me that cursor did not refer to the use of bad language.

Should I click and send? I tapped my finger lightly on the mouse. What kind of door was I opening? This was a whole new world I was entering and I didn't mean only the cyberspace. With this message, I would be encouraging a relationship with Arnie. Would Russell approve of this if he were here? Of course not, I chided myself. If Russell were here, a relationship with Arnie would be unthinkable. Russell was not here. Memories of Russell were. I had to remind myself of that if I sent this.

Lord, do I send the message? My finger jerked a bit and I heard the mouse click. Just like that the message was gone. There was no turning back. Like the message to Tommy, the words had disappeared from the screen.

How long does it take, I wondered, to travel from my computer in Ohio to his in Indiana? Tommy said my DSL was fast. But no matter how fast the DSL, I expected it would be some time before Arnie would respond with an answer, if he still wanted to write to me.

Wonder if the Purple Dragon is e-mailing him too? Before I could answer myself, I heard Elma's familiar "hellooo!"

"Back here," I yelled. Elma followed my voice and found me without any trouble. She's pretty comfortable in my house, makes herself right at home. I'm not so familiar with hers, but that's probably because she has Warren roaming around. I respect his privacy and I wouldn't want to surprise him in an awkward situation by barging into his house unescorted.

"Hey chick! How's it going?" Elma was in her girlfriend mode.

"All right I think," I said. I leaned back in my chair and clasped my hands behind my head. "Tommy's got everything in place and I sent a message to his box to test it out. I just sent one to Arnie as well. We'll see what happens."

"Well, while Warren and I strolled through the mall this morning, we ran across some things we thought you might like." She reached into the shopping bag in her hand, pulled out a book with a yellow cover, and handed it to me.

A big-eyed black and white cartoon character stared at me and pointed to the title, *The Internet for Dummies*. A bit puzzled, I held it in my hand until the words finally clicked in my head. A smile spread slowly across my face.

"So are you and Warren commenting on my IQ?"

Elma grinned. "How much do you know about the Internet?"

"Only what Tommy tried to teach me this morning."

"So, the title applies, I rest my case." She reached in her bag again and pulled out another book. This one was blue, but I couldn't see the front of it because Elma held it to her chest. "This one is from me. Warren said he wanted no part of it. But I think it was a good buy."

She handed me the book and I turned it over. *Dating After 50, the Definitive Guide for Mature Singles.*

"Elma!"

Chapter 15

During January, the snow had come and gone, and come again. It was a strange winter. There was talk of breaking an all-time record for total snowfall. With almost six more weeks of winter left, it was a certainty. I didn't know whether to wish for record-breaking snow or not. I loved the fluffy white stuff, but too much of a good thing wasn't always a good thing.

Elma and I had kept busy the past few weeks with church activities. Everyone demanded my cinnamon rolls for Wednesday night dinners, so my overworked oven kept the house nice and toasty. The two of us joined a new prayer and Bible study group on Tuesday mornings. We studied women in the Bible, starting with Eve. Poor Eve. I really felt sorry for her sometimes. She always seemed to get the brunt of the criticism for eating the apple, like Adam wasn't standing there saying, "Go ahead. Let me know how it tastes."

I took advantage of our frequent snow showers to make a few more ski trips to Snow Trails. This year, with a continuous supply of fresh snow, buying a ski pass had paid off. I was amazed at the popularity of snowboarding. You didn't see so much of it during the morning and early afternoon unless there was a day off from school for the kids. It was one of those things that distinguished the younger generation from the oldsters. The times I went, the slopes were host to adults and the bunny hill was littered with young tots who learned to get their ski legs under the watchful eye of very patient instructors.

I stopped my ruminating and took the last tray of fresh baked cinnamon rolls from the oven. As I set them on the cooling rack on the kitchen table, I glanced out the window. Large snowflakes floated down once more. A new layer of snow was on its way to cover the old one with a white comforter of downy softness. Boy, wasn't I waxing poetic today?

The temptation to play in the new snow was just too great. The rolls were finished so I donned my coat and cold weather gear, and headed outside for a little fun. There was still a lot of kid inside this 65 year-old body.

I looked up at the white sky and watched the large flakes cascade down to my cheeks where they melted icy-hot on my skin. I stuck out my tongue and caught a flake or two. It was safe. It wasn't yellow snow until it hit the ground and a dog found it.

On the sleeve of my jacket, the snowflakes lingered long enough for me to wonder at the intricate designs. How could God make each one so different? I guessed it was a lot like how he made people so different. Mary Jane never got out in the snow unless she absolutely had to, and continually grumbled about every trace of accumulation. Elma liked the look of the snow but would rather enjoy it from the kitchen window of her home with a hot cup of coffee in her hand. Russell had been a cold weather guy like me. Guess that came from being an Alaskan. We use to sled on a hill that was in the middle of where the development was now. Russell would put me on the sled and pull me for a wild ride to the hill and then we would both race up and get on the sled together for an exhilarating slide down, only to get up and do it again and again amid giggles and snowball fights.

I found a flat spot in the yard and sat down. Did I still have the knack for making snow angels? I laid back, extended my arms and swished them and my legs back and forth in the snow. There was no graceful way to get up when I finished. I'm not as agile as I used to be. My snow angel was a little hard to distinguish. I walked a little farther away and decided to try again.

Sitting down carefully, I went through all the motions again. This time I lay still for a minute enjoying the softness of the snow layers beneath me, and the gentle flakes that floated down from above. I felt like I was drifting in a world of white, just drifting...

"Annie? Annie, are you all right?"

I flinched. The voice sounded familiar. I raised my head to see a figure race through the snow to where I lay.

"Stop!" I yelled. "Don't get too close."

The figure stopped within a few feet of me. It was Arnie. I started laughing. Wouldn't you know he'd pick this moment to visit? What in the world was he going to think of me now? The picture of the crazy lady on my cruise card flashed before my eyes. I was living up to character. I laughed all the more.

"Are you all right?" Arnie asked again. Worry tinged his voice.

"I'm, I'm fine. I just made a snow angel and I'm trying to figure out how to get up without ruining it." I tried unsuccessfully to stop the spasms of laughter. "C-can you help me out?"

Well, that set Arnie to laughing, probably from relief that I hadn't fallen and done bodily harm. Mary Jane wouldn't have found it so funny, so I guess I was lucky it was Arnie who'd come and not Mary Jane. He wasn't much help standing there doubled over though.

"Are you going to stand there laughing at me or give me a hand up?" I asked.

"A snow angel? Where is my camera when I most need it?" Arnie walked slowly toward me and stood at my feet. I gave him my hand and he gently pulled me to my feet. I carefully stepped out of my creation and then turned back to admire it. It was perfect.

"Nice job if I do say so myself," I said, my hands on my hips.

Arnie chuckled. "You make a mighty fine snow angel, Annie."

I turned to look into those smoky blues that were crinkling at the corners. "I didn't expect you to stop in so soon. I just got your e-mail yesterday that said you might be passing by sometime in the future."

"The future has arrived, m'lady." He bowed and made a sweeping gesture with his hand. I was beginning to understand and enjoy Arnie's sense of humor. He could be very gentlemanly one moment and totally like a child the next. I wasn't one to talk as I stood like a kid, looking at my snow angel.

"How about a cup of coffee?" I offered.

"Sounds good." We moved toward the house.

"So, where are you really headed?" I asked.

"Here. I came to see you."

"That's flattering but, if I remember correctly, you said something about taking on a case that had an Ohio connection."

"Okay, you caught me. I'm really on my way to Columbus to file some papers, but don't I get points for stopping by?"

"You get coffee, and a fresh baked cinnamon roll," I said as I reached for the handle on the side door of the house.

"A sweet roll and coffee. That's got to be worth the trip." Arnie followed me into the house.

We were enjoying our cinnamon rolls and coffee, and talking about the farm and the garden plots I rented when I heard, "Hellooo!" I rolled my eyes at Arnie and whispered, "It's Elma. Are you ready for this?"

"I'm up for a good grilling." He patted my hand just as Elma walked into the kitchen. Her eyes zeroed in on the gesture. I knew she would think we had been sitting there holding hands. Oh brother! Now she was going to go further off the deep end about Arnie, if that were possible.

"Well, hello. I didn't realize you had company," Elma claimed innocently.

Sure she didn't, I thought. "Elma, Arnie's car is parked in the driveway."

"Sorry. I thought maybe Mary Jane had a new car." She turned to Arnie. "So, you're Arnie." Elma held out her hand as he rose to shake it.

"Yes, I'm Arnie." Elma moved to the table and Arnie pulled out a chair for her. She was duly impressed. I could tell by her grimace at me. Thank goodness she didn't point a thumb over her shoulder.

Arnie returned to his seat. "You must be Annie's friend, Elma. She's told me a lot about you."

"And all of it's true, knowing Annie." Elma beamed and patted my arm without taking her eyes off Arnie.

"Coffee and roll, Elma?" I asked.

"I'd love it. Thanks." She turned her attention back to Arnie. "So, tell me all about yourself."

I busied myself with the coffee and roll and hoped she didn't make Arnie too uncomfortable. It sounded like he was handling things quite well, probably came from all that experience with women on cruise ships. The color purple swirled through my head. Guess that Purple Dragon thing still bothered me some.

Elma was only half way through her coffee and roll when Arnie said he needed to leave.

"I have to get to Columbus before the clerk of courts office closes, so if you ladies will excuse me, " He rose and extended a hand again to Elma. "It was nice meeting you, Elma. I'm happy to know that Annie has such a good friend just across the street. Someone needs to supervise her snow angel production."

"Snow angel?" Elma gave me a bewildered look.

"I'll explain later," I said to her and turned to Arnie. "Let me walk you out."

Elma had the good grace to sit at the table and sip her coffee so I could see Arnie out on my own. I grabbed my jacket off the hook and walked him to his car.

"Thanks for stopping by. It was good to see you again." I suddenly felt an overwhelming sadness creep up. I immediately scolded myself. You're just saying goodbye to a friend, and he'll be back again.

"Your cinnamon rolls are the best. Next time I want to sample your pickles," Arnie said, as though he sensed my melancholy.

"I didn't think pickles mixed well with cinnamon rolls or I would have offered."

Arnie chuckled. He placed his hands on my shoulders. "Well, Miss Snow Angel, I'd better go." He gave me a little hug and a soft kiss on the cheek before settling in behind the steering wheel of his car. "Keep those emails coming," he called through his opened window just before he backed down the driveway.

I stood and waved until he turned onto 47. Taking a deep breath, I returned to the house to face Elma, the friendly interrogator. She was wiggling in her chair when I came back into the kitchen. I refilled my cup of coffee. I was going to need it.

"Wow. He's even nicer that you described. Did you see how he pulled out the chair for me? Warren hasn't done that in years."

"Warren gets the door for . . ."

"And he's sooo good looking! Blue eyes, silvery hair, and he must work out."

"Goodness, Elma, how could you tell that with him dressed in a suit?"

"And that suit! Tailored just right, charcoal gray pin stripe, kinda reminded me of James Bond, the good-looking one, Sean Connery." She sighed like a groupie teen-ager.

"James Bond didn't have silver hair," I pointed out.

"But Sean Connery does now," Elma argued. Sean Connery was the only man who could give Warren any competition as far as

Elma was concerned. She loved Sean Connery despite his thinning gray hair and middle-aged paunch.

"Arnie did look nice, professional." I savored the picture of him in my head.

"So, what was he doing here? Did you see that Lexus he drives? Did he ask you out again? Is he coming back soon?"

I wanted to tell Elma to breathe. The questions just kept rolling out of her.

"This must mean he's interested. Why else would he just stop by? This isn't exactly on the direct route to Columbus. Do you still think he's just a friend?"

"Elma, slow down. He's just a friend who happened to be close by and decided to stop in and say, 'hello.' Nothing more, nothing less."

My non-committal answers got to her. I could tell by the exasperated look on her face. They got to me too. Seeing him again had stirred up a lot of old emotions and inner conflict. Somehow I had to resolve this and keep my sanity.

"Well, I think you're not seeing the whole picture here. I saw the way he looked at you when you talked, and how he held your hand." Now she grinned like a mother who'd caught her daughter with her hand in the cookie jar. My face flushed. Good thing I'd given up on that blusher.

"That wasn't hand holding. It was just a gesture of . . ."

"Gesture, shmesture, I saw what I saw. I wouldn't be surprised if the next time he showed up it was with flowers, asking for a date."

I had to laugh at her. Her intentions were good. I was just glad I wasn't interested in Arnie that way. Or was I? I could be very disappointed if I dreamed of flowers and a date. Better to play it safe and not dream.

"And what's this about snow angels?"

I explained to Elma my escapade in the snow and Arnie's timely arrival. I challenged her to go out with me and see who could make the best snow angel but she declined, said I was crazy. Maybe I was.

Early the next morning, I sat at the table, my Bible opened before me. I enjoyed my time in the scriptures, but I missed my walk and talk time with the Lord. There weren't too many breaks in the weather to make it safe enough to walk 47. I'd ventured out a few times, but it got a little harrowing as I was forced to weave around the growing snow piles along the side of the road to avoid traffic.

Then an idea struck. I smiled. Russell used to say he could hear the thunder when the lightning struck in my head. I decided it might be a good idea to drive to the entrance of the development, park and walk. Why hadn't I thought of that before? Russell also used to say, "Necessity is the mother of invention." I needed a good ambidextrous outing, a good walk and talk. There were issues to be sorted out. Decisions to be weighed. Those weren't the sort of things you did while you sat drumming your fingers on the table.

The sidewalks in the development were fairly clean but I slowed my pace so I could keep an eye out for icy spots. Kids dotted the driveways as they waited on the school bus. I looked for Sarah and her mother but they must have kept watch from inside their warm house. Snowballs flew through the air in a couple of places. Crazy lady that I was, I felt the urge to join in, but I restrained myself. Some mother might not appreciate a stranger pelting her child with a snowball. If I got hit though, there would be no holds barred.

Lord, what a wonderful creator you are. There is no way anyone could duplicate this kind of fun in a toy store. Snow has got to be one of your greatest creations, every flake so different, you can mold it into all sorts of shapes, and even make angels in it.

That made me think about Arnie and the snow angels he discovered me making. I smiled. What did he really think when he realized what I was doing? It must have been good thoughts, he called me "Miss Snow Angel."

Russell used to call me "Pumpkin. "It had something to do with me growing pumpkins. If Russell were still here, would he call me "Pickle" now? I wasn't sure I would like that pet name.

Miss Snow Angel was kind of nice. I liked it, or rather I liked the way Arnie said it. I remembered the little flutter in my tummy when he hugged me, and then, that soft kiss again. Get a grip, Annie. You're beginning to sound like a teenager. You are a grown woman, a widow. You've had that young love thing. It only comes once.

But, what about mature love?

I mulled that over for a bit. Russell was my one true love, the man of my dreams as Elma would say. A person could only have one true love, right?

I'm your one true love.

Now I really thought I was going crazy. I was hearing voices in my head. Wait, not voices. Voice. And it was in the part of my head that was connected to my heart, the very heart I had given to Jesus so many years ago.

Lord, you are my one true love. I didn't mean to think otherwise. It's just, I don't know, you gave me Russell, and, and I truly loved him as my friend, my husband, and my lover. He was a gift from you. I'm just not sure there's room for another man in my life like that.

I looked up in time to see a wife kiss her husband good-bye at the door. My heart sank. I was really missing Russell again, or was it Arnie I missed? Conflict!

There's room in your heart.

There is?

Lord, I really need your guidance. I know Arnie's a good man. He's also one of yours. Show me Your will for our relationship.

It was good to be ambidextrous but I wasn't sure my talk was done when my walk was. I got back into my car, still a little conflicted, but feeling better now that I had talked with God. Arnie and Russell were both good men. God had given me a double blessing. I drove the short distance back home, and pulled into the drive next to the sheriff's car.

The sheriff's car?

What was he doing here?

Chapter 16

The sheriff stood at the door and watched as I pulled my car past his and got out. I tried to chase off the flutter of embarrassment I felt rise at the thought of our last encounter involving the "bird burglar."

"Hi, can I help you?" I called out. I watched him pick his way across the slush in the driveway.

"Hello, Mrs. Pickels. Nice to see you again." He touched his hand to his hat and nodded a bit. Sheriff Stewart looked like he'd worked on whittling his waistline since last fall. He looked a bit thinner.

"Do you have a few minutes to talk? I need to ask you some questions about your pickles."

"Of course," I said. "Let's go in out of the cold." I led the way to the door. "Mary Jane, my niece, told me you'd stopped by while I was away."

"How was your trip?"

"It was great. The Queen Mary 2 was a beautiful ship and I met some very nice people."

Sheriff Stewart followed me into the house. He stomped his feet and wiped his boots on the entry rug but he didn't take them off like Tommy always did.

"I keep meaning to take my wife on one of those cruises. Someday we're going to do it. Maybe when I retire." He tapped his middle with both hands. "She's got me on a diet so I'll live long enough to enjoy it."

"Don't wait too long. You never know what the future holds," I warned him. "Can I get you some coffee or tea?"

"Just a glass of water would be fine, if you don't mind," the sheriff said as he stood and surveyed my kitchen. Must be old habit, I thought, one of those things a policeman does naturally, always on the lookout for anything unusual. He removed his hat and brushed his red hair back into place.

"Why don't you have a seat?" I nodded to a chair by the kitchen table and reached for a glass from the cupboard. I handed him the water and he took a long swig before he sat down and opened the little notebook I remembered from his visit before.

"Your pickles were delicious, by the way," he said as he flipped pages, "But I noticed something in the brine after we polished them off. I'd like to ask you about it."

"Oh dear, I hope I didn't leave anything in there I shouldn't have. I keep a very sterile area when I'm pickling, don't want any problems like you hear those fast food restaurants having."

"No, it wasn't anything like that. It was, well here, let me show you." He pulled a little plastic bag from his breast pocket and set it on the table. "Do you recognize this?"

I was relieved. It was something that was meant to be in the pickle brine. "Of course. That's my secret ingredient, marjoram."

"Marjoram?" He frowned. "Are you sure?"

"Of course I'm sure. I get it from one of my garden plot renters. He has more than he needs, so I snip a little now and then. I thought it looked real pretty floating in the brine. I think it gives the dill a little more zing."

"Zing." Sheriff Stewart wrote in his little notebook. "Who is this renter who grows the, um, marjoram?"

"His name is Tommy. He's a very nice young man, always pays me on time and in cash, very respectful, and helpful. He's been keeping my driveway shoveled this winter."

His head nodded as he wrote. "What's Tommy's last name?" I thought for a moment. It had never been necessary to know Tommy's last name.

"I don't know," I told the sheriff, "I never asked him."

He looked at me in disbelief.

"Where does Tommy live?"

"I don't know, I never asked him."

"What do you know about Tommy?"

"Well, he's a nice young man." I felt like the sheriff had turned into the male version of Elma.

"Mrs. Pickels," the sheriff interrupted. "We've been through all of that, he's a nice young man. But what do you know about Tommy that might help me find him?"

I could sense his impatience. Why would he want to find Tommy? Surely it wasn't because of his marjoram. What would the sheriff want with that? Was there something I didn't know about Tommy? That was obvious. While I didn't know a lot about Tommy, I could tell Sheriff Stewart what I did know. But if Tommy was in some kind of trouble, maybe I shouldn't, at least until I could see if I might help him out.

"Mrs. Pickels, do you know *anything* about Tommy?" the sheriff's pen tapped rapidly against his little notebook.

"I know that he drives an old Chevy, and he's very smart. He knows a lot about computers. And he has a girlfriend. Her name is Mary Jane, just like my niece."

Sheriff Stewart scratched his head. I looked at his hair. Thankfully, the scratching didn't seem to be making him balder.

"We had a conversation once about how our Mary Janes help us out."

"And how does Mary Jane help him?" the sheriff asked. His eyebrows narrowed slightly and caused his forehead to furrow.

"It was very sweet. He said his Mary Jane helped him get through life."

"I'm sure *she* does." The sheriff seemed a bit sarcastic. He hadn't even met Tommy. I hated it when people drew conclusions about someone without taking the opportunity to get to know them, and the sheriff hadn't even seen him. What would Sheriff Stewart think once he saw Tommy's metal piercings and tattoos?

"And how does Mary Jane help you?" The sheriff looked at me strangely.

"Well, Mary Jane helps me print the labels for my pickle jars."

"Uh-huh." The sheriff wrote something down. "And Tommy's been supplying you with the marjoram for your pickles?"

I nodded and wondered about that trace of sarcasm again.

"There's nothing more you can tell me that would help me find Tommy?" He sat back with a big sigh.

"Sorry."

"Will he be renting a farm plot again this year?"

"I assume so."

"When will you know?" He put his pen down and stared hard at me.

"Well, usually people start reserving their plots in April so that they can begin working the soil or even planting cold weather crops. I should know sometime around then."

"Okay, Mrs. Pickels, I guess that will have to do." The sheriff closed his little notebook and plopped his hat back on top of his head. He rose and pushed in his chair. "Thanks again for the pickles. They were real good."

The sheriff stopped just short of the door. He turned. Something was bothering him. His lips were pursed and he rubbed his chin for a moment.

"Mrs. Pickels, " He cleared his throat.

"Yes?"

"Your pickles are good, but I wouldn't use anymore *marjoram* in the recipe. It doesn't really affect the taste and it just might have an adverse effect on some people. You wouldn't want that."

"Adverse effect? No, of course not."

That was a cryptic message if I'd ever heard one. Adverse effect? Were people allergic to marjoram? No one had ever complained to me. I'd never heard any reports on the news about people who had allergic reactions to marjoram. Certainly not like the peanut allergy problems. I was still mentally scratching my head as the sheriff opened the door to leave.

"Have a good day, Mrs. Pickels." The sheriff closed the door behind him.

As Russell would say, "Something was rotten in Denmark and it wasn't the cheese." But then Russell usually meant the barn needed cleaning out. I was really confused. What did putting marjoram in my pickles have to do with Tommy except for the fact that he grew it?

I suddenly remembered I had Tommy's cell phone number. I could have given that to the sheriff. But, if Tommy were in trouble, I'd like the opportunity to help him out before the sheriff got involved. For the life of me, I couldn't imagine that nice young man being involved in any kind of trouble, unless it was a traffic violation. Maybe that car of his really could burn up the highway.

I dialed his number. A mechanical voice told me to leave a message. I didn't know what to say so I hung up. Besides, something like this should be talked about over hot chocolate and a cinnamon roll.

A few days later, the sheriff's visit still kicked around in my head as I carried my second cup of coffee into my ambidextrous room, the one I used for computing and sewing. The modern conveniences of the Internet had become a part of my daily morning routine. After my breakfast, I would pour another cup of coffee and boot up the computer. That was a term I'd learned from my dummy book; then sip my coffee while I checked my e-mail.

Arnie was pretty good about e-mailing almost every day. It was fun to correspond with someone so frequently like that.

This morning I had two e-mails, one from Arnie and one from Tommy. Since Tommy was fresh on my mind, I opened the one from him first.

Mrs. A,

Hi! How are you? I haven't heard from you for a while so I assume you are doing well with your computer and the e-mail. I am getting anxious to get started on my garden plot. I hope the weather gets better. I will be out to see you soon. I need to ask a favor of you but I'll wait until I visit. Take care. If you need any help, call me.

Tommy.

A favor? I wondered what kind of favor Tommy could want. Maybe he planned on asking his Mary Jane to marry him, and wanted me to help him with the proposal. My romantic side took over for a moment and let my imagination take a ride in that direction, made me feel like an Elma. Or did the favor have something to do with the sheriff's cryptic visit?

I clicked on the reply button and wrote:

Tommy,

Good to hear from you. I'm having fun with the e-mail and learning to surf the net thanks to the book my friend bought me. It's one of those books for dummies, but this dummy is learning a lot from it. Ha. Ha. Looking forward to seeing you sometime soon. How about hot chocolate and a cinnamon roll?

Mrs. A.

I was going to tell him about the sheriff's visit but thought better of it. If the favor he wanted to ask me had something to do with being in trouble, I didn't want him afraid to tell me because I'd talked to the authorities.

My cursor—I learned all sorts of new words now, traveled up to the e-mail message titled *Greetings*. I clicked on it and leaned forward to read Arnie's morning message.

Good morning to my favorite Snow Angel!

Hope this finds you feeling chipper and ready to play in the snow. Did you get any of our late winter snowfall? We have about 2 inches here. My case in Ohio has finally come to an end. Everyone found an amiable settlement, the lawyers are paid, and I'm back into retirement. With all this free time, the wanderlust is hitting again. Do you have any trips planned? This is the season for some good bargains on cruises. Guess I'll do a little bargain hunting this morning. Care to join me? I would love to spend some time with you.

Have a happy day!

Arnie.

Snow Angel. The name had stuck to me like good packing snow did on a winter wool coat. It did sound special the way Arnie said it though. What did he mean, "Care to join me?" What was he asking of me? *Lord, don't let me make a fool of myself here.* How do I answer him? It wouldn't look proper to go off on a vacation with him. Who knows what people would think? And yet, what was wrong with being on the same ship together but separately? It wasn't like we'd be sharing a room. Mary Jane would have a real fit if I seriously considered a trip with Arnie. She was sure he was after my money.

Just the other day she came for one of her routine elder checkups on my ability to care for myself and told me some big story about a lady who was duped out of her savings by some gigolo, as Mary Jane put it. "I wouldn't be surprised if Arnie fit the description," she had said snidely.

"You have to be careful of men like him. They're out for your money."

"Hah! What money?" I had replied.

"You have quite an investment from the property you sold, and there is still a lot of value in this farmland," Mary Jane responded. "Do you want to risk losing all of that?"

"First of all, Mary Jane, you're assuming I have more than a friendly relationship in mind with Arnie. That's certainly not the case. We just . . ."

"It doesn't take more than a friendly relationship," Mary Jane protested. "I've seen women interviewed on TV who were just friends with some con artist, and they came to trust him enough to let him have access to their funds."

"Arnie's never mentioned money. I'm sure with his professional background he doesn't even need it. Lawyers make a good buck." I could feel my face begin to heat up. I refused to let her get to me.

"I worry about you, Auntie," Mary Jane changed her accusing tone to one that almost sounded compassionate.

"I know, MJ, but you have to understand that I'm not senile yet. I can still discern the bad guys from the good."

"I'm not so sure about that," she said. She stiffened.

"What do you mean?"

"Tommy." She said it like she was dropping a bomb on me and waiting for it to explode. She couldn't miss a chance to take a few shots at him as well as Arnie.

"Tommy?" I asked innocently.

"There's something not right there, Auntie. Even the sheriff was curious about him when I mentioned his hanging around here while you were gone."

"Mary Jane, he was just doing me a favor shoveling the driveway. If he wanted to steal something, he's had plenty of opportunity to do so by now. Nothing is missing."

Mary Jane sat quietly and pouted. Any moment I expected little curls of steam to escape her ears.

"MJ, if Arnie ever mentions money, especially my money, I will tell you immediately. Then we can decide together if he is some kind of a threat," I touched her arm gently. "I promise."

Now as my attention returned to the e-mail message displayed before me, I considered Arnie's invitation. It would be fun to go on another trip, fun to be with Arnie. There were just too many things besides Mary Jane's reaction to consider at the moment. Would it send the wrong message to Arnie? I didn't want to encourage anything more than friendship if I still wasn't ready for it. Emotions can be ambidextrous sometimes. You feel one thing on the outside but on the inside you feel something entirely different. While it appeared I handled my friendship with Arnie well on the outside I still felt a little guilty on the inside, like I was cheating on Russell.

Of course the greater challenge might be Elma. If I went off with Arnie on another cruise, she'd have the caterer, the flowers, and the church lined up before I got back. That woman absolutely itched to plan a wedding.

I created a new message box and began writing:

Dear Arnie,

Yes, we got more than our share of the late winter snow. I love it but I am getting a little anxious about spring getting here. It's time to start thinking about planting and my garden renters.

I do not have any travel plans at the moment. The bargain cruises sound tempting but I need to be here for my pickle planting and to see the garden renters get a good start. All of that feeds my travel fund. Good luck with your bargain hunting. Let me know where you are off to.

Warmly,

Annie

I sat back and reread what I'd written. It looked all right. I didn't tell Arnie I wouldn't go, just that I couldn't go. I clicked the send button.

Returning to my homepage on my browser (I was really into this Internet vocabulary now) I entered "cruise bargains" in the search box at Yahoo and watched as the search results registered. Arnie was right. There were a lot of bargains. I began surfing. If the Internet had been around earlier, the surfing songs of the Beach Boys might have sounded a little different. "Let's go surfing now," could have meant something entirely less romantic than water, waves, and sun.

There were so many places in the world that invited exploration by cruise ship, the Norwegian Fjords, the Antarctic, the Orient. I filled out the forms to receive brochures. What else was there to do between now and Easter besides ski and color eggs?

Chapter 17

Easter came a little early, in March rather than in April. It snowed so much that week that everyone half expected a white Easter, which would have been appropriate. After all, the Bible says Jesus washes away sin to make you white as snow. Most people groaned at the possibility of a snowy Easter. Most people, not me. But then, I love the snow. A lot of folks like Elma don't. Elma wears a sweatshirt in the winter that says, "Let it snow. Let it snow. Let it snow, somewhere else!"

Just after Easter, a new pile of travel brochures arrived in my mailbox. I found it easy to request brochures from the Internet. Having the ability to surf fed my travel bug. England looked especially inviting. Maybe it was because of my Queen Mary 2 cruise. Meeting all those English folks and indulging in a bit of the culture made me a little curious to see the country. I wanted to experience a real "cream tea"—one with fresh scones and real clotted cream.

I dumped the pile of brochures on the kitchen table. I'd have to get a bigger mailbox if I kept this up. The lid barely closed on all that the poor mailman stuffed in there.

If you could declare a national day for hot chocolate, I decided, this was the day. I sat down with a steamy cup, gave the marshmallow a swirl, and sorted through the colorful brochure pictures of pastoral countryside and bustling cities. In the midst of deciding whether one pamphlet should go in my keep pile rather than the don't-keep pile, I heard a siren wail. Out in our rural area, a wailing siren usually meant a fire somewhere. The sound got closer and closer. I assumed it was headed to the development, but suddenly it stopped. My heart beat quickened. Was my house on fire and I didn't know it? I sniffed for smoke. Nope.

Elma and Warren!

I ran to the front window and looked out. Sure enough, lights flashed across the street but they weren't from a fire engine. It was an ambulance! My heart sank to the pit of my stomach. I hesitated only a moment as I rattled off a quick prayer and made a mad dash for the door.

The snow had melted with the morning sun but I still had to puddle jump as I made my way across 47. Questions assaulted my mind. Who? What? How bad? Had Warren taken up woodworking again and cut something vital this time? Or did Elma insist on climbing that rickety ladder to get to the top of the cupboards and this time it gave way?

I rushed up the driveway and pushed past the deputy sheriff who arrived with the ambulance. He reached out to stop me but the look on my face must have made him think better of it.

Elma stood in the middle of the living room. Her hands looked like they were holding her face together as she watched the paramedics leaning over Warren who was stretched out on the floor. I gently put my arms around her. She leaned into the comfort of knowing her friend was there.

We said nothing for a few moments. I took in the enormity of the situation. "What happened?" I whispered.

She stared straight ahead, her eyes fixed on Warren. "He was having some chest pain, thought it was indigestion, argued with me not to call the squad." She reached into her pocket and retrieved a tissue to dab at her eyes. "He went to the kitchen for some water. He, he just doubled over."

She shuddered and I gripped her tighter.

"He didn't argue with me then. I called the squad."

I rubbed my hand up and down her arm gently. She glanced at me. "Thanks for coming."

"You knew I would," I said.

She nodded.

We stood and watched the EMS team start an IV and take all Warren's vital information. They reported everything to the county hospital on a walkie-talkie type cell phone.

"Mr. Thompson," the young lady with a stethoscope around her neck said loudly. "We're going to take you to County General. They want to see what's causing you all this discomfort. Do you understand me, Mr. Thompson?"

Warren kind of moaned and nodded slightly. He didn't argue. The EMS team got him onto the gurney and wheeled him outside to the ambulance.

"Mrs. Thompson would you like to ride along?" the blonde EMS guy asked as he finished stuffing some things back into his medical pack. She nodded and he helped her into the ambulance.

Elma turned to me and called through the back doors of the ambulance. "Annie, would you lock up for me, and call Cathy too?"

"Sure. And I'll be along as soon as I can. Love you." The doors closed and the ambulance moved down the drive to 47 where the deputy sheriff stood in the middle of the highway and made sure that traffic stopped so the emergency vehicle with its precious cargo could pull out safely.

I went back in and found Cathy's work number next to the phone where Elma kept all her important numbers. Thank goodness she was so organized. Cathy was understandably upset when I called, but fortunately I was able to calm her down. She said she would be on the first flight home.

I hung up and surveyed the living room floor where the emergency team had worked on Warren. Empty packages and swabs lay scattered where the paramedics dropped them in their haste to help their patient. Elma and Warren don't need to come home to this. I grabbed the waste can from the kitchen and picked up. Afterward, with Elma's coat and purse in hand, I locked the door behind me and went back home. One more phone call. I found the number for our church prayer chain and then I was out the door and on my way to County General. The drive was a lot longer than I remembered but it gave me time to talk with the Great Healer.

I found Elma in the ER waiting room sitting in a plastic chair and staring at the noon news on television.

"Anything new?" I asked as I sat down beside her.

"No. Looks like we're done with the snow and it's going to get warmer."

Elma was obviously not herself. She had kind of a vacant look on her face and her skin color was bad, like she'd used a foundation with too much yellow in it.

I put a hand on her forearm. "I was asking about Warren," I said gently.

"Oh, I'm sorry. I kind of got lost there for a minute." She reached for her purse and coat, and took them from me. "They think he had a heart attack. Maybe now he'll start getting the checkups I've been on his back about."

A little of the usual stubborn I-know-best Elma began to show through. I relaxed some.

"How's he doing?" I asked.

"He's doing all right. They're running all sorts of tests and he's being unusually good about it." Teary-eyed, she looked at me. "I think he's really scared. So am I."

"Mrs. Thompson?" A doctor dressed in blue scrubs with clipboard in hand entered the waiting room.

"I'm Mrs. Thompson," Elma said. She raised her hand and then pointed to me. "This is my friend Mrs. Pickels."

He nodded his head at us and pulled up a chair. Hair grayed at the temples and little crow's feet around the eyes, he appeared to be middle aged. It's hard to tell sometimes with doctors. They age a bit faster than the rest of us. It's probably all those years of studying late in medical school and then all the crazy hours they keep when they go into practice. I guess if a doctor looks too good for his age, you ought to be worried if he's practiced enough.

"I'm Dr. Tery." He extended his hand to Elma. "Your husband is resting a bit," he said as he flipped through the pages on his clipboard. "We still have a few more tests we want to do but for now he doesn't seem to be in any danger. We'll keep him a couple of days for observation and to finish our evaluation. Right now, I'd say he's suffered a mild heart attack. Sometimes that's not a bad thing. It alerts us to some health conditions that need to be addressed, a wakeup call of sorts."

"Warren certainly had that this morning," Elma commented. "Maybe he'll listen to me now."

The doctor smiled. There was a sense of weariness in it. Either he was tired or he'd heard this all before.

"Well, here is my card. I'll be taking care of Mr. Thompson while he's here unless you have another doctor you would rather call in. Your husband didn't indicate that he had a primary care physician."

Elma took the card and nodded. "Warren hasn't been to a doctor since Dr. Boardman retired a few years ago. Thank you, Doctor Tery."

"You're welcome." The doctor placed his hands on his knees as he prepared to get up to leave.

"Mr. Thompson will be put in a room shortly. Would you like to visit with him a bit first?"

Elma nodded. Dr. Tery led her back into the hall to the patient cubicles.

I sat and focused on the midday sports report. The Indians had already lost their first pre-season games, the Cavaliers were out of the playoffs, and the Browns promised a good draft for new players. Nothing new there. I shuddered. I hated being in the hospital again. The smells, the announcements, the noises, the shuffling of crepe soles. It all brought back too many bad memories. Russell, I wish it had been different. Busy corridors and quiet rooms. Waiting. Wondering. Hearing the results of. . .

I looked for a distraction. There was a pile of magazines on another chair. Maybe I could find a unique recipe for my pickles.

Half way through a *Woman's Day* issue, Elma reappeared.

"Warren keeps drifting off. Why don't we get something to eat? I'm actually feeling hungry."

"Cafeteria or the McDonald's up the street?" I asked.

"McDonald's. I smelled the hospital food in the corridor. No thanks." Elma wrinkled her nose.

A few minutes later, we sat at a table under the watchful masked eyes of the Hamburglar and sampled the new salads the fast food chain had added to the menu to prove it was interested in good healthy eating. The food they offered couldn't be that bad for you. There were plenty of people in white medical coats lined up to place orders for lunch. Surely they wouldn't be eating unhealthy food, would they?

After lunch, we returned to the hospital and went up to Warren's room. He looked small and vulnerable in hospital garb with an IV running into his arm and pillows fluffed around his head. The drapes had been pulled partially closed giving the room an eerie mixture of cloudy sunshine and fluorescent hospital lighting.

"You girls have a good lunch?" Warren's voice crackled and his mouth appeared dry.

"We did," Elma said as she reached for a cup with a bent straw in it. She offered Warren a drink of water. He sipped a bit then waved her off.

"We celebrated your promotion to the fifth floor by eating healthy at McDonald's." I quipped.

Warren gave a weak grin. "Healthy? At McDonald's?"

"We had salads. Those new things with the apples and walnuts." I said. Elma was being unusually quiet. I expected her to jump into the quipping, but she didn't.

"And here you are bragging about it to a man who's not had anything solid to eat since breakfast. They told me if I was good, they'd make sure I got a dinner tray."

"Mmm. Sounds like a gourmet meal coming your way in a bit." I teased.

"What color do you think the Jello will be?" Warren smirked. "I hear they like to mix 'em together and create their own."

I looked at Elma but she was still as silent as a TV with the mute function turned on. She continued to fuss around Warren, tucking in sheets and smoothing his hospital gown. I think the poor man just wanted to go to sleep.

Warren turned to me with a little wink and said, "Annie, could I impose upon you to take Elma home? I'd like to have some of my own things here, something that doesn't have a slit up the back, and I know she doesn't have our car."

"I'm not leaving you," Elma said sharply. Tears came to her eyes. She blinked furiously, but that only made them spill over to her cheeks.

"Elma, I'm fine," Warren insisted. "The doctor said he just wants to observe me a day or two and get back some of the test results. I'll get a little nap and you can gather up some stuff from home for me. By the time you're back, I'll be ready to take you in a game of Scrabble. Bring that portable game you have and paper to keep score on."

She nodded. I don't think she trusted herself to say anything more. She kissed him on the forehead, and retrieved her purse and coat from the visitor's chair.

"Take care, Warren," I said. "If you need me for anything, you know my number."

"Just keep an eye on Weepy Woman over there." He pointed at Elma who stuck her tongue out at him.

"Thanks, Annie."

When I got Elma home, her phone was ringing. It was Cathy. She was due into the Columbus airport at 7 p.m. I volunteered to pick her up and drop her off at the hospital so she could visit her dad, and drive Elma home. I figured that way Elma only had to drive once by herself. She worried me.

Lord, look after Elma, I prayed on the way back to my house. *She needs Your care as much as Warren does right now. Thanks for taking care of him. Guide the doctors. Touch him and heal him, Lord. Elma would be lost without him.*

Chapter 18

Three days had passed since Warren's heart attack. The results the doctors shared with Elma and Warren confirmed the diagnosis, mild heart attack. Everyone looked and felt much more relaxed. The mild heart attack was a warning, the doctor said. If Warren behaved himself, there was no reason for his quality of life to change. Elma was satisfied that she had been right all along. She would be a tough old watchdog now. I felt sorry for Warren. Elma would hold a magnifying glass to everything he did from now on.

When Warren told me he would be released the next day, I replied it was on his own recognizance. I liked the sound of that phrase. So did Elma. She told him his bail bond was the diet and exercise they expected of him as well as faithfully taking his cholesterol-lowering drug. If he failed, he would be jailed.

Cathy planned to stay a few more days until Warren got settled at home and she was sure Elma could handle everything. I think she may have read some of those same articles Mary Jane did on elder care. Elma enjoyed the company of her daughter, though. I knew the only thing that would make her happier was to convince Cathy to have a baby. But Cathy seemed determined to hold firm to putting her career goals first before supplying the requested grandchild.

We played a couple of rousing games of Scrabble while Warren was incarcerated. Elma ended up taking the big board instead of the travel game. We all had a little trouble seeing the letters on the travel version, even Cathy. Warren was in rare form.

"A-r-t-t-e-r-y, artery!" he exclaimed.

"There's only one 't' in artery, Dad," Cathy said patiently.

"Yeah, but if you put my doctor's first name with his last name, artery is spelled with two 't's."

"Your doctor's name is Arthur Tery," Elma said.

"Not if you shorten it to Art Tery."

Warren howled at his own joke. It was good to see him back to his old self. Warren came up with a few more questionable words but, since he was the patient and we didn't want his blood pressure rising, we let him get by. He was warned however that, once out on parole, Webster would become the judge.

Everyone looked and felt much more relaxed. The mild heart attack had not done any major damage to his heart. Under Elma's watchful eye, Warren would be just fine.

The morning Warren was due to be released, I figured Cathy and Elma could handle the trip home with him, so I spent my time washing and ironing the white tablecloths from a church banquet the week before. The tablecloths were some kind of wrinkle-free material that had the free part destroyed by someone who didn't wash them correctly. Now they wrinkled freely even if you got them out of the dryer in a hurry and tried to fold the wrinkles away. Elma usually did the tablecloths, but I told her I needed something to keep myself busy and out of trouble, so she gave them to me.

The morning television news programs kept my mind occupied as I labored with the tedious task of ironing all the linen. Why they called them news programs was a mystery. After the first half hour or so, everything else was fluff. Cooking, makeovers, garden tips. I guess it was programmed to resemble the sections of a newspaper. Once you got it out of that little orange bag.

I was half finished with the last tablecloth when the phone rang. It was Elma, but I didn't recognize her at first. She was crying so hard she could barely talk.

"Elma, what is it? Slow down and breathe," I pleaded. "I can't understand you."

"Warren, he's gone." she wailed.

"Gone? Gone where?"

"He's gone. Died." Elma sobbed deeply into the phone again.

"Is Cathy there?" I wasn't getting anywhere with Elma. She didn't make sense. Warren was coming home this morning. I suddenly had a sick feeling inside, as if I was free falling and there was no net below me for a safe landing. My friend was hurting, deeply. My mind struggled with what I feared.

Another voice came over the phone. "Annie, it's Cathy." She sounded upset but at least she spoke more clearly.

"What's wrong, Cathy? Why is your mother so upset?"

"Dad died this morning."

I sat down on the closest chair. *No, Lord! No!* I put my hand to my forehead to support a head that suddenly felt too heavy for my neck. He was coming home, he was fine, he won Scrabble last night.

"Annie?"

"I'm here. What happened?" I asked.

"The doctor thinks it may have been an aneurism, a blood clot, I don't know. I went down to bring the car around to the exit. Mom stepped out of the room for a minute to get a cart for his flowers and stuff, and, when she came back, he was, he was lying across the bed." Cathy's voice caught in a hiccup. "He was gone just that fast."

"Do you want me to come down? Can I help?" My head spun as I tried to absorb what she was telling me, tried to force reality into a mind that refused to believe Warren could be dead.

"Thanks, but I'll need you more when we get home. Pastor Simon is here now." Cathy took a deep breath. "There are some papers, and things we need to do. We'll probably be home in an hour or so."

Tears wet my eyelashes. "I'll be praying for you and your mom."

"Thanks, Annie. Talk to you later."

Empty static crackled through the receiver in my hand. I slowly hung up the phone. The void was back, the deep black void that engulfed me when Russell died. That's what Elma was feeling now too. It hurt in the pit of your stomach and caught in your throat. My heart was breaking for my friend. Like a programmed mechanical robot, I walked to the ironing board, finished the tablecloth, and then turned off the iron. I needed to pray. I promised Cathy I would.

I gathered my Bible and my reading glasses and went into the kitchen. Sitting at the table, I opened the book that I knew was comfort to those who seek solace. The pages swam before my eyes. The words of comfort might have been there, but I couldn't read them. Warren was more than the man of Elma's dreams. He was the love of her life. And now he was gone. I knew that pain, and it consumed me again, fresh and sharp as the day Russell died. Everything I thought I had put aside, had learned to live with these many years, came back in a flood of painful memories.

I got up and paced the kitchen. I reached for the phone and held it midway to my ear. Who would I call? Elma was always the first person I thought of when I was down. I weighed the thought of calling Arnie. On the ship, we had talked a bit about his wife Ruth who had died of cancer and my Russell. He would understand how I felt. The load of sadness was too great. I needed to share it with someone. I dug out his card from the drawer and dialed the number. The phone rang for so long that I expected the answering machine to give me its spiel and beep, but instead I heard a breathless, "Hello."

"Arnie?"

"Yes." He paused a moment. "Annie?"

"Yes, um, is, is this a bad time?" I asked hesitantly.

"No, no. Not at all. I just came in from shoveling my drive. I don't have a nice young man to do that for me," he teased.

I tried a smile but my lips quivered. There was a sour feeling in my throat and I swallowed hard to try to rid myself of it.

"Annie, is something wrong?" I could imagine Arnie's forehead furrowed with concern.

"Elma, Elma's husband, Warren, he, he, passed away this morning." The words sounded strange, unreal.

"I'm so sorry. Oh, Annie, that's awful." I could hear the surprise in his voice and a touch of sorrow. "I thought he was coming home, everything was all right."

"We did too. It was sudden. They think it was a blood clot."

My mind drifted back to the phone calls I'd made after my Russell died, the disappointment I'd heard in the voices of people who were so sure he would pull through. While they were saddened at the news, they didn't feel the deep dull empty pain that went to your very core.

"This is hard for you, isn't it?"

"Yes. I feel badly for Elma but I keep remembering Russell, his death." I swallowed hard again and reached for a tissue from the box on the kitchen counter.

"Tell me about it, Annie. Maybe it will help."

"Are you becoming a Dr. Phil now?" I asked, trying to lighten the conversation. Surely he didn't want to hear all the details.

"Would you deny me that opportunity?"

"Well, as long as I don't have to be on TV." I smiled slightly through my tears.

"Promise. This is just between you and me. Tell me what happened when Russell died," he coaxed.

"It was just after our fifth anniversary. Russell began to complain that he just didn't have any energy. By the end of the day, he was exhausted and asleep in his chair. I knew something was wrong even before the other signs showed up. He was a very active person who suddenly couldn't do a full day's work. Then he got these itchy red patches on his skin and a fever that finally convinced him to see a doctor. The doctor found a lump in his armpit."

"Russell hadn't noticed the lump?" Arnie asked.

"He thought he'd hurt himself jumping off the tractor. Anyway, Dr. Bedford decided to treat the symptoms as a virus until we got the test results. We went home with a prescription for the rash, and instructions for rest and fluids. We prayed a lot for God to heal. When the test results arrived, the doctor had us come back to the office. I knew that wasn't good. He changed his diagnosis to Non-Hodgkin's Lymphoma."

"A fancy way of saying cancer," Arnie said.

"Those were Russell's words too. The doctor went on to explain that it was cancer of the lymph nodes but could be treated, and that survival rates were improving. There was hope for remission." I remembered sadly the ray of hope we clung to. My tears flowed freely now.

"What kind of treatment did they decide on?" Arnie asked.

"Chemotherapy and radiation. Dr. Bedford said it was a pretty tough combination, but Russell was young and it was our best chance. Russell wanted to start immediately. I think if the doctor could have led him right into the treatment room that day, he would have gone. The treatments sapped what was left of his energy, took his hair and, more often than not, caused him to lose his meals."

"How long did he have to go through the therapy? I assume the treatments didn't work."

I remembered Arnie talking about how Ruth didn't respond to any treatment.

"Russell seemed to rally around spring time. The swelling under his arm was gone and, from all indications, he looked like he was in remission. His hair grew back, and he began working the farm again. We began to think God had truly answered our prayers. Then the glands in Russell's neck swelled and the lump under his arm came back."

I stopped and wiped my nose, got another tissue and dried my eyes and cheeks before going on. Arnie waited patiently.

"We listened to Dr. Bedford tell us what we already knew, the cancer was back. We thought we could beat it again." My voice cracked. "The chemotherapy weakened Russell even more this time. It was evident we were losing the battle. Finally, Russell said, 'No more. I want to enjoy whatever life is left.' So I brought him home. There was some renewed energy once the treatments stopped, but before long he could barely make it out of bed to his recliner."

"Annie, that must have been so devastating."

Arnie was right. It had been. But, even in his weakened condition, I knew Russell loved me beyond all measure.

"We went over the finances and he explained them in detail," I continued. "Then we drew up a plan for me to follow once he was gone. The pages were tear stained, we cried a lot together, but his plans for me kept a roof over my head and food in the refrigerator."

"He was a good provider, a good husband," Arnie observed.

"He was. We learned to laugh, even through the pain." I chuckled a bit as I remembered.

"Russell began to collect hats. Anytime someone came to visit, they always asked very somberly, 'If there's anything I can do,' and Russell would answer very somberly, 'Yes, there is one thing.' When they asked what he needed he would simply answer, 'Your hat.' They would look bewildered for a minute and then take it off their heads and give it to him. Then he would tell them, 'If you can give me your hat, you can give your problems to Jesus. Some of them are a little harder to part with than others, but he'll take care of them all.' Sometimes I think he should have been a preacher."

"I'll bet he had quite a collection of hats. What did you do with them?"

"We started hanging them on the walls of the bedroom. The funny part was, people started showing up in the craziest things, ball caps with ponytails stuck to them, straw hats with fake mule ears or tin cans tied on them. Even the visiting nurses joined in the fun. I knew the end was near when our favorite nurse arrived in a decorated hard hat she'd stolen from her husband. When we had to point it out to him, we knew he was pulling away from us."

I paused. The memory of that last day was as clear as if it were yesterday. That afternoon, Russell had opened his eyes while I sat in the overstuffed chair in the bedroom. I pulled the chair next to the bed so I could hold his hand. It took me a moment to realize he was looking at me.

"Hey, honey," I said. "Need a drink?"

"Sure," he replied. I got the cup with the bent straw and put it to his lips. He gave me a little smile, something I hadn't seen in a few days.

"I love you," I said as I stroked his soft new hair.

"Love you too," he replied slowly. "I smell apple blossoms."

It was a cold November day. There were no apple blossoms. I could feel tears begin to form and I blinked them away as best I could.

"I remember the apple blossoms," I said.

"You are. . .my love. . .forever." His words were coming slower. "Sorry can't. . .stay longer. . .love you." He smiled a little again.

"It's all right, Russell. I know you have to go." I swallowed hard. "Just rest. I love you."

He closed his eyes and relaxed. A few moments later his face looked peaceful. His breathing had stopped and I fell into the black void.

"Annie? Annie, are you there?" Arnie asked urgently.

I fought my way back to the present. "I'm sorry. I'm here. Thanks for listening."

"Annie, do you want me to come?" he asked anxiously. "I'd be happy to be there with you if you need a friend."

"I'm all right, Arnie. Thanks. Just talking to you helped. Once I get busy helping Elma out, I won't have so much time to think." That was what I truly hoped for.

"I'm right here, Annie. Call me if you change your mind."

Arnie sounded earnest. He was sweet to listen, I thought as I set the phone back on the counter. I hoped I didn't make him uncomfortable sharing something so personal. If he were truly a friend though, he'd understand.

Somewhere in the middle of all my feeling sorry for myself emerged the realization that it wasn't about me, it was about Elma and her loss. I wanted to pray. Elma needed prayer. But words wouldn't come. My old friend, anger, was back though. It had been a close companion when Russell died. If I were to pray, it would be to rail at God for the unfairness, the bad timing, and the circumstances, all the things that made me angry when Russell died. I couldn't do that again. It would drain me, physically and emotionally, and I needed to be strong for Elma.

I rose from the chair where I sat reflecting on my selfishness. I needed to be busy. I walked into the kitchen and began pulling out ingredients from my cupboards to make a fresh batch of cinnamon rolls. I mixed the flour, yeast, and other ingredients in a large bowl and turned it out onto the clean spot on my counter. The yeast dough took a beating like it hadn't since, well, when Russell. . .

I needed to concentrate on something else besides Russell's death. I turned on the television again and listened as I mixed the filling for the rolls. A well-dressed weather woman gave the forecast, sunny and warmer. I hoped the warm days would coax the daffodils into bloom. Daffodils are hardy creatures. Their leaves begin to poke through the dirt in early spring and, more often than not, they have to survive a spring snowfall. This year's spring snow had been heavy and deep. Still, as soon as the snow began to melt, they reappeared, poking through the leftover icy cover in anticipation of glorious blooms.

It doesn't take much sunshine to coax the daffodils to flower once the buds have formed. Their blossoms splash color throughout the landscape, a signal for all the new birth that comes with the onset of spring. They were a happy lot, those daffodils, despite the trials they went through every year.

The phone rang. I jumped.

"Annie," Cathy said when I answered. She sounded so tired. "I have to go out and pick up Jeff at the airport. He managed to get a flight right after I called him this morning. Could you come over and sit with Mom? I hate to leave her alone right now."

"Sure, Cathy. I'll be right there." I covered my yeast dough with a cloth and hurried out and across the street. I found Elma asleep on the couch when I arrived. She looked like a little child. Cathy had covered her with an afghan.

"The doctor gave her a light sedative," Cathy whispered. "We figured she was going to need some rest before we dig into all the arrangements."

"It's going to be hard on her, no doubt about that." I shook my head. Life could be so cruel.

"Thanks for coming, Annie." Cathy hugged me and left to pick up her husband.

Lord, give Cathy a safe trip to the airport. We don't need any more grief right now. That sounded a little sharp, but God knew I was angry. I was going to need a little time to get past this. He would have to understand that.

Elma slept quite a while. I moved around in the kitchen putting away the clean dishes from the dishwasher and replacing them with the dirty ones from breakfast. I brewed a pot of coffee and was about to throw together a batch of cookies when Elma shuffled in.

"Is that coffee I smell?" she mumbled. She pulled out a chair and sat down at the table, burying her head in her hands.

"It is. Want some?" I asked.

"Please," she answered weakly. She propped her elbows on the table.

I poured a cup of coffee for each of us, and set the milk and sugar on the table for Elma. I always teased Elma that she needed to drink her coffee like a woman, but she insisted on putting in the milk and sugar. I didn't mention it this time. I sat quietly blowing on the hot coffee in my cup.

Elma slowly stirred the milk and sugar into her coffee. She shook her head slowly back and forth. I thought for a moment she was following the spoon around in the cup, but then I realized she was just trying to understand what was happening, trying to understand that Warren was gone.

"I know he's with Jesus," she said. "He might not have gone to church except for Sunday, but he loved Jesus just the same."

I nodded.

"We were going to stop and get those new McDonald's salads for lunch," she continued. "You know, those walnut and apples ones you and I had that day."

She sipped a bit of coffee noisily. "He said he supposed that was as close to fast food as he was going to get on that newfangled diet."

She sipped more coffee. The sleep hadn't erased the dark circles under her eyes. "He was just standing there putting the last of his sports magazines into a bag when I went into the hall. I wasn't gone a minute."

She took a deep breath that shuddered from her head to her toes.

"I didn't get to say, goodbye."

My heart was breaking. Elma's words were slow and deliberate as if she were trying to grasp the meaning of what she was saying before she said it. Warren was gone.

That opened the floodgates for both of us. I reached for the box of tissues on the counter and we both went through a handful. When the sobbing subsided, I warmed our coffees a bit, and we reminisced about great Scrabble games and summer outings and Warren's offbeat humor.

Before long, Cathy was coming in the door with Jeff and the two of us met them with the sweet-sour smiles that come in the midst of grief.

I left them to plan Warren's funeral, to work on all those details that keep you moving forward when you just want to curl up and stop life from moving on. At home my dough had risen enough. My cinnamon rolls were ready to be baked. I wanted to fill the house with the smell of sugar and spice and warm sweet dough. I sought comfort in that smell. But would I find it?

Chapter 19

Elma made it through the funeral with a strength that was larger than her small frame. Standing tall, she greeted visitors and comforted those who broke down. Warren was deeply loved by many. She appeared to listen intently while Pastor Alkins delivered the eulogy and a little sermonette. Those pastors never missed a chance to tell about Jesus, especially when the audience was a group of mourners faced with their own mortality.

Elma even helped Warren's old fishing buddy pull a chair close to the casket so that he could "sit a spell and jaw with my friend." I half expected Warren to sit up and start arguing with him about the fish stories he was telling.

"Yeah, Warren, that old muskie like 'ta pull my boat half across the lake. I just played him real good." The chair teetered as he pantomimed the adventure. I noticed a few boys in the corner snickering and pointing to the old fisherman. I shot them a look of disapproval. The old guy didn't notice them. He just kept on as though Warren were a rapt listener.

"Well sir, I got him all the way up 'ta the boat and reached for the net. That ole ugly face of his poked outta the water and looked at me. I seen his gills spread out, like he was taking a big breath, and then, and then, he just spit that lure right back at me. Gave me such a jolt, I plumb jumped backwards!" His arms flew out to his sides and his chair fell over pitching him out onto the carpeted floor of the funeral parlor. Several men rushed to his aid and the snickering boys ran from the room as if they had caused the whole thing.

"Nuttin broke," the fisherman said. He brushed himself off. "I was jist tellin' Warren how the big ole muskie we use 'ta fish for sent me into the lake for a swim. Guess I got a little too excited again."

He righted the chair, reseated himself, and finished telling Warren his story. Somewhere in heaven, I was sure Warren bellowed with laughter.

After the service was over, I stood with Elma, Cathy, and Jeff at the casket before the undertakers closed it. Cathy reached into her large handbag and pulled out the traveling Scrabble game, and tucked it under the satin sheet covering Warren from the waist down. Elma reached into her purse as well. She came up with a small Webster's dictionary.

"And no cheating," she said quietly as she placed the pocket-sized book next to the scrabble game.

A week of sunshine and mild weather had encouraged the daffodils to trumpet the arrival of spring. They were in full bloom. Despite my poetic feelings about the change of seasons, it didn't take long for my thoughts to turn to Elma. Cathy and Jeff had left the day before. Cathy had already missed two weeks of work and was afraid she might lose her job if she stayed much longer. When it came time for Cathy and Jeff to leave, Elma's tenacity showed through as Elma assured them she would be fine. She would take one day at a time and call them often. Cathy made me promise to look after her mother, as if I wouldn't. She just needed to be reassured. It was hard for her to leave Elma behind in an empty house filled with reminders of Warren.

I snipped daffodils while the early morning dew was still on them and put them in one of my old pickle jars. It wasn't fancy but it was quaint. Elma's house was old country style in its décor so the pickle jar fit right in. Elma didn't keep any of the funeral flowers, just the planters. She didn't want the house to smell like the funeral parlor and keep reminding her of the whole business. Elma had assured her daughter and son-in-law that she would take one day at a time and call them often. I knew how hard that one-day-at-a-time stuff could be. That's why I picked the daffodils for her.

Bouquet in hand, I crossed 47 and knocked on Elma's door. There was no answer. I knew she was home. Her car was still in the garage. I knocked again and then tried the knob. The door was locked. Odd, I thought, Elma and Warren never locked their door. I fished under the juniper bush next to the steps and found the jar with the key in it. I knocked again, and when I didn't get an answer, I used the key.

"Elma?" I called out setting the jar of daffodils on the counter in the kitchen. I stepped into the living room and yelled again. "Elma!"

"Oh, good grief!" Elma exclaimed coming out of the back hallway in a robe, a towel thrown over her head. "You liked to scare the life right out of me."

"I'm sorry." Relieved to see her, I began breathing again. "You didn't answer. I wanted to make sure you were all right."

"Okay, Mary Jane, did you think I'd fallen and couldn't get up?" A little smile brightened her face. Humor. It was a good sign.

"Touché," I said. "Have you had breakfast?"

"Yesss, Mother." She rubbed her hair vigorously with the towel. "Cathy sent you, didn't she?"

"No, actually I was out picking daffodils this morning and I thought they'd look nice with your country farmhouse look."

"You have the farmhouse, I just have the country."

My but we were feisty this morning.

"What time would you like me to pick you up for church this afternoon?" I had determined that I would not let her sit at home and brood. Besides she was needed to command the Wednesday night dinner.

"Is it Wednesday already? I've lost track of time." She wrapped her wet hair with the towel and thought for a moment. "I might beg off this week, thought I would start rounding up some of Warren's things."

She sighed. A shadow crossed her face.

"There's plenty of time for that, Elma. The girls will be shorthanded without you. Besides, this is stew night. They'll peel all those potatoes down to where there's nothing left to put in the pot."

"You're right there. Not a one of 'em's learned to use a potato peeler." She shook her head. "How about 2 o'clock? That should give us enough time to peel potatoes before they need to go in the pot to stew, and I'll still have time to do some stuff around here."

"Would you like any company?"

"No offense, Annie, but I've had company for two weeks. I love my daughter and son-in-law and you too, but I need some space right now."

When your best friend says she doesn't need you it's a bit deflating. Maybe I was another Mary Jane. Maybe I needed to be needed.

"Well, call me if I can help, or just to talk. You know."

"I know," Elma said. She hugged me tight for a moment. "I'll be over at two."

Tears stung my eyes. I went home wondering what I would do with myself until two o'clock. I had planned to spend the day comforting my friend but she seemed to need less comfort than I did. I crossed back over 47 and ambled up my driveway and into the house.

Inside, I wandered back to my ambidextrous room to do some surfing on the 'Net. I also needed to write to Arnie. He told me he wanted to come for Warren's funeral, but I didn't think that was a good idea. He and Elma only met once and he never met Warren at all. I let him know I was going to be real busy helping out with everything and thanked him for his thoughtfulness. I didn't want him seeing me all weepy-eyed and upset.

The computer whirred and clicked while it booted up. I managed to get myself a cup of coffee and a leftover cinnamon roll while the electronic wonder busied itself with its morning exercises. Goodness, if I did as much thinking as that computer did before I got going in the morning, I'd be tired out before breakfast. The Network.com homepage told me there was mail waiting for me. I clicked on the first message.

Mrs. A,

I stopped by last week but you weren't home. I wanted to talk with you about renting my garden plot again, but I have a problem. I hope you can help me. I'll stop by again this week and see if I can catch you. You are one busy lady.

Tommy

He must have stopped by the day of Warren's funeral. Had Tommy ever met Warren? In his last e-mail, he mentioned a favor. Now he was saying he had a problem. Whichever it was, he needed help. I hoped I was up to the task.

There was some junk e-mail next. Spam was easier to get rid of than the paper stuff that filled my mailbox and ended up in my trashcan that had to be carried to the street for pickup. But at least the printed paper ads in the mailbox didn't offer me aid for body parts I didn't have or want to enhance. I became experienced at spotting those offensive ads in the e-mail box without reading them. One click and they disappeared.

The next message was from Arnie:

Hello Annie,

I hope the sunny days and warmer weather are helping to cheer you. Losing a close friend is a difficult thing. Is Elma coping well? We both know how that goes in the early stages.

I'm aboard the Celebrity Millennium for a quick cruise of the Eastern Caribbean. I couldn't pass up the deal--$100/night. Where else can you sleep, eat, and be entertained for that kind of money? Wish you could have come. It would be a lot more fun with you here. (At least there are no purple dragons on this trip.)

Have a happy day!

Arnie

I had to smile at his reference to the Purple Dragon. We had quibbled back and forth about her capability to spit fire. I likened her to the harmless creature in the song, Puff, the Magic Dragon. "According to quite a few opinions," Arnie said, "Puff is a reference to marijuana." I argued with him that Puff was nothing more than a small boy's imagination at work—a sweet song with a catchy tune. I'm not sure I won the argument.

I replied to Tommy that I looked forward to seeing him soon and I'd have some cinnamon rolls in the freezer ready to be microwaved when he came. Then I wrote to Arnie and wished him a good trip, saying I looked forward to a full report on the ship as I had never cruised on the Millennium. Cruisers always like to compare ships and services. It's the topic that usually starts off conversations at the dinner table on the first night of a cruise.

The mention of Arnie's trip started me thinking about my own travels. I was still in the planning stages for my excursion to England. If I chose a cruise, I would have to go during the summer. That would interfere with the pickle-growing season. If I went too late into the fall, I worried I would run into bad weather. I certainly didn't want to be running around London in a slop of cold rain possibly mixed with snow. You never saw pretty pictures of snow in London, not like at home. I worried about leaving Elma, too. Sooner or later that brave front she put up would crumble. I didn't want her to face her fears of a future without Warren alone.

My stomach rumbled. Lunch was overdue. Lacking English fish and chips, I fixed myself a ham sandwich and popped open a can of diet Coke. The ham was left over from the funeral dinner at church. Elma and I had split all the leftovers the church ladies so diligently wrapped up for her. We froze what we could. Cathy and Jeff helped her eat the stuff that wouldn't keep.

Sandwich in one hand, I leafed through my London brochures with the other. I kept them handy for when I had nothing better to do than dream. Dreaming helped to keep your mind occupied when you didn't want to think about things that made you sad. Red double decked buses and Bobbies in tall black hats dotted the pages of the brochure. How tall was Big Ben? Were there chimes in Westminster Abbey that sounded like a grandfather clock? I popped the last bite of sandwich into my mouth just as I heard the door open.

"Hellooo."

It was two o'clock. Time to stop dreaming and go peel potatoes. Wednesday night dinners would stop soon for the summer. What would I do to get Elma out of the house after that?

Chapter 20

The month of May was just a week away. Elma put on a brave front. I knew she hurt inside but she wouldn't admit it. Nothing of Warren's sat around the house any more. I assumed it was either packed away or sent off to charities. Elma was very efficient.

The sun warmed my face as I sat on the step outside my kitchen door. A slight breeze picked up the sweet scent of spring soil mixed with earthworms and loam. It was time to turn over the soil and plant seed. I leaned back and waited for Herb to arrive. He worked at the Taylor Rental near Sidney. A few days ago, I drove up there to see if I could rent one of those tillers like Tommy used last fall. Sid, who had lived up the road from me and used to do my spring plowing, sold his farm, and then auctioned off all his equipment last fall. He decided he was done with farming and moved to Florida. He used to come each year and plow my little acre of land where I planted my pickles and a few tomatoes. Nothing tastier than homegrown tomatoes, so I always stuck a few plants in with my pickles. Now that he was gone, it was necessary to find another way to get my garden acre turned over so, I sat and waited on Herb and his tiller.

I needed to get my cucumber pickle seeds planted soon or my early crop would run into my late crop, and I'd be up to my neck in pickles by fall. When I drove up to Taylor Rental, it was Herb who showed me all the different kind of tillers I could rent. He talked about horsepower, from two horses to seven. I pictured seven horses pulling a plow. That seemed like a lot to handle even if they were mechanical.

Then he talked width. Tillers were anywhere from twelve to twenty-four inches wide. Did I want rear tines and front wheels or rear wheels and front tines? I could tell Herb was really into tillers, especially when he talked about the souped up tiller he was working on in the back of the store.

"I'm racing it in the annual Tiller Thriller," he said with enthusiasm.

"The Tiller Thriller?" I asked.

"Yup. My buddy and I go every June. It's in Arkansas at the Purple Hull Pea Festival. We used to enter the Rip Roaring Tillers of the 90's category but this year we've built a real beauty. We're going for the Super Duper Dirt Slanger category, no holds barred." He took his cap off and wiped his arm across the top of his large forehead. The thought of all that excitement made him sweat. "Would you like to see it?"

He looked so eager, like a kid who just created a masterpiece from Crayola crayons and paper and needed praise. I hated to disappoint him, so I followed him out to the back of the store. Herb pulled a blanket off a contraption that was all shiny chrome and bright red paint. It didn't look anything like the ones in the store. I had to agree with him. It was a beauty, a mean-looking machine. I politely declined his offer to fire it up.

"Oh, I can just feel the power by looking at it," I said.

Herb puffed with pride, took a hanky from his back pocket and swiped at a speck of dust on the chrome. I gently directed him back to my problem of needing a way to till my garden. We finally decided that he would deliver two machines. One was a seven horsepower, 24-inch tiller with wheels in the front, tines in the back. The other was a two horsepower, 14-inch tiller with tines in the front, wheels in the back. Whichever one I could handle, he would leave with me for the day. I looked forward to the challenge, sort of.

Herb's SUV turned into my driveway with his trailer full of tillers following behind. The seven horsepower tiller looked a little bigger than I remembered it, but Herb assured me that once it got going, it wouldn't be hard to handle. He removed the gas cap and showed me where to pour more gas in when I needed it. Then he started it up.

I could barely hear myself think over the roar. My lawnmower didn't make that much noise.

Herb drove it (I guess you drive those things) to where I needed to start tilling. One more quick lesson on starting, stopping, and lowering the tines, and he was ready to hand over the reins.

Okay, I can do this. I put my hands on the handle and released the lever to start forward. The monster in front of me sprang to life pulling me behind it. Every inch of me bounced and vibrated as the tiller spewed dirt every which direction. I could hardly see with my eyeballs jiggling in their sockets like the plastic eyes of a stuffed teddy bear in the clutches of a running toddler. I struggled to keep up with the menace. It felt like I was behind a team of runaway horses, seven to be exact.

The machine picked up speed as the garden slanted in the direction of the creek. I felt a new sensation in the pit of my stomach other than the jiggling, doom.

"Whoa!" I yelled, but it wasn't listening. Where was that brake? I was afraid to let go with one hand to grab it. Could I turn it around?

Too late! The creek was in front of me!

Yucky creek water splattered me as the tiller dove in. Like a hapless water skier, I forgot to let go and dove in after it. The tiller sputtered and died after hitting the water. I sputtered but managed to survive my plunge into the cold creek. Herb looked like he had just been through a haunted house and met a real ghost as he fished us both out of the muddy waters.

Once I was on my feet again, I retrieved two old towels from the laundry room and wiped creek slime from my face and hair as I walked back to Herb who was evaluating the damage.

"I think we'd better try the smaller tiller," Herb offered as he patiently dried the seven horses off with the old towel I offered him.

"I think I'm done for the day," I said as I kneaded the sore muscle in my back. I'd had enough fun. "How much do I owe you?"

"You didn't have it a full hour, Mrs. Pickels," he said sympathetically as I stood there in a wet flannel shirt and jeans, picking wet rotted leaves off my clothes. "There won't be a charge."

"But I dumped your tiller in the cr . . . "

"It's a hardy critter. I'll have it dried and re-oiled and working again in no time once I get back to the store," Herb grinned. He straightened up and took a deep breath. "Tell you what Mrs. Pickels, I can come over after work one evening next week and till your garden for you, that is, if you don't mind my bringing the Thunder Down Under."

"The Thunder? Oh, you mean your souped up model."

"It'll give my buddy and I some practice and we can run some time trials. Did I tell you the record for a 200 foot run is 7.47 seconds?"

For a middle-aged man he sounded like such a kid.

"No." I stood amazed. "That's pretty fast."

"If ol' Thunder cooperates, we should have your acre done in a little over an hour, two tops."

"Well, I would certainly appreciate the help," I said, "and it would be fun to watch your Thunder Down Under in action. Thanks!"

Herb managed to pull the nightmare tiller with the seven horses up the ramp and onto his trailer. He shut the gate, gave me a wave, and hollered, "See ya' next week!"

I smiled and waved back, all the while telling myself what a crazy old woman I was for thinking I could handle something as monstrous as a seven horsepower tiller. I watched Herb navigate around Elma who was headed in my direction. I was sure she wanted to see what the devil was going on.

"You are a sight!" Elma almost doubled over laughing. "Your hair is every which way, there's mud streaking down your cheeks, and, what's this?" Elma plucked a gob of some kind of slimy plant life off the sleeve of my damp flannel shirt.

"You don't like my new look?" I turned about like a model.

"You better get into the house and get cleaned up before anyone else sees you like this," Elma warned.

"Too late," I said. I nodded over her shoulder. "Arnie's car just turned into the drive."

Elma spun around and we both watched as my handsome friend dressed in a nice clean pair of blue jeans and a plaid cotton shirt opened casually at the neckline, emerged from his car. His cruise tan still bronzed his skin. He had written that he would be by sometime soon but didn't say when. Guess it was now.

He took off his sunglasses, wiped at his eyes, and squinted at us.

"Annie?"

"No." Elma giggled. "It's actually the monster from the muddy lagoon."

"Annie, what in the world have you been up to now? You're not making mud angels are you?"

Everyone had a good laugh at my expense, me included. I figure if you can't laugh at yourself, you're taking yourself too seriously.

We went into the house. Elma started some water to boil for tea. I mumbled off a few prayers while I showered and changed into some fresh jeans and a lightweight sweater. Mostly, I thanked the Lord I wasn't hurt and Herb was going to help out with the tilling.

Elma talked with Arnie in the kitchen while I dressed. I could hear the mumble of voices but I couldn't hear what they were saying. Their voices were too low. I hoped it wasn't something I would have to straighten out later. You never knew with Elma. Just as I entered the kitchen, laughter exploded from the two of them. Was I the humorous subject that brought such levity to my two friends? I noticed Elma dab at her eyes with a tissue. Was she crying or had she just laughed too hard? I hoped the latter even if the laugh was at my expense. It was good to hear my friend's laughter again.

"Hey, now that's the woman I remember," Arnie exclaimed. He rose for a moment as I neared the table. "I was just telling Elma that I'd like to take you two fine ladies out to lunch if you'll let me."

"Oh, I don't think so," Elma said quickly. "You two need to be alone."

Arnie and I both looked at her. I rolled my eyes and stuck out my tongue. Arnie just smiled at her.

"Nonsense, Elma," Arnie insisted, "You're coming along. We'll be the three Musketeers, or the three Stooges if Annie decides on another escapade."

I playfully hit him in the arm.

"No, really, I. . ." Elma protested.

"Arnie's right," I said. "You're coming with us. Maybe the two of you together can keep me out of trouble."

"I can't promise to keep her in line on my own." Arnie prompted. His raised eyebrow challenged Elma to help him.

"Well, you're right. Trouble does seem to follow her. I'm not sure we won't need some backup as well." Elma gave a smile of resignation. "Just give me a minute to grab my purse and lock up at home."

"We'll pick you up in ten minutes," Arnie called after her as Elma scurried out the door like an excited little girl who's been invited to go to the carnival.

There was a moment of awkward silence after the door closed. You could hear the birds chirp outside as they fought over the bird feeder. The squirrels chattered at the chipmunks, and a mourning dove added its low "coo" to the ensemble.

"So, how was the Millennium cruise?" I asked to break the spell.

"Nice, but the ship wasn't near as luxurious as the Queen."

"Food good?" I eased into the chair across from him.

"Very."

I fidgeted with the spoon Elma had used for her tea. Why was it suddenly so hard to talk? We e-mailed each other easily enough. Maybe we said all there was to say on the Internet or had Arnie and Elma shared something he was keeping from me?

"Elma seems to be coping quite well," Arnie observed breaking into my thoughts.

"Yes, it seems that way. I worry that she hasn't gone through that anger stage yet. I keep watching for signs of it. You remember," I said knowing Arnie had experienced the same thing after Ruth's death. Everyone did. It was one of the normal steps of grief, or so I'd been told by Elma herself years ago.

"Boy, do I remember. I have a spot in the wall at home that I had to patch. Good thing the plasterboard was weak there or I'd have broken my hand. The paint is just slightly different in that spot, but it's a reminder of my struggle with God's decision."

"I got mad at Russell as well, ranted and raved at him as I walked the fields he left behind for me to take care of." I smiled a bit sourly as I remembered. "Then I decided Russell wasn't the one who'd made the decision to leave, God decided to take him. I exploded in the middle of the potato field. I could have dug that whole field up by hand that day."

"Maybe you need to get angry again."

I frowned at Arnie. He broke into a grin. "If you got angry enough, you wouldn't need that tiller. You could just rip through that garden with your bare hands, could save you another dunking in the creek."

"You're incorrigible!" I got up smiling and pushed my chair in. "I think Elma's ten minutes are up."

Arnie was good for me. He reminded me not to take myself so seriously. I loved him for it, as a friend, a very good friend.

Lunch with Arnie and Elma was at a restaurant in a building that looked like an old barn. Gift shops offered a unique shopping opportunity on the lower floor and the restaurant on the second floor offered a cozy ambience. It overlooked a grassy knoll with pine trees lining what must have been a cornfield at one time. I took a deep breath and inhaled the wonderful fragrance of fresh baked rolls. The rolls and the homemade vegetable soup were a winning combination.

I felt very ambidextrous that afternoon. I managed to eat and talk and not splatter the front of my shirt with soup. We kept the conversation light. I noticed Elma managed to finish all of her turkey sandwich on fresh baked sourdough bread without much effort. It was the most I'd seen her eat in the last few weeks.

"I haven't made sourdough bread in ages," Elma said. "That was really good."

"If you made some, I wouldn't mind helping you eat it," I offered.

"I don't have any starter. I threw it out long ago," Elma said wistfully.

"I have some I can share with you." I kept a little container going in the refrigerator. It was an old habit my mother taught me. I liked making pancakes with it.

"What's this starter stuff?" Arnie asked.

"It's like a yeast concoction that you use to bake with," I explained. "It ferments and grows its own yeast so you don't have to start from scratch with store bought yeast, gets its own unique flavor and it's something you can share with one another, pass it along."

"This stuff grows in your refrigerator?" Arnie asked. He got a look on his face like he'd just sucked the lemon from his iced tea.

"Well, yes, sort of. It ferments. You can see little bubbles of gas build up in it," I went on.

"Bubbling in the depths of the refrigerator." Arnie tapped a finger on his chin. "Hmm, boil and bubble, toil and trouble," He spoke in hushed tones, stirring a finger in the air.

"Behave, or these two witches will have to cast a spell on you," I teased.

"Oh no. With your luck I'd probably turn into a charming prince instead of a frog."

Elma seemed to enjoy our banter. She was tuned in sharper than an FM radio station.

"At least I wouldn't have to kiss a frog." I stopped short. Maybe that was out of line.

After we left the restaurant, Arnie dropped Elma at her door and then pulled across the street to take me home. He didn't want me crossing 47 on my own, like I didn't do that every day. Arnie walked me to the door and stopped.

"Annie, it was so good being with you today. I've missed you."

My heart raced. Was he going to press on toward that kiss we'd bantered about at the restaurant? Did I want him to? He took a step closer.

"Arnie, I ..." His arms went around me and drew me close.

"You make this frog feel like a prince." His eyes softened. "You're a special lady, Annie Pickels." He hugged me tightly for a moment then released me. "Thanks for a wonderful afternoon." He brushed my cheek with the back of his hand and then turned to walk to his car.

"See you soon?" I called out haltingly.

He turned.

"Soon." He smiled, got in his car and waved before driving off.

The afternoon passed quickly. I ran errands. With Herb coming back on Thursday to till my pickle patch, I needed to get fertilizer, some weed killer that would keep the weeds from sprouting, and a new pair of garden gloves. I hated to give up on my old pair. They were soft and leathery but, after three years of working with a hoe and a shovel, and pulling weeds, the seams had begun to pull apart, and now there was a hole that was big enough for my finger to pop through.

It was hard to part with those gloves, almost like trying to replace an old friend you loved very much. I went to several garden stores and the big hardware store on the outskirts of Sydney. I finally found a pair in the seed store that was very similar to my old one. The store also sold unusual varieties of flower and vegetable seeds. I was partial to a special seed called Pickling Cucumbers that had been around since Russell planted my first row of pickles. Last year, the company that distributed the tiny seeds changed the name. The seeds had been cultivated for so long that they were now known as "Heirloom Cucumbers, The Preferred Pickles." The fancy name went with a fancy new price of course.

The sun dipped below the horizon by the time I was ready to head home. My lunch had worn off and hunger was nibbling at my insides. I saw the Tinkers Tavern sign that advertised home cooking and decided I didn't want to cook at my home tonight. I slowed down and made the turn into the gravel parking lot. I found a spot in the shade of a tree and rolled down the windows some to keep the smell of the fertilizer from building up too much. As I looked over my shoulder to the back passenger window, I saw a familiar sight, an old car with flaming wheel wells. What was Tommy doing here?

Chapter 21

Tinkers Tavern was rustic, resembling a large log cabin. It sat on the edge of a creek that could get nasty in the springtime if God decided to bless us abundantly with rain. Amazingly enough it had survived many floods. I climbed the stairs made of split logs and entered. The dining area was to the left of the entry. Tinkers had separated the bar from the dining area to make it a more family friendly place. I stepped in and surveyed the room but did not see Tommy.

"Are you looking for someone?" a young lady with auburn hair and big hazel eyes asked. She was about the same height as Elma and had a winsome look about her that made you wonder if she wasn't a cheerleader at the high school.

"Yes," I replied. "I saw a friend's car parked outside and I thought he might be eating here."

"Did you check the bar?" She gave a disapproving huff as she pointed a thumb over her shoulder. "There are a few men over there enjoying their afternoon beer before going home to their wives."

"Thanks, I'll check and then I'll be back for dinner." I smiled politely.

"I have a table by the window if you like." She pointed to a wall lined with windows and tables in the empty dining room.

"Thanks! Save it for me," I responded as if she would be doing me a great favor. It didn't appear that Tinkers would fill up quickly at this hour. She smiled shyly and went back to the table where she was cocooning silverware in napkins and I turned to go into the bar.

It took a moment for my eyes to adjust to the darkened barroom. The yeasty smell of beer mixed with the stale smell of cigarettes. My stomach rolled. I could put up with the smell of beer better than the acrid smell of second hand smoke. There were two men dressed in denim shirts unbuttoned to expose dirty T-shirts underneath. It appeared as though they'd worked in the dirt all day. As I walked in, the two raised their heads quickly with a look as though they'd been caught misbehaving and then went back to their conversation. Maybe they thought I was a wife come to pull one of them home by the ear. I smiled at the thought.

At a table in the corner, I saw Tommy hunched over some papers, holding a pen in his hand with a half empty glass of beer beside him. As I walked across the room, I sensed the men behind me turning in their seats to watch. They must have figured Tommy's grandmother was there to scold him. Sorry, fellas, I'm not the entertainment today.

"Hi, Tommy," I said as I approached the table. "I thought that was your car out there in the parking lot."

He looked up at me.

"Hey, Mrs. A." Surprise registered on his face. Then he smiled. His smile brightened the room. "What are you doing here?"

"Decided I would treat myself to dinner out. I don't feel like cooking tonight."

"The world is in trouble then," he teased. "I can't imagine it without your cooking."

"Careful," I came back at him. "You've only tasted my breakfast."

I glanced down at the papers in front of him. He poked the pen at them.

"I'm filling out an employment application." His face reddened. "Got a little problem with my cash flow and I need to find some more work."

Was this the problem he alluded to in his e-mail? Why not seize the opportunity and talk to him about it?

"Tommy, I'm eating alone. Can I get you to join me?"

"Aw, I don't know, Mrs. A," He wiggled uncomfortably in his chair.

"My treat. C'mon. I'd rather not eat alone tonight."

"Well, okay. Thanks."

He gathered his papers together, grabbed his beer, and followed me to the dining room. The little gal I had met on my way in led us to a table by the window. She set down the wrapped silverware and menus and grinned at Tommy. The dummy didn't notice. I felt sorry for the little gal. She probably didn't realize he already had a girlfriend, Mary Jane. I ordered iced tea and Tommy passed, saying he would finish his beer.

We sat and peered out the window overlooking the creek that ran swiftly over the protruding rocks. I'm sure if the windows had been open, we would have heard a rush of water rather than creek babble. Purple and white phlox bloomed here and there. Their colorful heads waved slightly in the breeze. I sipped my iced tea and watched as Tommy finished the last of his beer.

"What kind of job are you applying for?" I asked.

"Bartender." He placed his glass back on the table. "I figure in a place like this, I wouldn't have to know a lot of fancy drinks. Bill, the owner, has decided he'd like some hours off and is looking for part-time help."

"Do you need money that badly? I thought you'd be able to get a good paying job with your computer skills."

"I've applied, but no one seems to be hiring right now."

I refrained from suggesting that a haircut and less metal piercing might help the job situation. Even in today's permissive society, I was sure it made a difference. We ordered our meals. Tommy asked for a Diet Coke with his.

"I don't think I'm going to be able to rent my garden plot this summer," Tommy continued when our waitress went off to put our orders in with the kitchen. "I just don't have the money."

He fiddled with his paper napkin, rolling the corners up tightly between his fingers. I hesitated for a moment, thinking hard. Mary Jane would have my hide for this.

"Tommy, why don't you come and work for me?"

"Huh?"

"You could earn your garden rent by cutting my grass. You need to come and check on your plants regularly anyway. You can cut my grass on those days."

"Wow, Mrs. A. That would be great!" Excitement sparkled in his brown eyes.

"It's a deal then." I extended my hand and we shook on it.

Dinner arrived. We both had the special for the night, spaghetti with meatballs and a crisp green salad accompanied by warm toasted garlic bread. Tommy dove into his mound of steamy pasta with enthusiasm. I couldn't tell if he was that hungry, or just relieved to have his problem solved. I waited until we were half way through our apple pie alamode to ask him about his girlfriend.

"How are things going with your Mary Jane?" I asked before shoveling another bite into my mouth.

"I'm afraid my Mary Jane has run out," he said sorrowfully. He looked crestfallen.

"I'm sorry to hear that." I wasn't sure what to say to console him. You'll find another nice girl, just didn't seem appropriate.

"It's all right. Having my garden plot will help if I get it planted soon enough."

I couldn't imagine how gardening was going to take the place of a lost love, but I knew from experience that it would at least be a distraction. It was good to have something to keep you busy when you were down. I changed the subject by asking a few questions about the Internet and Tommy happily lapsed into a running commentary on search engines or some such thing. I just listened and nodded my head now and then as if I understood everything he said.

We parted in the parking lot. I watched his old heap head into the sunset as smoke poured from its tailpipe. I opened the door of my Escape. Whew! The open windows didn't keep the fertilizer from smelling up the inside. I hurried onto the open road to get some fresh air circulating. On the way home, I reviewed the conversation I'd had with Tommy. Not once did he ever mention a family. In fact, in all the times we'd had coffee and rolls, never once did he say, "my mom" or "my dad" or "my sister or brother." Where was his family? Was he alone in this world?

I hated to leave the fertilizer in the Escape overnight but I didn't think I was up to tossing the bags out of the back end and onto the little trailer that hitched behind my John Deere lawn and garden tractor. I didn't think the Escape could smell any worse than it did now.

I was wrong. It could. After a whole night with the windows closed to keep the critters out, the smell was enough to knock you over when I opened the door. As soon as I'd had my morning walk, I hitched the trailer to the John Deere and positioned it right under the back of the Escape. All I had to do was pull out the bags and let them drop onto the trailer. It usually worked well.

The first couple of bags fell with a thud that rattled the trailer and the John Deere both. I didn't notice that the hitch had come loose until the final bag hit the trailer. The trailer upended itself and sent bags of fertilizer sliding to the ground. One caught on some metal that sliced a gaping hole in the bag spewing its contents onto the driveway. I stood back, my hands on my hips, in disbelief. It's terrible when everything goes wrong and there's no one else around to blame, or whack with a newspaper. I went over to the landing and sat down. I needed some time to contemplate the logistics of the problem before me.

I heard the gravel between the driveway and the road crunch as a car turned into the yard. I brightened at the thought that it could be Arnie and then dimmed as I realized he would find me in another fix. On one hand I was disappointed it wasn't Arnie, but then I was also relieved to see that it was Tommy.

"Hey, Mrs. A. Looks like you had an accident here." He approached me with a worried look. "Are you all right?"

"Yeah, thanks, Tommy. I'm just trying to decide what I want to do with this mess." I looked at the pile of bags that lay strewn on the driveway.

"Let me help you get the trailer righted and then we can clean up the mess in the driveway." He sauntered over to the pile of bags. "I think we'll have to unload it first."

I joined him in the disaster area. It took a few minutes to get the remaining bags off the trailer and hook it back onto the John Deere. Once it was securely hitched, we started loading the bags back on the trailer again. They were only fifty pounds each, but it certainly helped to have two extra hands to do the lifting.

We were almost done when Tommy dropped his end of the bag we were lifting and yelled out in pain, his face white and contorted. He grabbed his back and wobbled to the tailgate of the Escape and leaned against it.

"Tommy! What's wrong?"

"I'll be, all right, Mrs. A.," he said through clenched teeth. "Just, my back." He let out a long slow breath like a woman in labor.

"You don't look all right. Here," I rushed to him. "Let me help you over to the landing. You need to sit down." He leaned on me as we shuffled toward the house. He carefully lowered himself to the step.

"Thanks." Tommy was breathless. He reached in his pocket and pulled out a brown prescription bottle of pills.

"What are those?" I asked.

"They're muscle relaxers and pain killers," Tommy explained. He shook two round white tablets and one oblong pink tablet into his hand.

"Here, let me get you some water." I scrambled up the steps into the kitchen and returned quickly with a glass of water.

Tommy swallowed the tablets. "Thanks, Mrs. A. I just need to sit for a few minutes and let these little babies work. Then we can finish."

"I don't think you need to finish anything. Tommy, why were you lifting if you have trouble with your back?"

"I hate to act like an invalid. I'm usually good to go if I remember to take my medication. I guess I just forgot it was time to take some. It's times like these I miss my Mary Jane."

His comment had me wondering if Mary Jane was a nurse or a massage therapist. I was about to ask when I heard the phone ring inside.

"I'll be right back. Don't you move," I warned.

"Annie," it was Elma. "I need to go to the store to grab some more onions for church. Can we leave a little earlier this afternoon so I can stop on the way?"

"Sure, Elma. As soon as I'm sure Tommy's all right, I'll finish up the mess I'm in and get ready."

"What's wrong with Tommy? What mess?" Elma asked.

"He hurt his back lifting some bags of fertilizer."

"Oh, that sounds nasty. Did he pull a muscle?"

"I'm not sure what's going on exactly. I need to ask a few questions, kind of grill him like you would if you were here." I chuckled.

"That's not nice, Annie. I would only ask questions because I was concerned with his back." She sounded offended. It wasn't like Elma to take offense to what was obviously a little teasing from her friend. "Call me when you're ready then."

"Will do. See ya' later." I hung up wondering what was wrong with Elma.

Another glass of water in hand, I went back out to Tommy.

"Are you feeling better?" I asked him. He seemed to have some color back in his face.

"Yeah, those little babies really do the trick. I just have to be careful not to drink when I'm on them."

I thought back to his beer in Tinkers and hoped he hadn't mixed the two that night. "How long have you had a problem with your back?"

"Since about forever," he said caustically. "When I was about ten, I was in a car accident. They said my mother fell asleep at the wheel. She didn't see the semi-truck stopped in front of her on the highway. I was asleep with my head down on the seat. That saved my life, but," he inhaled deeply. "But they had to cut me out of the car. My legs were broken. Needed pins to hold 'em together. Something went haywire with my back too. They never could decide what caused the pain then or what causes it now."

"And your mother?"

"She wasn't so lucky, or maybe she was. It killed her instantly. Crushed her."

"I'm sorry." I put my hand on his shoulder. I wanted to hold him. He looked like a little boy at that moment, a little ten-year-old boy. His story explained the absence of a mother in his life, but what about the rest of the family? I pressed a bit but Tommy seemed reluctant to share too much more. Perhaps someday he'd tell me everything.

Chapter 22

"So, how's Tommy's back?" Elma asked when I slid into the passenger seat of her white Honda Accord. It had been Warren's car. Elma alternated between driving that and her Civic. She claimed she didn't want the Accord to sit idle and rust away, but I think it had more to do with her mood swings than rust problems. When she was feeling her oats, she'd drive the Civic but when she wanted to feel closer to Warren, the Accord was her vehicle of choice.

"Tommy's medicine kicked in after a while, and he seemed fine. We lifted the last bag onto the trailer, and, and he went off to, to . . ."

Elma got stuck behind a tractor on the road and was making me nervous swerving over the yellow line to see if she could pass. "He went off to work in his garden plot the rest of the morning."

"That seems strange. Usually people with problems like that are flat on their backs for a few days." Elma started to pass and then slowed to pull back in behind the tractor. I tensed, relaxed, then tensed again.

"He's had this problem since he was ten. He was in a car accident."

She didn't' take the hint as I emphasized *car accident* and moved in real close to the tractor again.

"His legs were broken and his mother was crushed to death."

Elma swerved left and then right again.

"He had to be cut out of the car." Would more details keep her from swerving again? I was beginning to feel ill.

"Poor kid. What an awful thing to have to live with."

The tractor pulled off into a field and Elma stepped on the gas. I let out a deep sigh of relief.

"So it was just him and his father after that?" Elma asked.

"No, actually his father was gone from the picture before the accident. He said his parents had separated. He and his mother were on their way to live with her parents for a while. That's where he eventually ended up after all the surgery and therapy for his legs."

"Raised by grandparents. That's sad. Grandparents should be something special in a kid's life not the replacement for parents," Elma said wistfully. I knew she was still prodding Cathy about having kids. "What about his father's parents? Were they around?"

I couldn't answer for a moment. To my horror, an Amish buggy was bouncing along the road in front of us. Was Elma ever going to slow down?

"He didn't say. I didn't ask. Elma? Isn't that a buggy up ahead?"

"Yeah. We'll have to pass it." She sped up.

I closed my eyes and felt the car swerve left then right. When we seemed to be on a steady course again, I peeked to see if we were past the buggy. The road ahead was clear. I exhaled. What was wrong with her? She never drove this recklessly before!

"Well, has he been to any other doctors about his back problem?" Elma continued unaffected by my loud exhaling.

"I assume so. He had those pills."

"Hey, you can get pills on the Internet. I've seen them talk about that on TV. Are you sure he got them from a doctor?"

I was distracted again. I saw a truck waiting to pull onto the road. *Buddy, don't do it. For the love of Mike, don't pull in front of Elma.* He must have heard me because he stayed put.

"The pills, Annie," Elma repeated. "Did he get them from a doctor?"

"I don't know. I didn't ask." I was tempted to wave a thank you at the truck driver as we passed.

"Does he still live with his grandparents?"

"I don't know. I didn't ask."

"Does he ever see his father?"

"I don't know, Elma. I didn't ask." I felt so incompetent. I could never be an investigative reporter. I never asked enough questions. "Look, I just let the boy talk. I didn't feel like I wanted to pry."

"Okay. Okay. Don't get your girdle all in a twist. I was just curious."

"I felt he needed to talk. I didn't want him to clam up because I asked a question he didn't want to answer." Thankfully, I saw the Kroger sign ahead. We could get off this subject and onto something else, like what onions were best for soup.

Elma turned into the Kroger Superstore's lot. We parked near the door and hurried in to find her onions. She was making her chicken soup again for the Wednesday night church dinner. I didn't tell Elma that I had invited Tommy to dinner at church. "It's a good deal," I told him. "For a buck fifty, you can get a nice warm meal, dessert and all." He told me he'd think about it.

I hoped he would come. Wednesday night dinners were a good way to get people in the doors of the church to see that church folk weren't weird sorts that went around spouting scriptures and thumping Bibles. It dispelled a slew of stereotypes that seemed to cling like a nylon slip full of static electricity.

I hustled after Elma to the produce department. The manager of the department was up to his elbows in oranges, arranging them in rows that built up to the back of the display. It was a delicate operation. One wrong move and they would all tumble down. Don't ask me how I know that. I just do.

"Howdy, ladies," chirped the manager. He wiped his hands on the white full-length apron he wore. "You ladies need some help?"

"We just need some onions," Elma answered as she passed him. She stopped in front of the bin full of yellow onions, opened up a plastic bag and began picking the best from the pile. The manager looked at me, a flicker of recognition in his eyes.

"Need some oranges today, ma'am?" He held one up and grinned.

"No, thanks, just here to help my friend." I flushed pink, then red.

"Elma." I nudged her. "I need to grab some salt. Meet you at the checkout." I hurried to the seasonings aisle leaving the produce manager with his Cheshire cat expression guarding his orange pyramid.

We arrived at the church with plenty of time for Elma's soup to brew. Everyone loved Elma's soup. Who wouldn't? It was so full of chunks of chicken and noodles, you could almost eat it with a fork. Elma always managed to get good deals from the local grocers. Sometimes she would make a trip to the Sam's club just outside of Columbus, and buy her staples in bulk. She frequently filled the freezer and pantry that the church had dedicated to the Wednesday Night Dinner Committee with her bargains. That's how we kept the price down to a dollar fifty.

At five-fifteen, diners began to arrive and pay for their meals. We expected about a hundred people, but made enough for about a hundred and fifty so no one would go away hungry. Leftovers were sent to shut-ins and our pastor's family. It gave their food budgets a break.

At five-thirty, we opened our serving line. Bowls of hot chicken soup were paired with rolls and fresh vegetables from a tray of celery, carrots, broccoli, and cauliflower. There was cake for dessert this week. I usually made cinnamon rolls, but since there were rolls for dinner tonight, we chose cake for dessert. I kept my end of the table full of servings of chocolate and carrot cakes. There was always a surge of people at six. I scrambled to cut cakes so I wouldn't fall behind. I didn't notice the fellow with the black ponytail who stood before me until he spoke.

"Hey, Mrs. A." Tommy was neatly dressed in a blue T-shirt and jeans. His black hair shone like he'd just shampooed it and there was no trace of a five o'clock shadow.

"Tommy! You came!" I quickly tried to rein in my enthusiasm and surprise. "What's your pleasure, chocolate or carrot?" I held a plate of cake in each hand.

"Chocolate'll do. I already got my vegetables." Tommy pointed at his pile of carrots and celery on his tray. "I met your pastor. He's a nice guy."

"Hey," said a young man about Tommy's age. "You met me, too. I'm a nice guy."

"Yeah," Tommy smiled at his new friend. He pointed a thumb at the young man next to him. "Mrs. A, do you know Kirk?"

I looked at Kirk. He was a few inches taller and a lot more mischievous looking than Tommy even without any tattoos or metal studs. But I figured I was prejudiced. I'd known Kirk since he was about knee-high. I'd seen him at his best as well as his worst.

"Oh, I know Kirk all right."

"Now, Mrs. Pickels, you wouldn't tell stories on me, would you?" Kirk pleaded. "I just made a new friend here. I want to make a good impression."

I looked at Tommy. "You're safe as long as he doesn't have a squirt gun in his back pocket." I laughed at Kirk's grimace. "You two better move along. We got hungry people behind you."

"Save you a seat?" Tommy asked.

"Sure, but don't wait on me. Go ahead and eat."

I watched the two of them walk off to find a table. Tommy couldn't have met a nicer kid. Kirk was home from Ohio State

University for the summer. He and Tommy would have lots to talk about. Kirk was into the world of computers and hoped to get a degree in that field.

I went back to my cake slicing and serving but I caught a glimpse of the boys now and then with their heads together probably communicating in some kind of computer lingo. At six-fifteen, Patsy relieved me, and I took a tray of soup and rolls to the table where Kirk and Tommy still sat.

I took a seat and bowed my head for a quick moment of grace before asking, "So, how are you two getting along?"

"Great!" said Kirk, "I've finally found someone who speaks my language."

"So that's why I could never understand you in Sunday school." I nudged Kirk with my shoulder. He had been one of the brighter students in the preschool class where I'd helped as an assistant teacher years ago. They all loved to say my name and snicker every time it crossed their lips.

"Missus Pickles," little Kirk had said pertly one morning with a giggle. "What was Noah's wife's name?" I was shocked. Why would a three year old need to know Noah's wife's name? The story didn't give her a name. How was I to know what it was?

I looked him straight in his twinkling little eyes and said, "Mrs. Noah."

He went running up to his dad, from whom a lot of the mischief originated, and excitedly reported, "Mrs. Noah!"

As a college student, Kirk had spent his first summer away from home with Campus Crusade for Christ as a beach missionary on the east coast. This summer, however, his parents insisted he get a summer job and help out with the cost of his education. He was working at a local trucking company helping them switch over to a new computer program and setting up a website for them. I assumed that was what much of the conversation with Tommy had been about.

"Hey Tom, I gotta go set up for our class." Kirk stood and grabbed his tray. "Sure you won't join us?"

"Not this time, Kirk. Thanks." Tommy smiled uncomfortably. He seemed a little uneasy about the invitation.

"Okay, catch 'ya later." Kirk sauntered off.

"What class is Kirk in?" I asked raising a piece of buttered roll to my mouth.

"Something about clean living, spiritual living. I don't remember. It sounded interesting but, but I need to get some resumes together tonight." Tommy fidgeted a bit. "Kirk gave me some ideas for job possibilities."

"Terrific. I hope something works out for you." I fished the last noodle out of my bowl, balanced it delicately on the plastic spoon, and successfully made it to my mouth. Just in time, too. Pastor Alkins walked over to the table and leaned down.

"Tommy, it was good to meet you. Please don't be a stranger. If you don't have a church home, we'd love to have you come on Sunday. I promise not to keep you past noon. If you're like my son, your hunger alarm sounds off about then." He clapped Tommy on the back and walked off.

"I gotta go, got a lot to do." Tommy rose hastily. His usually cheerful countenance was clouded with emotion.

"Sure, Tommy." I was puzzled but I didn't question him. Elma would be disappointed in me. "See you next week, you'll still cut my lawn?"

"Sure." Tommy hastily took his tray and dumped the paper and plastic products into the trash barrel. He set the tray on the stack of empties and sped toward the exit with his hands in his pockets, shoulders hunched. Something was bothering that boy.

I skipped dessert. The chocolate cake was gone and I didn't want to waste calories on a piece of carrot cake even if it did sound healthier. Elma was busy directing the cleanup in the church's kitchen when I entered. She sat on a high stool, her bowl of soup perched on the counter, and barked orders in between spoonfuls of chicken and noodles.

"Patsy, give that extra jar of soup to Mrs. Alkins," she ordered. "She said one of her boys would run it over to Mr. Miller tomorrow when he gets home from his physical therapy session."

I watched as Patsy dutifully obeyed. We all kind of bowed to Elma. She was a good leader and a great cook. Everyone's willingness to let her lead made the whole Wednesday night operation move smoothly. She was the head. We were the hands and feet. It got the work done.

Since Warren died, however, Elma had become bossy. She barked orders rather than ask for something to be done. No one complained though. Maybe I was the only one who noticed it or maybe they were all more forgiving. We finished up early and slipped into the sanctuary for the last of the praise and prayer service. I liked the "popcorn praise" time. Pastor Alkins asked for people to stand up and give a one-sentence praise then sit down again. People popped up and down all over the sanctuary on a good Wednesday night.

"Praise the Lord for the beautiful spring weather!"

"Praise the Lord, my tests were negative!"

"Praise the Lord for his goodness!"

"Praise the Lord, our son got a job!" That one got a laugh. It came from a man whose son had moved back in with them when he lost his first job.

Suddenly Elma jumped up.

"Praise the Lord I know Warren's in heaven with Jesus!"

The sanctuary was quiet for a moment after Elma sat down. Warren may have been in heaven, but he was still missed by this earthly crowd. A few more praises rang out before the organist started up with the chorus we always sang at the end of the service.

Something beautiful, something good.

All my confusion, He understood.

All I had to offer Him was brokenness and strife,

But he made something beautiful out of my life

Life was beautiful with God in it no matter what you faced throughout the week. I thought about Tommy. What did he face this week? Financial problems? Physical problems? Girlfriend problems? God and I were going to have to do some serious talking about that boy.

KAREN ROBBINS

Chapter 23

It seemed that everyone realized at the same time that spring was here. Thursday evening, my driveway looked like the parking lot at the convenient store when they had "Ten Cent Hot Dog Day." The day care center wanted a plot of land to grow vegetables. It kept their older summer kids busy. A local florist wanted a plot to grow some fresh flowers as well as some she could preserve for winter floral arrangements. The teen group from our church asked for a plot to grow tomatoes and corn to raise money for a mission trip. I didn't charge the teens. I considered it my contribution to their cause.

Then there were the regular folks who just wanted a spot to grow some fresh vegetables for eating and putting up for the winter. It was heartwarming to see younger women were eager to carry on the art of home canning.

Herb from Taylor Rental and his buddy had arrived as well. The pair resembled Laurel and Hardy. Herb was short, stocky, and smiled a lot. George, his buddy, towered over him but, unlike Stan Laurel, he was more muscle than skin and bones. They unveiled their huge souped-up tiller to the awe and wonder of the teen group that was just about to leave. Herb basked in the glory of their praise and adoration as he and George zipped into denim jumpsuits and unloaded their mean looking machine.

"Yup this here's The Tillernator. That's what we renamed the monster." Herb took a rag from his back pocket and wiped off the name painted in black and white on the red enameled machine. "It's a Super Duper Dirt Slanger."

"Man, how many horses you got there?" one wide-eyed beefy teen boy asked.

"Oh, I'd say about 75. There was a 100 horsepower limit. We think we can get the job done with 75. Right, George?"

George nodded and continued stowing the chains that had held the monster in place on its trailer.

The youth pastor gave in to his group of teens who begged to stay and watch the action. I was tempted to start selling tickets as the driveway filled with more cars. Where were all these people coming from?

"Hi there, Ms. Pickels," Herb said as he saw me approach the group. "I hope you don't mind. George and I invited a few friends to watch The Tillernator make its debut."

"I guess it's all right," I told him.

I figured it might take all those friends to help Herb and his killer tiller out of the creek if he couldn't control it. The crowd followed Herb and George as they pushed and pulled The Tillernator down to the field to plow. Once they were lined up on the field, they pushed the button and we listened to the engine crank a few times then die. The expectant onlookers groaned in unison.

Herb made a few adjustments and they pushed the starter again. This time the monster sprang to life, trembling with anticipation. Herb donned what looked like a motorcycle helmet. He pulled down the face guard and gave a wave to the cheering throng. George stepped back and Herb thrust the machine into gear.

The Tillernator took off in a cloud of dust, dirt, and exhaust fumes. It kicked up so much debris that no one could see Herb. Halfway down the 200-foot stretch of field, the engine died again.

When everything settled, we could see Herb pick himself up off the ground about 15 feet behind his 75 horse-powered wonder. George and a few friends ran down the field to him. Herb appeared unhurt, just dirty. He waved a hand at the rest of us like the signal a racecar driver gives when he's just survived a spinout on the track.

Herb and George talked things over, and Herb took the controls again. This time he kept the Tillernator reined in a bit. He finished the row, and returned to his starting point.

"I need a little more practice," Herb said sheepishly to the admiring group of spectators. "Good thing we put that little safety stop on there." Herb held up what looked like a chain for a pocket watch. One end was attached to his belt and the other end had a plug that fit into a hole near the starter button. George grunted his approval.

"It's like a jet ski," Herb explained. "If you fall the plug comes out and the engine stops."

The kids oohed and aahed over Herb's foresight, or perhaps just the mechanics of the whole thing.

"Let's run a time trial," Herb said to George. "Got your watch?" George nodded. Herb flipped down his face shield and started the Tillernator again. Just as before, we couldn't see anything but a cloud of dirt and dust. When the cloud reached the far end of the field, George pushed the button on the stopwatch.

"Wow!" the beefy teen said looking over George's shoulder. "Ten seconds flat!" Everyone seemed duly impressed and congratulated Herb upon his return. My field was getting plowed in spurts of speed, but the accolades slowed progress. I flinched as a heavy hand on my shoulder spun me around.

"Auntie Ann! What in the world is going on here?"

"Mary Jane! What are you doing here?"

Mary Jane stood with her hands on her hips. The tone of her voice and her deep frown made me feel like a teenager who'd been caught at a party she didn't have permission to attend.

"I've been calling all evening," she explained angrily. "When you didn't answer, I decided to come over and check on things." She looked at the evening's entertainment. "What is this, this, thing?"

"It's a tiller," I told her. "Herb from Taylor Rental graciously volunteered to come and till the garden for me. I would think you'd be happy that I wasn't doing all that work myself." My voice held a sting. I didn't mind when Mary Jane berated me in private, but I wasn't going to take her guff in front of all these people.

Cheers rang out as the Tillernator took off again down a new row with Herb panting behind it. He needed to get in better shape to keep up with all those horses.

"Auntie Ann, Auntie Ann!"

Mary Jane stood beside me and demanded my attention. I continued to watch Herb and ignore her. When I didn't answer, she stepped in front of me, her back to the field and the Tillernator, which was making a return trip.

"Auntie Ann, why isn't that farmer up the road plowing for you? He always did a NICE JOB." Her voice got louder as the Tillernator got closer. "THIS IS A RIDICULOUS DISPLAY OF, OF. . ." She was digging for the right word.

The right word was lost in the noise of a 75 hp engine and the screams of the crowd as Herb fell again and the Tillernator jumped forward. Mary Jane suddenly disappeared before my eyes.

George saw the monster machine headed for her and in a burst of super hero speed, he tackled her pushing her out of the way just as the Tillernator died a few feet from where she'd been standing. The odd couple landed in a stack of straw bales. Mary Jane spat straw out of her mouth and spewed fire from her eyes as she fought to get out from underneath George.

"What do you think you're doing?" she shouted at him.

"The, the Tillernator, I was afraid it wouldn't stop in time." George sputtered.

He held out a hand to help her up. Mary Jane refused and struggled on her own to stand. Indignantly, she brushed straw bits and pieces from her sweater and pants. She lifted a foot to discover a coating of rich black mud on what looked like brand spanking new sneakers. Her dismay was evident.

"Why don't you come into the house and let me help you clean up?" I suggested. I steered her in the direction of the house. Mary Jane was beet red, anger, I supposed, or maybe embarrassment. More than likely it was a combination of both. Little puffing sounds escaped from her mouth as we made our way to the back steps.

"I'm glad you weren't hurt." I put my arm on her shoulder. "That tiller could have done you major damage if it had run you over."

"It stopped before it got to me," She grumbled as she stooped to take her shoes off before going into the kitchen.

I picked up her soiled shoes and took them to the utility sink in the laundry room. A wet rag and little soft scrubbing cleanser took most of the dirty stain away. The stitched areas were impossible to reach even with the old toothbrush, so they remained a little more defined now that they were a darker shade than the rest of the shoe. I hoped Mary Jane wouldn't notice before she got home.

Mary Jane stood at the kitchen sink and stared out the window, a glass of water in her hand that still shook slightly from her near-death encounter. She turned as I came in.

"This has got to stop," she said.

"What does?"

"This habit of collecting rag-tag characters from, from who-knows-where and, and bringing them into your house."

"First of all, MJ, a good part of that group are the teens from church along with the youth pastor." I paused to let that sink in a minute, not too long lest Mary Jane get rolling again.

"Some of the others are the same people who have rented garden plots from me for years now. They are people I know and trust."

"Those two characters with the monster machine aren't, and there are guys standing around drinking beer and smoking! I'm sure the parents of those teens wouldn't appreciate that!"

"Don't exaggerate. There were only two men I saw with a can of beer and only one of those was smoking," I scolded. "Do you think Pastor Ted would have let the kids hang around if it were a beer party?"

I had let Mary Jane have her way for far too long. Her need to be needed was turning into a need to control. It was clear to me as I watched her search for a come-back answer.

She harrumphed a few times before she sat in a kitchen chair and put on her shoes. The laces were drawn so tightly I was afraid the circulation to her toes would be stopped.

"Auntie, I just can't be responsible for you if you continue to surround yourself with questionable people who have no good reason to be here except to take advantage of your good nature."

I felt my blood pressure rise.

"I never asked you to be responsible for me. I'm old enough and capable enough to be responsible for my own actions." I took a deep breath and lowered my voice. "MJ, I just want your love and respect. I appreciate the help you give me and your concern for me but I'm not ready to give up living my life my own way yet."

Just when I thought Mary Jane was softening, she stiffened her back and stood up abruptly. An index finger wagged in the air at me.

"Auntie Ann, you mark my words. You are going to get hurt if you keep befriending these people. That Tommy is going to cause you some kind of trouble and, and, that Arnie, I know he's after something, the farm, the bank account, there's something he wants. Mark my words."

She stomped to the door.

"You're not getting rid of me, you know. I will be back."

The screen door slammed behind her.

"I'll be back. I'll be back." Wasn't that one of Arnold Schwarzenegger's lines?

I hurried outside to see if the Tillernator was finished yet. The crowd had thinned. A few men helped George and a sweat-streaked Herb put the Tillernator back on its trailer. I looked at my field. The monster had certainly turned up the soil. I was going to have to put the rake on the John Deere and smooth it out.

"Thanks Herb, George," I said with my hands in my pockets. I wasn't sure I wanted to shake their grimy hands that were covered in oil and dirt. Thankfully, they didn't offer to shake hands either.

"It was our pleasure. Gave us a chance to show off a bit to our friends too." Herb clipped the last chain in place.

"Your friend okay?" George asked quietly.

"She's my niece and, yes, she's fine. Just a bruised ego." I smiled.

"Your church group wants us to bring the video from our Thriller Tiller competition to one of their meetings. The kids were really into this." Herb beamed proudly.

If I knew those kids, they had seen a chance to get two guys to church as well. I waved to Herb and George as they pulled away from the drive and started up Route 47. The sun was setting in a glorious explosion of reds and pinks tinged with some purple.

"Red sky at night," I repeated to myself, "Sailors delight." Tomorrow would be a nice day for farmers too. I could finally get those pickles planted.

I turned to go into the house and call it a day. I looked back at the sunset one more time. The glory of God's beautiful sunset held great promise for tomorrow.

KAREN ROBBINS

Chapter 24

Just as the sunset had predicted the evening before, the morning arrived with the promise of a perfect day. The birds chirped happily all along my route as I did my ambidextrous morning exercise. I breathed the clean sweet air of spring and listened to the harmony in the choir of birds. I reveled in their musical talent.

The sun warmed my face. Its light fell to earth intensifying the colors of the spring blossoms, deepening the green that had begun to explode in the trees. Sunshine spread itself over the fields and grassy lawns, beckoning to the winter weary to come and find new life. A slight breeze crossed my cheek with its soft velvety touch. As I walked, I talked and marveled poetically until nothing else came to mind. *For now, Lord, that's all the poetry I have in me. I need to get to pickle planting. If You don't mind helping with the old bones today, I'd be much obliged.*

When I got back home, I exchanged my sneakers for a pair of work boots and hitched the rake to the back of the John Deere. It did its job on the lumpy field, turning chunks of earth into smooth topsoil. I had to make a couple of passes in a few areas to get the ground leveled out where the hungry Tillernator had taken bigger bites.

The sun was getting high in the sky as I finished the last row on the edge of the field. My back needed a rest. It wasn't so easy sitting on the John Deere all morning and bouncing around. Didn't anybody sell shock absorbers for a lawn tractor? I'd tackle the seed planting after lunch. I parked the JD in the old barn and took the rake off so it would be ready for Tommy when he came to cut the grass. The John Deere was wonderfully ambidextrous.

As I rounded the house to go in for lunch, I glanced across the street at Elma's yard and stopped dead in my tracks. Both cars were pulled out of the garage and parked to one side of her driveway. Her garage door was wide open, and it looked like there were tables set up where the cars had been. What was she up to?

I waited to cross the street. A semi whizzed by blowing dust. I blinked furiously and swiped at a spec in the corner of my eye. My vision was clear by the time I reached Elma's garage, clear enough to see what looked like a flea market.

Men's shoes were lined up on one table, Warren's, I assumed, with belts neatly arranged beside them. Another table held a collection of hard backed books. I recognized some of the titles. They were the books Warren often commented about reading and offered to lend to me. His tastes covered everything from the classics to science fiction, with a smattering of sports biographies thrown in. He loved books. These titles were the ones he savored and reread. Tools were laid out in neat rows on Warren's workbench, all tagged with prices. I drew my finger down the neck of a hammer with a $2.00 sticker on the handle. While he wasn't necessarily the handiest man around, he prided himself on having the right tool for the right job. Elma and I always joked that it was a testosterone thing.

The door to the house opened. Elma popped out, her arms loaded with Warren's shirts and pants.

"Elma, what's going on? What are you doing?"

Her hair looked like it hadn't seen a brush that morning and her eyes were a bit puffy. I was more than a little concerned. This wasn't like Elma. Her morning routine included much better grooming habits than that.

"I'm having a garage sale," she said flatly, almost like one of those computer voices that call on the phone occasionally.

"A garage sale?" I looked around. Everything on the tables and hanging on the clothes rack had belonged to Warren. There was nothing that belonged to Elma.

"I'm tired of picking up all this stuff and moving it around. It's time to get rid of it." She sounded angry, a lot like she used to when Warren would get involved in a project, and leave his tools and things sit out. This was different though. It had a ring of desperation to it.

She dropped the pile of shirts and pants onto a nearby table, and began to fold them, laying them out like a store display. I picked up a chess piece from a set that Warren had made himself. He'd found a box of old tubes from the days when radios and TVs weren't all electronic, and turned them into pawns, knights, rooks, bishops, queens, and kings.

"Are you sure you're ready to get rid of all of this?" I asked gesturing with the large tube in my hand that was meant to be the king.

"Yes," she replied curtly. She fussed with the shirt she was folding.

"Did you ask Cathy if she might like some of these things?"

Elma didn't answer. She fought to get the shirt's sleeves tucked into the folds without wrinkling them.

"You know, she might like to have something to remember her father by." I ran my fingers over the chess board.

Elma picked up the next shirt and shook it so hard it snapped loudly. She laid it face down, smoothed it out, and began folding again. I could see her mouth drawn tightly, her lips pressed together so hard they were losing their color.

"Elma don't do this. Don't sell everything before you've had a chance to think it through."

Warren had only been gone a few months. I knew she'd hid the grief in a closet, locking the hurt behind a door in her heart. It appeared the closet door had opened.

"I've thought about it, a lot. I've thought and I've thought 'til I can't think no more." Her voice began to rise. "I have to face it. He's gone. I can't bring him back. I can't keep these things around to remind me every day that he's not here."

"But, Elma."

She turned to me, her face distorted with the anger that raged within her.

"I can't be an Annie Pickels and, and cling to a memory for 30 years!" Elma grabbed the chess piece from my hand and threw it across the garage. The vacuum tube exploded into shards of glass against the concrete block wall.

My breath caught in my throat. My heart stopped. I could feel the blood drain right down to my toes.

Elma looked at me with a fury burning in her eyes that I'd never seen before.

"Get over it Annie! Russell and Warren are both gone!"

Her words felt like a slap in my face, a knife to my heart. I turned and numbly stumbled down the drive, past Warren's car, and across the street to my house, the house Russell had built for me.

The place I felt safe.

The place I felt loved.

I sat in Russell's recliner. It didn't recline anymore and I had to keep it covered with an afghan because the upholstery was worn so thin, but I kept it when all the other furniture needed replacing. It was the place I curled up with a book on a cold winter night. It was the place I sat to watch a silly TV sitcom, or my morning shows. It was the place where I felt Russell's arms around me.

A shiver went down my spine. I pulled the edges of the soft afghan around me to warm the cold I felt creep through my limbs. Elma was wrong. It was thirty-five years I had kept his memory alive. But she was right too. Everything I did was balanced against what Russell would have done, how the two of us would have worked out a problem, relaxed together, enjoyed an evening. I held onto whatever I could that was his just to feel him near. I didn't want to let go. I was afraid of what might happen to me if I did.

Yes, Elma was right. My Russell was gone.

I pulled my knees up and rested my forehead on them. All these years I'd wandered in a desert of my own making. I'd never realized how truly alone I was. I cried for my loneliness. I cried for Russell being gone. I cried for Warren's death. I cried for Elma. And then, I just cried.

My head was buried for a long time. The shadows of the evening began to lengthen. The house grew dusky with the fading light. Still, I couldn't move. What was the purpose? Who needed me anymore? I was just an old lady, shriveling up like a pickle that had been discarded.

There came a knock on the door so slight that I barely heard it. I was determined not to answer it. I put my hands over my ears and squeezed my eyes shut. Go away.

A hand touched my shoulder lightly.

"I'm all out of tissues. Would you have any extras?"

I opened my eyes to see Elma kneeling beside the chair looking as cried out as I felt. Her face was blotched and swollen, her nose red and raw.

"Annie, I am so sorry. I… " Elma began. She couldn't finish. Her body wracked with sobs.

I got out of the chair and went down on my knees next to her. I hugged her tightly.

"I know, Elma. I know."

I reached for the box of tissue I kept on the coffee table and passed it to her.

"Here, there's plenty more of these if we need them, and then, we can start on the toilet paper."

She smiled at that. We knelt there for a time. The beauty of a friendship like Elma's and mine is that it doesn't always need words. We cried together. Much as I hate crying, I couldn't stem the tide of tears. I think there were thirty-five years of them dammed up inside of me. Elma passed me a tissue when the river turned into more of a trickling stream. She smiled weakly. I inhaled deeply and held my breath for a moment determined to gain control again. I hiccupped, a squeaky little hiccup that made us both chuckle.

"You know, while we're down here on our knees, how about we take this problem to the Lord?" I suggested.

"Good idea," she whispered.

We held hands and prayed. We prayed for our friendship; we prayed for the loneliness we both suffered from missing our husbands; we prayed that God would mend our hearts.

When we were prayed out, Elma looked at me and said, "Now who is going to help whom off this floor?"

We managed to grunt and groan our way to stand on our feet.

"How about a cup of tea and a cinnamon roll?" I suggested.

"Sounds great." Elma hesitated. "friend."

"Friend. Sounds good." I hugged her.

We sat at the table a while sipping our tea and watched the birds fight for the sunflower seeds at the feeder in the back yard.

"Are you going through with the garage sale?" I asked tentatively.

"Not right now. I'll take your suggestion and ask Cathy first what she might like to have. There are a few books and things I think I might want to hold on to, just a little while longer."

"When you decide to hang out the garage sale sign, I have a few things to add to your inventory. I need to do some housecleaning too."

There were some closets that had things I would never use and Russell had no need of now. It was time to pass them on.

"Are you sure Annie? You know I didn't mean what I said. I was angry with Warren for leaving me, angry with God for taking him when I thought he was coming home. You just happened to be the only person who was there to yell at."

"I know. I've had my bouts of anger over Russell leaving me behind, alone and with no one to share the grief. At least you have Cathy."

"I'm sorry, Annie." Elma reached over to pat my hand.

"That's why I've always said you were God-sent, Elma." I covered her hand with mine. "You arrived just when I needed a friend and you've never given up on me."

"Until today." Elma hung her head.

"No. Even today. It was time I faced up to what I've done with my life. I should have moved on long ago, stopped clinging to what is only a memory."

We looked at each other as tears clouded our eyes again. I reached for the box of tissues. It was empty.

"Looks like we need to scrounge up some toilet paper."

We laughed and grabbed some paper napkins instead.

KAREN ROBBINS

Chapter 25

It had been a few weeks since Elma and I had our marathon cry. My pickle plants leafed out nicely. Spring had been kind to us. It rained just enough to water the fields but not enough to wash out the seeds. The lawn turned greener and thanks to Tommy, it was neat and trim. He sported a smile and talked about his Mary Jane again. I assumed their relationship had blossomed anew. My Mary Jane dropped in a few times. The day she saw Tommy on the John Deere, her litany began.

"What's he doing here again, Auntie?"

"He's cutting the grass for me."

"I see that, but I thought you liked cutting your own grass. You wouldn't let my boys help you with it."

Mary Jane's boys were more interested in driving the tractor than they were in mowing the lawn. Half the time, they'd forget to put the blade down. When they finally finished, I had spots in the lawn that looked like little clumps of forest where Leprechauns could live. Twice was enough to learn that Mary Jane's boys were more work than help to me.

"Tommy is cutting the grass in exchange for his garden plot rent this year. He's a little short on cash right now," I explained.

"I'll say he's short. It looks like he can't even afford a haircut." Mary Jane shook her head and clucked. "Does he ever bathe?"

"Mary Jane!" She was exasperating.

"Well, look at him Auntie. His clothes look tattered and dirty and he's got smudges of dirt crusted on his forehead. I'll bet he hasn't seen a bar of soap in weeks."

"I'll have you know that boy cleans up really nice when he comes to church."

Mary Jane whirled around and faced me.

"He goes to church? Our church?" she asked incredulously.

"Yup. Twice a week," I replied proudly. "He comes for Wednesday night dinners and Sunday school and worship service. I believe that's more than you do."

The last comment was probably a bit mean-spirited but I enjoyed Mary Jane's consternation.

"I don't like those dinners and all that noise, the kids running around." She flailed a hand in the air. "Besides, I have other things I have to do."

Mary Jane seemed deep in thought for a moment, perhaps trying to remember what was on her to-do list. She turned back to the window to observe Tommy again.

"I don't care if he is going to church. I still don't like the idea of him hanging around here all the time." She shook her head. "He looks so, so unsavory."

"Mary Jane, looks can be deceiving. There is many a prim and proper churchgoer who appears to be an upstanding Christian but doesn't practice what Jesus preached." I didn't want to be pointing any fingers, but I hoped Mary Jane would think about what I said.

She did, think, but not about what I hoped.

"Prim and proper, that reminds me, that man hasn't been around here anymore, has he?"

"What man?" I played dumb. At my age it's credible. People always suspect Alzheimer's or dementia.

"That, that Arnie. The one who seems to be taking an interest in your farm and house and well, your assets."

Now, I would have been pleased if I'd thought by assets Mary Jane meant my girlish figure, my silken hair, and my peaches and cream complexion. Since I had none of those assets, I was left to assume she was insinuating that he was after some financial gain. So far, I'd been the only one to gain monetarily. Arnie had always paid when we went out together.

"Arnie hasn't been around for a while. We still e-mail each other on occasion." Actually I meant every day, but I didn't want Mary Jane's sweet-tart attitude turning to vinegar.

Mary Jane sighed. "Auntie, what am I going to do with you?"

Was she giving up already? That would be highly unlikely.

"Well, if you're looking for something to do, you could make me some more of those flyers to send out to restaurants. I hear there are some new places opening up in that huge shopping center near Shelby. I thought I might branch out a bit."

"You know, you're getting good enough at that computer that you could do this yourself."

That was a switch. Was Mary Jane actually telling me I could capably do something on my own? The world was surely going to end soon.

"I know, honey, but you have better eyes than I do for design, and I can't get the stuff in that program to cut and paste and stay in the right place long enough to print out." I hoped flattery would get me somewhere.

"Okay, I'll go see what you have."

Mary Jane pulled herself away from the window and went off in the direction of my spare room where the computer was set up. I didn't follow her. She always lost me when she tried to show me how to do the labels or flyers. She didn't explain things as clearly as Tommy did.

The noise of the John Deere had stopped. Tommy was done with the lawn. I filled up a glass with fresh ice cubes and water and took it out to him.

"Thanks, Mrs. A." He gulped the cold water down quickly. "It's warming up. Summer will hit us soon."

"Don't wish us all that humidity yet." I looked at his empty glass. "Need a refill?"

"Oh, no thanks. I need to check on my plants, pull a few weeds. Everything is growing pretty good this year so far." Tommy handed me the glass of ice.

"Care for cinnamon rolls and coffee when you're done?"

"I don't want to keep you from your company, Mrs. A." He nodded at Mary Jane's car.

"That's just my niece. You can join us for a snack, can't you?"

"Really, Mrs. A." He pulled at his dirty shirt. "I'm not exactly presentable today. I'll meet her on another day when I'm cleaned up. I'll just check on my plants and be on my way."

He hobbled off in his clunky boots that never seemed to be tied. I had tried to talk him into taking a garden plot closer to the house so he wouldn't have to trek so far, but he insisted again that I should reserve those for the folks who couldn't walk that far. Today, he looked like one of those folks as I watched him limp down the path beside the creek.

That boy and I needed another good talk over some hot chocolate and cinnamon rolls. He didn't seem to have any connection to family. I knew his mother had been killed in the accident that caused his back and leg problems, but what of his father? The grandparents he'd lived with? Where were they now? He needed to have a sense of belonging, a sense that someone cared about him. He seemed like such a lost soul.

I went back in the house to check on Mary Jane. She was fussing with her purse when I entered the kitchen.

"Oh!, Auntie!"

I seemed to have startled her.

"What's the matter, MJ?"

She wouldn't look me directly in the eye but continued to fuss with the zipper on her purse trying to close it. If she had taken the time to reorganize the papers that were popping out of the top, the zipper would have worked easier.

"Nothing, I just remembered I need to get home for the boys." She tossed the purse strap over her shoulder and grabbed her keys. "Your flyers are in the printer. If you need more, well just call me."

"Thanks, Mary Jane. I think I can manage to print them. It's the designing that's beyond me."

I moved aside as she rushed past me like a hornet that had been swiped at with a newspaper. I was innocent. It wasn't me doing the swiping. My mind hadn't gone near a rolled up newspaper in quite a while. I stood in the kitchen a moment while the dust settled from her hasty departure. No disrespect meant to my gender, but I wondered if she might be experiencing a little PMS or early menopause. I shrugged it off. She was just being Mary Jane.

A cup of coffee in hand, I wandered back into my ambidextrous retreat to sit in front of my computer and do some surfing. A trip to London still beckoned to me. I sat back and sipped my coffee as I daydreamed and thought about searching for places to visit over there.

The coffee in my cup was gone by the time I turned my attention back to my computer. I set it aside and wiggled the mouse to stop the crazy squiggles my screen saver made. Mary Jane still had the program up with the flyer on it. When I went to close it, the little warning box appeared and asked if I wanted to save the design. I was surprised that Mary Jane hadn't saved it and closed it up. She must have been in one big hurry. I clicked on "yes" and saved the flyer as "newpicklefly" before I closed the program. When the screen disappeared, it revealed my e-mail box was open. It was displaying my new messages. Eagerly I searched for a message from Arnie. I hadn't heard from him yet today.

I glanced through the list. There was a message with his name on it in my box already. The subject line read, "Picked a peck of pickles yet?" It appeared that I had already read it. Strange, I couldn't remember reading it. Was this another senior moment? I opened the message.

Hello Pickle Lady,

How are your plants doing? I hope you've planted enough for me to buy a few jars of those delicious pickles. My mouth waters when I think of how wonderful they taste.

I was remembering our day together last week. I loved being outdoors and taking in the beautiful scenery with you at Indian Lake. Your picnic lunch was delicious. Thank you again.

I'm trying to find myself a hobby. There are fewer cases coming my way and I can't be off cruising all the time, so I really need to find some other things to occupy my mind. Any suggestions?

I spent the day working in my yard, cutting grass and the like. Has Tommy been out to cut yours this week? Have you learned any more about his family? I like the way you care so much about people. It puts me to shame. I keep praying for a more caring heart.

I'm sure I won't find anything around here to measure up to the memory of your picnic lunch so I guess I'll go out and try to find some fast food to fill the void at least. You are one good cook, Annie Pickels.

Fondly,

Arnie

I sat back refreshed with his kind words. What a dear friend. He was so complimentary. I'd only thrown together some chicken salad on wheat bread and tossed in a couple of pickles with a container of Cole slaw. I didn't even make any fresh lemonade. We drank canned ice tea. Indian Lake had been a wonderful time. I clicked on "reply" and began a message to Arnie.

Dear Arnie,

You are such a gentleman. That picnic wasn't anything to hold a candle to. I'm sure your fast food will be just as good, although maybe not as healthy.

Tommy finished my lawn today and went off to check on his plants. I didn't get a chance to see him before he left to go home. I'll try to catch him the next time for some gentle questioning. Don't want to become a griller like Elma.

Speaking of Elma, I'm thinking of getting her involved with quilting this winter. That's a good hobby. Are you interested?

Thanks for your faithfulness in writing each day. I always look forward to your messages.

Your Pickle Lady,

Annie

I hit "send" and the message disappeared. Whoosh! Gone! Just like that. It still amazed me how the whole thing worked.

The flyers Mary Jane printed out were stacked in the printer next to the computer. I reached over and rescued them from becoming permanently rounded by hanging over the paper holder. I flipped the stack of printed material over to check out the finished product. Surprisingly, the first page was almost blank.

I examined it closer. There were only a few lines of print at the top. I read them:

void at least. You are one good cook, Annie Pickels. Fondly, Arnie

Those were the last lines in Arnie's e-mail message. Mary Jane had printed out Arnie's e-mail!

Surely it was by mistake. I went through all the possibilities. Unless there was something very strange I hadn't learned yet about this computer, she would have had to do it deliberately, open the mail program and the message, and click on the printer icon. An imaginary roll of newspaper was not going to solve the anger that stewed now. How dare she invade my privacy? Evidence in hand, I marched into the kitchen to grab the phone and punch in Mary

Jane's number. The phone rang four times before anyone picked up.

"Hello." I recognized Harold's young voice on the other end.

"Hello, Harold. How are you? This is Auntie Ann." My voice sounded strained. I could feel the veins pulsing in my neck.

"Hi, Auntie Ann. I'm fine," he said and sighed impatiently.

"Is your mother there? I need to talk with her."

"Naw. She's gone shopping."

"What about your father? Could I talk to him?" I needed to talk to some adult. I needed to vent. Besides, Bud should know what his wife was doing. Maybe he could talk some sense into her.

"Dad's on a business trip. He won't be back until next week." I could sense Harold's impatience with me. I had probably interrupted one of his video games.

"Oh." I tried to think of what to do next.

"That all you want?" Harold asked rather rudely.

"Can you remember to tell your mother I called?" I replied rather rudely myself. I wasn't setting a very good example but at that moment I was too riled up to care.

"Yeah, sure. Bye." Harold hung up.

I stared at the phone for a moment. What would ever compel Mary Jane to break a trust like that? What was I going to do with her? A knock on the door broke my train of thought. Through the window I could see a man in a uniform. I recognized him immediately. It was Sheriff Stewart.

Now, what did he want? Was he still after my pickle recipe? My heart sunk as I remembered it was probably Tommy he was after. But why?

"Hello, Mrs. Pickels," Sheriff Stewart greeted me when I opened the door. "I was wondering if your garden renter, Tommy, was around?"

I looked past the sheriff to see that Tommy's car was gone. "No, I'm afraid you missed him. He was here earlier. He cut my grass and checked on his herbs and corn."

"Hmmm," he looked down at his feet. "I hate to do this to you, Mrs. Pickels, but I need to have a look at that garden plot you tell me this Tommy is taking care of." He reached in his back pocket and pulled out a legal-looking paper and handed it to me. "I have a search warrant."

I took the paper in hand and glanced at it. Search warrants always meant a crime had been committed. Any good TV crime watcher knew that. What did Sheriff Stewart suspect? I closed my mouth when I realized it was hanging open, and looked back at him.

"You still can't give me any information on this *Tommy*? *Tommy's* name? *Tommy's* address? *Tommy's* phone number?"

Every time he said "Tommy" he made it sound like I had made him up. While I may imagine that I swat people with a bagged newspaper, I knew I didn't make Tommy up. After all, Mary Jane and Elma saw him too. On the other hand, I supposed it did seem a little strange. The sheriff was never there when Tommy was and I truly didn't remember his phone number when he asked me.

"I'm sorry you missed him," I said. "You're welcome to have a look at his garden plot, though. You didn't need this." I held up the search warrant. Did he think Tommy had stolen something and buried it there?

"Just want to keep everything legal. These days you have to be careful." The sheriff cinched his pants up and tucked in the back of his shirt. Would you be willing to show me where this plot is?"

"Sure. Give me a minute to switch shoes." I took off my sandals and hastily got into my old sneakers then joined the sheriff outside. He stood at the edge of the driveway looking out into the distant garden plots. He lifted his hat as his fingers scratched at the spot in the middle of his red head again.

"The teens from our church have that one over there," I began to explain. I pointed to a square of land that blossomed with zucchini plants, green beans, and tomatoes. "They're raising money for their mission trip. And that one over there belongs to a family with six kids. The mom homeschools and I think they're saving some money on groceries by doing a lot of canning. They're also learning about nutrition."

I continued to point out other plots with varieties of produce and flowers as we walked toward Tommy's plot of land. Weeds and tall grass partially hid Tommy's plot since no one else had rented plots and cleared them anywhere near his. There was a well-beaten path through the grass and weeds, a testament to Tommy's diligence.

We reached the small clearing that held Tommy's corn and marjoram plants. The sheriff stopped to take it all in. The corn stalks were about 10 inches high and between the stalks of corn were the marjoram plants almost as high as the corn. That boy did have a green thumb. Russell would have been proud of him.

The sheriff stepped between two rows of plants and bent down to examine the marjoram. Honestly, I could not understand why he was so fascinated with herbs. Why was he out here to begin with? Did he think Tommy had a body buried beneath the sweet corn? If he suspected that, he was worse than Mary Jane. Sheriff Stewart hadn't even seen Tommy yet. Reaching for the microphone on his shoulder, the sheriff stood and spoke into it.

"Henry? You there?"

"Yup," came the reply. "I just pulled in."

"We're in the back northwest corner. Bring those bags with you. I think we hit pay dirt."

The receiver on his shoulder crackled. "Sure. Be right there."

Pay dirt?

The sheriff bent over and grabbed one of the marjoram plants. He gave it a jerk and the plant came out roots and all. I gasped.

"Sheriff, you can't be pulling up this boy's plants. He's worked hard to get this all growing so well."

"I'm sure *he* did," the sheriff said dryly. He shook the excess dirt from the roots of the displaced plant. "Now, Mrs. Pickels, you want to tell me again about this *Tommy*? Or, do you want to tell me how hard you worked to grow this marijuana?

I stared blankly at him. Marijuana?

Chapter 26

Marijuana? No. It was marjoram. The sheriff was mistaken. He squatted to look at another plant. I tapped him on the shoulder. "Sheriff, I'm sorry to tell you this but that's marjoram. I'm sure of it. Tommy said it complimented the corn."

"Actually, the corn is helping the marijuana." He rose with a groan and brushed his hands together to get rid of the loose dirt. "We find that marijuana growers hide their plants among the corn. It's harder to spot from the air."

The sheriff's eyes narrowed as he looked at me. I'm sure my face was pale. I didn't understand why he seemed so suspicious of my every move.

"This Tommy is pretty clever," he said.

"No, he isn't. I mean, it can't be. It's not marijuana."

My tongue wasn't working for me. My words didn't seem to come out right. I remembered taking the last leaf from a package of marjoram I had bought at the store. The leaves were dry but I thought they looked similar to the dried leaf I took from Tommy's plant. I told the sheriff.

"They looked alike to me."

"I'm not an expert on marjoram," Sheriff Stewart said, "but I do know how to recognize marijuana. We find enough of it planted out in the county's undeveloped land."

He half closed one eye as if he were trying to figure something out.

"I'm surprised at you, Mrs. Pickels. Why would you have stuck it in your pickle jars? Were you trying to sell it?"

"Yes. No!" I was confused. Shock at this discovery was playing havoc with my brain cells. "I wanted to sell my pickles not marijuana. I was sure this was mar, jor, . . ."

My voice trailed off as I realized the sheriff was not convinced of my innocence. I was in deep trouble. I was sure of it. The more I said though only seemed to make it worse.

Henry, the sheriff's deputy, arrived on the scene with an armload of black garbage bags. He let out a low whistle as he stood and surveyed Tommy's garden plot.

"Mighty nice little garden ya' got here."

"It's not my garden," I mumbled.

"It's yer land. Must be yer garden," Henry pointed out. He stood there nodding his head up and down, appraising the value of their find. "That's a lot of Mary Jane."

"Mary Jane?" I looked at him, the question written on my face. Suddenly a large melon seemed to grow right in the lower half of my stomach.

"Yeah. Mary Jane. Mary Ann. Mary Jonas. Mary Weaver. Marijuana. Whatever you want to name it, it's still illegal."

The sheriff handed Henry the plant he had pulled up. He waved his hand over the rest of the garden plot. "Finish up here, Henry. I'm taking Mrs. Pickels back to the house."

Mary Jane. *My Mary Jane helps me get through life.* Was my Mary Jane right? Tommy was just a pothead? No. I couldn't believe that.

My Mary Jane helps me too. My words echoed in my head. Oh no! Tommy thought I was using his marijuana! Well, I was but not that way! I followed the sheriff back down the trail to the driveway where Elma stood on tip toes trying to see what was happening out in the far end of the field.

"Annie! Annie, are you all right?" Elma sounded relieved to see me. "I was thinking all sorts of crazy things." Her hands shook and her lips trembled as she fought back tears. She must have thought I was hurt or dead and lying out in the field. I tried to reassure her with a smile but I could tell by the look on her face, I hadn't succeeded.

"What's going on?" Elma asked.

"The sheriff says he found marijuana in my pickles," I said numbly.

"Marijuana? Annie, what were you doing with marijuana in your pickles?"

I shrugged. "I thought it was marjoram."

"Marjoram?" Elma looked thoroughly confused.

"Ma'am, I'm going to have to ask you to leave," the sheriff said to Elma. "I need to question Mrs. Pickels about what she's been growing back there." He jerked his head in the direction of Tommy's garden where Henry was collecting the plants.

"Oh." Elma shook her head. "I can't leave my friend if she's in trouble." She moved to my side and wrapped her arms around me.

"It's okay, Elma. It's just a misunderstanding. I'll call you when we get this straightened out." I patted her hand and unwrapped her arms.

"Are you sure, Annie? 'Cause I'll stay right here with you if you need me." Elma searched my face then gave the sheriff a sideways look that challenged him to just try and move her.

"I'm sure." I smiled with faked confidence. "I'll call you later when this is all over."

"Before you leave ma'am, I need your name and address. I'm probably going to want to ask you a few questions too." The sheriff dug out his little notebook and pen. I moved between him and Elma.

"Elma's just a friend and neighbor. She has nothing to do with my pickles or my garden plots." I puffed up my chest. He wasn't going to intimidate my friend.

"Elma Thompson," Elma volunteered as she stepped out from behind me. "I live across the street and I assure you Annie has done nothing wrong." Her uplifted chin dared the sheriff to dispute my innocence.

"Thank you Ms. Thompson. Now, if you don't mind, I need to spend some time with Mrs. Pickels."

Elma backed away reluctantly. She turned around and slowly walked in the direction of her house, glancing over her shoulder one more time before crossing the street. I nodded at her for reassurance.

"Mrs. Pickels," the sheriff said sternly. "I'm going to give you another chance to tell me how I can contact this, this Tommy. Otherwise, I'm going to have to take you in for possession of marijuana, growing it on your property, and possible charges of selling it, even if as you claim, it was in your pickle brine as a spice."

My mind raced. That sounded like a heap of trouble. But if it was that much trouble for me, how much more trouble was it for Tommy? How could I let the sheriff go off and drag that boy away just when I had begun to make him feel like someone cared about him? No. I wouldn't do it. The sheriff would just have to arrest me. I'd take my chances.

"I don't know how to get in touch with Tommy." I said defiantly.

"Is there a Tommy?" The sheriff raised an eyebrow. "Or were you just growing it for yourself? I hear some older folks like to use it for their arthritis."

"I do have trouble now and then with my arthritis. Mary Jane does help me out those days." I looked him squarely in the eye. "But Mary Jane is my niece."

"Mary Jane is your niece?" He pursed his lips and exhaled loudly. "Okaaay." The sheriff closed his little notebook and pocketed his pen. Reaching behind his back, he produced a pair of handcuffs. My heart leapt to my throat. I was about to be arrested.

"Annie Pickels, you are under arrest for possession of marijuana, growing marijuana on your property, and the sale of an illegal substance. You have the right to remain silent. . ."

He continued on just like I'd heard so many times on the police shows on television. While he was still reciting his memorized speech, he put one cuff on my wrist drawing my arm behind my back and cuffing the other wrist. I stared straight ahead and refused to give in to the salty feeling of tears.

Sheriff Stewart helped me into the back of his car and shut the door. I sat and looked through the screen that separated the back seat from the front. I've been arrested. I'm sitting in the back of a police car in handcuffs. This is not happening. *Lord, give me courage.* My lower lip quivered. You will not cry, I commanded myself.

Henry appeared with three bags full of young marijuana plants. He opened the trunk of his car and retrieved some tape. I watched as he and the sheriff sealed the bags with tape and labeled them. I felt like I was in the middle of a TV drama, but without the cameras and the guy who yells, "Cut!"

"What about the house?" I heard Henry ask the sheriff.

"Just do a run through. Make sure there aren't any houseplants. Check out her pickling paraphernalia. Make sure there's no stash. Give John a call to help you out."

This would be the second time today my privacy had been invaded. I became more indignant which helped keep the tears at bay. It did nothing for my helplessness though.

"I'm going to run her in and book her. Be sure you lock up when you're done."

"Ee, yup!" Henry said as he turned to go into my house. The sheriff got into the front seat of the car.

"Okay, Mrs. Pickels. One last chance to give me the information about Tommy."

I sat quietly. He told me I had the right to remain silent. I was going to use that right. He started the car and we headed for the county jail. As we pulled out of the driveway, I saw Elma sitting on her front step. I would have waved but my hands were bound behind my back. Elma's hand flew to her mouth as she realized I was in the back of the police car. She started down her driveway but we were quickly past it before she got to the street.

We arrived at the jail about twenty minutes later. The sheriff parked his car in his designated spot. Before he got out, he called Henry one more time on his radio to find out that the search of my house revealed no more marijuana or Mary Jane, the niece or the plant. While I sat there waiting to get out of the car, I noticed a curly haired fellow in jeans and a yellow cotton shirt lean against the wall near the door marked "Entrance." He studied the police car. I'm sure he wondered what the sheriff was doing with his grandmother in the back seat.

When the car door opened and the sheriff pulled me out, I heard a couple of suspicious clicks coming from the direction of the young man next to the door. The last time I had heard clicks like that, I'd had an awful picture taken on board the Queen Mary 2. Sure enough, when the sheriff turned me around, I saw a camera pointed in my direction.

"Sheriff!" the young photographer called out. "Is this the big drug bust I heard about on the scanner?"

The sheriff kept his eyes fixed straight ahead.

"What'd she do, put coke in her cookies, a little bash in her brownies?" The young man laughed. "Come on. She's somebody's grandma. What'd ya have her in handcuffs for? Is she dangerous?"

"You can read the arrest report when it's done." The tone of Sheriff Stewart's voice quieted the heckler long enough for the sheriff to open the door and push me through. We quickly turned into a room with two desks, each manned by an officer in uniform. They both looked up.

"This Pickels?" the older one said with a smirk on his face. He leaned back in his chair and pointed at me with his coffee cup.

"This is *Mrs.* Pickels," the sheriff answered.

His tone indicated that he expected them to give me some respect. I was grateful but how did you respect someone in handcuffs? I saw the look the two exchanged. In another minute, I expected them to be on the floor rolling in laughter.

"I'll handle the booking," Sheriff Stewart said with authority. "You boys help Henry out when he gets in with the evidence bags."

"Sure," answered the younger officer.

The youngster exchanged a grin with the older coffee drinker. They both started shuffling papers on their desks. I heard muffled chuckles as we went into the next room and the door closed behind me. The room we entered had a long counter about chest high that separated the entryway from a work area full of computers. No one manned any of the half dozen workstations. It reminded me of a control center in a science fiction movie after the aliens ran everyone off.

The sheriff moved behind me and unlocked the handcuffs to remove them from my wrists. He tapped the top of the counter.

"Please empty your pockets, Mrs. Pickels, and put the contents on the counter."

I reached in my pockets. All I had was a wadded up tissue and a piece of hard candy. I set them on the counter. The sheriff looked at them and shook his head slightly. "No jewelry, watch?"

"I don't normally wear jewelry when I'm working around the house or in the yard." Thankfully, I had left my engagement ring on the counter on the ring holder when I'd done the dishes this morning and planned to go out to work in the garden. That seemed so long ago. Still, I was glad that I didn't have to hand over Russell's ring and have it stowed away by the sheriff.

He looked back down at the well-used tissue and the red and white striped candy in its cellophane wrapper.

"You can keep the tissue," he said stiffly. I put it back in my pocket. The sheriff deposited the peppermint candy in a small manila envelope, wrote my name on it and locked it away in a drawer. "Have a seat here, Mrs. Pickels." He pointed to a chair next to a computer.

Stashing the handcuffs somewhere behind his back, he sat in the cushioned chair in front of the computer monitor and wiggled the mouse. Studying the screen, he clicked the mouse a few times, and typed in some information.

"Name," he said blankly, still focused on the screen.

"Annie," I replied.

He stared at me for a moment. "Full name."

"Ann Louise Pickels." I cringed at having to give my middle name. I hated it. It sounded so nasal. I still didn't know where my mother had come up with it. Some distant relative?

"Date of birth."

The sheriff stared at me as if he defied me to lie about my age. No problem. My age didn't really bother me. I gave him my birth day, month and year.

"Height."

"Five foot six." I assumed he wanted the measurement in stocking feet.

"Weight."

Now he was getting personal. I didn't mind telling my age but my weight—well. . .

"About 140."

He looked me over, head to toe.

"145." His fingers clicked on the numbered keys.

My face flushed. It was really closer to 150. He finished recording the rest of the pertinent information that identified me, white hair, brown eyes, slight scar on my right cheek. I reached up to my cheek and swiped my hand across it. The scar turned out to be a streak of dirt. He deleted the information.

When the sheriff finished with his computer, he led me to a spot by the counter where he pulled out an inkpad and a piece of paper with little boxes printed on it.

"This will go easier for both of us if you just relax."

He took each of my fingers, one at a time, and rolled the tip across the inkpad and then across a corresponding block on the white paper. The moist towelette he handed me hardly budged the ink off my fingertips. I swiped furiously to no avail and gave up in disgust.

Next he took me to the other end of the room where a chart was mounted on a wall with lines drawn across it to indicate various physical heights. I held a plaque with numbers written on it while he snapped my picture, front and profile, with a camera mounted on a tripod. He never told me when to smile. Does one smile for a mug shot?

"Mrs. Pickels, I'm going to put you in a holding cell until I run a background check. This shouldn't take too long, but in the meantime, if you happen to think of anything that might lead us to your, your *Tommy*, give a rap on the door and one of us will get you out."

I sniffed like royalty would if they had suffered such indecency. I wasn't going to let him have the upper hand.

"I think you'll find my background to be very simple. I'm a farm girl from Mansfield."

He led me down another hall to the holding cell. I envisioned a cell with cold iron bars. I could see myself clinging to them, my chin resting on a crossbar, a tin cup in one hand. I remembered Mayberry's town drunk running his cup across the bars of his cell to get Barney Fife's attention. Wonder how much noise I can make?

The holding cell was nothing more than another room with a bench in it and a door that swung shut behind me with a click that told me it was locked. I looked through the glass in the door and saw the sheriff disappear down the hall. For all my bravado, I felt a little weak in the knees. The bench was hard but a welcome support. What do I do now?

I tried to recall the crime shows I'd watched. Bail was next, wasn't it? But who would post bail? There was no way I'd call Mary Jane with my one phone call. I couldn't remember Arnie's number. Besides, I didn't think they'd let me make a long distance call. Elma was the only choice left. I hated to involve her in this, but I could picture her at her kitchen table with the phone in front of her waiting for it to ring. When they made the offer for my phone call, I'd call her.

With that decided, I felt a little calmer. I leaned back and closed my eyes. How many jailhouse prayers did God get? Certainly this would be the first from me. And the last, I hoped. God and I had a good heart-to-heart and when I was finished, I felt at peace. Whatever came, I knew the Lord would help me handle it. I nodded off.

The noise of a key in the lock and the doorknob turning startled me into consciousness again. It was Sheriff Stewart. Was it time for a jailhouse meal or was he coming to tell me I could make a phone call?

"Mrs. Pickels, will you follow me please?"

I rose and fell into step behind him. Was he leading me to the real jail? I had visions of striped jumpsuits and badly fitting slippers, standard issue, I assumed, for prisoners. I did hope the food would be edible. I glanced at a clock on the wall. It was 8 p.m. No wonder I was hungry. It was three hours past my dinnertime and I couldn't remember eating lunch either.

To my surprise, instead of a ride to jail, we ended up back in the big room with all the computers. I sat in the same chair while Sheriff Stewart busied himself with more papers at the counter. Finally, he sat down next to me.

"Mrs. Pickels, I've talked with the judge and he's given me permission to release you on your own recognizance. We didn't feel you'd be a risk for flight. You have an arraignment scheduled for Monday."

I nodded as if I understood all that he was telling me. I guess he wasn't convinced because he went on to explain.

"That's where you will enter your plea and have a court date set for trial. I strongly suggest in the meantime that you get yourself a good lawyer."

I hoped he would give me my discharge papers with all the instructions written out like they did in the hospital. In my state of mind and hunger, I wasn't sure I'd remember the details.

"So, I can go home now?" I asked.

"Yes," He answered.

I hesitated.

"I'll need a ride," I told him.

"You'll have to call someone." He moved the phone closer to me and turned to work on his computer.

"Can't you return me to my home? You're the one who brought me here."

The sheriff's face tightened. He turned to me. "Mrs. Pickels, you'll need to find your own way home. I can't spare anyone right now to give you a ride." He pushed the phone further in my direction. "Isn't there someone you can call?"

"There is but I hate to have her drive this late in the evening." I felt my dignity come back and my dandruff raise up. "I think it's very rude to bring me all the way here and keep me so long, then tell me I have to find my own way home."

"Mrs. Pickels." The sheriff's neck began to color. "You have been arrested on some very serious charges. You have been uncooperative in answering my questions and helping our investigation. I suggest you not push your luck trying to get a ride home from me."

I slowly reached for the phone and dialed Elma's number, all the while staring at Sheriff Stewart and his red hair that was now blending with his skin tone. He went back to his work. Elma was more than willing to come for me. Luckily she knew the way. The jail was next to the courthouse where she'd had to take care of some things when Warren died. I hung up the phone and drummed my fingers a bit on the desk. The sheriff sighed and looked up and sighed again.

"What is it now, Mrs. Pickels?"

"I hate to bother you, sheriff," I said with honeyed words. "But would it be too much trouble to give me back my personal items?"

He laid his pen down and slowly rose. He sauntered over to the drawer that held the envelope with all the worldly goods I had on my person when I was booked. He returned and tossed the envelope on the table in front of me.

"Thank you," I said politely. I tore it open and shook out my peppermint. It wasn't much but I hoped it would help the rumbling in my stomach. Next time I got arrested, I'd try to time it better so I could get fed. I was on a little sugar high by the time Elma came to pick me up. We stopped for a bite to eat on the way home and I filled Elma in on the jailhouse routine while I enjoyed my late night dinner.

At home, I fell into bed, exhausted but wide-awake. My to-do list began to form. I would call Arnie in the morning. The sheriff said I needed a good lawyer. He was the best one I could think of, actually, the only one.

But what would he think of me now?

Chapter 27

The night seemed short. I woke feeling like I weighed a ton. My body resisted my attempts to lift it out of bed but I forced my feet to touch the floor. Ignoring the protest of my legs and back, I stood and plodded into the kitchen. There was no fresh coffee. I hadn't prepared it before I went to bed. I rinsed out the old and started a fresh pot. The laundry basket was still where I left it, on a kitchen chair, when Mary Jane had arrived yesterday. It seemed so long ago. I fished out a clean T-shirt and the pants from an old jogging outfit, threw them on, and went out for the paper while the coffee pot made its gurgles and spits as if it too had had a bad night.

Even though my world was turned upside down, I could still count on a rolled-up newspaper inside an orange plastic bag tossed in the middle of the driveway. This morning it was almost a comfort to see it just where I expected it to be. I picked it up and slipped off its protective wrapper. Friday's news unrolled in my hands. The bottom of the front page caught my attention. Smiling up at me were Herb and his buddy, George. The Bugle sent a reporter and photographer out to capture their excitement over the planned trip to the Tiller Thriller in Arkansas in a couple of weeks.

They stood beside the Tillernator, which was looking a sight cleaner since the last time I'd seen it. George and Herb looked happy. My eyes continued to scan the bottom half of the page.

The weather was expected to be sunny and pleasant. The pollen counts were low. Rain was expected for the weekend. Good. We needed the rain. It was too bad it had to come on the weekend. The Indians had won. The Reds had lost. See page C1.

I flipped the paper over to look at the top half of the front page.

I gasped!

GRANDMA ARRESTED ON DRUG CHARGES
Marijuana found in her pickle recipe

There I was pictured plain as day, being led into the jail, my hands cuffed behind me. I looked closer. Actually, it was a better picture than the crazy lady on my cruise card. If I were counting blessings, that was one. I hurried into the house. I needed a cup of coffee before I faced this. My hand shook as I poured the steamy black liquid into my cup. I was front-page news. Everyone would know how stupid I was. Or would they think I was truly growing and using the marijuana? Either way, I still came out a few brain cells short. With the front page spread out before me, I began to read:

Sixty-five year old, Annie Pickels, found herself in a pickle yesterday when the sheriff raided her farm to find that she had been growing marijuana in the back acre of her land just off Route 47. Pickels claims she thought the green plants were marjoram. She was using the leaves as a spice in her pickle recipe.

The reporter mentioned my small pickle business. He had interviewed a few of my customers and gotten the consensus that I was just a harmless old lady who made great pickles.

"What a hoot," Bill Barker, the bartender at Tinkers Tavern said. "I didn't realize the green leaf in the jar was marijuana."

"I can't believe Annie would be involved with drugs. It's just not in her character," remarked Sally Imalas at Amy's Deli.

Imalas has been one of Pickels' customers since she started selling her pickles locally a few years ago.

The article went on to innumerate the possible penalties that faced me, imprisonment, fines, and one that made my blood run cold. My house and farm could be confiscated under the new tougher drug laws. *What am I going to do, Lord? I can't let them take Russell's house!*

I knew I had to call Arnie right away. No matter how embarrassed I was, I needed to know what to do. He was the best one to tell me. I grabbed the phone.

"Annie!" Arnie sounded genuinely pleased to hear from me. "What a surprise. I was just thinking of you."

"Good thoughts, I hope, because what I have to tell you isn't so good."

Arnie recognized the edge in my voice. His tone changed immediately. "Annie, what's wrong? Did you hurt yourself? Is it Elma?"

"I need your help." I swallowed hard. I couldn't go on.

"Annie, take a deep breath and tell me what's wrong." Arnie's concern was evident in his voice.

"I got arrested yesterday." I stopped to wipe my nose with a tissue. Talking to Arnie, hearing his voice, brought tears to my eyes.

"Arrested? What? No. Were you speeding in that sporty little Escape of yours?"

There was the ring of amusement in his voice now. He must have imagined I was upset over some little thing that was easy to straighten out. I hated to disillusion him.

"No. I got arrested for possession and cultivation of marijuana."

There was a long silence.

"This is a joke, right? Did Elma put you up to this?"

I smiled slightly. I could only wish it were a joke.

"No, Arnie. In fact it's front page news in the Bugle this morning." I glanced down at my picture again. If it was a joke, it was a bad one.

"Wow."

There was silence again. I could hear him exhale slowly.

"Arnie, I need to hire a lawyer. I was, I was hoping that, that…"

"You're not going to use anyone but me," he injected quickly. "I don't want to trust your welfare to someone else."

He paused. "Annie, how did you get mixed up with marijuana?"

I told him briefly what happened. The way he questioned me, I could tell he was taking notes, being lawyerly. When I was done with my story, I waited for him to say something. The silence was unnerving.

"Arnie, are you still there?" I asked.

"Annie, I'm not going to sugar coat this. It could be very serious. On the other hand, we have lots going for us. Tommy was actually doing the growing, the cultivating. I think, with character witnesses, we can prove that you truly didn't know what marijuana was."

"I'm sorry, Arnie. I know you want to blame this on Tommy, but I don't want to involve him."

"But Annie," he protested.

"No. That young man has been through enough in his life. I'm just beginning to see him open up and make new strides in his life. I don't want to ruin that."

"I can appreciate that but—"

"I know. I'm risking a lot." I bit my lip. I could sense Arnie's frustration. "Will you still help me?"

"Of course I will. You're just not making it very easy."

"I'm sorry."

Before I hung up, Arnie promised to come and talk with the prosecutor, the sheriff, and anyone else he deemed important, and then help me decide what to do for the arraignment. I felt so relieved. A burden is always easier to carry when it's shared.

The next thing on that to-do list that had kept me sleep deprived was the pickles I'd distributed in the fall. I needed to offer to let people return what they had for a refund. I couldn't let them get into trouble possessing something with marijuana in it. I began calling the customers I knew would be open early.

It was noon when I finished the list of delis and restaurants that carried my pickles. The list wasn't that long but everyone wanted to talk about what had happened. They were all very supportive and sympathetic, all but one. Patricia who ran a little shop that sold mostly souvenirs and homemade items at Indian Lake was irate. She ranted on and on about the possibility of someone suing her for discovering marijuana in their pickles. It turned out she hadn't sold any of the jars she had that contained the marijuana. Thankfully, I kept very good records. When she said she still had six jars on the shelf, I looked it up and saw that she had only ordered six jars. I promised to pick them up as soon as I could and refund her money. She was still indignant but agreeable to the solution.

My hands were shaking when I finished talking to Patricia. I wasn't sure if it was from her railing at me or from not having breakfast. I assembled a bologna and cheese sandwich, grabbed a few potato chips, and popped open a soda. Half way through my sandwich, the phone rang. It was an ominous ring. With a feeling of dread, I answered it. A voice screamed back at me.

"I knew it! I just knew that, that creep was going to get you into trouble!"

"Thanks, Mary Jane. I'm fine and how are you?" I took a bite of my sandwich. I knew I'd have time to chew it.

"What do you mean, how am I? How do you think I am? I'm, I'm steaming mad. That's how I am! I pick up the Bugle this morning and what do I see? My aunt splashed across the headlines.

And then, and then your line was busy all morning. I couldn't get through."

I swallowed and took a sip of my soda.

"Mary Jane calm down. You are not in any trouble. I am. And I will take care of it. Thank you for your concern."

"You and Dad are both alike! You think you can do whatever you like," she said. Her tone was accusatory but at least she had stopped screaming.

This was the first hint I had that my brother caused Mary Jane any consternation. I figured she got along much better with him than with me.

"Well, I'm about to wash my hands of the both of you. Neither of you listens to a word I say."

"Easy, MJ. What has your father done to make you so upset?"

"He's dating some floozy and expects me to like her. I think he plans to marry her. I don't need a stepmother at my age."

So this was what was bothering her so much lately. It wasn't just me. My brother was dating? I needed to find some time to catch up on his life with him. Where had the time gone since I'd last talked with him?

"I'd ask you to talk to him," she continued, "but you don't have any more sense than he does with you dating that, that sheep in wolf's clothing."

I was pretty sure she meant wolf in sheep's clothing, but I let her rant on a bit more without correcting her. Besides, it seemed she confused Arnie with my brother's girlfriend the more she talked. My sandwich lost its taste the longer I listened to Mary Jane's ranting. I decided we both needed to move on.

"Mary Jane, I really need to go. I have some more calls to make this afternoon." I didn't want to have this conversation go on any longer.

"Well, what do you expect to do about all this?" she demanded.

"Please don't worry about me, MJ. I have a lawyer and he assures me everything will be all right."

It sounded good to me. I hoped I convinced her. Maybe I could still convince myself.

"Well, stay away from Tommy. He's trouble. I hope the sheriff has him."

I hadn't even told her Tommy was involved. She just assumed.

"Maybe now that sleazy cruise guy will leave you alone too if he thinks you're spending all your money on lawyers."

Poor Mary Jane, if you only knew. The sleazy cruise guy is my lawyer.

I tossed the rest of my bologna sandwich. It wasn't going down very well any more. I needed to get out of the house, to do something. Indian Lake was not so far away. Maybe I could drive over and pick up those pickles from Patricia. I called Elma. Her chatter would keep me company and I wouldn't have to face Patricia alone.

Elma and I enjoyed the ride to the lake. We talked about everything except pickles and marijuana. Patricia wasn't there when we arrived but her salesgirl had the jars for us in the back room. I paid her and made her sign a receipt just to make sure everything was legal.

"Yeah, now you worry about legal," Elma said with a grin when we got back in my Escape.

We both laughed. On the way home, we swung around to the Pinetree Barn where we'd had lunch with Arnie a while back. There was nothing like comfort food in a time like this. Elma and I delved into the fresh homemade bread and soup special they offered.

"Are you worried about what's going to happen now?" Elma asked softly.

"Yes and no," I replied. "I surely don't want to lose the farm, or do jail time. Arnie seems to think I'll get off lightly. He wanted to involve Tommy but I told him not to."

Elma looked surprised. "Why did you do that? He was the one growing the stuff. Don't you think he should take responsibility for his actions? He knew exactly what he was doing."

"Elma, look how far he's come in these past weeks. We've got him coming to Wednesday night dinners at church and he's even gone to class with Kirk a couple of times. He's beginning to know people care about him."

"I know. He's been there on a few Sunday mornings too, but he's the one who got you into all this trouble."

"I just don't want to see him locked up. He's not going to get the kind of attention he needs behind bars. He needs a family, a sense of belonging to someone. Now that I know Mary Jane isn't the name of his girlfriend, I'm not even sure he has one of those."

"You can't be his savior," Elma said sternly.

"No, but I can help him find one."

Our coffee and pie arrived and Elma changed the subject. I guess she figured there was no talking sense into me. She could join Mary Jane and Arnie on that opinion.

When I got back to the house, I found my answering machine blinking its signal to me that I had a message. Actually there were two messages. The first was from Tommy.

"Hey, Mrs. A. I just read the article in the Bugle. Wow. I am so sorry I got you into so much trouble. I'm going to go down to the sheriff's office and straighten it out."

"No! Don't!" I yelled at the machine, then realized he couldn't hear me.

Tommy's message continued. "I didn't realize you were using the marijuana in your pickles. I thought you were using it like I was, for the pain. Would you mind, um, well, you know, praying for me? I'll try to call and let you know how it all turns out."

The praying part gave me hope, but I was still concerned. My fears eased a little more with the next message. It was from Arnie.

"Annie, it's me. I just got a call from the sheriff's office that Tommy turned himself in. The sheriff wanted to let me know since it affects your case. Tommy doesn't have a lawyer and I offered my help. The kid took me up on it. I'm on my way over there now. Keep a light on for me. I will stop by as soon as I'm done talking to Tommy and let you know how things went. Annie, it'll all be okay."

Okay? Will it ever really be okay again?

I sat in Russell's old chair, my Bible in my lap. It was closed. I knew I should open it. There should be some verse that would lift me up and out of the uncertainty that gripped me. I felt suspended in time, not able to look forward. The future seemed a blur. I needed to pray, wanted to read, but didn't know where to begin. Like the apostles in the garden, I fell asleep.

A knock on the door startled me and my Bible slid to the floor as I ran to answer it. I glanced at the oven clock on my way through the kitchen. It was midnight. Guess I was catching up on my lost sleep. Arnie's silhouette appeared in the light that shone down from the eaves over the kitchen door. Did he bring good news or bad? His shoulders were slumped and he was rubbing his eyes when I threw open the door. He straightened and gave me a tired smile. I stepped aside to let him in.

"How did it go?" I asked anxiously. "Is Tommy all right?"

"Tommy's fine. I posted bail for him." He set his briefcase down in the kitchen and I motioned for us to go into the living room. "The fact that he turned himself in was a help in convincing the authorities he wasn't a threat to run anywhere."

Arnie sank into Russell's chair. He leaned over and picked up my Bible tucking an old bulletin back into it. "Been keeping watch I see," he said as he placed the Bible on the end table.

"Not very well. I fell asleep."

"Sleep sounds good. I need to find a motel close by. I'm not up to driving all the way back to Indianapolis tonight. Besides, I need to meet with you and Tommy tomorrow and work out a plan for your defense now that I'm representing both of you."

"Why don't you stay in the extra room tonight?" I offered. "You won't find a motel close by, and you look too tired to get back out on the road."

"I don't want to put you out," Arnie said politely.

"You won't. I'll worry too much if I send you back out on the road." It was past midnight and who knew how long it would take him to find a place to stay? There was nothing nearby.

"Are you sure?" He raised his eyebrows and cocked his head as he looked at me. "How's it going to look to the neighbors, me staying with you?"

"The only neighbor around here to see anything is Elma, and she'd be delighted to think you were staying here. She knows us well enough to not think poorly." Although I inwardly cringed at the teasing I knew I would have to take.

"Well, if you're sure it's not inconvenient."

"Oh, it's terribly inconvenient, but you're worth it." I felt myself smiling at him, a flood of new affection in my heart.

"All right, then. I'll get my things out of the car and we can both call it a night."

I hurried upstairs to the extra bedroom and quickly threw some sheets and a blanket on the bed. I was just putting fresh towels in the bathroom when I heard Arnie call out, "Annie? Where did you disappear to?"

"Up here. I was just making sure everything was in order," I yelled down the stairs.

Arnie came up the stairs with a small overnight bag in one hand and his briefcase in the other.

"This is nice," he said as he surveyed the room. He set his briefcase on the old desk in front of the window. "Nice desk. I like the trim." Arnie ran his hand lovingly around the scrollwork on the drawers.

"It belonged to my father." I stood awkwardly in the middle of the room. The presence of my father's desk recalled the parental rules of not letting boys visit in my room. But this wasn't my room and I wasn't a vulnerable teen-aged girl.

"Annie, thank you. I appreciate your keeping me for the night." He sank onto the bed and ran his hand over the soft blanket.

"It's the least I can do after all you've done for Tommy and me. I'm so grateful." I started out to the hall but turned with my hand on the door. "If you need anything else, just holler and thanks again, Arnie."

"Good night, snow angel," he said softly.

Snow angel. I loved the way he said those words.

"Good night," I said and closed the door. I may be sixty-five on the outside, but I felt like sixteen on the inside. I went to bed with a renewed feeling of confidence, comfort, and companionship. I fell asleep as my head hit the pillow. The morning would bring good things, I was sure of it.

Chapter 28

The next morning, I awoke to the sound of footsteps overhead. Quickly I dressed, splashed some water on my face, and brushed the night's tangles from my hair. I dashed to the kitchen and started a pot of coffee to brew. What would I make for breakfast? I'd never had breakfast with Arnie. I had no idea what he might like.

Bacon and eggs sounded like a good bet. Most men were fond of that. I pulled out the package of bacon and the carton of eggs from the refrigerator and grabbed the tub of margarine before the door closed. By the time Arnie appeared in the kitchen, it smelled of fresh cooked bacon and hot toast.

"That smells great!" Arnie said. He took the cup of coffee I offered him.

"How do you like your eggs?" I asked.

"Over easy." He closed his eyes and savored the first sip of his hot coffee. "Mmmm. Good."

It felt so natural with him in my kitchen, a cup of coffee in his hand and a warm smile on his face.

"I should have offered to take you to breakfast," he said.

"Are you afraid of my cooking?" I asked.

"No. Looks to me like you handle yourself pretty well in the kitchen."

He leaned back against the counter, one leg crossed over the other, and watched me crack the eggs into the skillet. I turned the eggs over in the pan hoping this wouldn't be one of the times when the yolks broke. The eggs made it from pan to plate without a leak and I proudly set them before Arnie as he sat down at the table. I settled in a chair next to him with my own plate, and we both dove into the food as if we hadn't eaten in weeks. It was pleasant to share breakfast with someone. For those few moments of peace, I almost forgot the reason Arnie was there. Two short raps sounded on the kitchen door.

There was a pause.

I waited, fork poised in midair. Three more quick raps made my face pale.

"Is that a secret knock?" Arnie asked with a grin.

"It's my niece Mary Jane."

Of course she would pick this moment to show up. I hurried to the door before she could have a chance to get her key out and let herself in. I was almost too late.

"Whose car is that in the driveway?" Mary Jane asked. She pointed over her shoulder at Arnie's Lexus.

"Hello, Mary Jane." I said ignoring her question. She brushed past me and stopped short when she reached the kitchen and saw Arnie. He rose and extended his hand.

"Hello, Mary Jane. I don't believe I've had the pleasure of meeting you yet. I'm Arnie." Arnie's hand hung in the air waiting for Mary Jane's response.

Mary Jane's face flushed with red as though someone had thrown beet juice at her. She was flustered. She started to reach for his hand and then held back. Her glance took in the half eaten breakfast. She turned to me.

"What's he doing here?" she demanded.

"Arnie came in late last night to help out with the legal mess I have here," I said matter-of-factly and then asked in the most pleasant voice I could muster, "Would you like some coffee, MJ?"

"What do you mean 'help out'?"

I hated the snide tone of her voice.

"Arnie is my lawyer." I explained.

"Your what?" she sputtered. Her eyes bulged until I feared they were going to pop out of her head and bounce on my kitchen floor.

"My lawyer."

Mary Jane clutched her forehead as though a pain had cut across it. "I don't believe this!"

"Mary Jane, why don't you sit down and have a cup of your aunt's delicious coffee while we talk about this?" Arnie suggested.

Mary Jane looked at him with a fury that burned in her eyes. At any moment, I expected smoke to roll out of her nose and ears. She slid her jacket off and hung it over the back of a chair all the while keeping an eye on Arnie as if he were about to take something more than a second cup of coffee.

"I will have some coffee, Auntie. Thank you."

At least she hadn't lost her manners completely. I got a cup out and poured the morning brew into it. It almost drained the pot. I should have made more but I didn't count on extra company.

Arnie ignored her stares and finished up his eggs while I gave Mary Jane her coffee and refreshed our two cups. Somehow I had the feeling that there was a connection between these two. Maybe it was the way they sized each other up like two boxers who had studied their opponent and were about to begin their sparring. Something unspoken between them hung in the air. I shrugged the idea off. They'd never met. I would have noticed a glint of recognition in Mary Jane's face if that were true. Still she had seemed awfully rattled when she met him.

"What makes you think you can help my aunt with her legal problems?" Mary Jane asked Arnie bluntly.

"If you had truly done your homework, Mary Jane, you would have found that I was one of the top prosecutors in Indianapolis before my wife died. I'm only semi-retired and I spend most of my time taking on cases that others don't want because they won't get paid or they don't bring any prestige. Instead of prosecuting people, I'm now defending them, trying to get them the fairness they deserve in a court of law."

"Hmph! Doesn't that sound noble," Mary Jane sneered.

I inhaled deeply, preparing to defend Arnie, but he touched my arm to quiet me.

"I'm concerned about your Aunt as much as you are," he continued. "She stands to lose a lot here if her case isn't handled properly. I've had the experience that qualifies me to help her and Tommy as well."

Uh oh, shouldn't have mentioned Tommy.

"Tommy? Tommy? You're defending that, that pothead too?" Mary Jane threw her hands in the air in disbelief.

"Everyone deserves the right to be represented in court. It seems to me, Mary Jane, you're passing judgment before you know all the facts," Arnie responded.

"I know he planted all that pot on my Aunt's farm and got her into all this trouble." She stared at him with an icy glare. "Auntie Ann doesn't seem to be able to judge for herself the kind of company she should be keeping."

I felt my hand form a fist. My knuckles turned white. I wasn't going to be able to hold back much longer.

Arnie's foot tapped mine gently, another signal to let him handle it. It was like we were in a courtroom already where you had to let your lawyer do all the talking for you. His patience amazed me. Mine was running short.

"I assume you are referring to me as well as Tommy by that remark." Arnie leaned forward narrowing his eyes a bit. "But, for your aunt's sake, we won't go there right now. Mary Jane, you've been a big help to your aunt and I respect you for that however. . ."

"You, sir, are not going to tell me to leave," Mary Jane spat out.

"No, in fact," he said, "I was going to ask you to stay, for everything. I want you to see that neither Tommy nor I are out to take advantage of your aunt. But you have to give me your word that you will not interfere, and you will not talk about what goes on in our discussions of your aunt's defense. If you say or do one thing to the contrary, you will be closed out. I can't afford to have you jeopardize your aunt's case. Understood?"

While Arnie waited for an answer, he turned to me and asked, "Annie, you have to be in agreement. I can't have her in on our lawyer/client conferences without your permission."

I don't know, Arnie," I said. Mary Jane could be volatile. Arnie seemed able to handle that, but what if she made up her mind to strike back somehow? Her distrust of Arnie and Tommy was evident. While I was deep in thought, Mary Jane spoke up.

"I'll abide by your terms but, if at any time, I see you take advantage of my aunt, I'll be sure to bring it to the attention of the bar association." She stated the threat as if it were a challenge to a duel.

"Fair enough. Annie?" Arnie asked me.

He looked so calm and collected. Did he know what he was getting into with Mary Jane? Obviously not but I bowed to his judgment.

"I guess it's all right with me," I said to Arnie. Mary Jane looked smug. I pointed a finger at her. "Mary Jane, promise me you won't do anything rash."

"When this is all over with, we'll see who was right," Mary Jane said. She sat back with her arms folded across her chest. "I just hope it doesn't cost you everything, Auntie."

"Okay, let's get started then." Arnie reached for a yellow legal pad he had set on the counter. "Your arraignment will take place on Monday. That's when you enter your plea to the charges. I want you to plead not guilty."

"Not guilty? But I am!" I was confused. How could I look a judge in the eye and say I wasn't guilty of having marijuana on my farm when it was right there, plain as day!

"Technically, you are guilty. But there are extenuating circumstances. You did not intentionally let marijuana grow on your property."

"You got that right," Mary Jane mumbled.

Arnie gave her a look to remind her of her vow of non-interference then continued. "You did not intentionally sell the marijuana, it was a by-product, so to speak, of your pickling process. The charges read as though you had criminal intent. Did you?'

"No, of course not," I insisted.

"I didn't think so. That's why you need to plead not guilty. After your plea, the judge will set a court date." Arnie noted something on his legal pad.

"Will that be with a jury and everything?" I had visions of being drilled by a prosecutor while twelve people watched me squirm.

"It could, but it probably won't go that far. The Bugle has already helped your case by painting you as a grandmotherly figure." Arnie grinned. "The prosecutor isn't going to want to be known as the guy who sent Grandma to jail for a little pot. He'll be willing to make some deals if you will change your plea."

"I'm confused," I said. "Am I guilty or not guilty?"

"You've heard about plea bargaining, Annie. I know you've watched enough movies and TV to know a little how it works. You are guilty, but not of what they have charged you with. Therefore, we will work with the prosecutor until the charges are what you can honestly say you are guilty of."

I scratched my head and immediately understood why Sheriff Stewart did it so often. These legal things could be confusing.

"Okay. It may take a bit for it to set in, but I think I'm getting it." I could be a sly old gal when I wanted to and saw opportunity.

Avoiding eye contact with Mary Jane I asked Arnie, "Is that like someone who sits down to someone else's computer and happens to read what's on the screen as opposed to someone who intentionally goes into a program and opens e-mail? It's just a matter of the degree of guilt?"

From the corner of my eye, I could see Mary Jane squirm. Point made and taken.

"Yeah," Arnie said. He looked straight at Mary Jane. "It's something like that."

Mary Jane sat stoically at the end of the table, puffed up like a rooster ready to take on the competition for rule of the chicken coop. There was definitely something going on between the two of them. What was it I had missed?

Arnie and Mary Jane left at the same time. Neither wanted to leave the other behind to talk to me alone. The urge to scratch my head returned, but I scratched the leftover breakfast off of plates instead and loaded the dishwasher.

Chapter 29

Monday morning arrived along with claps of thunder and flashes of lightening. The late spring storm left behind a smell of damp, freshly turned soil. The rain would be good for those who got their crops in early. I assumed I hadn't frightened off too many of my renters. Most of them had already invested in seeds or small plants for their plots of land. I hoped the land would still be mine to share with them once this legal issue was over.

Arnie had promised to pick me up for court by 10 o'clock. I was sitting down to a second cup of coffee, still in my morning walking clothes, when Elma yelled, "Halloo!"

"Come on in, Elma!" I yelled back.

She came into the kitchen with a shopping bag hung on each arm and a garment bag clutched in her hands.

"What in the world are you doing?" I asked. Was she getting ready for another garage sale or had she been bargain hunting in someone else's garage?

"What time do you have to leave for court?" she asked. Elma draped the garment bag across a chair and dropped the bags to the floor.

"Arnie is picking me up at ten," I said.

"Good. Then we have some time." She bent over a bag and pulled out two pairs of shoes. Both pairs were obviously orthopedic, big and cloddy-looking. She held them up. "Which color do you like? The brown or the black?"

"I don't like either." I wrinkled my nose. "What are you doing with those? Surely you're not thinking of adding them to your wardrobe."

"Just humor me," Elma said patiently. "Which color?"

"Depends on what you're wearing with them."

Elma put the shoes down and reached for the garment bag. She unzipped it and pulled out two dresses. One looked like an old mother-of-the-bride dress that had seen much happier days. It was maroon with a billowy lace top that was made for a large-bosomed matron. The skirt had tiny pleats that had lost their crisp crease. Little cloth buttons accented the front of the ensemble making it appear to close in the front when actually it had a zippered back.

The second dress reminded me of the old flower sacks from which women used to sew clothes years before fabric stores provided a variety of materials. It was a shirtwaist dress made of a cotton flowered print that had faded to a powdered blue color.

"Lovely, Elma. What's the occasion?" I asked.

"Your trial." The gleam in her eye told me I was in trouble.

"You're wearing that to my trial?"

"No. You are." She held the flour sack dress up to me as though checking to see if the color complimented my skin tone. "After all, the Bugle called you a 'grandma' and your defense will be that you're an old lady who didn't know any better. I think you need to dress the part."

"I don't think . . ."

"Actually, I'm surprised Arnie didn't suggest it," Elma ran on. "Isn't it part of a lawyer's job to make sure their clients come to court dressed appropriately?"

"I think my Sunday-go-to-meetin' clothes will do just fine." I smiled and nodded my head to affirm my opinion. Elma was right about grooming clients for the courtroom though. Arnie had asked Tommy to remove some of the metal and get a haircut. I was eager to see how short he would have it cut. Elma cleared her throat loudly.

"Well, I expected an argument. Soooo, since you won't dress up like an old grandma, you certainly won't be able to convince the judge that you're innocent. Therefore, you'll probably end up incarcerated. But, not to worry." She reached in another shopping bag. "I have the perfect outfit for those days spent socializing with other felons behind bars."

Elma whipped out a pair of silk pajamas that were striped to look like a prison outfit you see in the old movies.

"Voila!"

"Elma, they're perfect!" I grabbed them from her hands and held them up to me. Laughing, I paced back and forth like a caged animal in front of her. "How many steps do you think there are in a cell?"

"How should I know? You're the one who spent time in the slammer."

"That was only a holding cell. It doesn't count." I glanced at the clock on the oven. "Oh, look at the time!"

"You'd better get dressed," Elma said. She reached into her bag again. "Which shoes do you want to wear?"

"My own, thank you." I picked up my coffee cup and started to rinse my breakfast dishes. Elma took them from my hands, and turned me in the direction of the bedroom.

"Go. Git. I'll take care of these. Arnie will be here soon and you don't want to keep a gentleman waiting, even if he is your lawyer."

"Thanks, friend." I gave her a big hug and skipped off to the bedroom.

I didn't hear Arnie come in. When I got back to the kitchen, dressed and ready for whatever lay ahead, he and Elma were sipping tea at the table.

"You're right, Elma. There's no way I'm going to pass her off as an old granny." He beamed a bright smile in my direction.

"It's okay," I said. I grabbed the striped pajamas and held them up to my neck. "Elma's taken care of me in case my lawyer doesn't get the job done right."

"Ouch. Guess I'd better be at my best." He walked over to me and hugged me close. "We'll make this work. It'll be all right."

As we left Elma was rinsing out teacups and promising to start the prayer chain. This morning was just the arraignment, but a little prayer never hurt. The storms had passed and the sun dried the damp pavement. It was a pleasant ride to the courthouse. We even spotted a rainbow in the distance.

Tommy met us on the steps of the building. I didn't recognize him at first. That boy cleaned up real nice! He was clean-shaven. His hair was cut short, parted, and brushed to one side on top. He had removed all his metal studs but opted to keep one small hoop earring in his right ear. Black slacks and a crisp blue shirt made him look like he was off to work in an office on Casual Friday.

"Hey, Mrs. A." he greeted me.

"Tommy!" I looked him over appraisingly. "You look, you look. . . "

"Conventional?" He blushed.

"Handsome. You look handsome." I smiled proudly at him.

"Mrs. A., I haven't had a chance to tell you how very sorry I am about all this." Tommy's eyes filled. He bit his lower lip.

"It's all right, Tommy. You didn't mean any harm," I assured him.

"But you could lose your whole farm and be fined."

"Hush. We got ourselves a great lawyer." I poked Arnie with my elbow. "And he's not going to let that happen."

"We'd better get inside," our great lawyer said. "We need to be seated when they call your names."

The arraignment took hardly any time at all. I recognized the reporter who'd taken the picture the night I was arrested. He was sitting in the back across from a scowling Mary Jane, his curly head bowed over his notes. Did I still look like a grandma to him?

The prosecutor stood before the judge and enumerated the charges he had against us. The judge asked us to stand and tell him how we pleaded. I almost choked on the words not guilty. I still couldn't understand why I would say that, but I trusted Arnie. Tommy pled not guilty as well. The judge rifled through some papers, looked at his court recorder, and said, "Trial will be set for three weeks from today. Is that agreeable with counsel?"

Both Arnie and the prosecutor answered, "Yes, Your Honor."

The judge talked with Arnie and the prosecutor some more, but my mind kind of wandered off trying to envision what it would be like during a real trial in the courtroom. Suddenly, I realized the judge was asking me something.

"I'm sorry, Your Honor. Would you repeat that?" I asked politely.

"Mrs. Pickels, your lawyer has said you waive a jury. Do you agree?" I looked around.

"Your Honor, I'm sorry. I don't see a jury to wave to," I said innocently.

From the corner of my eye, I saw Arnie's hand fly up to cover his mouth. He looked like he had tried to cover a sneeze but I knew what it meant when those eyes twinkled. What had I done?

The judge cleared his throat a couple of times and then slowly repeated his question. "Mrs. Pickels, I'm asking you if you waive, give up the right to have a jury hear your case and decide it. If you do, then it will be up to me to make the decision when your case comes to trial. Which way would you like to do this?"

He steepled his fingers and peered over them at me intently. Now it came to me. Arnie had talked about this waiver thing. I'd forgotten. He said that since we'd probably plea bargain, it would be fine to just waive the jury. We could always change our minds later.

"Well, Your Honor, I'm sure that by the time our case comes to trial, you ought to be able to handle it," I told him. "There's no sense making people take off work to serve on a jury if we don't really need them."

There were some noises in the courtroom behind us. I didn't turn around but the judge eyed some people like a father who was correcting his children with a look that had an "or else" attached to the end of it.

Tommy agreed to waive a jury as well and the judge banged his hammer down on a block of wood on his desk. "Court adjourned. It's time to break for lunch."

"That's it?" I asked Arnie as he gathered his papers and stuffed them into his briefcase.

"That's it for you for now. I'm sure the prosecutor will be contacting me soon," he said. His briefcase snapped closed with a practiced motion of his hands.

"Tommy, what are you doing for lunch?" I asked.

"I've got some lunchmeat in the fridge at home." He fussed with his collar. "I'll probably make a sandwich."

"Arnie, do you mind if Tommy joins us for lunch?" I asked.

"Sure. He's . . ."

The prosecutor, Jim Spizegud, approached and interrupted Arnie with a knuckle rap on the table.

"Arnie, can you join me for a working lunch? I'd like to talk to you about the Pickels case."

The man talked right past me as though I wasn't there. I thought that was rather rude, but when I started to say something, Arnie took my arm and squeezed it a bit. I took that as a signal to keep quiet.

"Sure, Jim. Your office?" Arnie asked.

"Yeah. Italian subs good for you?"

"Fine."

Spizegud walked away swiftly without an ounce of acknowledgment that Tommy or I stood there. I guess that's the way it worked. Lawyers talked to lawyers and judges, not to the people on trial.

"Tommy," Arnie said. "Can you get Annie home for me? I don't know how long this will take and she didn't bring her car."

Great. Now Arnie was talking past me.

"Not a problem, Arnie," Tommy said. He actually seemed to stand taller with a little responsibility put on his shoulders.

"Thanks." Arnie picked up his briefcase and turned to me. "Annie, I'm sorry to have to bow out of lunch, but this will get the ball rolling sooner and maybe we can all breathe a little easier once we know where the prosecutor's office stands on plea bargaining."

"I know," I said. "But before you go," I fumbled in my purse and pulled out some foil wrapped tablets. "Here. You may need these. Italian subs. You're sure to get heartburn."

Arnie smiled, deposited the antacid tablets in his pocket and left me standing with Tommy in an empty courtroom.

"So, where do two felons fresh out of their arraignment go to eat around here?" I asked Tommy as I searched the back of the courtroom for Mary Jane. She was gone. Off to make her father's life more complicated by helping him plan a wedding. Bless his heart, my brother offered to keep her busy and out of my hair for the trial by asking her to help him plan for the upcoming nuptials. I hoped to be able to be there in a few weeks.

"How about Tinkers? It's on the way home and I can get my employee discount," he said.

"Employee discount? Really? You got the job?"

"Well, not the one I applied for. I'm not tending bar, I'm bussing tables and washing dishes." He shrugged. "It's a job."

"I'm proud of you." I patted him on the back before I walked through the swinging doors of the courtroom he held open for me. "It's an honest day's work and something to get you through until the right job comes along."

We had a light lunch at Tinkers. Tommy took some good-natured harassment from his fellow employees about his new preppy look. I noticed the sweet little gal who was hostess glance in his direction with a soft look in her eyes every so often. I wondered if Tommy knew she was enamored with him. It was obvious to me.

The thrill of the afternoon, however, was the ride in that old jalopy of Tommy's. It needed some new shocks and maybe springs as well. The muffler didn't sound like it was long for this world either. The inside was neat and clean though, and smelled of some sort of polish, almost like a new car would smell. I looked for one of the usual scented fir trees that hang from the rear view mirror in a car like that but Tommy didn't have any. Thank goodness. I hated the smell of fake pine.

After lunch, I asked him to drop me off at Elma's house. I figured she needed an update and had probably held her breath all morning. She had surely turned blue by now. I was right. She shot out of the door as soon as we rumbled to a stop in her driveway.

"They let you two go off together?"

"Yep. Regular Bonnie and Clyde we are." I smiled at Tommy who had opened the car door for me and helped me out. He was back behind the wheel again. I don't think he knew who Bonnie and Clyde were.

"Thanks for the ride!" I shouted after him through his open window.

"Thanks for lunch!" He waved and then turned to see his way clear as he backed out the driveway.

"Whew!" Elma said. "That boy sure cleans up nice!"

"The outside's lookin' more like the inside now." I didn't need orthopedic shoes or matronly dresses to feel like a grandmother. Just being with Tommy was enough. The muffler chortled as he drove away.

"He's a good boy," I said to Elma, "just needs a little fine tuning, like that car of his."

Chapter 30

The computer played its familiar notes as it booted up that afternoon. I watched the little icons materialize. Booting up, icons. I was amazed at how bilingual I could be. Computer language wasn't too hard once you got the hang of it. I still didn't understand though why the plural of computer mouse wasn't computer mice.

My mailbox only had two new messages. One advertised drugs I knew I didn't need, and the other confirmed an order I'd placed online for more pickle jars and lids. Now that Tommy had taught me to surf, I found all sorts of places where I could get supplies cheaper than at the local discount stores or grocery.

No messages brightened my day from Tommy or Arnie, but I hadn't expected there would be. I was with Arnie in court that morning and had lunch with Tommy that afternoon. We talked enough, then but I was curious about the outcome of Arnie's lunch with the prosecutor. Would he call and tell me? Or would he e-mail? Up until now I had never wanted one of those newfangled phones but a text message would be faster than even an email message.

I composed a message to send to Arnie to thank him for all his help, and another one for Tommy to tell him how great his new haircut looked and how proud I was that he'd found a job. When I finished, I got up and meandered through the living room, straightened the afghan on Russell's chair, and then stacked the magazines I'd read and hadn't yet decided to discard. Outside the skies turned gray and darkened. While we needed the rain, I hoped it wouldn't last too long. The dark skies seemed foreboding.

In the kitchen, I lit a candle that resembled a big jar of preserves. It smelled good, like peaches and cream. The glow of the candle added a little cheer to the kitchen without turning the lights on. I started a kettle of water to heat and plopped a blackberry tea bag into my favorite mug. One hand on my hip, I stood at the stove and stared at nothing in particular while I waited for the kettle to whistle. The air seemed heavy, almost too thick to breathe. A knock on the door broke the spell of doom and gloom.

It was Arnie.

I brightened.

"Hi," I said as I let him in. "I was just thinking about you."

He hugged me tightly for a minute. "I've been thinking a lot about you."

The whistle of the teakettle was like an alarm going off. I scurried to the stove and pulled it off the burner. "You look like you could use a cup of tea," I said. Arnie had circles under his eyes. He was worn out.

"I could." He sighed and picked up the box of blackberry teabags and examined it. "You wouldn't have anything a bit more manly around here, would you?"

"Darjeeling work for you?"

He nodded. I fished out another mug and the manly teabags. Arnie sat down heavily in one of the kitchen chairs. He rubbed his eyes with the heels of his hands then ran his fingers up through his hair and down to the back of his neck.

"Tough afternoon?" I asked as I set the two steamy mugs on the table.

"Tough." Arnie reached for his mug and blew across the top before taking a quick sip. "I'm not so certain the prosecutor is going to give us a break. He's dead set on taking this to court on the original charges."

"But I thought," I started but stopped. My empty mouth hung open in disbelief. It wasn't supposed to happen this way.

"Maybe you should have dressed up in those granny clothes Elma brought you." He tried a smile but it faded quickly. He took another sip of tea and winced from the heat of it. "The prosecutor is painting you as a lady who knew exactly what she was doing. He's thinking conspiracy between you and Tommy to grow the marijuana and then eventually hit the streets selling it big time."

"I didn't mean to sell it," I protested.

"I know. And it's ridiculous to think you'd put it in a jar of pickles to market it. But, he seems to think it's a viable idea." Arnie shook his head. "And, if you knew it was marijuana, you certainly wouldn't have given the sheriff two jars of pickles."

We sat quietly for a few moments. In the distance, we could hear the faint rumble of thunder. A storm approached. I watched the wind bend the trees and scatter broken bits of twigs across the yard.

"So?" I asked tentatively. I could read the defeat on Arnie's face.

"So, he's refusing to accept any plea bargain from you or Tommy. He's focused on moving forward with the evidence in hand. His staff assures him that this will be a good example of what happens to people who think they can live outside the law."

Arnie's words got sharper. I sensed his frustration. This was a whole new side of Arnie I'd never seen before. He always seemed so confident, so calm and collected.

"He's done nothing to learn what kind of person you are or to find out anything about Tommy's background, which, by the way, is clean, no arrests, not even a traffic violation."

The floodgates that held back Arnie's frustration burst open. The more he talked, the more animated he became. Anger. Another facet of the man who had become I now realized, an important part of my life.

"Arnie, it's all right." I placed my hand on his arm. "You did your best. Some people are just unreasonable and you can't get them to change."

"It's not all right, Annie." He rose and walked to the window, staring out at the darkened sky. Black clouds blocked the late afternoon sun. The wind picked up even more. "You stand to lose too much if he gets his way. It's just not fair!"

I let him rant a bit longer. His energy seemed to match that of the storm that now pelted rain against the windows and lit the sky with flashes of bright light. I didn't understand some of the legal stuff he spouted, but I could understand his anger, his frustration, his despair.

A loud clap of thunder made us both jump. The lights flickered and went out. The candle I had lit kept us from plunging into an eerie darkness. Arnie retrieved it from the counter and placed it on the table in front of me.

"Arnie," I said when he was again seated next to me at the table, "let's spend some time together in prayer."

"You're right, Annie." He put his head in his hands. "I've not prayed enough. I've never been good at that."

"You've prayed by yourself. I've prayed by myself. We haven't prayed together. The Bible says, 'when two or three are gathered, well, I count two, that meets minimum." Arnie's mouth curled up slightly. It was the best smile I could expect for the moment. We held hands and bowed our heads and prayed back and forth as we thought of things to say to God. We prayed right through the storm that raged outside the window. When we were done, I noticed the sky had started to clear. In the twilight, a ray of sunshine pierced the clouds. I felt closer to Arnie than ever before.

A click and some whirs announced that the electricity was back on. Funny, you don't really notice the hum of a house until it's been gone for a while.

"Hungry?" I asked him.

"Yeah, I am," he replied.

"How about some comfort food?"

"What's that?"

"Well, my mother always used to fix grilled cheese sandwiches and tomato soup when we needed some cheering up."

"Sounds perfect," Arnie said. "Would you mind if I used your upstairs bath to change my clothes and freshen up?"

"Not at all. In fact, you're welcome to spend the night if you don't think a pot-pickling grandmother would ruin your reputation." I cocked my head to one side and fluttered my eyelashes, trying to look the picture of innocence.

"I'm not sure I have a reputation left to ruin." The corner of his mouth tried to smile. He was still a little down on himself. "Thanks for the invitation, but I have reservations at that motel that leaves the light on for you."

"Well, if you prefer their hospitality to mine, you just go right ahead." I tried to act indignant.

"It's not that." Arnie looked down at his shoes. "I don't think we need to chance Mary Jane finding me having breakfast here again."

"Mary Jane? What's she got to do with you staying here?"

"I just don't think you need any more trouble right now."

Arnie went out the door to fetch his clothes which left me to wonder again whether the two of them had something they were keeping from me.

The tomato soup and grilled cheese sandwiches lent just the comfort we needed. I fixed a little coffee and we finished off my last two cinnamon rolls. Tomorrow I would keep busy and make one more batch for the last Wednesday night dinner before Memorial Day. After that, the dinners were suspended for the summer. If I weren't around in the fall, someone else would have to learn to bake the rolls. I'd leave my recipe with Elma if need be.

After he helped me with the dishes, Arnie left. He placed a gentle kiss on my forehead before he got in his car. I touched the spot as I closed the door behind me, cherishing the tenderness he exhibited. God was good to have put Arnie in my life. I felt so much closer to him. Maybe it was the prayer. Prayer draws people together.

I assembled my ingredients and started preparing the dough for my cinnamon rolls. The recipe allowed the dough to rise overnight. It was much more convenient than waiting all day for the yeast to do its work. Just about the time I was elbow deep in dough, I heard someone at the door.

It was late and the rhythm of the knock ruled out Mary Jane. Elma wasn't apt to come traipsing across the street at this hour. For a moment, all of Mary Jane's warnings sprung to mind. "And Auntie, with the traffic picking up on 47, well, anyone could be passing by and decide this looked like a promising place to hit."

I approached the door cautiously. Had I locked it? It was too dark to see more than a black silhouette against a night sky. I glanced at the doorknob. I hadn't locked it! My heart thumped a little faster. I flipped on the outside light and saw it was a man covered in slimy mud, Arnie! I whisked the door open.

"What in the world happened to you?" I exclaimed. I covered my mouth. He looked such a sight. I wanted to laugh.

"Can I come in or would you rather hose me off first?" A shiver ran through him and he struggled to keep his teeth from chattering.

"Come in, of course. Come in." I struggled to contain the giggles that wanted to surface.

"Go ahead. Laugh," Arnie said. "I know you want to."

I held a hand to my mouth again and squeezed out the words, "Oh, I hate to laugh at another's misfortune, but I sure would like to know what happened."

"I ran out of gas."

"I didn't know you could get so, so," I stepped back and examined his appearance. There was mud on the knees of his jeans, his white Nikes were now brown and squishing when he walked, and rivulets of water dripped from his hair making clean tracks in the dirt on his face.

"I ran out of gas. Then I tried to phone a gas station, but every one of them on the list my navigation system gave me was closed." He swiped at the muddy water on his face. "So, I decided I'd hike back here, but when I got out of the car to fetch my briefcase, my foot slipped on the wet grass and I went sliding down into the ravine on the side of the road."

I couldn't hold back any longer. Laughter burst out of me.

"Okay, okay," Arnie said. "Now that that's over with, can you help me out?"

He bent to slip his shoes off. He held each one out the door and poured off the excess water. He did the same with his socks, squeezing the water out of them before draping them across his wet shoes.

I wiped the tears from my eyes and took a deep breath. "How can I help?" I asked.

"You wouldn't have any dry clothes would you? I didn't want to carry my suit all the way through this drizzle." He resembled a wet puppy dog begging for a place to curl up and dry off.

"I'm sorry, I don't have any of Russell's clothes left. I sold them all at Elma's garage sale." I thought for a moment. "I do have a robe you could slip on though while I wash and dry your clothes."

"Guess that'll have to do," Arnie said resignedly.

"Take your clothes off and put them in the washer."

Arnie stepped into the laundry room while I fetched the robe. When I returned, I knocked on the door and Arnie reached a hand out to grab the robe. The door shut again and I heard, "You have to be kidding! I can't wear this!"

"It's all I have. I'm sorry." I suppressed a string of giggles behind my closed fist.

Arnie emerged a moment later dressed in my pink chenille robe. Thank goodness Mary Jane had bought it too big. It wouldn't have gone around him otherwise. As it was, the hem just brushed his knees exposing muscled calves.

"Nice legs," I said nonchalantly. I looked down at his bare feet. "I do have matching pink slippers."

"Don't push it," Arnie said as he clutched the robe to keep it closed.

"Why don't you go up and shower while I get the washer started?" I offered.

"Thanks." He started toward the stairs and turned to wag his finger in the air. "Just assure me there won't be any cameras going off when I come back down."

Fifteen minutes later, Arnie sat at the kitchen table, legs demurely crossed, waiting for me to pour some fresh coffee in a couple of mugs.

"Can I borrow your car to get to the motel when my clothes are dry?" Arnie asked sheepishly. He was not the kind of man who enjoyed being in a helpless condition. "I don't think I'm going to find gas at this hour."

"No, you may not," I said firmly. "You're staying here tonight."

"I thought we settled that before."

"Well, that was before you forgot to fill up your gas tank and decided to take a late night swim in the mud." I took his hand. "Look, you're exhausted, besides, I'm not giving you your clothes back until tomorrow morning. So, that's that."

His shoulders slumped. "You're right. I am tired."

"I think you ought to get to bed. You may have a long walk to the gas station in the morning." Arnie looked at me in disbelief. "Just kidding, we'll take the Escape and a gas can and get you on the road again."

Arnie thanked me for the coffee and washing his clothes. He pulled the pink chenille robe tightly about him and lumbered off to bed. I stuck his clothes in the dryer, and set the rest of my dough in the refrigerator for the morning.

It had been a very long day. I yawned and stretched. My morning could start a little later tomorrow. I set the alarm clock for seven and slipped between the covers on my bed and listened to the quiet settle over the house. Tonight that quiet was a little different. Tonight I shared it with someone else. It was a nice feeling.

Chapter 31

There was a little bounce to my step in the morning as I circumambulated my daily route. "Circumambulated" was a new word for me. I was trying it out in my head. It had a nice sound, like ambidextrous, but it wasn't easy to say aloud.

I waved to a few kids as they waited for their school bus and smiled at a mother who stood with her youngster and fussed with last minute dress details. It was a great morning. The spring air was on the cusp of summer's warmth. Memorial Day was Monday. The anticipation of a long holiday weekend created a stir of excitement among the school kids this morning. Will I be enjoying these mornings out much longer?

I would not let the events of yesterday weigh me down. Instead, I remembered Arnie and his unexpected appearance on my doorstep late last night. The anticipation of making pancakes for him for breakfast when I got back to the house buoyed my spirits. I looked forward to a great day. Then I saw Mary Jane's car parked in the driveway.

I didn't need to go into the house to know there was a heated argument inside. I could hear it from outside through the screen door.

"You can't tell me what to do!" Mary Jane shouted. "I've been taking care of her long before you came along. She's too trusting, too vulnerable to snakes like you!"

"Are you taking care of your aunt or trying to control her?" Arnie shouted back. "You're not happy unless she's doing everything you tell her to do."

"She lives life too dangerously. She's going to, to hurt herself, or be hurt by someone." Mary Jane sputtered. "She's already been hurt, hurt by that pot head of a kid she lets hang around here. In the end, I'll probably have to take her in to live with me when she loses all she has to the courts and you!"

"She's not losing anything to me," Arnie shot back. "I'm not charging her for my services. She's my friend."

"She's your mark!" Mary Jane spat. "You spotted her on that ship and decided you could clean her out. Why else would you be in there on her computer checking into her private records?"

"I was checking my e-mail, if you must know. And how would you know where her private records are? Did you check into that when you printed out her private correspondence from her e-mail box?"

My hand flew to my mouth.

"There was no other way to know what was going on," Mary Jane hissed.

So Mary Jane admitted she printed out Arnie's e-mail message. My suspicions were confirmed.

"How else was I going to stop you? I needed to know what was going on and how to contact you to tell you to stay away."

"Well, your threatening e-mails are automatically deleted from my mailbox," Arnie said. "They are doing you no earthly good except to perpetuate your need to feel in control."

I put my hand on the screen door to open it. This didn't need to go on any longer. It would only get uglier.

"I warn you, I promise you, if you do one thing to hurt my aunt, I'll have the police on you faster than flies on . . . "

"Who's going to hurt whom?" I burst in. "What's going on here?"

Mary Jane was livid, her face contorted and beet red. Arnie's color looked better but his forehead was furrowed so deep I thought his eyebrows might get lost in the creases. Both of them clammed up. I looked from one to the other and back again. Finally, Arnie spoke up.

"Mary Jane and I were having a discussion about computers and if they were secure enough to keep your private financial records on them."

Mary Jane shot him a look that would have made the Wicked Witch of the East melt without the water.

"Well, I wouldn't trust myself to keep financial records there," I said. "I'm not skilled enough to know how to do all that fancy bill paying and banking online. I'd be afraid to wipe everything out with one click on the wrong icon." There, at least Mary Jane can't think Arnie was using my computer to find out about my money.

"Well, Auntie, mark my words,"

I hated it when she said that.

"this sleazy character is going to get you into trouble just like Tommy did. He may not have all the piercings and tattoos, but he's just as much trouble. Do you really believe he ran out of gas last night?"

I looked at Arnie. He must have told her why he was here.

"Yes," I said firmly. No one would have gone through all that muck last night just to ingratiate himself to me. "And as soon as I make him some breakfast, we're going to go get the gas he needs."

Mary Jane grabbed her purse and slung the strap over her shoulder. "I just can't get through to you anymore."

She brushed past me to leave. The door slammed behind her. A few moments later, we heard loose gravel kick up as she zipped out onto Route 47.

"I'm sorry," Arnie and I said at the same time.

313

"No, really," Arnie insisted. "I shouldn't have lost my temper with her."

"She's going through a difficult time right now. Not that that's an excuse for her behavior." I reached in the refrigerator and pulled out my sourdough starter to mix in the pancakes. I began to add ingredients and beat it with a whisk. "Her father is getting married and MJ is not looking forward to the prospect of having a stepmother at her age."

"Well, she shouldn't be taking it out on you." Arnie sounded like his anger still simmered.

"I know. But I'm a tough old gal. If it saves my brother some heartache, what's the hurt?" I scooped a measure of pancake batter and poured it onto the heated griddle. "Plain or chocolate chip?"

"What?"

"Your pancakes, plain or do you want a few chocolate chips in them?"

"What is it you women say? Never turn down chocolate when you're in a mood?"

I whacked him with my dishtowel.

Either Arnie was not a man to brood over things or the chocolate in the pancakes did its job. Our breakfast was pleasant. We cleaned up the dishes together and set about getting Arnie the gas he needed to get him on the road again. I was sad to see him go. I enjoyed the presence of someone else in the house, more specifically Arnie's presence.

Chasing after Arnie's gas took all morning. When I got back, I started right in on my baking. I hoped my cinnamon rolls would come out all right. The dough sat neglected until noon. I got my production line set up, spreading butter and sprinkling cinnamon mixture, then rolling up the dough to slice into individual rolls. Even with the busyness of baking, I couldn't help but think of Mary Jane and the argument I'd overheard. I was going to have to do something with her. I just didn't know what.

The kitchen filled with the delicious scent of baked yeast dough and cinnamon. I hummed and prayed as I worked. In the midst of all this turmoil with the court and with Mary Jane, I felt at peace. Prayer had a way of doing that, giving you peace and the confidence that someone more capable than you was in control.

While I waited for the last batch of rolls to bake, I found the orange-plastic-bagged newspaper I'd carried in this morning and not looked at yet. I discarded the bag with disgust and unrolled the Bugle to expose the headlines.

GRANDMA PLEADS NOT GUILTY TO POT CHARGES
Waves right to trial by jury.

I was front-page news again. Why couldn't it have been for a spectacular pickle recipe or business success or anything but a felony? I read on.

Annie Pickels, a sixty-five year old pickle entrepreneur, pled not guilty to charges that she grew marijuana on her property and sold it in her pickle jars. Her alleged accomplice, Thomas Madison, 25, also entered a plea of not guilty. Both waived the right to a trial by jury. As Ms. Pickels put it, "I'm sure that by the time our case comes to trial, you [Judge Oswald] ought to be able to handle it. There's no sense making people take off work to serve on a jury if we don't really need them.

Thank goodness he didn't quote me about waving to the jury. The reporter went on to give more information about the years I'd been an upstanding member of the community and my church affiliation and volunteer activities. He had done some research into Tommy's background as well.

Though he's young enough to be her grandson, Madison is not related to Pickels. His mother, Agnes Madison, died in an auto accident in 2001. She was a realtor in the Columbus area. His father, Benjamin Madison, is serving time in Lucasville for grand theft auto. He was caught running a chop shop out of his auto mechanics garage.

Tommy's father is doing time? The article continued with information about Tommy's clean record, no arrests, and about the car accident that killed his mother. It also mentioned his injuries in the accident and the fact that he was using the marijuana for relief from the chronic pain in his back. I could see people looking at that statement and his age and saying, "Yeah, right." Would the judge be skeptical, too? But where had the reporter gotten all his information. Arnie had warned us about talking about the case to anyone.

I paged through the rest of the paper more out of habit than interest. I pinched the corner of the editorial page and was just about to turn it when the bold print on the editor's column caught my eye.

PROSECUTOR'S ELECTION HINGING ON GRANDMA'S CONVICTION?

The editor of the Bugle seemed to think that in his quest to be hard-nosed with the drug issue, the prosecutor, Jim Spizegud, was "crucifying a naïve and harmless grandmotherly woman." He warned the prosecutor's office that, while the fight against drug traffickers and users was a noble cause, this was not the case that would elevate his position and assure his re-election.

If Spizegud continues his hard-nosed attitude toward this woman, he's not the same man this paper endorsed for prosecutor in the last election.

Whew! Was this a threat by the editor to withdraw support of the prosecutor? The editorial supported me as the front-page article had done. But, would it do any good? I was guilty no matter how you looked at it. The marijuana was there, growing out of the ground on land I owned. I remembered how pretty I thought it looked in those pickle jars as well. Whether I'd intended to sell it or not, I had.

The timer on the oven signaled me to attend to the last batch of rolls. I pulled them out the same time Elma hallooed me as she came in the door.

"Where've you been, Elma?" I asked over my shoulder as I closed the oven door. "I thought the smell of cinnamon rolls would have brought you over sooner. This is the last batch."

"The wind isn't blowing the right direction or I'd have been here earlier." She closed her eyes and inhaled loudly. "I'm not too late though. Those are fresh, aren't they? Oh, how Warren loved your fresh baked cinnamon rolls."

I looked closely at her to be sure she hadn't been crying. Once in a while she would have a weepy day but they didn't happen that often. Elma wasn't one to wallow in self-pity or depression too long.

"Yup, Warren could certainly down his share of cinnamon rolls. I'm ready for some coffee. Join me?" I reached for some coffee mugs.

"You bet!"

Elma poured our coffees and took them to the table while I pulled two rolls apart from the rest and set the warm yeasty concoctions on plates. I joined her at the table and watched as she eagerly forked a piece of roll and placed it in her mouth. Her eyes rolled to the back of her head as she savored the buttery sweet taste of sugar and cinnamon against her taste buds.

"Mmm. You are the queen of cinnamon rolls. Hands down."

"Thanks. I'll add that to my list of titles, Mud Monster, Snow Angel, Tiller Tamer, Pot Pickler."

"Come on now. Don't be so hard on yourself. The Bugle says you didn't do it. Don't you believe everything you read?" She pierced her lips, raised her eyebrows and crossed her eyes, made me wish I had a camera.

"Say, did I see Arnie here today?" she asked as her face returned to normal.

"You did. As a matter of fact, he stayed the night again." I laughed as I pictured him in my pink chenille robe. I shared it all with Elma including the argument I overheard between Arnie and Mary Jane.

"What are you going to do?" Elma asked. "You can't let Mary Jane spoil your relationship with Arnie."

"I don't know that she will. Arnie seemed to be holding his own when I came in. If he can stand up to MJ, it shows he's not afraid to be my friend." I picked up my cup and looked wickedly at her over the brim. "You haven't scared him off yet either."

"Me? I'm just a pussycat compared to Mary Jane. Besides, I'm not about scaring him off. I'm about making sure he makes an honest woman out of you."

I knew what she was getting at but I asked, "You mean get me off the hook with the law?"

"You know what I mean." She started humming a wedding march.

"Elma! That will scare him off faster than Mary Jane!"

"Oh, I'm not so sure, I'm not so sure." She hummed her way over to the sink with her dishes and rinsed them. "Catchy little tune, isn't it?" She laughed and hummed her way out the door.

Is that where I was headed, down the aisle? Where did I want to go? Certainly not to prison. Who would want to marry a jailbird?

Chapter 32

The trial date loomed before me casting a shadow over everything I did. As it drew closer, I weighed the value of tending to my pickle plants against packing up boxes of my belongings. I had visions of moving everything into storage while I served time and then found a place to live when I was paroled. I chose optimism over pessimism and pulled weeds in the pickle patch. Down on my knees in the dirt, I alternated between praying and thinking about all that had happened since the day the sheriff cleaned out Tommy's marijuana plants.

Tommy cut my grass regularly. He now kept his hair trimmed and, except for two earrings, the rest of his metal had not reappeared. The most encouraging difference in Tommy however was his regular attendance at our church services. He came on Sunday as well as Wednesday night. I often saw him with Kirk, the two of them with their heads together deep in conversation. I was glad Tommy and he had common interests in computers. Tommy needed a friend his own age especially now.

I looked up from my pickle plants to see a lone figure picking his way through the rows of my garden. It was the Bugle reporter.

His curly hair made him easy to recognize. I stood and brushed the dirt from my hands on my bib overalls.

"Can I help you?" I asked.

"Hello, Mrs. Pickels," he greeted me cheerily. "I hate to bother you, but I was looking for some more information to follow up on the story we did on your brush with the law."

"What kind of information?" I asked warily. My guard went up. Arnie had warned us about talking to the press.

"I'd like to do a feature story about you and your pickle business. Just a little about how you got started, what you do, and what your plans are for the future." He picked up a foot and looked at the moist soil clinging to it. It was obvious he hadn't expected to walk through a field of pickles today.

He looked harmless enough and he had written stories that were supportive. All he wanted to talk about was the pickle business, not the trial. I felt I owed him something.

"Okay, but let's go up to the house where we can talk, Mr, Mr, You know, I don't recall you telling me your name."

"It's Roger, Roger Maxwell. Just Roger is fine." He fell into step beside me as he picked his way carefully among the plants.

"Well, Just Roger, would you like some coffee and a cinnamon roll?"

He smiled at my attempt at humor. "I'd love some. Thanks."

We reached the drive and stomped to get some of the dirt off our footwear. When we went into the house, I stopped to slip out of my garden shoes, but Just Roger walked on into the kitchen. He was certainly not as well-mannered as Tommy or he would have taken off his shoes. We sat down to coffee and rolls and I answered his questions on pickling and how I'd started my business. Then he began to ask questions about my opinion of marijuana use.

"I don't see how my opinion of marijuana has anything to do with pickling, Roger." I wasn't as dumb as he may have thought.

He could stir up lots of controversy with an answer to his opinion question and I wasn't going to take a chance on being misquoted.

"I do have an opinion to share with you however, about the Bugle's paper delivery. Your circulation department made me put up a box for its delivery but your delivery person rolls it up in a plastic bag and throws it in the middle of my driveway." I waited for him to respond.

"I'm sorry for the inconvenience," Roger said as he rose. "I'll make a note of that." He never did. The interview was over.

When Just Roger's car was back on 47 and headed for wherever, I returned to my work in the pickle patch. Would Arnie be happy that I gave an interview to Just Roger? I hadn't seen much of Arnie in the three weeks following my arraignment in court. He kept me informed of his non-progress through his e-mails. He still pestered the prosecutor about the plea bargain. The prosecutor still stood on his convictions and spouted his views on justice being blind, "giving fair and equal administration of the law, without corruption, avarice, prejudice, or favor." In short, he wanted to throw the book at Tommy and me. I assumed it was one of those heavy law books. The question was: would we be able to duck?

I missed Arnie, just as my friend. If I didn't see Elma for three weeks, I'd miss her too. In fact, I'd probably call her. I took a break from the garden and went into the house. To call or not to call? I circled the phone once or twice. If it were any other friend, I would call without hesitation. I picked up the phone and dialed his number. There was no reason I couldn't call and see how he was, let him know I thought about him, appreciated his help. The phone rang twice.

"Hello," a female voice answered.

"Oh! I'm sorry, I must have dialed wrong," I said, embarrassed at my mistake. I hung up and dialed again. This time, I punched the numbers slowly to be sure they were correct. The same female voice answered.

"I'm sorry. I think I must have the wrong number. Is this 765-555-2215?"

"Yes," she replied.

I paused. Who was this woman? Arnie's daughter?

"Is this Pamela?" I asked.

"No," she said. I waited for her to say her name. Nothing.

"Is Arnie there?"

"No, Arnie's not here. You wanna leave a message?"

Her voice wasn't the least bit professional, like a secretary or a receptionist. Besides, this was Arnie's home phone number. He didn't have an outside office or a business phone other than his cell phone. Who was this woman?

"Yes, no, I don't know," I answered her. Did I want to leave a message with a stranger? "I, I, um, guess I'll call back later."

"Kin I tell him who called?" Her voice was salted with curiosity.

"No. That's fine, I'll just try back later. Thanks." I dropped the phone in its place like it was a hot potato and backed away from it. Who was that woman?

All afternoon, I tried in vain to put the phone call out of my head. *Arnie's not here* played in my head like a tape recording with no stop and eject button to push. The more I heard it, the more it sounded like she was very familiar with Arnie. I tried folding laundry. It didn't help. I sat down to read a book. Reading didn't help. Sweeping off the back steps worked off the frustration but not the sound of her voice.

The only sure way I knew to get my mind occupied was to do some pickling. I had my first yield of cucumbers all picked and stored in the cool basement. I was still trying to choose between pickling them and selling them at the roadside. If they carted me off to the hoosegow after Friday's trial, I planned to have Elma sell the pickles at another garage sale.

Scissors in hand, I went out to the south side of the house where the dill plants grew. They were a nice lacey background to the petunias and snapdragons I usually planted in June. I hadn't done that yet. The uncertainty in my life interfered with my normal planting schedule. I cut enough dill to get a couple dozen jars of pickles done and carried the pungent bundle into the house.

I gathered some wide-mouth quart canning jars from the basement and loaded them into the dishwasher to sterilize the jars and lids. Meanwhile, I organized my kitchen counter with my large agate kettle, jar lifter, vinegar, canning salt, the fresh dill, and my pickling spices minus the funny looking marjoram. I picked through the cucumbers and set aside those that were too small or too large to use later for relish or bread and butter pickles. I felt ambitious.

Once in a while, I'd find a cucumber that was too smooth. Cucumbers right for pickling have to have bumps, warts. You can't trust them to have the right texture or flavor for pickling if they don't. It's kind of like people. If they are too smooth, too perfect, you can't trust them. Could I trust Arnie? Is Mary Jane right? Is he too smooth? Who was that woman? I shook my head to clear it. Too much clutter there.

Through the open window, I heard the lawnmower start up. Tommy was here to cut the grass. Maybe he was getting things done in preparation like I was, just in case. I'd give him about a half hour and call him in for some cinnamon rolls and coffee. It could be the last chance we would have to talk for a while, maybe a long while.

I washed up the chosen cucumbers, sliced off the blossom ends, and cut them lengthwise into wedges. There were enough to fill about a dozen jars. I considered that sufficient diversion for one afternoon. I put the extras and the rejects back in their cool storage area in the basement, and then made a pot of coffee.

Just as Tommy finished up I waved to him from the kitchen door. He strolled over to me. The laces of his boots dangled dangerously between his feet as usual, a broad grin spread across his face.

"Hey, Mrs. A." He wiped his hands on an old rag. "How are you doing?"

"I'm fine, Tommy," I answered. "I wondered if you'd like a cinnamon roll and coffee before you go?"

"Sure thing, Mrs. A. You bet! Just let me put the mower away and I'll be right in."

He sauntered back to the John Deere and drove it into the old barn where I kept it. I noticed he walked a bit straighter than usual. It made him look taller. As he always did, Tommy removed his boots before he came into the kitchen.

"You look awful busy, Mrs. A.," He said as he surveyed my pickle production line.

"Just doing a little pickling," I said nonchalantly.

"You're not using any of my marjoram, are you?" He gave me a wicked wink.

"I decided to stick to my original recipe, thank you." I gave him a mock scowl as I put two cinnamon rolls in the microwave and set the timer. "How's that back of yours been lately? Still giving you trouble?"

I poured two cups of coffee and set Tommy's cup in front of him. The microwave binged and I pulled out two nicely warmed rolls with icing glazing the tops.

"It's a funny thing, Mrs. A. I don't seem to have near so much trouble any more. I haven't missed my Mary Jane at all. Once in a while I have to take a pain pill, but they seem to get me through all right." He took a bite of his cinnamon roll and leaned over the plate as the sweet warm icing oozed over the other end of the roll.

"That's great news." I studied him. Something was different besides his haircut and the absence of metal studs. His face was aglow with the look of a little boy who had a secret to tell. He finished chewing and carefully tasted the hot coffee.

"Kirk says it's the power of prayer."

My grand-maternal antennas were sensing something important going on here.

"Kirk's right. Lots of people have been praying for you, you know." I blew across my coffee while I waited for him to continue.

"I know. I've been prayin' too." His face reddened slightly and he studied his coffee cup.

"That's good, Tommy," I said.

"We have plenty to pray about, haven't we Mrs. A.?" He glanced shyly at me then finished off the last bite of his cinnamon roll.

"Yes, we do." I could feel him building up to tell me something. He stared into his coffee cup and chewed on his cheek a bit.

"Mrs. A, Kirk helped me pray about Jesus, too." His face flushed. "I, I asked Jesus to be my Savior."

Tears flooded to my eyes. I blinked them back. I felt such a surge of love for this boy. "Tommy, I can't tell you how proud I am of you for making such an important decision in your life." I felt around in my pocket for a tissue.

"Yeah?" His eyes looked a bit teary. He nodded his head. "I'm proud of me too."

Tommy explained that the Wednesday night class Kirk coaxed him to attend had prayed for the pain in his back. One of the women in the group worked in a clinic that specialized in chronic pain and she talked one of the doctors into taking Tommy as a patient on a pay-as-you-can basis. His first appointment was next week.

"I almost think I don't need to go. My back is so much better." He straightened in his chair and moved side to side with ease.

"Go. See the doctor," I said. "God doesn't put you in the path of others for no reason."

"I know that now. If I hadn't met you, I wouldn't have started going to church and I wouldn't have met Kirk." He swallowed hard, trying to stem the wave of emotion that threatened to surface. He looked at me, eyes wet with tears. "Kirk says Jesus forgives me. Will you forgive me, too?"

I got up and put my arms around him in a gentle hug. "Of course, Tommy, of course."

Somewhat embarrassed by the sentimentality, Tommy rose and wandered over to my pile of pickles.

"Hey, I'm sorry. I've kept you from all your work." He picked up the jar lifter and played with it, opening and closing it to see how it worked. "Anything I can help you with?"

"Sure. An extra set of hands and some good company will make this project go a lot quicker."

I took the jar lifter from him and put it back on the counter. Men fidget with gadgets too much.

We passed the rest of the afternoon putting pickles into hot jars, adding the vinegar and spice mixture, and sealing the jars. I demonstrated for Tommy the proper use of the jar lifter as we took the finished products from the boiling water in the kettle and set them on a dry kitchen towel to cool. He was an apt student and seemed to enjoy the learning experience.

"Wow," Tommy remarked. "That's a lot of work for just twelve jars of pickles. How many jars do you usually sell?"

"Oh, I don't know, about, 300 a year, I guess. I'd have to go look at my sales records."

"What do you charge per jar?" He asked.

"Two-fifty." I was a little embarrassed to tell him I charged so much.

"Two-fifty? For homemade gourmet pickles? Mrs. A, you got to be kidding!"

"That's too much?"

"That's not enough." Tommy grabbed a pen and an old receipt from his pocket. "Let's see we've just spent two hours putting these in jars and processing them. You probably spent close to another hour just preparing them. At $2.50 a jar,"

He did some calculations, sat back and shook his head slowly.

"What's wrong?" I asked, my eyebrows knit together.

"Today you only made $10 an hour, and that's considering that I worked for free. If you subtract from that all your costs, vinegar, spices, jars, cucumbers, dill, you can't be making more than two dollars an hour, if that much." He tossed his pen on the counter. "You could make more than that waiting on tables at Tinkers."

I sat stunned. It wasn't so much the news of how little I was profiting but how quickly Tommy had put it all together. He seemed to have a head for business.

"I know you grow your own pickles and dill, but you still have to pay for seed, fertilizer, water when it doesn't rain, and then you spend time taking care of the field. We didn't even figure all of that in. Then there's delivery, bookkeeping."

Tommy kept ticking things off that I had never considered. I was just happy to take everyone's two dollars and fifty cents and put it into my travel fund.

"Bottom line, Mrs. A," Tommy said as he tucked his pen and paper into a pocket, "You need to charge more."

I stood in awe at the business wizard before me. Where had he been hiding all this time?

Chapter 33

GRANDMA'S POT TRIAL BEGINS TODAY
Prosecutor perseveres in prosecution of pot pickler

If people only get fifteen minutes of fame by now, I should have used all my allotted time. Maybe the saying only applies to the famous, not the infamous. The article on the front page of the Bugle mostly repeated the previous news in reference to my pot-pickling escapade. The reporter had done a little more homework though. He mentioned that Tommy and I would be tried together, and that the prosecution would call the sheriff and his deputy, and an old girlfriend of Tommy's who agreed to testify that she saw him smoking marijuana. Tommy told Arnie that the girl was actually the one who had given him his first marijuana joint and encouraged him to try it to relieve his back pain. When it came to who supplied the illegal substance, it was his word against hers.

The article quoted the prosecutor as saying that he seized only the garden plot where the marijuana plants grew and left my home alone in deference to my age. He was "allowing Ms. Pickels to stay in the house until the court made a decision of her guilt."

Arnie assured me the trial would last more than one day, but I arranged with Elma to keep a key so that she could have my things put into storage in case I didn't come back. It would be difficult to leave the house on the day the verdict would be given, not knowing if I'd return.

Arnie called to say he had a few last minute things to do. I wondered if they included the woman on the phone. Tommy picked me up in his old heap. He looked sharp dressed in his trial clothes. He smelled good too. On the way, we talked about pickles, and the cost of supplies, and how I'd gotten started pickling. He'd seen the feature story the curly-haired reporter wrote along with the photograph of me on my knees in the garden in my dirty bib overalls and plaid shirt. Just Roger must have snapped it before I saw him approach me in the field.

Tommy reviewed my need to raise prices to increase my profit margin. "If you raise your prices, you'll have more to spend on that trip to London you talk about. You'll have more pocket money and be able to afford a nicer hotel."

I smiled at his concern.

Arnie met us on the steps of the courthouse. He looked different to me. Perhaps I saw him in a different light now since I'd talked to the woman in his house. We moved off to one side and took a minute to whisper a prayer for what lay ahead. As we raised our heads and started toward the door, a microphone was thrust in front of us and a bright light illuminated our faces.

"Ms. Pickels, how do you feel about the way the prosecutor is pursuing this case against you? Do you think he's being fair or just trying to make a name for himself with the election coming up?"

"I, I," My mouth wouldn't form words. I couldn't think of what to say. The reporter had startled any logical communication out of me. The Bugle was one thing. Now we had to deal with the local television station. My world seemed much more complicated. When I didn't answer quickly enough, the microphone pointed back to the reporter as he asked more questions.

"Mr. Madison, do you have any comment on your role in this? Do you think that marijuana should be legalized for medicinal use?" The microphone pointed at Tommy who immediately lost all color in his face.

Arnie recovered from his surprise and stepped in. "Excuse me, but my clients have no comment at this time. If you don't mind, we need to be in the courtroom. Thank you for your interest."

Arnie took my elbow and gently pushed me ahead of him making sure that Tommy got in step as well. We could hear the reporter as he turned to his cameraman and summarized his encounter with us. "Be sure to tune in at noon. We'll have an update on the pot-pickling trial. This is Tom Wilcox reporting for ActionNews 14."

Those fifteen minutes of fame were expanding.

I waited for a free moment when I could mention yesterday's phone call to Arnie. I hoped he would explain the other woman. It was needling me. What was she doing there? Who was she?

Arnie marched us directly into the courtroom and up to the table where we were to sit. The room was almost filled to capacity. As we walked to our seats in front of the wooden railing, I recognized faces from my church and the community, friendly faces, faces that smiled with encouragement. When I sat down, I felt a hand clasp my shoulder. I turned to see Elma seated directly behind me. She clucked like a chicken and shook her head.

"Honey, where are those clothes I got you. You don't look anything like the grandma they're talking about in the paper this morning."

Arnie snapped his head around at the mention of the newspaper.

"There's more in the Bugle today?" he asked.

Elma passed the paper to Arnie who scanned the article intently.

Elma smiled. "She's still being called a grandma, she just doesn't dress the part."

"Elma, I wouldn't wear those clothes to a Halloween party," I said.

"Well, now you've gone and hurt my feelings. But that's okay. I got you something else, I thought you'd enjoy."

She handed me a shopping bag. I pushed aside the tissue paper to look at what Elma had done now. A fluffy purple feather popped up. Startled, I jumped back. When I stuck my nose down to look again, I saw that the feather was attached to a bright red straw hat.

"Gotcha," Elma said. Before I could answer her, the door to the judge's chambers opened.

"All rise," bellowed the bailiff. My heart beat a little faster. I hoped my morning walks had strengthened my heart for this.

Judge Oswald took his seat and banged his gavel on the block of wood on a desk that sat higher than anything else in the room. It all happened in one swooping motion, showing years of practiced habit. He scooted his chair in and peered over his reading glasses at us.

"Gentlemen, I have before me the lists of witnesses to be called and your various motions." Judge Oswald shuffled papers, scanned a few, and patted them into a neat pile on the desk before him. He folded his hands on top of the papers and looked from one lawyer to the other. When they didn't respond, he cleared his throat. I thought he was about to say something when he took a deep breath, held it, then let it out slowly. I could feel my foot begin to tap involuntarily. My anxiety level rose. Everyone in the courtroom waited for the word from the bench to begin.

"Mr. Johnston." At the mention of his name by the judge, Arnie stood abruptly. "I assume you have discussed a plea bargain with Mr. Spizegud?"

"We talked, Your Honor. Mr. Spizegud made no offer."

"Mr. Spizegud?" The prosecutor jumped to his feet as well.

"Your Honor, this is a cut and dried case. Both defendants have been caught red-handed. There's no room for bargaining," he stated.

A long loud gush of air escaped the judges lips making them vibrate as if he were giving the lawyers the raspberries. He tapped his fingers and looked around the top of his desk a moment for something he never found. Finally, his gaze returned to the two lawyers who still stood before him waiting for a response.

"I'll see counsel in my chambers before we begin."

It was an order, not a request. Judge Oswald rose and strode to the door by which he had entered. Arnie and the prosecutor scrambled to grab their legal pads and follow him. Before Arnie left, he bent toward Tommy and me with a puzzled look.

"I'm not sure what's going on, but it may not be all bad. Take a look at today's editorial." He put the Bugle in front of me, and then left to follow Jim Spizegud into Judge Oswald's chambers.

Tommy and I leaned over the editorial page and read what Arnie had pointed out.

Is there no mercy in justice any longer? Apparently not in the case of Jim Spizegud, prosecutor for the county, who is about to crucify an otherwise upstanding member of our community for her one minor mistake: not knowing the difference between marjoram and marijuana. How many of us, I wonder, would recognize the illegal substance if we'd never used it?

But Mr. Spizegud will not stop there. He intends to put away a young man with an otherwise clean record for as long as he can. Whatever happened to rehabilitation? Second chances? Three strikes before you're out?

The editor went on to remind people that Spizegud was up for reelection and speculated how well he would do at the polls if he pursued his present course in this case. He certainly did not paint a pretty picture of Mr. Spizegud, and I pondered the advisability of the editor making an enemy of the prosecutor's office.

The last paragraph of the editorial held out hope in the form of the judge whose record of fairness, reported the editor, was well-recognized in the community.

Judge Oswald has always been a man of foresight and compassion while still maintaining a balance of justice in his courtroom. It is our hope that his record will not be smudged by the persistent intentions of an overzealous prosecutor.

"What do you think?" I asked Tommy.

"I don't know. I don't think a judge is going to be swayed by public opinion. He has to follow the law," Tommy replied.

"What's up?" Elma hissed at us.

I turned and leaned toward her. "Don't know. Arnie wasn't sure either, but he pointed out the editorial in the paper."

The longer we waited, the louder the stir in the courtroom became. Finally the men returned and the courtroom hushed, without the judge hammering on his wooden block. The judge did not even sit down. He just leaned over his desk, surveyed the courtroom and said, "This court will be in recess until tomorrow morning at 9 a.m. when I expect you gentlemen will have some good news to tell me."

With a quick rap on the block with his hammer, the judge turned and left.

Tommy and I turned eagerly to Arnie who scooted his chair out of the way of Elma who hung over the wooden rail that separated us from the onlookers in court. Her position appeared precarious and I checked to see that her feet were still planted on the floor. Arnie cleared his throat.

"The judge told us we have to come to some kind of plea agreement," Arnie explained. "He doesn't want to try this case. Said it was a waste of time and money. I think he's really upset with Spizegud."

"So what do we do?" I asked.

"You all get to go home. I get to eat more Italian subs with our friendly prosecutor over there. I'll let you know what happens as soon as I can." Arnie picked up his papers and stuffed them in his briefcase. "Tommy, can you stay at Annie's this afternoon so I can meet with the two of you later?"

"Sure, Arnie. I got the whole day off for the trial." The little boy inside Tommy beamed through in his smile.

"Great." He grabbed his briefcase and left.

Even with Tommy and Elma at my side, I felt abandoned. I might have even welcomed a little of Mary Jane's banter as a distraction but she was off picking out a daughter-of-the-groom dress and wasn't due to check in with me until the afternoon.

A few people from church came up and wished us well. Bill Barker from Tinkers Tavern reminded me that he needed some more pickles, with or without my special ingredient. He winked at me and slapped Tommy on the back. The courtroom was pretty empty by the time we turned to leave.

"How about lunch?" Elma suggested. "My tummy's starting to rumble."

"I don't know." I started to say. I felt off kilter. The question about the woman who answered Arnie's phone still niggled in my brain and that, added to the unexpected turn of events in the trial, made my head spin. Or maybe I was hungry too.

"I'm a little hungry," Tommy said as he put a hand to his midriff. "What do you have in mind, Mrs. Thompson?"

"There's a little place around the corner." Elma jerked her head in the direction of the street. "It has a bit of a foreign flare. Caribbean, actually."

"Oh yeah?" Tommy's face lit up with expectation. "A little reminder of sand and surf and palm trees sounds like fun. What do they have to eat?"

"I hear they have a special dish." Elma paused effectively. "Jailhouse Jerk Chicken."

Poor Tommy! He'd been had by one of the best. The only one who could deliver a better one-liner was Warren. Elma had learned from the master.

The restaurant turned out to be a Denny's. There were no palm trees, sand, or Jerk Chicken, jailed or otherwise. I ended up having a second breakfast. I wasn't in the mood for anything too heavy and the French toast special looked too good to pass up. Elma had a BLT with coleslaw and French fries. There was a dill pickle accompanying the sandwich. Elma picked it up and started to bend it back and forth like a rubber chicken.

"Look at this pickle. It's in bad shape. Nothing like yours, Annie," Elma observed.

"Bad quality control, I'd say." Tommy took the pickle from Elma and held it straight up between his fingers and watched it curve to one side. "Been processed too long, ya' think?"

Elma looked from Tommy to me, eyes wide and full of surprise.

"Tommy helped me put up a batch of pickles yesterday," I explained. "He did a nice job, too." I smiled at him proudly.

"Well, seems to me this manager ought to be buying his pickles from a local producer, get 'em fresh and a whole mite tastier!" Elma looked around as if she was going to summon the waitress.

"Elma, I couldn't supply enough pickles for them if I wanted to now. I have trouble keeping up with the customers I do have. Besides," I added, "who knows where I'll be doing my pickling in the next three to five years."

"I could see you being another Martha Stewart," Elma said. She waved her hand in the air as though she were painting the picture. "You could turn that prison into a productive pickle supplier."

"Annie Pickels Prison Pickles," Tommy announced. His hands spread out as if he'd created a neon sign.

Great. Now Tommy was into the whole scene. I shook my head. I was outnumbered.

"You two need help." I drank the last of my coffee and left a tip on the table for the waitress. It was time to leave before things got out of hand.

The time had passed quickly. I wondered if Arnie enjoyed his Italian sub and if he still had the antacid I'd slipped him. More than that, what kind of plea bargain could he set up and would he ever tell me who that woman was?

Chapter 34

Back in the courtroom the next morning, the hands on the big round clock on the wall pointed out 8:57. The seats filled again with friends and curiosity seekers. We made it into the building without any microphones thrust in our faces, but we had noticed one camera flash. When I turned to look, the now familiar reporter from the Bugle saluted me with a wave of his hand. I smiled back at him.

The seconds hand on the big round courthouse clock jumped spastically as it ticked off the remaining time before our future was to be decided. Tension thickened the air and made it hard to breathe. Everywhere heads bent together and people talked in hushed tones. Even Elma remained quiet this morning, no jokes about jailhouse food or clothes or fancy hats. Tommy picked at his cuticles until I was sure they would bleed. I may have looked calm, cool, and collected, but this morning I had layered on the antiperspirant after my shower. At least my underarms wouldn't give away my nervousness. I heard the clicks from the clock as time inched forward. My nerves twitched in sync and my pulse rate increased.

Arnie's meeting with Jim Spizegud the day before had been successful. They came to an agreement and once Tommy and I approved it, the deal was set. Now we awaited the judge's reaction. Would he agree to the terms? Right next to my concern for the trial, there still lingered the matter of the mysterious woman who answered Arnie's phone. Getting Arnie alone had not been an option these past few days, and the topic needed private discussion.

The minute hand hit the 12 on the clock making it officially nine a.m. The door to the judge's chambers opened. I marveled at his punctuality. The audience collectively rose to their feet with us and waited for the sound of the gavel on wood as their cue to be seated again.

Judge Oswald peered over his glasses at the assemblage before him. His expression appeared to show the lack of a second cup of coffee or perhaps he just wore his practiced blank look that kept others from guessing his thoughts. He cleared his throat and began.

"Council, I assume you have had ample opportunity to talk." Judge Oswald raised his eyebrows causing his forehead to furrow right up to the place where there used to be hair.

"We have, your honor," the two lawyers answered in unison.

"And?"

Arnie looked at the prosecutor who walked forward with papers in his hand to formally present to the judge. Spizegud returned to his desk but remained on his feet and began to read from his notes.

"The state is prepared to reduce the charges in this case in exchange for guilty pleas entered to the following," Spizegud read the reduced charges that Arnie had explained to us the day before. When he finished, he adjusted his tie and sat down.

Judge Oswald gazed at Arnie, Tommy, and me. Arnie prompted us to stand with him. "You've heard the charges as they have been read by the prosecutor. Ms. Pickels and Mr. Madison, how do you plead?"

"Guilty, Your Honor," we answered together.

"Thank you," the judge said. "Court will reconvene in thirty minutes at which time I will render judgment in this case." He started to leave and then reached back to bang his gavel on the wood one more time.

"What's he doing?" Elma said leaning over the rail. "I thought it was all decided."

"It is to a point," Arnie replied. "The judge still has to agree to the conditions and state them formally. He doesn't want to appear to be soft on the drug issue or hasty in his decision. I'd say he's playing to the audience a bit." Arnie nodded his head in the direction of the folks who looked on anxiously.

"I think he didn't get his second cup of coffee this morning," I said. I winked at Tommy. "I should have brought him one of my cinnamon rolls."

"You mean you still had some?" Tommy feigned indignation.

"You haven't cleaned me out yet." I tugged on his ear being careful not to pull on his earring.

Thirty minutes seemed like an eternity. I watched the second hand again as it bounced slightly each time it skipped over another slash mark on the clock. It seemed to step back before it leapt forward as though hesitating to bring us into the next hour. I drummed my fingers on the table to some erratic rhythm in my head. Then, finally the door opened again.

"All rise."

The words calmed the torrent of voices in the room, but accelerated a sudden rush of adrenalin through my veins. For a moment I felt like a feather that would take to the air with the gentlest wisp of a breeze. Arnie's hand on mine kept me from floating away. Judge Oswald finished his ritual hammering and shuffled papers in front of him.

"I've reviewed this case and the recommendations of the prosecutor's office, and find that they have reached an amicable agreement with the defendants." He cleared his throat. "First, Ms.

Pickels, I hope you understand now how important it is to be aware of what's happening on your property."

I nodded my head slightly. Arnie had cautioned me not to say anything unless the judge addressed me directly with a question.

"While you didn't actually plant the marijuana you are still responsible for allowing it to be grown there. You are very fortunate, Ms. Pickels, that you did not lose all of your property since marijuana was found on your land as well as in your pickle jars. By the way, I strongly suggest you change your pickle recipe."

Hushed giggles spread through the room behind me. I could feel my ears turn pink.

"The court fines you $3,000 dollars and sentences you to six months in jail."

I heard Elma gasp. My stomach turned over faster than it would on a roller coaster. I thought I wasn't getting any jail time. What was he doing? He checked something on the page with a pen and then looked at me again.

"I am suspending your sentence and reducing your fine to $1,500 provided I have your word that you will learn to recognize the difference between marijuana and marjoram, and not grow it, the marijuana, on your farm, or put it in your pickle products."

I didn't realize I was holding my breath until it came rushing out of me. I wasn't going to jail.

"Ms. Pickels?"

"Yes, Your Honor. No more growing marjoram. No more pickling marjoram." The crowd roared with laughter. What had I done? The judge hammered it quiet again.

"Not marjoram. Marijuana, Ms. Pickels, marijuana."

"I'm sorry. Yes, sir. Marijuana."

Judge Oswald looked straight at Tommy whose complexion looked every bit as pale as the white shirt he wore. The judge sighed deeply as he shuffled papers again.

"Mr. Madison, you, sir, took advantage of this nice lady's ignorance of the difference between marjoram and marijuana. You grew the marijuana on her property putting her in danger of losing all she owned because of the drug laws in this state. You have openly admitted smoking marijuana." He studied Tommy a little closer. Then pointed his pen at him. "I don't care if it was medicinal. You were smoking it. To your credit, however, you did not try to sell it." The judge looked down at his papers again. "The court fines you $10,000 and sentences you to 2 years in jail."

The whispers spread from onlooker to onlooker created a strange hum in the room. I wondered if it was because they thought that was too much, or not enough.

Judge Oswald continued. "Mr. Madison, the court will reduce that sentence to one year of probation if you agree to a drug rehabilitation program."

"Yes, sir. I will," Tommy said. His voice sounded squeaky, uncertain, like a young boy whose adolescent voice is about to drop an octave.

"Now, it's my understanding that Ms. Pickels has agreed to pay your fines." Tommy's surprise registered as he flashed a look in my direction. "Is that correct?"

"I don't know anything about that, sir," Tommy answered looking back to the judge.

"Your Honor," Arnie said interrupting the dialog that had developed, "Ms. Pickels has agreed to pay both hers and Mr. Madison's fines."

"Well, young man, I'd say that was pretty generous. However, I don't feel that's entirely fair to Ms. Pickels." The judge narrowed his eyes. "Therefore, I order you to spend the next year working for Ms. Pickels on her farm to repay this generous lady whose only reason for being in this courtroom today is your doing. Furthermore, I will reduce the fine to $3,000 provided you work at least ten hours a week there. If you do not comply, you will be personally responsible for the full amount of $10,000 and subject to having your probation suspended. Is that clear?"

"Yes, sir, that's very clear. Thank you, sir." Tommy nodded his head emphatically.

"Don't thank me, son. Thank Ms. Pickels. And don't make me have to come after you." He pointed his pen at Tommy again. "Part of your probation includes random drug testing. Those tests had better be clean."

The block of wood on the judge's desk got hammered one last time as the judge declared, "Court is adjourned."

There was a rousing cheer. I gave Tommy a congratulatory hug. Tears brimmed his eyes. Arnie reached around me and shook his hand.

"Thank you, thank you." Tommy said over and over.

The judge had surprised us. Tommy was supposed to get a reduced sentence not probation and the reduction of the fines was more than what we expected. I looked over at the prosecutor's table. Jim Spizegud was smiling and shaking hands with people. Ever the politician, he acted as though the whole thing had been his idea.

I knew better than that. The whole thing had been an answer to prayer. It was really God's idea. And God had been very ambidextrous in crafting his plan. Not only did it get Tommy out of a fix, but it also gave me an opportunity to care for him as though he were family.

"Let's celebrate!" Elma shouted. She jiggled around like someone had tossed a bunch of spiders down her panty hose.

"Tinker's Tavern?" Tommy suggested. "I have to make sure Bill hasn't given away my job, my other job." He looked at me and grinned.

"Looks like my training you in the fine art of pickling is going to pay off for me," I teased. I turned to Elma. "We'll finish our business here and meet you at Tinkers."

There were papers to sign and a check to write out. When it was all done, Tommy and I walked out the door feeling blessed. The air smelled sweeter and the sky looked bluer.

"I'll meet you two there," Arnie said at the bottom of the steps and turned to go to his car. For the second time in two days, I felt like he had abandoned me. I straightened my backbone, lifted my chin, and took Tommy by the arm.

"Guess you're stuck with the old lady," I said trying to keep emotions in check.

"The last thing anyone could ever call you, Mrs. A, is an old lady. The honor is all mine." He wrapped my arm in his and escorted me to his car as if he were taking me for a grand ride in a luxury limousine.

We spent the half hour ride to Tinkers Tavern discussing the future of my pickle business. Tommy insisted I raise prices to insure I made a profit for all my hard work. I talked about planting more pickles now that I knew I would have help with the pickling. Somewhere along the way, the "I" became "we" and I knew that Tommy and I were going to begin a partnership that involved more than his paying off a debt.

The parking lot was full when we reached Tinkers.

"Business is good," I observed. "I think your job here is probably secure. Bill's going to need you."

We walked up the old wooden stairs and entered the hallway that separated the bar from the restaurant. The little gal that had her eye on Tommy the last time I was there greeted us. She blushed when Tommy said, "Hey, Ginger. How's it goin'?"

"We're here to meet some friends," I said. I had passed Elma's car in the parking lot so I knew she was here. Arnie's Lexus however, was missing.

"Oh, yes, I know," Ginger said cheerfully. "They're already here. Follow me."

We entered the restaurant. A cheer exploded in the crowded room. A chorus of "For she's a jolly good fellow" followed as

Elma rushed forward to grab my hand and lead me to a table in the center off all the friends gathered there. She thrust a plastic champagne glass full of a bubbly drink into my hand.

"Elma! Champagne?" I said surprised at my tee-totaling friend.

"Sparkling apple cider," she said with a wink.

"To our pickling queen and her protégé!" Elma shouted.

Everyone raised their plastic glasses and yelled, "Here! Here!"

"Soup's on!" Bill announced from the back of the room. I turned to see a table laden with all sorts of sandwiches and salads and a huge pot of Bill's finest homemade soup. "Don't forget to sample the pickles," he yelled over the din of noise.

They made Tommy and me go first. Elma was close behind us. Everyone was congratulatory, even Mary Jane who brusquely said a quick hello to Tommy before she disappeared from the party. I think she was disappointed that the judge let him off so easily and that he now would be an integral part of my life.

Those who didn't know Tommy introduced themselves and told him they thought he was a fine young man. I think he was a bit overwhelmed. I saw Kirk and him go off to a table in the corner with Ginger and another girl from our church. It was good to see him with friends, good friends.

"Where's Arnie?" Elma asked between bites of a corned beef sandwich that was too big for even her to get her mouth around. "I thought he was coming with you."

"He said he'd be along." The irritation in my voice was evident.

"What's wrong, Annie?" Elma set her sandwich down and wiped her mouth.

"Oh, I don't know." I could feel my lower lip quiver. When had I turned into such a wimp? In my defense, it had been a long two days. I was tired and I still hadn't solved the mystery of the other woman.

"Something's bothering you. Did something happen at the courthouse? Are you all cleared with the legal stuff?" Elma was a bloodhound. If I bled the least little bit she would sniff it out.

"Nothing at the courthouse. It happened the other day." I sighed. "I called Arnie's house to talk with him and a woman answered."

"His daughter?"

"That's what I thought at first, but it wasn't. She never gave me her name, just said Arnie wasn't there. Did I want to call back."

"There's a reasonable explanation, I'm sure," Elma said. She picked up her sandwich again. Sauerkraut juice and Thousand Island dressing dripped down her hands.

"She sounded awfully familiar with Arnie. Something in the tone of her voice. I don't know. I haven't had a chance to ask him about it." I played with my coleslaw.

"Hmph," Elma had a mouthful. "Um sure, muthin' worry 'bout."

"What if Mary Jane's right, Elma. What if he is slick and is trying to take advantage? Maybe I should start worrying."

Her mouth full again, Elma could only telegraph a look to me and shake her head. She was right. There was probably nothing to worry about. Still, I needed to know. Who was that woman?

Chapter 35

I sulked in the passenger seat of Elma's car on the way home. Arnie never showed up at Tinkers. I tried to tell myself it didn't matter. Still, if he truly considered himself a friend, he would have joined in the celebration. At the very least, he could have come just because he was my lawyer.

I concentrated on how much I had to celebrate. I still owned my home and my farmland. I wasn't going to jail and neither was Tommy. Tommy was excited about coming to work for me even though it was court ordered. What more could I ask for?

"You're awfully quiet, Annie," Elma observed as we neared my house.

"Oh, I guess I'm just a little tired out from all the day's events."

I stared out my window not trusting my face to conceal my emotions. I couldn't deny my disappointment in Arnie. That woman, whoever she was, must really have a hold on him. He couldn't even say good-bye to an old friend. Elma turned into the driveway.

"Isn't that Arnie's car?"

A Lexus, the same color and make of Arnie's was parked in front of the barn.

"Yes, yes. I think it is," I said haltingly not ready to trust what my eyes saw or my heart felt.

"Well, this is where I leave you," Elma said. Her eyes lit up like fireworks on the fourth of July.

The eternal optimist. Elma supposes there's some kind of redemption here. He probably just left something behind.

"Why don't you come in with me?" I suggested. I wasn't sure I wanted to face Arnie alone, not just yet.

"Oh, no. I think you two probably have something you need to talk over, another woman perhaps?"

Elma shooed me out of the car with the back of her hand. I got out and closed the car door, but I bent down to the open window. I wanted to give Elma another chance.

"Sure you won't come in? You too, could learn the secrets of the mystery woman, if he tells me anything."

Elma leaned across the seat. "Honey, give him a break. Let him explain. Arnie's a great guy. Trust me."

She left me standing there in disbelief, abandoned again. I watched her back out of my driveway and all the way up to her garage. My leaden feet trudged up to the door. It was time to confront my fears. Time to confront Arnie.

It suddenly occurred to me that Arnie was inside. Did he break in? I didn't remember giving him a key. I tried the door. It was unlocked. Maybe I left it that way. I made a mental note to get in the habit of double-checking the door. If a little bird could wreak havoc in my life by getting in uninvited, what could a full-grown lawyer playing with my emotions do?

I walked up the three steps into the kitchen. On the counter was a bouquet of white carnations with one red rose in the center. I set my purse down next to it and inhaled the wonderful scent.

My eyes caught the sight of another bouquet of carnations, pink this time, sitting on the kitchen table with one red rose in the middle of them. I turned. There were more bouquets of carnations of various colors scattered throughout the rest of the kitchen and into the family room, each with a red rose in the center. Amid all the flowers stood Arnie. He was grinning from ear to ear. In his hand was a single red rose. He held it out to me.

"I miscounted. There were only 11 bouquets. This one needs to find a home."

"Oh, Arnie." I sounded like a gushy schoolgirl but it was all I could muster.

"I'm sorry I didn't make it to Tinkers. This took a little more time than I expected."

"I, It's . . .You're for—" The tears came. Arnie rushed to my side.

"Hey, Snow Angel, I didn't mean to make you cry."

"They're ha-ha-happy tears." I managed to squeeze out between sobs.

"Well, dry those tears and go change into one of your dancing dresses. I'm taking you out for our own little celebration." He dabbed at my face with a handkerchief. "And, Ms. Pickels, the woman you are so worried about is my cleaning lady, has been since before Ruth died. She thinks she's my mother sometimes, so she was just checking you out when you called."

I looked up in amazement at him. "How did you know?"

"Elma, of course. That woman will do anything to keep the two of us together. She has some cockeyed notion we might get to like each other." He smiled warmly.

"Let me guess. She gave you the key to get in here, too?"

"Like I said, she's given us her blessing." He stepped back and pointed to my bedroom. "Now move along. We have some celebrating to do."

"Yes, sir, that we do." I hustled to the bedroom trying to decide which cruise dress would be appropriate. Elma was going to get a tongue-lashing. Then I was going to kiss her.

Early, too early, the next morning I heard pounding on the door. I wrapped my pink chenille robe around me and ran to see who it was. Elma! Of course. I opened the door and she rushed in.

"I didn't have my key," she said. "Sorry, did I get you up? I just couldn't wait any longer. How was last night? Were you surprised? Where did he take you? What did you have to eat?"

The string of questions was out before I even closed the door. I shook my head. Gotta love her.

"Can we have some coffee before I answer?"

"Oh, I'm sorry. I thought you'd be up by now. You're usually done with your walk and everything." Elma's mouth hung open in awe as she surveyed the bouquets of carnations. "Did Arnie do this?"

"Yes. I thought you knew, Ms. Here's-the-key-to-her-house." I poured two cups of coffee while Elma smelled all the flowers.

"He didn't tell me exactly what he was doing. Just that he wanted to surprise you with something."

"Well, he did. Thanks." I gave her a hug and kissed her on the forehead.

"You're most welcome." Elma sat down at the table and reached for her coffee. "So, what else happened?"

"He had reservations at a really nice restaurant just outside of Columbus. We ate dinner, listened to the band, danced a bit." My voice began to sound dreamy.

"Mmmm. Dinner and dancing. Perfect." Elma was lost in her own fantasy. Coming back to reality she asked, "So what's the significance of the rose in the center of each bouquet?"

"He said he wasn't ready to give me the full bouquet of roses yet. The single roses are to say that he wants to develop this relationship further, maybe past just friendship, but," I was blushing.

"But? But what?"

"But he wanted to make sure I wanted that as well."

"Do you?"

"I think so. I have feelings for him, Elma. I just don't know if they are the right kind of feelings for something other than friendship."

"Friendship is a good start. I don't think Warren and I would have had so many happy years if we hadn't been such good friends." Her eyes became teary. She hadn't talked about Warren in a while, a long while.

I patted her hand. "You two were the best example of married friends I've ever seen."

All of a sudden she started laughing. I pulled my hand back, puzzled.

"I'm sorry," she said as she wiped away the residue of tears on her eyelashes. "I just had a picture flash through my head of Mary Jane's expression as she heard about Tommy getting off and now will find out Arnie gave you all these flowers."

"She'll pop a cork when she hears about Arnie, and it won't be a champagne cork."

"She'll get over it."

"She'll have to," I said. "More coffee?"

"Any cinnamon rolls?" Elma asked.

"Now you sound like Tommy."

"When does he start working for you?"

"We haven't worked out his hours yet. He's going to get his schedule from Bill first. I can work him in around his regular job." I zapped two rolls in the microwave and grabbed a tub of margarine.

"I'm excited," I said putting the warm cinnamon rolls on the table. "Tommy's got a head for business. I think I may be expanding my output and raising my prices. There could actually be a profit in this pickle venture."

"Well, I can give you a line on a few new customers." Elma sounded like a salesman. "I've seen some places that could use a good pickle or two."

"So, now I have a business manager and a marketing manager. Guess I'd better get the Tillernator out here to plow up some more space. I'm going to have to increase production."

"I don't mind helping out," Elma said seriously enough to make me sit up and take notice.

"You don't? What about all the other stuff you do at church?"

"I did all that stuff when Warren was around and still had time to spend with him. Now, well, now I just have extra time."

She got weepy-eyed again. I wasn't much better. When your friend hurts, you hurt. Then an idea struck like a lightning bolt. I excused myself for a moment and went to fetch something I thought might lift Elma's spirits, and give me something to look forward to as well. I came back and plopped a stack of brochures and travel books on the table.

"What's all this?" Elma asked.

"This, m'lady, is our trip to London." I opened one of the pamphlets to a picture of the palace with the fancy guards standing in front of a wrought iron fence.

"London? I, we, I couldn't." She picked up another brochure and started thumbing through it.

"Sure we could, but not until late October early November, after pickling season. What do you say?" I paged through a glossy travel magazine. "Look here. It's a picture of Pickle-dilly Circus with all the red double-decker buses and black taxi cabs."

"Pickle-dilly?" Elma started laughing. "It's Piccadilly Circus not Pickle-dilly. You have pickles on the brain."

"And here, here's Westminster Abbey, the Tower of Big Ben."

"The rosey red cheeks of the little children," Elma sang. The Beatles' fan in her emerged.

I could feel my enthusiasm get through to her. "Come on, Elma. Think of it, the two of us in London, walking down to Trafalgar Square, feeding the pigeons, watching the changing of the guard at the palace while we munch on hot roasted chestnuts."

"Do you suppose the queen would invite us in?" Elma put her hand to her hair and primped.

"Only if we wear our red hats with the purple feathers and remember to hold our pinky fingers up when we sip our tea."

We both erupted in laughter.

"Look, I found this bed and breakfast place that's not too expensive and it's right in the middle of everything near Pickle-dilly Circus."

"P, P, PICCA-dilly." Elma was laughing so hard she could barely speak. Tears ran down her cheeks.

"Why do I keep saying Pickle-dilly?" I thought hard for a minute. There must have been something, "Oh! I remember!"

My exclamation quieted Elma for a moment.

"There's a new recipe I wanted to try. It's for pickled green tomatoes."

"What's it called?" Elma asked as she wiped her face dry.

"Piccalilli, and it doesn't call for any marjoram!"

THE END

ABOUT THE AUTHOR

As a full time mom, a teacher, a businesswoman, a paralegal student, a travel addict, and diver, Karen has had a wealth of experiences that contribute to her story ideas and speaking topics. In 1987, she sold her first written piece for publication in *Standard*, a Sunday School take-home paper. Since then she has published over 250 articles and essays in various publications and written columns for a local newspaper and several regional magazines. For two years she produced a newsletter for new adult readers in the Project: LEARN organization of Cleveland. Karen has been a contributing author to many compilation books including the Chicken Soup For The Soul series. She coauthored *A Scrapbook of Christmas Firsts* and *A Scrapbook of Motherhood Firsts*. Her previous novels include *Divide The Child* and *Murder Among The Orchids*.

Karen has been married to her husband Bob for 44 years. They met at Put-In-Bay, OH, where Bob drove cab for a summer and Karen worked in a pizza shop. They have five children (grandchildren being added regularly). Now that their children have grown and left the nest, Bob and Karen have been able to travel extensively having visited all of the seven continents. Follow their travel adventures at http://karenrobbins.blogspot.com.